The

STEPMOTHER

———❖———

Diana Diamond

ST. MARTIN'S PAPERBACKS

THE STEPMOTHER

Copyright © 2005 by Diana Diamond.
Excerpt from *The Other Woman* copyright © 2006 by Diana Diamond.

Cover photo © Stefano Oppo / Photonica

Library of Congress Catalog Card Number: 2004061908

ISBN: 0-312-93944-2
EAN: 9780312-93944-1

Printed in the United States of America

St. Martin's Press hardcover edition / July 2005
St. Martin's Paperbacks edition / May 2006

St. Martin's Paperbacks are published by St. Martin's Press, 175 Fifth Avenue, New York, NY 10010.

10 9 8 7 6 5 4 3 2 1

Praise for Diana Diamond

THE STEPMOTHER

THE FIRST WIFE

THE GOOD SISTER

MORE . . .

One

"T ime!" Charlene Hendricks announced, clicking the button on her stopwatch.

"Another minute," Steven Armstrong gasped. His breathing was labored as he pedaled furiously on the stationary bicycle. "I can go for another minute!"

"That's enough!" she insisted. "Let's not overdo it. You strain something and you're back to square one. Just stay with the program."

Steven stopped pedaling and slumped forward over the handlebars. Charlene draped a fresh towel over his shoulders and offered him an open bottle of water. He took a drink, then wiped his face with the towel. "You know I can do a lot more than you're letting me," he said.

"You're doing more than enough. I don't want you trying to break the world record for knee surgery. It takes time, and patience."

Steven managed to laugh even as he was gasping for breath. "I don't have a lot of time, and I've never been big on patience. Believe me, Charlie, the knee is fine. I'm just trying to work off the paunch I got from all that time in bed."

She looked at him skeptically. "What paunch? You're in great shape."

"Nah! I used to ride twice as long without even breaking a sweat."

"Sure," she agreed, "when you were in your thirties and forties. But for a man in his sixties you're way above the curve. You know the rule in personal training: Act your age."

She took her warm-up jacket out of her backpack and put it on over her tank top. "Tomorrow at one o'clock, Mr. Armstrong?"

"Steve!" he snapped angrily. "I keep telling you to call me Steve."

"Okay, Steve, I'll see you tomorrow, same time, same place." She started toward the open door that connected the gym with the rest of the house.

"Charlie! Do I really look like I'm in my sixties?" When she looked back, he seemed desperate.

"No, Mr. Armstrong, you look twenty years younger. And now that you're shaving your head you look like a stud!"

He smiled and ran his hand over the dark haze that had been a crown of wild hair surrounding a bald pate. "You like this?"

"It's a turn-on," she smiled. "I can hardly keep my hands off you."

She was out the door when he called to her again. "Charlie!" She poked her head back into the room.

"I'm going to swim some laps. Why don't you stick around so you can tell me what I'm doing wrong?"

She raised her hands in a gesture of helplessness. "I have to pick up my kid. You can hold off on the laps until tomorrow. We'll do them as soon as you finish stretching." She pulled back through the doorway. Steven was still looking at the space she had vacated when he heard the front door snap shut. A few seconds later he heard the telltale rattle of her antique Toyota. She had just left, but already he missed her.

Charlene Hendricks had come into his life along with a steel and epoxy hinge that had been substituted for his fatally damaged knee. Steven had resisted the knee replacement for over a year, managing to get by on a combination of painkillers and grit. Hell, he didn't build his hardware empire by pandering to every ache and pain. Thirty-three years on the job and he had missed only three days of work—one when each of his children was born. Even after he'd taken the company public and retired to his role of disgruntled share owner, he still kept himself busy. He had designed his new home on the Fort Lauderdale waterway, and then become his own construction contractor. Every cement block, every plumbing fixture, every truss and tile had passed his scrutiny. Why not? He had spent his life in hardware. Nobody was going to put anything over on him!

Then the boat! He had bought a seventy-five-foot motor yacht with a planing hull and twin diesels, and then supervised every step of its construction from laying the resin to installing the running lights. He had been climbing the ladder from the after deck to the flying bridge when his knee buckled under him.

The doctors prescribed a new knee, a prosthesis that would replace the worn joint he had overworked. Steven had absolutely refused. There was nothing wrong with his knee that a little time wouldn't heal. He would simply suck it up the way he had always done when ailments threatened to slow his pace. The doctors shrugged. "When it hurts enough, you'll come back," they assured him. He had struggled for ten months, laboring to move around his house during the day, and sitting with his knee iced at night. Eventually, he had decided that the doctors were right and signed up for the knee replacement.

Charlene had visited him in the hospital right after the operation and introduced herself as his therapist. She had helped him out of bed and supported him as he took his first faltering steps on his new knee. Then she went home with him to help him in the arduous task of rehabilitation.

At first, Steven had wondered why he needed her. He could stretch his own muscles, do his own leg lifts, and climb aboard the stationary bicycle. Why did he need her to twist his legs and stretch his back, or count his repetitions? But slowly he had learned to value her advice and to welcome her company during the grueling hours that he would have been spending alone. Then, halfway through his recovery, he had begun to notice her not as a professional trainer but as a woman. A very attractive woman, totally different from his deceased wife, the mother of his children.

He noticed the rivulets of sweat that trickled down from her headband when she ran beside him, and the stains that spread down the sides of her tank top. He took in the sculptured muscles in her legs, the firmness of her thighs, and the tight buns that pressed into her leotards. Her waist, which frequently flashed as her shirt rose, was slim and flat. The breasts that showed when she bent toward him were firm and erect. Charlene, he had decided, was a new kind of woman, not soft, nor gentle, nor modestly ashamed of her femininity. She was spare, strong, and confident, invariably upbeat and annoyingly capable. As he had worked with her, he had realized that whatever other admirable characteristics she had, she could probably run him into the ground.

Steven found himself competing with her. He'd be damned if a woman young enough to be his daughter was going to be quicker, stronger, or more durable than he was. If she could demonstrate leg lifts with twenty pounds of weight, then he would do thirty pounds. If she could raise the treadmill to fifteen degrees, then he would turn it to twenty. He enjoyed her concern that he was pushing himself too much, and basked in the admiration she had for his determination. In the six weeks of his rehabilitation, Charlene had become his physical and emotional partner. So Steven was not surprised when he realized that he was falling in love with her.

But he *was* embarrassed. He had seen many men his age decide that they were still physically desirable to younger women, and then make asses of themselves as they pursued a ridiculous romance. Some had spent fortunes showering presents and trust funds on bon bons half their age. *No fool like an old fool,* he had thought, shaking his head in despair. Was that what he was becoming? An old fool! Charlie was in her thirties, the same age range as all three of his children.

He was old enough to be her father. Hell, he could be her grandfather! What was her first rule of rehabilitation? Act your age!

It's not the same thing, he tried to reason with himself. *Charlie and I are already partners.* Weren't they working together day after day? Weren't they matching each other pound for pound and stride for stride? Hadn't she told him time after time that he was way ahead of his age group in his physical strength and endurance? What was it she had called him—a stud! She didn't talk to him as if he was old enough to be her father. Maybe that wasn't the way she thought about him.

But then he laughed at himself. *Act your age!* What in God's name could he possibly offer a woman like Charlie? More than likely she had her pick of any number of guys her own age. Virile guys with six-pack abs and rock-hard buns, and erections that could lift a woman off her feet. Why would she be interested in an old man with bad knees?

On the other hand, there were things he could offer that most younger men couldn't match. He *was* worth $200 million, so he could provide her with a sense of security that she had never known and wasn't likely to ever know. That had to count for something! There was his house, a modern design on the inland waterway just north of Fort Lauderdale, that had made the cover of *Architectural Digest*. It had to be twice as luxurious as the nicest dream house she had ever imagined. There was the yacht, with its implied promises of faraway places. And the simple comfort of knowing she could have anything she wanted.

But Charlie wasn't mercenary. The most important thing in her life was her daughter, a thirteen-year-old whom she loved without reservation, and whose future was infinitely more important to her than her own. Steven knew that he could change the young girl's life. She could be in private school instead of in one of those left-behind public schools. She could be tutored in art, music, horsemanship, whatever might interest her. Her college education would be assured. Not many young studs could handle all that!

Was he trying to buy her? Perish the thought! Buying was when you wanted something and you paid the price it cost. All he was doing was tallying up the joys he could bring to her life. He was a man of means with global clout who would love, honor, and protect her. It was up to her to decide whether all that was more valuable than great buns.

If he decided to ask her, how would he do it? The easy way would be to simply keep her on as his personal trainer, three hours a day, six days a week. He could pay her lavishly so that she could afford to spend more time with him, perhaps bring her daughter to the house or out on the boat for trips to the Bahamas and the Keys. Foster the relationship until the next step was inevitable.

Or, he could do what he had always done with a difficult decision. Bite the bullet and put it to her squarely. *I love you. I can't bear the thought of you leaving. Please marry me so that you and your daughter can be my new family.* That's what he should do the next day as soon as she showed up at his door. Except she might break out laughing before she knew that he was serious. That would be the most crushing defeat of his entire life. Or, she might explain patiently that lots of men thought they were in love with their personal trainers. It was a hazard of the occupation, and she certainly wouldn't hold it against him. A patronizing evasion would be much more painful than an outright refusal.

What should he do? Steven vacillated during his dinner and during his evening walk along the beach. He tossed and turned the entire night. The one thing that he was certain of was that he couldn't live without Charlie nearby. The one thing he feared was that he was just another old fool.

Two

Charlie tapped the steering wheel to the beat of rock music playing through the tinny speakers of her car radio. She needed to get a new radio. One with a big bass speaker hidden behind the back seat, and a couple of tweeters buried in the doors. Heck, what she really needed was a new car. This one had been on its last legs when she bought it, and she had paid through the nose just to keep it running. New brakes, a new water pump, and a new head gasket, not to mention tires and windshield wipers. Worse, the air-conditioning had a mind of its own, deciding on the hottest days in South Florida to shut down and take a rest. She needed to figure a better car . . . maybe even something with a bit of pizzazz . . . into her budget.

The problem was that she had already figured a condo she couldn't afford into her budget. Two bedrooms and two baths in a landscaped enclave of town houses that had its own community clubhouse and swimming pool. She had saved two years for the down payment, and was carrying a mortgage that ate up half of her income. But it was a necessary expense. She had to move her daughter into a neighborhood where drug dealers were unwelcome, and into a school district that was as good as she could hope for in a state where the average taxpayer had no children. She needed a home where Tara could have the privacy of her own bedroom, and a living room nice enough to invite guests home to. The pool was a plus. Tara had one or two girlfriends over each Saturday for splash parties which kept her under Charlie's eagle eye and grew her daughter's circle of friends. The investment in the house seemed to be paying off. The girl seemed happy, easily adjusted, and reasonably popular . . . all values that a new car couldn't possibly deliver.

She watched the explosion of fledgling adolescents that burst out of the school's main doors. As in the big bang theory of the universe, the sudden expansion of energy quickly broke up into numerous constellations, each headed off into its own orbit. Tara was in a group of girls that seemed to be exchanging humorous banter with a nearby constellation of boys. But then she broke away, and with her backpack over her arm, sauntered toward the parked car. She opened the door and threw the backpack over the passenger seat. "Gross," she announced as she reached for the radio dial and tuned in an even more cacophonous rock group. "These guys are really bad!" Charlie smiled. She was adult enough to enjoy being a bit out of touch.

At home, Charlie went straight to the kitchen, took two rock-hard hamburgers out of the freezer and popped them into the microwave to defrost. Then she began to cut up some yellow squash. "Tara," she called in the general direction of her daughter's bedroom, "can you do the salad?" Tara sulked into the kitchen, certainly less cheerful than she had been in the car, and got out the wooden salad bowl. She ripped lettuce and chopped celery without her usual enthusiasm for working beside her mother.

"Something wrong, hon?" The girl shook her head. "Anything you want to talk about?"

"No . . ."

Charlie dropped the squash into a saucepan, and took the meat patties out of the microwave. "Do you want to grill these?" Her answer was a barely perceptible nod accompanied by a soft "Okay." *No point in pushing it,* she thought. Tara usually found a way to bring up subjects that were troubling her.

There had been the battle of the bare midriff. Tara was beginning to develop a figure and had the perfectly understandable urge to show it off. Low-cut jeans and shirts that stopped below the ribs had become many ninth-graders' announcement of adulthood. Tara had pooled her allowances to buy an outfit and then moped for days trying to get up the courage to show it to her mother. She had taken the plunge and worn it to breakfast on a Saturday. Charlie had hidden her shock and controlled her instinct to launch into a lecture. "Hey, that's cute!" she announced and watched Tara blush. "No, I mean it. It's casual, sporty, and it really emphasizes your slim waist. I like it!" Tara's eyes had looked up in relief, a smile beginning to play at the corners of her mouth. "Of course," Charlie had forged on, "it's a little *too* bare for school.

"Mom!" Her voice was heavy with frustration and despair. She began whining about what the other girls were wearing.

It had been on the tip of her tongue to announce that she didn't give a damn what anyone else was wearing but she had caught herself in the nick of time. "Okay, but you have to break me into this slowly. We'll shop for a top that reaches to your jeans. If it bounces up every once in a while to show some skin, I suppose that would be all right. And maybe after I get used to it I'll take you out for something just a speck shorter."

The whining had stopped. An understanding had been forged. Tara had agreed reluctantly even though she was secretly relieved. She would have been embarrassed to show up at school with a bare midriff.

There hadn't always been compromises. On coloring the tips of her dark hair blonde, Charlie had given in completely. She colored her own hair, and couldn't think of a defensible argument why her daughter shouldn't do the same. After all, the kid wasn't asking for spikes of purple and chartreuse. Nor was there a compromise on navel piercing. That discussion had ended in an unequivocal "No!"

What now? Charlie thought. Was Tara thinking of a tattoo?

"Are you at the gym tonight?" Tara asked while tossing the salad in nearly slow motion.

"Of course," Charlie answered. She ran a senior aerobics class three nights a week at a local health club, which was why they were eating early. "Is that a problem?"

Another head shake for a response. But then the girl added, "I'm sorry."

"Sorry? Is there something happening here tonight that I'm going to miss?"

Tara turned her back and carried the bowl to the table. "Just sorry that you have to work so much. I guess it's my fault. . . ."

"What's your fault, Tara?"

"That you're stuck with me."

"Stuck? What makes you think that I'm *stuck*? I love you. I love being with you."

Tara shrugged, studiously studying the table so that she was keeping her back to her mother. "If you weren't tied down with me, you wouldn't have to work so hard. You could do things for yourself."

"Like what? Go out dancing every night. How many times do I have to tell you that I'm doing exactly what I want to do."

The girl wheeled and hurried through the kitchen, picking up the hamburgers on her way out to the grill. "Like you could get the new car radio you want," she said in passing.

What's this all about? Charlie followed her through the sliders and out to the small patio, scarcely large enough for the grill and a small table. "I'm going to get a radio," she said. "And I'm going to get a new car to go with it."

"No, you won't," Tara said gloomily.

"I don't mean a brand-new car. Probably something a few years old. But with low mileage so that I won't have to keep getting it fixed. Something jazzy with a sports shifter and leather seats." Her decision was spontaneous, not that she hadn't been thinking of a new car. But this was the first time she realized that her daughter was ashamed of the car they were driving.

"It's not the car," Tara answered, refusing to climb out of her gloom. "It's everything. You could be doing lots of things without me. You could be having lots of fun. . . ." She dropped the burgers on the fire and heard them sizzle. Then she added, "I'm your unlucky penny."

"Unlucky?"

"Well, when you did it, you didn't *want* to have a baby."

"When I did what?"

Tara pushed passed her back into the kitchen, looking for an excuse to break the face-to-face confrontation. "You know. People do it and they don't have a baby. You weren't lucky."

Charlie followed at her heels. "You mean when I had sex with a man who wasn't committed to me, I didn't want to have a daughter."

Tara turned to her with the beginning of a tear in her eye. "Well, you didn't, did you? I was a mistake!"

"No!" She grabbed her daughter by the shoulders and held her face-to-face. "The mistake was sleeping with someone who didn't really care about me. That was a terrible mistake. But deciding to have you and become your mother wasn't a mistake. That was the best thing I've ever done. I love you! I love being with you! I can't imagine my life without you!" She drew Tara into an embrace and rocked her as if she were a baby. They were both crying when Charlie suddenly smelled smoke.

"What's burning?"

Tara broke out of the embrace. "My hamburgers!"

They jammed together between the table and the stove as they both rushed to the patio. Tara squeezed into the lead and found a column of flame curling up around the burgers. "Get some water," she yelled.

"Water doesn't work with grease," Charlie said, pushing her daughter away from the inferno. She took the spatula and lifted the flaming meat away from the fire. But she had hardly set the burgers back on the grill with another flame blazed up.

"Do something!" Tara begged.

Charlie lifted the burgers and tossed them over the rail and onto the back lawn. Then she reached close to the grill and turned off the gas. It had no effect. The grill was still on fire, and now there was the beginning of a new fire in the wild grass behind the house. She slammed the lid shut, dousing the high flame, but she could see that the fire was still raging inside.

"Get the hose!" Charlie ordered.

Tara ran off the patio, charged the garden hose, and aimed at the smoldering grass. In just a few seconds she had the yard fire out. Charlie was bent over the edges of the grill, coughing in the billowing smoke. "I think this one is out, too," she reported.

Tara came back to the patio, looked at her mother, and then broke out laughing.

"This isn't funny, Tara. It could have been serious."

The girl laughed all the harder, leaning against the wall for support. She tried to talk, but she fell into a new spasm of laughter and pointed a finger at her mother.

"What's so funny?" Charlie demanded.

"Your face . . . look at your face!"

Charlie turned into the kitchen, saw herself in the reflection of the hall mirror, cracked a smile, and then began laughing. The smoke had painted her into a comic black face, with white eyelids and bright white teeth. She turned back to her daughter and joined in the hysteria. They fell back into each others' arms, this time howling instead of sobbing. The soot wiped off onto Tara's face and then the two began painting white circles on each others' cheeks.

"Some pair we are," Charlie was finally able to say.

"You better marry a fireman," Tara teased.

Charlie shook her head. "I wouldn't have to if I cleaned the grill once in a while."

"Let's just have a salad," the girl suggested.

Tara set out the salad while her mother went to the bathroom and washed her face. "It's in my hair," she said when she returned to the table. "I'll take a shower at the spa after my class."

"You look good with dark hair," the girl said, now laughing easily.

Charlie was mystified. Where was the girl tormented with guilt whom she had been embracing only a few minutes before?

Three

———•—•———

Matthew Armstrong was standing over a slippery ten-foot putt when a cell phone rang a few yards behind him. His grip tightened and his arms stiffened as he brought the putter forward. The ball shot off line and didn't slow to a stop until it was eight feet past the hole.

"Whose fucking phone is that?" he demanded of his three playing companions.

"Yours," one of the men answered, "and you're damn lucky it didn't ring when I was putting. I'd have wrapped the club around your neck!"

Matthew stormed off the green to his parked golf cart ready to smash his cell phone to smithereens. It was vibrating in one of the cup holders, running around in circles, playing its cheery song over and over again. He snatched it up, about to scream at the fool who had called him during his regular golf match. But he saw "Steven Armstrong" printed out on the instrument's display. "Dad," he managed cheerily as he accepted the call.

"Hello, Matthew. Have you got a minute?"

"I'm on the golf course," he answered with the same sense of reverence as if he was in church.

"There's something I need to discuss with you. It will take just a couple of minutes."

Matthew eyed his playing partners who were seething at the interruption of their game. "Can't it wait?" he whispered to his father. "I'm on the sixteenth green."

"Yeah, sure," Steven growled. "My getting married isn't nearly as important as your golf game. I'd hate to take your mind off your next shot."

"Getting married?" Matthew blurted it out in a loud voice, drawing glares from the other players. He went back to his whisper. "Dad, let me call you back in half an hour when I can talk."

Getting married, he was thinking as he addressed his ball on the next tee. He nearly fell as he swung his driver, and then watched the ball take a duck hook into the woods. The prospect of his father taking a new wife was more than surprising. It was frightening. Matthew's whole existence was based on Steven's boundless charity. The last thing he needed was for his father to begin lavishing his attention on someone else. His next drive found a pond, and then he three-putted on the final hole. He didn't stop in the locker room but instead headed directly to the parking lot to call his father.

Steven Armstrong was a self-made man who had started as a clerk in a hardware store and ended up owning Ucandoit, a chain of giant hardware warehouses that sold everything a homeowner would need to maintain and expand his house. "You can do it" was the chain's motto as well as its name, but in case you couldn't, it offered classes in everything from carpentry to lawn care and sold all the tools and materials needed.

At first, Steven had mortgaged one store to put up the next. Then, three years ago, when he couldn't borrow enough money to finance his rapid growth, he had taken the company public. He had retired to the position of major stockholder where his main job, as he liked to put it, was to "just be a pain in the ass."

Matthew, who had grown up with the company, now held his father's seat on the board, a position which kept him fully occupied for a few days each month and left him plenty of time for golf, yachting, skiing, and fine dining—passions that had been fired during his spoiled youth. He had started as a stock clerk in his father's second store and, immediately on his graduation from college, been promoted to vice president of operations. In fact, he was little more than Steven's gofer, and pretty much a joke to the chain's executives and managers. But he had a large, well-furnished office, a company Cadillac, a country club membership, and an unlimited expense account. He could afford to join in the derisive laughter on his way to the bank.

Steven had written Matthew into the original public offering with a senior executive's position and a seat on the board. Matthew's position, as spokesman for his father's stock, assured that the board would never consider replacing him with a more competent executive, or discuss the value received for his high-six-figure salary. But if Steven should be so taken with a new wife that he lost interest in the company, or worse, if he sold his stock to finance a lavish new lifestyle, then Matthew's position would become precarious. How was he going to discourage his father's wedding plans without hurting the old man's feelings?

"Dad," he boomed into his cell phone while seated in his car where he wouldn't risk being overheard. "Sorry to have cut you off, but I needed a few minutes to digest the news. Did I hear you say you were going to get married?"

"What I meant to say was that I was thinking about getting married. In fact, I'm trying to get up the courage to pop the question today. I guess I was hoping for some encouragement."

"Well, go for it!" Matthew exuded despite the lump in his throat. "If that's what you want, then that's what you should do."

"You think so?" Steven said with a hint of a laugh. "Because at my age I feel pretty silly."

"Age isn't the question," Matthew answered. "It's really

an issue of lifestyle. Getting married would change everything you have now. Are you sure that's what you want?"

"Why would it change everything?

Be careful, Matthew warned himself. He had to be sure
not to sound critical because his father wasn't good at accepting criticism. Usually, it drove him into a sputtering rage.
"Well, take your new boat. You know how much you love
cruising. You've even been talking about long trips to the Caribbean. There aren't a lot of women who want to live on a
boat. The humidity makes their hair frizzy."

Steven considered the point. "I could stick to day trips
with an occasional overnighter."

"Even that might not work," his son cautioned. "Most
ladies at my yacht club like to party on board. They could
care less if the boat ever leaves the mooring." There was no
reply from his father so he ventured further into discouraging
possibilities. "You like to gamble."

"I don't gamble," Steven interrupted.

"Dad, you're always dialing into on-line poker games.
Isn't your handle 'Aces Wild'? And what about your day trading. Isn't that gambling?"

"Oh yeah, that." Steven allowed.

"Most women are death on gambling," the son suggested.
"That's something you ought to get straight right off the bat!"

"Okay, I won't dial into poker games. And no woman
would resent her husband checking on his investments."

"Another thing—and I hate to say this, Dad—but neatness
isn't one of your better traits. I remember that Mother was always on you to pick up after yourself and get your socks out
from under the bed. That drove you nuts for the few hours a
day that you were home. Imagine what it will be like when
you're sharing all your waking hours."

Steven bristled. "For a married man, there doesn't seem to
be much that you like about the institution."

Matthew backtracked. "Don't get me wrong. I just don't
want to see you get tied up in a lifestyle that isn't suited to
you. You can always find a woman to take out to dinner or to

a show. You can have a nice companion for social events. But you don't have to give up all the things you love for a little social companionship."

"I'm not interested in a social companion. And, anyway, I can't think of anyone who would want the job."

"Don't be silly," Matthew contradicted. "You're an attractive and very interesting man. Mother's friend, Madeline Rogers, would fly down in a minute to have dinner with you."

"Madeline Rogers? Why in hell would I want to have dinner with Madeline Rogers? She's older than your mother was, and she hasn't put on a pair of running shoes in twenty years. All she does is play cards, or that other game with the sticks and the tiles."

"Mah Jongg," Matthew provided.

"Mah who?"

"Mah Jongg. That's the name of the game with the sticks and tiles."

Steven was irritated. "I don't care what the hell it's called. The point is that I'm not ready to play it for the rest of my life."

Matthew rallied. "See what I mean. When you get married, you're going to have to take up your wife's activities. Women your age don't want half as much adventure as you want. Believe it or not, they actually enjoy playing Mah Jongg."

"For God's sake, Matthew, who said I was going to marry someone my age? The woman I'm thinking of asking is a lot younger than Madeline Rogers and she doesn't play Mah Junk, or whatever the hell it is."

"Younger?" There was genuine fear in Matthew's voice. "How young?"

"I'm talking about Charlie. You met her when you were down here."

Matthew swallowed. "Charlie . . . your therapist?"

"Yeah, but we're way past that now. My knee is fine. Now she's my personal trainer, helping me to get back in shape. I like her, and I think she likes me."

"Dad, she's younger than I am. What is she? Thirty?"

"Thirty . . . thirty-five . . . what difference does it make? She's a lot younger than I am, and I don't want to act like an old fool. But we're interested in the same things and we enjoy doing them together. Isn't that more important than how many years older than her I am?"

"Dad, you're a lot younger than your age," Matthew lied. "But doesn't she have a daughter? I think she mentioned a teenager."

"That's right," Steven said, "and she's absolutely devoted to the girl. That's one of the things I admire about her. She faces up to her obligations."

"Very admirable, indeed," Matthew agreed, even though he suspected that the comment might be a dig. Steven had often complained that his children never took their lives seriously and had commented, not completely in jest, that they weren't worth the powder it would take to blow them all to hell. "But if . . . when . . . you marry this girl, you'll also become the father of a teenage daughter. Have you thought of the changes that will bring into your life? You've been through it once. Are you sure you want to go back and do it again?"

"I won't be her father!" Steven snapped. Then he relented, "I'll certainly help her any way I can. Maybe get her into better schools and help with college expenses if that's what she wants. But I won't be waiting up all night for her to come home, or having a fit because she breaks curfew."

"And the first time you and your trainer are out of town, when she invites half her school over for a keg party, and they trash the place," Matthew recited, reminding his father of one of his blackest days as a parent. "What will you do then?"

There was a long pause that Matthew regarded as a sign of victory. He had touched on something that his father wouldn't be able to handle. Steven finally admitted, "I don't know what I'd do. Hell, it may never happen, but I get your point. I haven't really looked at this from every angle. It's more involved than just getting married. I'd be starting a whole new family. Maybe I should give this a little more thought before I jump into it."

Matthew couldn't suppress his smile as the conversation wound down. "Thank God," he yelled at his phone when his father switched off. But he would have to call his brother and sister and warn them of the bullet that he had just dodged. Their father could turn on a dime, and the others had to be ready to take the same line he had used if Dad called either one of them for advice.

Four

Charlie showed up a few minutes before 1:00, dressed for business in a leotard and tank top. Steven was already in his swimsuit and warm-up jacket, and he climbed onto the table where she helped him with his stretching. When they were finished, they went out to the patio where the swimming pool overlooked the inland waterway. He gestured to her backpack. "Do you have your swimsuit in there?

She was surprised. "No! I'm not the one who's going to be swimming laps."

"I thought you were going to help me."

"I am. From up on the edge where I can see you better. You swim and I'll take notes. Then we can talk about how you can get more out of it."

Steven took off the jacket and tossed it on a chaise. He made a stylish dive into the deep end and began swimming laps while Charlie walked back and forth on the edge of the pool watching his technique and evaluating his stroke. Almost immediately, she advised him to slow down. He was thrashing angrily and rolling too much. "It's not a race, Mr. Armstrong. You're the only one in the pool."

He *was* angry. He had been agonizing over the decision of what he should do. Ask her to marry him and risk looking like an idiot. Or keep his mouth shut and risk losing her. Matthew was right, of course. He hadn't given any thought as to how greatly his comfortable life would change. He'd be linking up with a woman whose age alone would dictate different interests. And a teenage girl? He couldn't begin to imagine all the disruptions she would bring to his household. At his age he shouldn't even be considering a cocker spaniel, much less a wife and daughter.

But then again, Matthew had told him that age didn't matter, and that physically he was younger than his years. So, maybe he would be able to handle all the problems that would come with a second marriage, just as he had with the first. Sure, there would be difficulties and frustrations, but he had married into those before and still found happiness with a woman he loved. Why couldn't he do it again?

"Let's switch to the kickboard, Mr. Armstrong," Charlie called from above. She extended the small board out over the water.

"Steve," he reminded her as he grabbed for the board.

"Okay, Steve," she agreed. "You were doing everything with your arms. I think you have to work your legs much more."

He nodded, pushed off with the board and kicked his way toward the other end. "You're right," he told her when he finished his second lap. "I can feel it in my thighs and abs."

"Good, how about three more laps?"

"I can do five," he answered.

"I know you can, Steve. I just don't want you to blow any gaskets."

She could sense that he was distracted. Steve was a natural athlete with great coordination and long, easy movements. Today he was churning. He was going through the motions but his mind wasn't in it.

"Ahh, screw it!" he suddenly decided. He pushed off from the board and caught the step of the ladder. "That's enough."

He bounded up and out of the pool, and snatched up his towel before she could hand it to him.

"Something bothering you?" Charlie asked.

"No!" he snapped, but then added in a softer voice, "Well maybe . . ."

She was about to ask what it was, but then thought better of it. She was his trainer, not his analyst. What was bothering him was his business. She should stick to her own field. "Well, then, forget the training. Just swim easily for relaxation. Take a walk outside instead of running on the treadmill. Maybe we both could use a day off!" She picked up her backpack.

"Don't leave," Steven blurted out. And then in a much softer tone, "There's no reason for you to leave. That's what's bugging me. I don't want you to . . . leave. There's something I want to talk about."

"Sure," Charlie said, and set the backpack down easily. But her guard was up immediately. At this stage of a patient's recovery, a long talk usually meant that her services were being terminated. *You've been wonderful, Charlie, But I think I'm ready to go it alone.* Or, *I hate to tie you down when there are people who really need your help.* There were any number of reasons and excuses, but they all added up to being let go. Sometimes she left with just a "thank you," and sometimes with a week's pay pressed into her hand. But either way, she had to start looking for another assignment.

This one had been a godsend. Steven didn't care about the hours, so she could drop her daughter off at school in the morning and then pick her up in the afternoon. He was easy to work with. Some of her clients had treated her as part of their servant corps, expecting her to keep the gym clean, take care of the towels and linens, and run personal errands. Steve had always treated her with the deference due to a professional.

There was no woman in the house hovering over their every move. Some wives seemed to assume that she would be throwing herself at their husbands—or that their husbands would try to take liberties with a hired girl. Hold a man's thigh while she was working his knee and the wife would appear instantly. Nor was she required to join in any conspiracy. With one client, the young wife was carrying on with the gardener during the husband's recuperation. She had been expected to provide cover for their liaisons. *Make damn sure he's pedaling that bicycle until at least three o'clock. And make a lot of noise when he finishes.* With Steven, everything was friendly, light-hearted, and strictly aboveboard.

And, of course, there was the house with its windows opening out onto the waterway, its gardens, and the shaded dock where his small boat was tied. She had free run of the place. Whether they took Steven's exercise mat out to the dock, did laps in the pool by the water's edge, or took a bottled water break in the kitchen, Charlie never had a better working environment.

"The thing is," Steven began, "that I'm past needing therapy."

"You certainly are," she agreed.

"And I probably don't need a personal trainer either. I mean we both know that I have all the routines down cold."

"True," she admitted. "I've really just been monitoring you." *Here it comes,* she thought.

"So, I suppose you've been figuring on finding another patient. You have to be guessing that I'll be letting you go."

Her mouth was too dry for a response. She simply nodded.

"And that's what's bothering me," Steven continued. "I don't want you to go."

"Huh?" She was startled. It sounded as if she wasn't being laid off.

"I'd like you to consider staying."

Consider it? She'd love to stay. But he was right. He didn't need a full-time trainer. "Well," she said, "We could cut back on the hours. Maybe get together just three days a week?" She had been about to say two days, but while the words were in her mouth she had decided to try for three. She would have to find something else to make up for loss in pay, but at least she could take a bit more time to find the right job.

"I'm not talking about cutting back on your hours. I'm

talking about you staying sort of . . . permanently."

Uh-oh! He wanted her to move in with him. And that wouldn't be just to keep count of his repetitions in the weight room. Steven was asking her to become his mistress. Which was flattering, because a man of his position and wealth could probably bring in the whole lineup from one of the topless joints. But it was out of the question. She had a daughter to raise, and she certainly couldn't hold the line on body piercing if she was in bed with the boss. It was also a bit insulting. Now that he didn't need her as a professional therapist, he was offering her an opening in another profession.

"What I'm asking," Steven went on, "is whether you would consider marrying me?"

"Marrying?" What was he talking about? Was this a high-class come-on?

"Well, yes . . . marrying."

"You and me?"

He had been twisting his towel in his hands. Now he was trying to tie it in a knot. "It must sound ridiculous, an old guy like me thinking a young, beautiful woman like you . . . And I know I'm saying it all wrong, because there was only one woman I ever asked, and that was forty-two years ago. So I'm a little out of practice."

"It's not ridiculous. It's . . ." She was about to say "sweet," but she realized how condescending that would sound. Or maybe she should say "impossible" except that would be too brutal. "It's flattering," she decided. "I'm out of practice, too. It's a long time since I've been asked."

"I don't believe that," he said. "Someone as terrific as you must get asked all the time."

"Oh, I get asked. But not to get married."

Steven tossed the towel aside and reached for her hand. "You must have known that I was attracted to you. You had to have some idea of my feelings."

"No." It sounded more definitive than she meant it to sound. "I knew that we liked each other and that we worked well together. But I had no idea."

"Then let me say it straight out. I love you very much, and I'm hoping that you'll consider marrying me."

"Steve, this is so sudden. So unexpected." Her hands were covering her mouth. In truth, it was a ridiculous idea, but she couldn't come right out and say so.

"I don't expect an answer right away," Steven hastened to assure her. "I know you have a life of your own, hopes, and responsibilities. There are a lot of things you have to consider. But maybe you could give it some thought. I'd hate to lose you because I never asked you to stay with me. But I'll understand if you decide that it isn't the right move for you."

He was offering her an escape. All she had to do was say that she would think about it. That would give her time to put her reasons into the kindest possible words. But that wouldn't be fair. She already knew the answer and it would be cruel to string him on. She had to tell him.

"Steven, I like you very much, and I certainly respect your integrity. But I've never thought that I was in love with you."

"I don't expect you to be in love with me. Just maybe that we could share our lives. I'd like to take care of you. I'd like to take care of your daughter. I'd like to be part of your life because, God knows, I don't have much of a life of my own. And maybe you could be part of the silly things I do. Like playing tennis, taking boat trips out to the Bahamas, and traveling to places I've never seen. I think we could be there for each other. Isn't that what love is? Being there for someone and trying to take care of them? Isn't it something you might learn?"

"In time, yes. It is something I could learn," Charlie told him. When he put it that way, there was no doubt that they could bring something to each other's life. And if that was love, then certainly she could grow to love him. But, to her, love had always been something more. Something she had experienced only once, with the young man who had fathered her child and then left her before the child was born. For a time she had thought that she couldn't draw her next breath without him. She had never felt that way about any other man, certainly not about Steven Armstrong.

"Look, if I'm being a complete ass, just say so," Steven offered. "I know all the reasons why it's a ridiculous idea. But I couldn't let you just leave without telling you how I feel about you. Because, if I did, I'd always be torturing myself about whether you might have decided to stay with me." He walked away from her as if he was afraid to make eye contact. "Anyway, I was hoping that you would at least think about it."

"I will," she said. "I'm very flattered, and I'll think about it."

What's to think about? she asked herself as she drove away from the house. *It's the best offer you've had, and the best you're likely to get.* Charlie thought about the implications for Tara. A better school, with all the extras that had been cut from the bare-bones budget of the school she attended. Music. Art. Theater. There had to be dozens of activities where a young woman could find her interests and her self-worth. And there would be new classmates—kids who were used to succeeding and were filled with confidence for facing new challenges. By herself, the best Charlie could offer her daughter was a fighting chance. With Steven's patronage, the girl could have the whole world. There was no doubt about it. Her marriage to Steven Armstrong would be the best break Tara could ever hope for.

And what about herself? She might keep working for another few years as an aerobics instructor, and might last a few more as a physical therapist. But then what? A dead-end job in the back office of a health spa? Or an attendant's job in the gym of a resort hotel? There were no business-suit jobs waiting for her. She would probably spend the rest of her life in sweats with a towel draped around her shoulders. What had Steven suggested? That she might join in his silly pastimes. Like taking his boat over to the Bahamas for a weekend in a five-star hotel. Or cruising down to the British Virgins to window-shop beaches and harbors that she had seen in travel magazines at the beauty parlor. His "silly" activities were more than she dared to dream about.

She would live in a house that was one of the residential stars of the Florida Gold Coast, featured in design and architecture magazines, and have a name that still turned heads on Wall Street and in the world of banking. She would carry credit cards backed by vaults full of cash, and drive cars that would never need an after-market radio. Was there a better life to be won through hard work and diligence?

What was there to think about?

Lots of things, she knew. Like how Tara would react to having a new father who was old enough to be her grandfather. Or how she would feel about her mother sleeping with someone she obviously didn't love just to earn room and board. Tara was beginning to face up to her own sexuality, and Charlie was battling to persuade her that it should never be for sale. So, how could she explain selling herself to get her daughter into a better school, and to get both of them into a better neighborhood?

Then there was the matter of Steven's children, most of them older than she was, and none of them ready to have a gym rat for a stepmother. They would see through the marriage in an instant and understand that their father was paying a very high price for an occasional roll in the sack. They would know exactly what it was that she saw in their father, and hate her for taking the old fool's money. They, of course, would expect that the Armstrong fortune was already theirs, and would see their father's new wife as a thief with her eyes on their inheritance.

And what about Steven's social friends? Charlie could imagine the first time that she arrived at a charity function on Steven's arm. "So she's the little gold digger," the ladies would whisper behind their hands. And the men, alone with their cigars, would wonder, "What do you suppose a fuck like that costs?" and "What the hell was he thinking? You can order up something like that by the hour over the Internet." She would never be accepted in his social circles, and he probably wouldn't be welcome as long as she was around.

The bottom line was that there would be troubles at every level of their relationship. It was ridiculous for Steven to think that she could "share his life." Most likely, she would end up ruining it!

She was turning into her condo community when she realized that she had driven right past Tara's school. "Damn it!" she yelled out loud. She was already losing her composure. She had built a decent, respectable life for herself and her daughter. What more could she expect? Reach too high and she would risk everything she had achieved. She turned around in her parking area and headed back to the school.

Charlie knew that she had made a remarkable recovery from her disastrous first romance. Deserted, broke, and pregnant, she had been staring at a life in public housing on the welfare dole. But she had found jobs first as a waitress, where the tips were good, and later with a telemarketing company that at least let her sit while she worked. A week after Tara was born, she was back on the job with her daughter in a basket under her desk. At nights, she had lugged the basket to the health club where she worked her way back into shape and, in the process, found herself a career. True, her adult life had been a frantic scramble between work demands and family needs. Also true was that her bank account had never allowed for a decent vacation or even provided a moment of security. But she was making it all work. She didn't need to slip into anyone's bed.

She was early at the school, so she slumped behind the wheel and searched the radio for a station that would deliver static-free music. It was the tinny sound of the rotted-out radio and the faded colors of the car interior that advanced the opposing argument. Sure, she was making it, but at a bare subsistence level, and that situation wasn't likely to change. Her earnings would edge up a few points each year. Tara's salary, when she was old enough to work, would be a windfall. But the expense side of the ledger would rise much more rapidly. Things weren't going to get a lot better unless her fairy godmother made an appearance.

She laughed at the thought. Steven Armstrong was her fairy godmother. He had stepped unexpectedly into her life, waved his magic wand, and offered to change all her pumpkins into coaches. Why would anyone hold out for the handsome prince when a fairy godmother was already on the scene?

The car door snapped open and Tara tossed her backpack into the back seat. She mumbled a greeting without so much as a glance toward her mother, and then stared morosely through the grimy windshield. Charlie reached out and turned off the radio before she started the car and slipped it into gear. "How was your day?" she began.

"I don't want to talk about it!" Tara snapped defiantly.

She made no response until they had turned the corner and come up to a red light. "Want to hear about *my* day?"

Tara shivered. "Not right now."

Charlie nodded, then took off quickly when the light changed. They drove in silence, both staring ahead as if the other wasn't there. Charlie hunted for small talk—anything to break the angry silence. "Do you feel like going down to the beach for a swim?" she tried.

"Harry asked Melissa to the class dance," Tara said as if that were the logical response.

Charlie rushed through her memory. *The class dance? Did Tara say anything about a dance? And who in God's name was Harry?* But she knew Melissa, a girl who had been to their pool and who had invited Tara to her family's yacht club. "Isn't Melissa one of your best friends?" she asked.

"I hate her," Tara answered instantly.

"Oh, I didn't know that. And I'm not sure I know who Harry is. Have I met him?"

Tara rolled her eyes. "He was at our house last week. Don't you remember? He came with Melissa and Janey."

She did remember. There was a skinny boy with dyed hair who was wearing an earring. "Oh, sure. Was he Melissa's friend? Or Janey's?"

"He was my friend until Melissa stole him. She asked him out on her father's boat, so *naturally* he had to ask her to the dance. It looks as if you don't get asked unless you have a boat or something."

Dear God, Charlie thought. *It's starting already.*

Five

Gary Armstrong stared in shock. The cell phone slipped through his fingers and landed on his well-oiled belly. "He said no!" he announced in a quiet voice.

"Who said no?" Courtney Davis asked. She was lying in the chaise next to Gary's, at the edge of the swimming pool, clad in only the bottom half of her bikini. She wore small, opaque goggles to keep her eyelids from tanning.

"My father. I asked him about the money and he said he didn't want to get involved now."

Courtney remained motionless to avoid casting a shadow over her bronzed body. "When?" she asked.

"When he hears from his trainer. He asked her to marry him and he doesn't want to make any commitments until he knows how his life is going to come out."

She sat up abruptly, plucking the goggles out of her eyes. "He what?"

"He asked his trainer to marry him. If she says yes, then he'll be restructuring his finances . . ." Gary was talking in a monotone as if he couldn't believe what he was saying.

"His trainer?" Courtney demanded. "The lady jock we met in Florida?"

Gary nodded. "That's the one. I'm sure she'll turn him down."

Courtney swung her feet around so that she was sitting on the edge of her chaise, facing Gary. "Why would she turn him down with all that money waiting to be spent?"

"Maybe she doesn't care about his money," Gary offered. "Maybe she wants romance and affection. He's a lot older than she is. That might be more important to her than just money."

She shivered as if a ghost had just passed between them. "Don't be an idiot! She can buy love and affection by the hour. It's the money that's hard to tie into."

He shrugged. "So she'll marry him. And if she does, he wants her to be part of all his financial planning."

Courtney was horrified. "Including the movie?"

He nodded. "That's why he wants to wait before advancing the money."

She sprang to her feet. "He can't wait. The studio gave us the green light. If the money isn't there, they'll move on to something else."

"I'll talk to Ira," Gary said.

"Ira! Don't you dare talk to Ira. If Ira thinks there's any doubt about the money he'll drop us faster than he dropped his last wife. The word will be all over town in half an hour."

Gary flashed an instant of anger. "Ira wouldn't bolt. He knows I can replace him. There are other producers that would kill to work with me."

She shook her head in despair. "Of course there are. As long you're putting up the money." Courtney stormed off toward the house.

"It's not just money," he called after her. "I bring a lot more than money to this movie."

She stopped and turned back to him. "For God's sake, Gary, what have you been smoking?" Then she strutted off, slipping on the bikini top while she was climbing the steps to the house.

He checked the impulse to rush after her. That would

only lead to a fight, with each of them making dumb threats. He'd scream that he was her only chance of ever making it in Hollywood. And she would counter that without the money he certainly wouldn't be making it with her. Best let her calm down a bit with a stiff drink before he again raised the topic.

But he hated it when she charged that he was only as good as his father's money. Gary Armstrong had been a Hollywood player for the past twelve years. He had been making pictures when Courtney Davis, or whatever the hell her real name was, was still wearing braces on her teeth. He didn't need Ira Straus, a producer at Whetstone Films, and he certainly didn't need her. She was the one who needed him.

Of course, that wasn't completely true, he had to admit to himself. Even if he didn't actually *need* her, he certainly enjoyed her. She was a perfect Ten, maybe even an Eleven. He attracted more attention with Courtney on his arm than he would if he was cradling an Oscar, and he always savored the envy that was so naked in other men's eyes. Certainly there was no shortage of attractively decorative ladies in Hollywood, but Courtney would be a standout on any runway. It was also true that she didn't really need him. Ladies like Courtney could always find a pretender to one Hollywood throne or another who would pay her bills and nurse her fantasies of becoming a star. Gary knew that, were he to die, Courtney would come to the funeral on some wannabe mogul's arm.

But for all its imperfections, their relationship worked. He was, in fact, involved in the process of making motion pictures, and did move easily among big-name producers, agents, and actors. That earned her a bit of recognition. And he had gotten her a small part in a mediocre film, so she could legitimately list herself as "actress." Now he had her slotted for a supporting role in his new picture with Whetstone, so she would soon be able to label herself "a star." For the time being, at least, he filled all her needs. For her part, she filled his need to live with a beautiful woman, which was every bit as important as his need to drive an expensive German roadster. And she faked a fabulous orgasm, which fulfilled his self-image as a stud. He certainly couldn't dismiss her lightly.

He also had to admit that there was more than a grain of truth in her charge that his role in Hollywood was founded, at least in part, by his ability to put up the money. Without doubt, he had a great eye for a script, was a finely honed critic of production and dramatic talent, and had the marketing instincts of an impresario. Some of the biggest names in the industry had told him so. But upon reflection he had admitted to himself that the compliments had generally come from people who were sniffing around for money. Not that the money was his most important contribution. It was just that the project in which he was to be a key player wasn't going to get out of rewrite until someone put up some seed capital.

Would Ira Straus really drop him if the money was delayed? Would he move onto a new project where the funds were already in the account? Maybe! Ira wasn't the kind of producer who ever went down with his ship. On the other hand, there weren't too many people with deep pockets waiting to make a movie. In Hollywood, a screenwriter was unemployed, an agent was a screenwriter with a telephone, and a producer was an agent who had a desk. Some of the industry's greatest acting was done by penniless producers who played the roles of high flyers, using Beverly Hills mail drops when they actually lived near the airport, and renting Aston-Martins by the hour so they could make memorable entries to luncheon meetings. There were any number of big players, but only a few who could sign a big check. Ira wasn't one of the few.

The downside of the situation was that if his father's little bodybuilder drew out the negotiations for the wedding, eventually, Ira would find something else. And when he did, then the current Whetstone project would go into that limbo where movies go when they die before principal filming. Should that happen, Courtney's star would fade and she would do the only sensible thing: Go find herself a new rainmaker.

He put on his bathrobe and walked back up to the house,

pausing for the glass of orange juice that his housekeeper had waiting on the patio. Then he went into the pool bathroom, where Courtney was just stepping out of the shower. She spent the next twenty seconds knotting a towel around her wet hair, and giving Gary a long, leisurely look at what he stood to lose.

"I'll call my brother," he announced. "He'll know what to do."

"Why would Matthew care? He doesn't have a movie about to go down the toilet."

Gary snickered. "Matthew has every bit as much to lose as I do. If Dad starts counting his money, he's going to notice how much Matt is costing the shareholders. Big brother could find himself out on the street."

He brushed against her as he stepped into the shower. Courtney pulled away reflexively as if he had delivered an electric shock. She tied another towel around herself, tucking the corner over the top and down into her cleavage. "Let me know what Matthew says," she ordered and closed the door behind her.

Gary recognized her signals. Several months earlier, when the Whetstone project was getting started, he had told her that there probably wouldn't be a part in the picture for her. She hadn't spoken to him for days, and she had so many bedtime headaches that he thought she might be developing a brain tumor. He had arranged a rewrite that gave more substance to a minor role and then announced to Ira that he was considering Courtney for the part. Straus had gone along with him, and Gary brought the script home for her to read. That night, they had made love in three different rooms. Her message had come across loud and clear. *If I don't get what I want, then you don't get what you want.*

He had recognized the threat when she abandoned him in the shower. If he didn't get the money from his father, he wasn't going to get her. He still had a towel wrapped around his waist when he dialed his brother's number.

Six

Charlie had decided to accept Steven Armstrong's proposal. She planned to be completely honest. She would tell him that she admired and respected him. That she enjoyed his company. That his proposal had been the most flattering moment of her life. That she looked forward to sharing his bed and would do everything she could to please him. That she hoped she would fall in love with him. But he would have to understand that she wasn't in love. She wouldn't say "love" until she was sure that it was true.

She wanted to be just as honest with her daughter. She wanted to tell her that Steven Armstrong was a fine man who would be a loving husband and father. That he would give both of them every opportunity to grow and prosper. That their lives, until now edgy and uncertain, would be completely secure. That Tara's future, now clearly marginal, would become boundless. But she would have to add that he wasn't the Prince Charming that a younger Tara had dreamed would come into her mother's life.

The issue she didn't want to face was the intimate side of her contemplated marriage. That would certainly be one of

Tara's first questions. "Are you going to sleep with him?" the girl would ask, meaning was she going to do all the things with Mr. Armstrong that she had warned her daughter against. Certainly, she would answer, that's what married people do. But if she was going to let him do all that even though she didn't love him, and just because he could buy things for her, wasn't that like being a . . . ?

What word would she use. Hooker? Call girl? Prostitute? Whore? What did kids her age call women who sold themselves? And how would she answer? That the difference was that she and Mr. Armstrong were committing themselves to each other? That theirs wasn't a quick commercial transaction but rather a binding, long-term relationship? How would those answers sound to a thirteen-year-old girl who was just beginning to explore relationships? Probably like so much smoke. To Tara, the issue would be simple. You didn't sleep with people you didn't love no matter how much they promised to give you. That was exactly what Charlie had told her daughter when they first discussed the realities of sex. That was the same standard Tara had every right to expect her mother to meet. So, maybe she should lie and say that she was madly in love with Steven, and argue that their age difference didn't really matter. Except this was too important a discussion to be launched with a lie.

It was how she was going to explain her decision to Tara that prevented her from making the decision. It would be much easier to tell Steven no, and then there would be no reason to discuss anything with her daughter. But . . . but . . . wouldn't that be throwing away the girl's future? And, if it was Tara's future that was in question, shouldn't Tara be part of the decision? And then her mental debate would start all over again.

Charlie picked her opportunity carefully—a school night after Tara had finished her homework, phoned a friend, and then settled at the opposite end of the sofa in front of the television.

"Anything special you want to watch?"

Tara shrugged and pursed her lips, an all too frequent gesture that generally meant *Why should I care?*

Charlie gave a synopsis of the movie she was watching.

The response was another shrug. The girl was still unimpressed. She clicked the "off" button on the remote and noted a flicker of consciousness in her daughter's eyes. "Well, maybe we should talk. I can't remember the last time that we had a decent conversation." Now she had Tara's attention. Her expression showed fright bordering on terror.

"Tell me what's happening in school. What are you and your friends up to?"

Tara stuck her tongue through her chewing gum and blew a bubble that she instantly sucked back into her mouth. "Nothing much," she decided. This was going to be even harder than she feared. Charlie pressed ahead, asking about the field hockey tryouts (they were going okay) and the math class that was giving her trouble (it sucked). She could see her daughter beginning to squirm. The girl couldn't stand being in a conversation with her mother for much longer.

"Well, I have something I'd like to discuss." Tara responded with a wary glance. What her mother wanted to discuss was usually some new prohibition in her lifestyle or a dreary new task that she was old enough to assume. The last lecture was on responsibility after she had forgotten about a dentist appointment. "What would you say if I told you that I was thinking of getting married?"

The girl's jaw dropped. She stared blankly at her mother who was doing her best to keep the happy smile that was so forced it was beginning to hurt. "Married? To who?"

"That was going to be the second part of my question," Charlie said. "But the first thing I want to know is just how you would feel about me getting married . . . in general?" *That was stupid. You can't get married in general,* she reproached herself.

Tara, too, thought it was pretty dumb. "How can I tell you how I feel about you getting married if I don't know who you're marrying? I didn't even know you were going with someone."

"I'm not. I haven't been dating anyone," she corrected. She would have labored through an explanation, but the girl cut her off.

"You're thinking of marrying someone you haven't even gone out with?"

Charlie was beginning to feel sick. Her rehearsed approach was getting nowhere. She couldn't break this kind of news piecemeal. She had to plunge in with the whole story and take her chances. "The man is a client of mine. I'm his therapist . . . his trainer. That's put us together several times a week, so I have been seeing him even though we haven't been going together. Then, out of the blue, he asked me to marry him. Well, I certainly couldn't give him an answer until I knew how you would feel about it. I mean, if I'm going to be his wife, then you're going to be his stepdaughter. So I'm asking you because I don't want to make such an important decision for you. You're not just a kid anymore." She reached across and touched Tara's hand. "You're still number one in my life, you know."

"Who is he?" Tara asked, pulling her hand away. "Do I know him?"

"Yes, as a matter of fact. You've been to his house twice. Once when . . ."

"Mr. Armstrong?" She made his name sound like Dr. Frankenstein.

"That's right! Steven Armstrong. He lives in the big white house right on the water. You remember that he had a knee operation, and that I was his therapist. Then . . ." Charlie intended to babble on about Steven's medical history so that her daughter couldn't get in a word. Her strategy didn't work.

"Isn't he like . . . ancient!" Tara interrupted.

"No, he's not ancient!" Charlie was offended. She had been weighing this decision more seriously than any since she had decided to keep her daughter. She didn't like the man she was seriously considering to be ridiculed by the child who would become his beneficiary.

"Well, kind of old," Tara said, amending her first reaction.

"He is a lot older than I am," Charlie admitted, trying to sound open and honest. "But we're both adults with the same interests. I think we could make each other very happy and be very good for one another."

"But would you have to . . . you know . . . do it with *him*?" Tara visibly shivered at the thought.

"If you mean would he and I make love, of course we would. That's what people who are married do."

Tara cut to the heart of the issue. "Are you in love with Mr. Armstrong?"

"I have great admiration for him."

The girl shook her head vigorously. "No! That's not what I asked. I asked are you in love with him."

"I'm not sure. But the more I think about it, the more it seems that I probably am." Even that was stretching the truth, but at least she wasn't telling a bold lie.

Tara was disappointed. "Isn't love more than a 'probably'?" At her age, it seemed that love should be the emotion that defined your whole life. "Probably" took all the excitement out of it.

"That's hard to answer. At every age, love means something different. It's not always a lightning bolt."

Tara jumped to her feet. "You do whatever you want," she snapped. "But I hope I never marry someone who I'm *probably* in love with. That's just a cop-out!" She stormed off to her room. Her door nearly exploded as she slammed it shut.

You certainly handled that beautifully, Charlie told herself. But she knew that the issue was far from settled. True, her first round had fallen miles short of the target. But at least she had raised the issue. Tomorrow, if she knew her daughter, Tara would mumble some sort of apology, claiming that she didn't want to be the anchor that kept her mother's ship from sailing. And that would give her the opening to introduce other considerations. She would tell the girl that if she decided to marry Mr. Armstrong, then they would both move into the big white house right on the water. Tara would give her "why should I care?" shrug. But she would immediately grasp that there would be big changes for her, and not all of them would be bad.

Then, maybe a night or two later, Charlie would reintroduce the subject. "What do you think about moving to a new house, and going to a new school? Think you can handle all that, or is it something you don't even want to think about?" But, of course, the girl would have been thinking about little else. She would have faced up to the days of loneliness when she parted from her friends. But she would also be intrigued by the opportunities that might lie ahead. Then it would be Charlie's job to help her over the transition. Promise her that her friends could come and visit as often as they wanted. Assure her that she could stay in her school until her graduation.

Was she manipulating her own daughter? Yes, damn it, that was exactly what she was doing. But wasn't that what raising a daughter was all about? Cajoling, and prompting, and manipulating until she saw things the way you did? Wasn't it her duty to help the idealistic little dreamer face up to reality? To understand that life with Steven Armstrong held a whole magnitude of opportunities that a personal trainer would never be able to provide? To show her clearly that all marital relations didn't begin with a lightning bolt?

She was climbing into bed when it dawned on her that the decision she was trying to make wasn't just about her daughter. For all her logic, she really didn't know how she felt about . . . doing it . . . with someone she didn't truly love.

Seven

At first, Trish didn't notice her phone ringing. Her radio was blaring so that she could hear the music above the roar of the wind, but still it was barely audible. At seventy miles an hour, and with the top down, the wind noise was deafening. It was the illuminated telephone keys on the dashboard that attracted her attention. She lifted the phone to her cheek, leaving her left hand on the wheel.

"Hello," she screamed.

A voice mumbled back in words that she couldn't understand.

"Hello!" she yelled louder. "I can't hear you. You'll have to speak up."

"It's Matthew," she was able to make out.

"Matthew, I can hardly hear you."

"I'm shouting," he howled back. "What's all that background noise? Are you in the shower?

"No! I'm on the Long Island Expressway on my way out to the Hamptons."

"Well, pull over to the side. I have news that's going shock you."

She eased off the gas, checked her mirror, and let the car drift into the slow lane. When the wind died, she heard the radio blasting and turned down the volume. "How's that?" she asked.

"Better," Matthew said. Then he asked, "Have you spoken with Gary?" She said she hadn't. "Well, then, let me be the first to tell you. Our father has asked someone to marry him."

"Shut up! You have to be kidding!"

"He asked her, and now he's waiting for her answer."

Trish laughed. "So who's the lucky lady? Anyone we know? Wait! Don't tell me! Let me guess! I can see her face. What was the name of that friend of Mother's? You remember, the baroque lady who used to dress like a sofa."

"Madeline Rogers," he supplied.

"That's it. Madeline Rogers. Is she the one he asked?"

"You're not even close," Matthew said.

Trish pouted. "Who then?"

"You remember the therapist who was helping Dad after his knee operation?"

"Sure! She had a man's name. Joey or something."

"Charlie. He asked Charlie to marry him."

An SUV came up behind Trish's Porsche and roared angrily around her, the passenger mouthing an insult. She realized she had slowed to fifty and added a bit of pressure to the pedal. "That's ridiculous," Trish said. "Why, she's our age. He's old enough to be her father."

"He doesn't think it's at all ridiculous," Matthew corrected her. "He's dead serious."

She considered. "Well, I suppose Charlie has to be a lot more fun in the sack than Madeline Rogers. I mean, he's still physically fit. So, if he's found a little bon-bon to lighten his load, more power to him. As long as he doesn't expect me to call her *Mommy*."

She chuckled at the foolishness of old men with their fancies of virility.

"Gary isn't as understanding as you are," Matthew announced. "It seems that Dad has decided not to invest in his new movie. At least until he knows whether he has a new wife and how she feels about it."

"He's not putting up the money!" Trish was shocked. But then she rationalized, "Of course it didn't sound like much of a movie when Gary told me about it. And his last picture didn't do well enough to pay back the principal. Maybe Dad is souring on Hollywood, as well he might."

Matthew laughed cynically. "Good thing for you he isn't souring on the art world? Did he buy anything big at your last show?"

"He wasn't able to come up for it," she said. "But I sent him pictures of paintings by a very exciting new artist. I'm sure he'll like them."

"What if Charlie hates them?"

"Well, Dad wouldn't let a bodybuilder dictate his taste in art. If she didn't like them, I suppose he would . . . he would have to . . ." Her car was already in the breakdown lane and headed into the guard rail. She straightened it in the nick of time, then oversteered back onto the road to the blaring of auto horns. "You don't think he'll stop investing in art, do you?"

"He's stopped investing in movies," Matthew reminded her.

She paused thoughtfully while she straightened the car and adjusted the speed to the traffic. "What's Gary going to do?"

"Gary thinks we all ought to be doing something to discourage the wedding. He wants us to get together right away." He mentioned a date and suggested her Manhattan apartment as convenient for them and close to the airports where Gary would land. It also offered a bit more privacy than his house where his wife would get involved. She pulled back into the fast lane but didn't bother to turn the radio on. She had to think. What *would* she do if her father stopped buying from her gallery? *He wouldn't,* she reassure herself. He loved her gallery and her artists. Hadn't she even named it the Armstrong Gallery, after him?

In truth, that was a bit of a stretch. She had been Patricia Bennet when she opened the gallery in Greenwich Village, but her marriage was already over and her husband had gone on to an even richer young heiress. That, too, was a stretch. The new wife wasn't actually worth more but she had a fantastic figure and oversized eyes. Trish knew that he had dumped her for better sex rather than greater fortune, but it was easier on her ego to think of him as a gold digger.

Not that she was unattractive. She was a bit too tall, and straight rather than curvy. Couturier dresses showed too much of what wasn't there. And her face was long and perhaps a bit masculine, nearly identical to her two older brothers. But her eyes twinkled, her smile gushed, and when she got a really great haircut, she was blonde and sporty. Trish didn't light up a room but, on the other hand, no man would be embarrassed to have her on his arm.

She had been an Art History major in college, which made her something of a disappointment to her father. "What in God's name does an Art History major do?" Steven had complained, and then tried to find a place for her in his hardware empire. Maybe he could add artwork to his decorating departments, or put her in charge of store decor. Instead, he had set her up in an artist's loft in Tribeca and paid her rent for the five years it took her to fail as a painter and find a husband. David Bennet had stuck around for a few years, long enough to convince her that her true talents were in judging artists rather than painting. When he left, she had opened the Armstrong Gallery in the Village with a generous down payment provided by Steven, and a mortgage that she could manage with even middling success. She had picked the name, "Armstrong," simply to announce her divorce.

Trish had succeeded. She had been received with open arms by the art set—stuffy critics, struggling artists, and easily duped buyers. She became a lunchtime figure at the tiny restaurants where art was discussed over wine and crepes, and a regular at gallery openings and shows. In the summer, when the whole set moved to the Hamptons like farmworkers following the sun, she was at all the fashionable cocktail parties. She was the first of her crowd to open a branch in the quaint village of East Hampton. True, that had required another transfusion of capital from her father, but she was paying off her notes faithfully. It was, she had convinced herself, a business deal that any shrewd investor would have jumped on. She had simply given Steven the first opportunity.

Trish parked in front of her gallery, which overlooked the park in the center of East Hampton, and went in for a quick chat with her store manager. The girl, also an Art History major, reported one sale for the week, to an interior decorator who thought the orange in a sunset at sea was a perfect match for drapes he was doing for a client. Then she drove to the small house that she rented as a business expense near the Maidstone Country Club. The cottage had a large deck overlooking a salt marsh and was perfect for evening cocktail parties.

Her father would never let his new wife dictate his taste, she tried to convince herself. Why, the girl was . . . what? A bodybuilder? An aerobics instructor? She remembered Charlie pushing on her father's legs to stretch out his back. What could she possibly know or care about contemporary art?

But then again, what could she possibly know about making movies? Her father wasn't investing in the new film until he had the girl's opinion. So, maybe he would cut back on his art expenditures. She didn't have to call her accountant to know what that would mean. Disaster, pure and simple! Steven Armstrong was the galleries' biggest customer.

His purchases assured the success of all her shows. She sent him photos of the paintings that were left hanging, glowing appraisals of their future value, and a price list that would cover the income she needed. Inevitably, he bought. Sometimes on behalf of the Ucandoit Corporation, whose directors were always thrilled to patronize their largest stockholder. The Ucandoit boardroom and most of its executive officers were decorated with the work of artists who had yet to be discovered by the mainstream. Others he bought as gifts for friends and business associates. Some he offered to Ucandoit's major suppliers, who generally were giddy in their enthusiasm for the work. And there were some that he hung in his own home to the dismay of his architect and interior decorator. All in all, he had bought over two hundred paintings from Armstrong Galleries, New York and East Hampton, accounting for better than six million dollars of her income.

Her other customers barely kept the galleries afloat. Steven Armstrong's purchases paid for her lifestyle.

Now, this hot-pantsed little gym rat might come up with other things for him to spend his money on. Insurance, so that she would be debt-free once she killed him with athletic sex. College tuition for that brat kid who had actually come to her father's house while he was in the midst of his recovery. A bigger yacht, so that she could cruise the world at his children's expense. It wasn't right! Any fool could see that all she was after was his money.

She lifted her phone and dialed Claudio Spector, an art critic for the *Village Voice*. "Claudio here," he answered.

"Claudio, this is Trish."

"Trish, darling. You're in a bit early. Should I come over right now?"

"I'm sorry, but I'm going to have to cancel," she said. "I have a petulant client who's toying with another gallery, and I have to bring him to heel. Be a darling and put it off until tomorrow. And would you call Terrence and Cynthia and tell them that I'll have to postpone."

She would have to call Gary and Matthew and decide how they were going to keep their father from marrying Charlie whatever-her-name-is. She couldn't wait until they got around to meeting in New York. She had a show coming up next week in the city. If her father didn't buy, the whole thing would be a bust!

Eight

Steven paced back and forth across the white-marbled foyer as if he were waiting outside a delivery room. Each time he passed the front door he glanced out at the circular driveway, expecting her car to materialize. She was late, and that wasn't a good sign. Or was it? Maybe it was for the best!

For a week, he and Charlie had gone on with their routine as if he had never mentioned marriage. She came to the house, set up his exercise schedule, and then led him through the repetitions. All their conversations had been business-related. "Keep your back straight, and keep those arms pumping," was the kind of thing she had said all week. His words had been just as banal. "I think my heart rate is going down. What was I yesterday? Seventy-eight?" She was the trainer and he was the client. Neither had given voice to what each was really thinking.

Then, the day before, he had broken. As she was leaving he had braved the taboo subject. "Have you given any thought to what I asked you?" His tone was offhand, as if he had asked her to change her hours. Charlie's response had been much more intense. "It's all I've been thinking about. And I'm sorry I haven't given you an answer. But please don't think I'm not appreciative. I'm terribly excited at the thought of marrying you, but it's complicated. I need more time."

He knew he should have taken her answer at face value and offered her all the time she needed. Of course it was "complicated." She was committed to her daughter. She had to weigh what was best for the girl. Even more difficult was that his proposal was forcing her to evaluate her feelings. Was she still hoping for Prince Charming who would sweep her off her feet? Was she still young enough to be romantic rather than practical?

"Is it going to be any less complicated a week from now?" he had asked her. "Or a month?" He had told her that in his business career he never put off tough decisions. "I'd allow myself one day. I'd weigh the facts and then give it my best shot. Usually, I was right. But even when it turned out that I had been wrong, letting the decision fester wouldn't have been any better."

Charlie had nodded. "You're right. I'm dragging this out, and that's not fair to you. I'll take one more day, and then I'll give it my best shot." She had stepped close and surprised him with a gentle kiss on his cheek.

Steven had been elated. The kiss! A personal gesture aimed to heal his spirit the same way she had healed his body. She had touched him before, always professionally, to aid his use of tissue and muscle. Now she had touched him personally to enliven his spirit. But during the night, he had begun to doubt. Perhaps it had been a good-bye kiss. Or a kiss aimed at strengthening him for the bad news she was going to bring. He began to regret that he had implied a deadline. He'd rather have a few more days of hope than to have the answer he dreaded.

Now she was late. She was always on time, but today she was late. Maybe that was her answer. She had kissed him good-bye because she knew that she wouldn't be returning. Probably she thought that this was the kinder way. Steven again glanced through the windows that bordered the front door. Still an empty driveway. Still no sign of her.

Well, maybe it's better this way, he rationalized. He had

his own doubts about the wisdom of marrying a woman half his age. He was frightened at the prospect of becoming a surrogate father to an adolescent. And his children were unanimously opposed. Each of them had warned of the grave dangers lurking ahead.

Matthew, he thought, had put it best. Get married if he wanted to, but be ready for his life to undergo drastic changes. His priorities would turn around so fast that he would probably suffer whiplash.

Gary had been less encouraging. It was too important a decision to make without at least considering alternatives. Take the summer in the Mediterranean, the way he had often talked about. Charter a boat in Sardinia and sail the Riviera. Window-shop the Greek Isles. You'll meet many women closer to you in age and more attuned to your interests. "Look, Dad! You've been cooped up in your house with the same woman, day in and day out, for all these months. Of course she seems wonderful to you. But you owe it to yourself to consider all the options. Get out and live for a while. Then decide what you want to do."

Trish had been downright hysterical. She had cried at the thought of him marrying again. "I just can't picture you with anyone but Mother. I don't think I'd recognize you. You've always been such an inspiration to me, and now this seems tawdry and beneath you." Steven had never considered that remarrying would be so devastating to his daughter.

The chorus of naysayers had begun to deflate his spirit. What they said, at least in part, made sense. Why should he be in any hurry to get married? Why should he risk becoming a public fool, or gamble with the affections of his children? As Matthew said, he was set in his ways.

If this is her answer, so be it! If Charlie had decided to kiss him good-bye, he would get along just fine. Maybe he would take a boat in Sardinia and see what the rest of the world had to offer. Except that Steven wasn't at all sure that he would be able to get Charlie out of his mind. Did he want to risk sitting aboard a boat in Sardinia while she fell in love with someone else?

He heard a car, and a glance to his driveway confirmed that it was her. He controlled his urge to rush to the door. He didn't want to appear too anxious, or even obsessed. Instead, he ran in the other direction, and hurried up the stairs to his bedroom. He should be in his sweats, ready for a workout, not in slacks and sport shirt.

He heard the door open. "Mr. Armstrong!" she called from the foyer. He didn't like the sound of that. Nobody married a person they called "Mister."

"I'm up here, Charlie," he yelled in no particular direction. "Just getting dressed. Be down in a minute." He hurried into his sneakers and tugged on the laces. A lace broke in his hand. "Damn!" Where was his old pair? In the closet? Or had he thrown them out? What a time to break a shoelace! He tied the two ends together in knot, but then the knot didn't fit through an eyelet. He took the sneaker off and backed the laces so the knot wouldn't have to fit through an eyelet.

"Steven! Are you okay?" She was calling from the bottom of the stairs.

"Yeah, sure. I guess I overslept!" He tied the lace and took a quick check in the full-length mirror, sucking in the slight bulge that he still had to work off his belly. He looked good. The sweatband around his shaved head made him look tough.

Charlie was in the kitchen, taking bottled water out of the refrigerator, when he came down. She was wearing her usual leotards and her warm-up jacket, her hair pulled back off her face. Nothing about her had changed. She still looked like a trainer, not like a woman who was about to accept a proposal of marriage.

She smiled when she saw him, which instantly made him aware that his heart was racing. Usually she came on like a prison guard, concerned only with getting him started on his stretching exercises. The smile seemed a bit giddy. He found himself beginning to smile with her. "What?" he said. "What are we laughing at?"

"Yes," Charlie said. "I'd be happy to be your wife. That's what I'm smiling at."

"You will?" He reached for the counter to steady himself. His knees were buckling. "No shit! You'll really marry me!"

She laughed at his choice of words. "No shit!" she answered.

Then Steven began to laugh joyously. "Damn!" he yelled. "I feel like a kid again. What do I look like? Twenty-five? Maybe thirty?"

"Be careful," Charlie said. "You'll begin to think that I'm too old for you."

He reached out and took her hands. She stepped toward him, expecting to be pulled into an embrace. Instead he held both her hands, and bent to kiss them. No one had ever kissed her hands before. Already she was getting used to being Steven Armstrong's wife.

But she wanted to be honest. He was a very decent man and she wouldn't want to deceive him in any way. She had to tell him that she was accepting his definition of love. That it was a commitment, not a feeling. Because she could make the commitment with a clear conscience, but she could never pretend to feel what wasn't really there. She had also been rehearsing a speech about her daughter's feelings all the way over in the car. Tara didn't want to share her mother with anyone, nor did she want them to be uprooted from their life together. She certainly didn't want a new father. Charlie had to prepare Steven for her surliness and indifference. Even though he would be giving her opportunities that she couldn't yet imagine or appreciate, she would more than likely act as if she was being martyred for her mother's pleasure.

Charlie wanted to start with a clear understanding. She intended to keep working to support herself and her daughter. Tara might live in a rich man's house, but she wasn't to have a rich girl's toys. She could imagine Steven lavishing every gift on the girl to try to win her over, which was exactly the wrong thing for him to do. Tara would resent a new sports car as a bribe. The only thing Steven should give her was time. In time, the girl would come to respect and admire him just as her mother had. She would even come to love him, just as Charlie hoped that she herself would.

"Now," she said when she retrieved her hands from Steven's attention, "there are some things we have to talk about."

"Sure! Sure!" he answered, daring to touch her hair with his fingertip. "But not now! This is a happy day for me. The happiest in as long as I can remember. I want to enjoy it. Let's go over to the beach and walk with our feet in the water. Or maybe take the boat out and run down to the Keys."

They decided on the beach. Steven backed his Cadillac out of the garage and Charlie climbed into the passenger seat. She set the water bottles into the console receptacles, and noticed the tuning buttons on the digital radio. She laughed.

"What?" Steven wondered. "What's funny?"

"Just that I was thinking of getting a new car radio. But this one wouldn't fit in my car. It's bigger than the dashboard."

"It's pretty good," he allowed, and clicked a button on his steering wheel. Instantly, the car filled with the sounds of a concert hall. "What do you like? Find any station that you like," he said.

"This is fine." She listened for a moment to a big band sound. "What is it?"

"Fifties stuff," he answered. "I used to play it on forty-fives when I was a kid."

"Forty-fives?" she had no idea what he was talking about.

"You know! The little records with the big holes. They came before the LPs." He wasn't sure whether that one had registered either. "Find what you want. I like all kinds of music."

Charlie fiddled with the buttons until she understood how the tuner worked. Then she switched to the station that Tara had set not only on her car radio but on every radio in their house. The twang of steel guitar strings vibrated in their ears. A bass woofer pounded out a drum beat that threatened to blow out the windshield. She tried to turn it down, but the blast of sound seemed even more deafening. "What should I do?" she screamed.

He used the button on the wheel to turn the music down to a dull roar. "What in hell was that?"

"Heavy metal," she laughed. "I didn't mean for it to come on so loud." But she stayed with the station, seemingly enjoying the same sounds that reminded Steven of a dentist's drill.

"Oh, yeah, I've heard of that," he said pleasantly. *It's happening already,* he thought. His neck hurt from the whiplash.

They walked the beach like any other couple, holding hands as the waves rolled in over their feet, pausing every few seconds to find a shell that he could skim out into the water. They had spent a dozen hours together each week since his operation. But the conversation, based on his recovery and training, had been built in. Now they needed topics that had nothing to do with their professional relationship.

"We should have brought bathing suits," Charlie suggested.

"I don't like salt water," he answered, leading to a moment of silence. Then he tried, "I suppose we could get chairs and just sit by the water," to which Charlie answered that she couldn't take a lot of sun. There was another pause in conversation with the silence becoming awkward.

They both found a topic at the same time. "When do you want the wedding?" they asked simultaneously, and then laughed at their foolishness. "How about Saturday?" Steven suggested.

Charlie was surprised. "So soon?"

"Do you have something better to do on Saturday?"

"No, but I need to get a dress. And one for Tara. I'm hoping she'll be my maid of honor."

"How long does that take?" He was teasing more than demanding.

"A wedding dress? Usually about a year. A month, anyway."

He nodded. "Okay, a month from Saturday. But not a day longer. I don't have as much time to waste as you do."

She knew he was trying to flatter her by suggesting that they marry right away. In truth, there was nothing she had to do that couldn't be completed by Saturday. "Will a month give your children enough time to get down here for the wedding?"

Steven smirked. "There's nothing any of them do that can't be wrapped up in an hour."

"Then it's set," she said. "A month from Saturday. I'll find a church and you get the license. And I'll have to plan a reception. Where do you want it? At the house, or at your yacht club? You know they may not be able to handle us on such short notice." She was babbling. From awkward silence, it didn't seem as if he was going to be able to get in a word.

"Wait a minute!" he said. He stopped walking and took her by the shoulders turning her toward him. "Before we get into all this, there's something I'd like to do."

She was puzzled. "Sure. What?"

He pulled her close and kissed her fully on the mouth, drawing her breasts tight to his chest. People looked up from their beach chairs. Walkers stopped to watch.

"Thank you," Steven said when he finally came up for a breath. "I'm thrilled that you've decided to marry me."

Charlie tried to compose herself, realizing that she was blushing. "I'm thrilled that you asked." But she knew that she wasn't. Even in his physical, passionate kiss she had felt nothing.

Nine

She doesn't love him," Matthew's wife, Hillary, said. "The only thing she's after is the money." There was an awkward pause. That was exactly what they all had thought of Hillary when she fell so madly in love with Matthew. Even now, after six years of marriage, she still seem obsessed with the stature and leisure that her husband's position could buy.

"I knew we should have moved faster," Gary offered, shaking his head in disgust. "What did I say to you, Matthew, as soon as I heard it? Didn't I say that we had to get together right away and figure out how we were going to stop this woman?"

"We can still stop it," Trish announced. "We'll all be there together, and we'll simply insist that he give this more time. If he has any regard for us, he won't rush into such an ill-advised marriage."

Matthew rolled his eyes. "I think we're past that, Trish. We've been invited to an engagement party. He's already made up his mind."

They were in a twin-engine business jet at thirty-two thousand feet over North Carolina, headed for the Boca Raton executive airfield. The cabin was configured with two seats facing another two seats over a table. Matthew and Hillary were side by side, their backs to the direction of flight. Trish was across the table near the window, facing the sister-in-law she could scarcely abide. Gary was next to her, across from his brother.

They had never managed to hold their meeting in New York at Trish's apartment. Steven's happy phone calls came while they were still working on the arrangements. "You have to meet her," he told each of his children. "Fly down Friday and I'll put you up at the yacht club. Sort of an engagement party." They had all met Charlie the afternoon their father came home from the hospital. But he was absolutely correct in saying that they had not gotten acquainted with her. After all, she was just "help" and no one really needed to get to know the help.

"Well, there will certainly have to be a prenuptial agreement," Hillary concluded. "I mean, he can't even think of marrying her without one." Another pause—Hillary had resisted any talk of an agreement before she married into Matthew's money.

Gary sneered. "He doesn't sound interested in a prenuptial."

Hillary bristled at the rebuke. "What I'm saying is that once the wedding is over, she can simply refuse to sign anything that limits her interests. It has to be done before the wedding." Trish glanced up. It seemed that Hillary was well versed on prenuptial contracts. Maybe that was why she had hustled Matthew off quickly on a whirlwind elopement. Hillary went on. "Do you realize that if something happened to Dad, his little bimbo could walk off with half the family fortune! In Florida, that much is guaranteed regardless of what his will says." *She's been doing her homework,* Trish laughed to herself. . . .

"Nothing is going to happen," Matthew told his wife. "Dad is in great shape. He'll probably outlive us all.

Hillary wouldn't be appeased. "Maybe she doesn't want to wait that long. For all we know she has a boyfriend. Someone has to be the little girl's father. And it could be that she and her boyfriend cooked this whole thing up together."

Gary turned away. "Jesus, Hillary, you sound like a late-night movie. That plot is so overdone I couldn't get it past a studio secretary."

"You don't think that slut would kill for a couple of hundred million? Think about it. She and your father are going to be alone together most of the time. And she's no wimp! She's a trained athlete. How hard would it be for her to throw him over the side? Or to give him a little push and send him tumbling down the stairs?"

"The girl's father deserted her before the daughter was born," Trish reported. Her father had told her so.

"And since then she's been a virgin!" Hillary mocked. "Are you all crazy. You think there isn't someone she'd like to live with if only she had the money? I'm telling you, this whole affair has the smell of a setup. We have to get a prenup if only to protect your father."

Gary laughed into his drink, sending up an explosion of bubbles. When Steven had gone into the hospital for his knee surgery, it had been Hillary who reminded everyone that if something should go wrong, their father wouldn't want them to use any special means to extend his life.

"I don't think that will work," Matthew said to Hillary. "Dad is in love with this girl. If you tell him that she's a liar who's planning to murder him, he's more apt to disinherit you than her."

Hillary huffed. "Then what do you suggest? That we all just wait around while the little lady screws us over?"

"I suggest that we all keep our heads," Matthew said. "We can't stop the wedding. But we can all impress on Dad how important a prenuptial agreement is. His life, his children's lives, his business, all his achievements could be lost. And we have to make it clear that we're not at all concerned about his new wife. It's just that he has to realize how vulnerable she would be if something should happen to him. Her relatives, even her daughter on the arm of a smart lawyer, might land on her. He should get everything set up in black and white if only to protect her."

There was a long silence as they weighed Matthew's suggestion. Gary held his glass up to the attendant, gesturing for another drink. Trish pursed her lips in an expression of deep thought. Hillary turned away and glowered out the window.

"Risky!" Trish decided. The others turned to her. "It will take us a month to get the message across to Dad, and then another month for him to get up the courage to raise the issue with her."

"Or," Gary considered, "she might resent an agreement. And if she's keeping him happy, Dad probably won't want to drive her away. So there might never be an agreement."

Hillary rejoined the conversation. "That's what I've been saying for the past half hour. We have to get it done before the wedding."

"And if we can't," Trish added, "we would have to make sure that if anything happened, it happened to her before it happened to him."

They drew deep breaths collectively because they all knew exactly what Trish meant. If anyone was going to be thrown over the side, or fall down the stairs, it would have to be Charlie rather than their father. And they were the only ones who could make that happen.

They landed in Boca Raton where a stretch limo was waiting to whisk them to their father's yacht club. They saw Steven's seventy-five-foot yacht, named *Idonit* as a play on the name of the business that had made him rich, tied to the pier and started toward it. They were stopped by their father's booming voice, bellowing from the deck that was outside the members' cocktail lounge. "Hey, you guys, the party is up here!" He was leaning against the railing, wearing a dark blazer over white slacks. The woman next to him was in a deep coral dress patterned with abstractions of shellfish. The two of them waved in unison. "Come on up!" Steven added.

"Jesus, where did she get that dress?" Hillary whispered to Trish.

"Florida tourist bureau, I imagine," Trish answered.

Gary stuck his head between them. "Just remember to call her 'Mother.'"

Steven was waiting at the top of the steps to embrace his daughter and his son's wife. Then he pounded the two boys on the back, pumped their hands, and dragged them across the lounge and out onto the deck. "Charlie, these are my children," he said with obvious parental pride. Then he introduced them one by one.

"My son, Matthew. He runs the business," Steven said, gesturing to his oldest child.

Charlie held out her hand. "Hi, Matt! I met you when you came down to see your father."

"We did," he agreed. "But then you were in sweat pants and a jacket. I had no idea how lovely you were." There were appreciative chuckles from the others.

"And Matthew's wife, Hillary . . ." the father intoned.

The women drew together and brushed cheeks. "How nice to finally meet you," Hillary oozed. And Charlie responded with a compliment that Hillary was even more lovely than Matthew had described. *Thank you,* Matthew thought to himself. He remembered clearly that he had never mentioned to Charlie that he was married. When he had seen her last, at his father's bedside, he had thought vaguely that she might be available for a seductive dinner and only God knows what might come after.

He introduced Gary as the "big-deal Hollywood producer," and mentioned his son's most important motion picture success. "Oh, I'd like to see it," Charlie said. "Is it still in the theaters? Or on video?"

Finally Trish was presented as the family art critic. Charlie had rehearsed what Steven had told her about the two paintings in his foyer. She admitted she knew little about art but said how much she enjoyed the paintings that Steven had shown her. With the introductions behind them, and everyone forcing Cheshire smiles, they adjourned to the bar for their pre-dinner cocktails.

Steven began by recalling the moment when he first knew that he was in love with Charlie. He had been on a macho kick, using more weight than he should for his leg lifts. She had pulled one of the weights off the bar and raised it over his head. "Next time you try to kill yourself, I'm going to help you," she had threatened. "I'll drop the damn weight right on your head."

Everyone howled at her impertinence. Obviously, threatening their father with a twenty-pound weight was a sure sign of love. "And when did you first know that you loved our father?" Hillary asked.

Charlie glanced at Steven. Then she answered, "Just a few days ago, when I had to decide how to respond to his proposal." She held out her hand for his support, and he took it in his hands. "I told him as honestly as I could exactly how I felt."

They oozed charm all the way into the dining room and through the rituals of ordering and selecting the wines. Charlie felt herself beginning to relax. Despite Steven's assurances that they would all be crazy about her, she had expected a harsh grilling. She knew that the difference in their ages would raise suspicions about her motives, and guessed that her position so close to the treasury would cause them some anxiety. Hillary's question about when she had decided she was in love seemed to be the opening salvo in the heavy shelling she was expecting. But there had been no cheap shots after that. Whatever Steven's children thought, they were all on their best behavior.

Trish complimented her on her dress and told her how well the color went with her tan. Hillary liked her healthy, outdoor look. "If I had your complexion, I wouldn't wear makeup either." Gary told her she could make it in movies. "Julia Roberts is the same age you are." He touched the well-formed muscle in her arm. "And you could do your own action scenes."

Midway through the meal, Charlie began to suspect that each of them was buttering her up. Whenever one of them paid a compliment, another would jump in to top it. Steven had to interrupt to remind them he wasn't "chopped liver." He laughed as he told them that if they blew any more smoke into Charlie's head "she won't think I'm good enough for her."

By dessert, she thought she had figured out the family dynamic. Each of them was vying for Steven's affection, and there was no surer way to earn his admiration than to admire the woman he had chosen. They were gushing affection on her for the benefit of their father and benefactor. Once she realized what was going on, Charlie felt completely safe. None of them would dare to insult their father's lady, even if they were livid to have her seated at their table. *Don't let it go to your head,* she warned herself. *It's all a game.*

It was in the ladies' room that she realized she had missed the most important message. Trish followed her in and yelled over the wall of the stalls. "I'm so glad that you like the paintings that I've been steering to Dad. He's simply crazy about most of those artists."

Charlie repeated that she wasn't a connoisseur of art. "All I've ever had were posters and reproductions. I won't pretend to understand modern artists, but I do find the paintings in your father's house sort of exciting."

"Exactly!" Trish said, and she continued the conversation while they stood together at the sink. "They're alive, and vital. Just like Dad. He loves them, but you know how self-made men are. He hates to spend anything on himself. He keeps saying he shouldn't be buying so much art, but he loves every piece. You should insist that he gets what he loves. There are all sorts of places where he can economize. Like I don't think he's ever gotten any pleasure out of the movies he backed. But he loves good painting."

Charlie followed that line without any help. If Dad wants to save money, Trish was saying, let him cut back on Gary's movies. But keep telling him how much you love my paintings.

Then it was Matthew over a nightcap at the bar. "The business is Dad's life work, and it's the underpinning of the family fortune. Trish and Gary would like him to sell his shares so that he'd have ready cash for their movies and art shows. But you know all about the goose and the golden egg. If he holds on, his shares will deliver dividends for years to come."

That was pretty transparent, too. Matthew ran the business, so the last thing he would want would be to find himself working in a company that his father didn't own. Screw his sister and brother. Just keep him in the executive suite.

Gary got her on the dock as they were returning to their cars. "I meant what I said about you making it in movies. I've got a project heading for production right now, and you'd be absolutely perfect for one of the parts. Let me set up a screen test. Even if you don't like the script, you'll have a test that I can show around."

They're all sucking up to me, she suddenly understood. They thought that she might become a gatekeeper for Steven Armstrong's attention and funding. Each one of them was trying to make sure that she kept the gate open to his company, her galleries, and his movies. *Jesus!* They thought she was going to have some say in how their father spent his money. Then it dawned on her. She was about to become Steven's wife. Of course she would have a say in how he spent his money.

Charlie had been embarrassed at the thought that he would be spending a good deal of it on her and her daughter. She felt as if she were going to be holding up a wooden bowl. Now it struck her that she was about to become a partner in a fortune. That gave her power, and that's why Steven's kids were kissing the hem of her garment.

She had to suppress a chuckle. This was ridiculous. She was a physical trainer. She knew nothing about making movies and even less about fine art. She was equally at a loss for the details of running a large corporation. She was marrying an important man who could give Tara and her a wonderful life with undreamed opportunities. She couldn't care less about what he lavished on his uppity kids, or where they stood in his pecking order. It wouldn't bother her if it worked out that she never saw any one of them again. But it was obvious that they intended to keep a very sharp eye on her. They would be looking for even a hint of what she might be whispering in their father's ear.

Ten

The last thing Charlie needed was to plan a wedding. It was to be a simple ceremony with a minimum of guests and just a cocktail party for a reception. But the details gnawed like termites into her already crowded schedule.

The invitations had to be done instantly. They were already late in getting into the mail. The yacht club manager had hundreds of questions—petty things like the size of the tent and the color of the tablecloths—that demanded immediate answers. The caterers needed to know whether she wanted the mushrooms stuffed with almonds or chopped beef, and had Charlie thought of tiny lamb chops as a finger food? The musicians needed her to pick the first ten songs. She was tempted to tell the caterer where he could stuff the damn mushrooms, but she knew she had to make the right decisions. Trivial as the questions seemed, the wedding would be her debut in Steven's circle of friends, and she wanted him to be proud.

She still had to contend with the everyday details of her single life. Tara still needed to be fed and prodded out the door each morning. Her aerobics classes needed her full energy and attention. Nor could she shortchange her therapy patients or ignore her personal training commitments. And there was a triathlon coming up a week before the wedding that she had to get ready for. Her daily running had her in shape for the marathon portion, but she had to find time to train for the bicycle and swimming events.

In the midst of this whirlwind, her car acted up, leaving her at the mercy of buses and taxis. It took three days and a new fuel pump to get it back into service. Steven had wanted to get her a new car, but she had insisted that the old Toyota would "get back on its feet." She was determined to make her own way, at least until they were well married.

When she found herself with a free morning, Charlie knew she should return frantic phone calls from the yacht club and from the woman who was going to do the flowers. But she had to give some time to the triathlon. She had practiced her swimming twice in the past two weeks. But that wasn't nearly enough.

She urged her daughter out of her room and past the breakfast table, then drove too fast on the way to school to keep her from being late. Next she went down to the beach to the place where the swimming event would be held. There was a thin haze across the surface so that she couldn't see the buoy, but that wasn't a problem. As long as she kept close enough to shore to keep the beach in sight, she would have no trouble. She wouldn't turn out to the buoy until she was close enough to see it.

She plunged in, stayed under long enough for the small wave to roll over her, and was already swimming when she reached the surface. She took long easy strokes, breaking the water with her forehead so that she could glance up and get her bearings between breaths. The haze made the water seem ethereal, and seemed to hold the silence close to the surface. The only sound was the rhythmic splash of her hands as they reached out for the next stroke.

She glanced up and saw the beach, just a white line of sand and rollers through the mist but enough to confirm her heading. She seemed to be making good speed, but there were no visible markers to tell her so. The buoy was still lost in the fog. Somewhere in the distance she heard the whine of a small engine, a Jet Ski starting up in the cove behind the barrier beach. Minutes later there was the rumble of a jet, an early-morning flight climbing out of Fort Lauderdale or Miami. Her world was beginning to wake up.

She saw the buoy, faint in the mist and further out to sea. She turned and headed straight for it. Now that she had a target, Charlie picked up her pace a bit. She wasn't racing. High speed had nothing to do with this part of the event. It demanded steady strong swimming in the hope of emerging from the water in the front half of the pack with enough energy left for the bicycling event.

The Jet Ski noise was louder, a metallic whine that fluctuated in pitch as the tiny, one-man boat bounced over waves. She would have to keep an eye out for it. A swimmer in the water wasn't easy to see, and thrill seekers who rode Jet Skis and wave riders weren't the most cautious of seamen.

She was moving well. Now she could make out the buoy clearly, and see that she was getting closer with each stroke. She guessed that she had been in the water for not much more than half an hour. If she could turn the buoy within forty-five minutes she would be setting a strong pace, a speed that might well get her ashore among the first dozen competitors.

The Jet Ski was getting louder. Charlie broke her rhythm to look up and locate it. It was coming around the point of the inlet, from the bay out into open water, and was headed in the general direction of the buoy. *Damn!* She didn't want to slow down but she knew she had to be careful. Jet skiers loved to make tight turns around markers, coming close enough to touch a buoy as they whipped around it. It seemed that they were both headed for the same marker.

She tried to recapture her rhythm but she was thoroughly distracted. *What in hell was he doing out at this hour, anyway?* These people generally stayed where there was boat traffic so that they could jump over wakes and go airborne. There were no boats out this early. She kept moving to the buoy but with her head up so that she could watch the intruder. For a moment, he seemed to veer off toward the beach, but the next time she saw him he had turned back to the buoy.

She was only a few hundred yards away so she kept swimming. Once she got near the buoy, he would certainly see her if that was where he was heading. He was directly behind her but still a good way off. There was no immediate danger.

But the situation changed rapidly. The tiny boat was closing on her faster than she was closing on the marker. At this rate it would reach her before she got to the safety of the buoy. She turned around, let her head bob up and began waving with both hands.

The growl of the engine was much louder, and the white splash of water that bounced out from under the hull was clearly visible. She could see the rider, a figure clad in a wet suit. The face mask was opaque so she couldn't really tell whether he was looking at her or had seen her. But the boat was skimming toward her in a straight line and at high speed. It wasn't turning away.

She screamed as she waved, but the cry was useless. Most likely she couldn't be heard over the godawful engine noise. Now she could even see the jet of cooling water that fired up behind the rider. The boat was within a hundred yards and charging with all its power. She rose up as high as she could out of the water and waved frantically. He must see her! Was this some crazy new game? Did he plan to speed right up to her, coming as close as he could before turning away?

Fifty yards, and then twenty-five. No time for her to swim out of the way. Charlie took a deep breath and dove under the water, kicking to drive herself further under. The white hull flashed by over her head, followed by the water jet that hammered against her back. She stayed down for a moment and then surfaced in the frothy wake.

She gulped in air. "You dumb son of . . . ," she started to scream, but she saw that the boat was turning abruptly, and then pointing back toward her. Then its engine peaked and it lurched back into high speed. It was coming back at her, and the faceless driver wasn't holding out a helping hand. He was trying to run over her.

Charlie took a bearing on the buoy and dove under again. Once more the hull flashed over her head, but this time it grazed the foot that was kicking behind her. She felt the sharp pain, knew that she had been cut and guessed that something might be broken. But she kept kicking and fighting to stay well below the surface as she swam in the direction where she had last seen the marker.

She was down a long time, burning up the air in her lungs both in panic and in the effort to keep swimming. But the water was murky and there was very little sunlight. She couldn't see the base of the buoy or the chain that descended to its mooring.

The sounds of the boat's engine and the banging of its hull were all around her. She couldn't get a fix on the direction, nor could she see the hull at the surface. She wanted to stay long enough to know where her attacker was, but she couldn't bear the loss of air any longer. Charlie shot up to the surface.

The first thing she saw was the buoy, only twenty yards away, a large steel tube dotted with rivets, the red paint beginning to fleck off. If she could get to it, it would serve as a shield. She could move around it so that the boat couldn't get to her without crashing into it. It was also about three feet in diameter. She might even be able to hide behind it.

Then she saw the boat, sitting idle, back where it had struck her foot. He must know that he had hit something. Was he waiting for her to struggle up? Was he looking for blood, or the shape of a dead body?

The opaque visor panned toward her, and then suddenly the head jerked. The engine roared and the boat nearly stood on its end as it pivoted toward her. She twisted in the water and dove under again. She had to reach the buoy. But the Jet Ski was on her too quickly. Before she could get enough depth, the hull glanced off the top of her head and then slammed into her back. The air burst out of her lungs. Her arms and legs were suddenly leaden. She was no longer swimming.

Eleven

Diego Cabanas turned the point in a flat-bottom rowboat powered by a five-horsepower outboard and swung the bow toward the channel marker. He blinked into the eastern sun that was beginning to burn off the haze. Then he cursed and threw up his hands in despair. One of those wild men on a Jet Ski was running in circles around the buoy, probably scaring off all the fish. Today was Diego's only day off, and he had spent the last three days anticipating a morning of fishing.

He had gotten up early and driven his pickup to the bait shop where he rented the boat. Fishing, he believed, had to be done in the early morning before all the boat traffic drove the fish into hiding, or at night when they felt they owned the ocean. But nighttime, when there was no way to see a sinking boat or a man overboard, could be dangerous. Morning, he had long ago decided, was best.

He had motored up the bay, enjoying the gurgling of the engine and the soft tap of the bottom against the flat sea. When he neared the channel, he heard the distant buzzing of a Jet Ski, and hoped that it was somewhere far up in the inland waterway. But as the sound grew louder, his fears mounted. Now, his worst fear had come true. The boat was racing back and forth over his favorite fishing ground. His day was ruined before it even started.

But what were his choices? Turn back to the bait shack, get the rental for the boat back, and spend the day ashore? Or head south along the barrier beach and maybe anchor at the next buoy? Or take his chances that the skier would go away and the fish might return?

The marker was dead ahead, and the guy was cutting around it like a crazy man, accelerating right up to it, and skidding around it at the last second. He was probably practicing for something, Diego reasoned. Well, he might not keep at it much longer. In fact, he had cut his engine to an idle and was sitting dead in the water. He seemed to be looking around for another challenge.

Charlie had no idea where she was until she saw the heavy links of the chain that disappeared down to the concrete anchor. She looked up and could see the bottom of the buoy. If she could just make her arms and legs work, and fight off her need to gasp for air! She had no time to look for the boat or think about it. She had to get to the buoy.

It seemed a desperately long climb, even though it was less than ten yards away, and perhaps six feet above her. She kicked and clawed until she touched the chain. Then she pulled herself to the surface. Instantly, she took in air, and only when she had a breath did she dare to look for the boat. She couldn't see it, but she heard the buzz of its idling engine coming from the other side of the marker. With her face pressed against the steel cylinder, she eased around it.

The rider was hanging off the side, with his face close to the water. He was over the spot where he had hit her the second time, looking carefully for any sign of her. He turned up his engine a bit and began a slow swing toward her, his concentration still beneath the surface. Charlie slipped back until she couldn't see him any more.

The sound grew louder. She knew he was coming around

the right side of the marker, so she kept sliding to the left. Then, when the bow of the boat came into sight, she took a breath and pulled herself under. She was holding the bottom edge of the buoy with her feet pressed against the chain. The hull eased up close, just inches above her, then continued around moving away from her. Charlie positioned herself on the opposite side and surfaced for another supply of air. The rider was easing back toward the area where he knew he had hit her, now hanging low over the other side of his craft.

Suddenly, he looked up, off into the distance. Charlie followed his gaze and saw what he must have seen—a small boat motoring out toward them, its bow slapping up a white spray each time it hit a wave. Instantly, the Jet Ski's engine roared, and it leaped off in the other direction, firing up its jet of cooling water.

In an instant, it was racing at top speed, carving a wide arc around the approaching boat. It moved in toward the beach keeping a distance from the newcomer. Then it turned and ran along the water's edge until it disappeared around the point.

Charlie concentrated on keeping the buoy between them until she was sure he wouldn't be coming back. Then she turned her attention to the small rowboat that had stopped, and was drifting about fifty yards away. A man was standing at the bow, lifting a mushroom anchor over the side.

It was a short swim, but she didn't have the strength to make it. She let out a scream and began waving a hand. The man seemed to glance up, but he quickly got back to the task of paying out his anchor line. She screamed again. This time he turned his head in a half circle searching for the source. He stopped when he was looking directly at the buoy. Charlie let go and waved with both hands. But she had to grab the barnacles on the wall of the cylinder to keep from sinking.

He was looking at her, and he yelled something that she didn't understand. She took a deep breath and threw all her energy into another cry for help.

The man began hauling in on the line, straining his arms and back and causing the bow to dip down into the water. His hand-over-hand motions seemed slow, and the anchor line looked as if it had no end. But after what seemed like minutes the iron mushroom broke the surface and he was able to roll it over the gunwale. He crouched as he stepped to the stern of the boat and sat at the engine. It started quickly, and the boat ghosted to the buoy.

He killed the engine when the side of the boat brushed the buoy and reached out his hand. Charlie grasped it firmly before she let go of her hold on the marker, and then was able to pull herself alongside. He was on his knees in the rowboat and had little leverage. Charlie didn't have the strength left to pull herself aboard. She was able to get her face up, and then the man got his hands under her arms. He almost fell backwards as he dragged her waist over the gunwale, and then she was able to swing her legs, one at a time, into the boat.

"Jesus!" Now that he could take a look he was shocked by her appearance. There was blood running out of her hair and over her face. Her back and shoulder were bruised and scraped as if she had been dragged by a horse.

"Thank you, thank you," she kept saying. "Thank God you came."

He dragged a duffel from under the seat and pulled out a small towel. "Hold this . . ." He gestured to the back of his own head. "Where you bleed." She put the towel on the top of her head and folded her hands over it to apply pressure. Next out of the bag was a first-aid kit, a plastic box with Band-Aids, antiseptic, some gauze and tape. Diego offered them to her although the bandages seemed much too small to do any good. She shook her head, still keeping the pressure on the towel.

"Can you take me in?" she asked.

"*Sí* . . . of course!" He started the motor and pushed the throttle all the way to the stop. They moved leisurely, the bow slapping up and down, back into the bay.

Twelve

Steven rushed into the emergency room, the nurse who had tried to stop him tagging behind. He poked at the curtains that separated the gurneys, glancing in for the instant it took to be sure that Charlie wasn't there. When he found her she was sitting in a wheelchair, wrapped in a blanket. There was a fresh bandage on her head, tied with gauze under her chin. Blood was beginning to ooze through.

He fell on his knees next to the chair. "Are you all right? Where are you hurt? How did it happen?"

"I'm fine," Charlie answered. "A few cuts and bruises. And I'm going to need a couple of stitches on my head."

"Well, how . . . ?" Steven started. But then he noticed a young man in a white shirt and tie, standing in the corner of the cubicle. He scrambled to his feet. "Doctor, is everything going to be all right?"

"It's not *doctor*," the man said with a smile. "It's *sergeant*. I'm with the Fort Lauderdale police. Sergeant Toomey. Jerry Toomey!"

"Police? Why?"

"Miss Hendricks was victim of a hit-and-run. A guy on a

Jet Ski. I'm following up." Then Toomey asked, "And you are the lady's . . . ?"

He was about to say, "father," but he thought better of it. There was no telling what kind of relationship an older man and a younger woman might be involved in, particularly on the Florida Gold Coast.

"The lady and I are engaged to be married," Steven answered. Then he gave his name and address. Toomey wrote in his notepad while Steven turned his attention to Charlie.

She started into the story of her morning swim along the course that would be used for the triathlon. She had just gotten to the distant sound of a boat when a doctor entered, announced that he was going to "close her wound," and asked the two men to leave.

Toomey brought Steven up to date. Charlie had claimed that the Jet Ski had attacked her, and had made two or three passes in its determination to run into her. She had described being hit and nearly knocked unconscious, her desperate scramble to the buoy, and her hiding while the tiny boat searched for her.

"There's no doubt that she was hit by the Jet Ski, and that the person driving the Jet Ski lingered in the area looking for her," the policeman said. "The man who rescued her," he flipped through his notes, "a Diego Cabanas, saw the Jet Ski circling the buoy, and he said it ran off as soon as he approached. But, of course, he couldn't say whether it had hit her intentionally or by accident, or whether the driver was searching for her to rescue her or attack her again."

"But why would anyone . . . ?" Steven wondered aloud.

Toomey nodded. "That's the big question. If we know why, then we could begin figuring out who. And if there's no why, then maybe there's no who. It could all be an accident."

That's what Steven wanted to believe. A near-fatal accident was bad enough. The thought that someone would want to hurt Charlie was more than he could bear.

"You and Miss Hendricks are getting married soon?" Sergeant Toomey asked.

"Two weeks," Steven agreed.

"Are there any jilted lovers? An ex-wife or husband who doesn't approve of the marriage?"

"No. We're both single, and both uninvolved."

"You're sure?" Toomey prodded.

"Yes," Steven said, and when he realized what the question implied, he added, "Of course I'm sure. Absolutely sure!"

The sergeant nodded and wrote in his notebook. "How about money?" he suddenly asked. When Steven seemed puzzled, Toomey explained, "Judging by your address, you have a bit of money. Does anyone get shortchanged when you marry Miss Hendricks?"

Steven's anger flared. "Sergeant, do we need to go through this?"

Toomey shrugged and closed his notebook. "Not at all. We can probably ignore the lady's claim that she was attacked. Chalk it up to trauma, and call it an accident."

Armstrong felt chastised. "No, that wouldn't be right. If Charlie says she was attacked, then I have to believe her."

The notebook opened again. "Will anyone get shortchanged?" Toomey repeated.

Steven took a deep breath and explained that his three children had been, up to now, his only heirs. With his marriage, he conceded, the new Mrs. Armstrong would become his principal heir. "But there's more than enough money. My children will still do very nicely."

"How much money are we talking about?" the detective wondered.

"A great deal!"

"Can you be a bit more specific?"

"Two hundred million, more or less," Steven answered. He was surprised at the flash of embarrassment he felt in mentioning his assets. "So you see, even after my wedding, each of my children will still receive a great deal of money."

Toomey nodded. "About half as much as they were expecting."

Steven suppressed his sudden anger. He spoke slowly, enunciating each word. "My children love my fiancée," he said. "And regardless of how much more or less any one of them might inherit, none of them would be capable of harming her."

"Anyone else who might be hurt financially? Creditors? Business partners?"

Steven shook his head.

The doors opened and an aide wheeled Charlie out of the emergency room. She forced a smile, and even tried a cheery wave. Steven ran to her and took over from the aide. "Are you all right?" he asked.

Charlie nodded and held up a folder of papers. "It's all here. My instructions, my prescriptions for painkillers, signs to watch for . . ."

He almost pushed her into Sergeant Toomey. "Oh, you've met, I'm sure."

"We have," the policeman said, smiling at Charlie.

"I told him all about the boat. Everything I could remember," she said. Then she added, "And if I think of anything else, I'm to call him."

They were almost to the car when Steven turned back and asked Toomey about the man who had rescued Charlie. "Do you have an address where I can reach him? I'd certainly like to express my gratitude."

Toomey turned to a fresh page and copied the name and address from his notes. He tore out the page and gave it to Steven.

When they were alone in the car, Steven pressed for details. As they drove to the beach pavilion to get her clothes out of the locker, he had her take him step by step through everything she had done. Was there anyone in the ladies' room where she changed? Or anyone on the beach who might have seen her begin her swim? He walked down to the water's edge and shaded his eyes as he looked out at the buoy. He could just make it out in the afternoon sun. In the morning haze, it would certainly be invisible. But so would a lone swimmer in the water. So even if someone was looking for her, how would they have found her?

How far out was she when she first heard the engine noise?

Could the Jet Ski have been out by the buoy waiting for her? She swam that route because it was the race course on which she was going to compete. If someone had been watching her, they would know that she always turned at the buoy.

Then the Jet Ski itself. What color was it? White, she remembered, and maybe the trim was red. One seat or two seats? Just one! The driver—a man or woman? Charlie had assumed it was a man, but in the wet suit it could easily have been a woman. She couldn't be sure. The best she could do was describe the suit as black with yellow borders.

She went through the details of the attacks, trying to remember the exact moment when she realized the rider was trying to run her down. "I thought he just didn't see me, until he turned around and came back at me." Then she told him about playing hide and seek behind the buoy, and how he had cruised right over her head.

He wondered about the moments when her attacker was searching the water, looking for her. Could he have been trying to rescue Charlie? If he had hit her by accident the most natural thing would be for him to search for whatever was in the water. That was possible, she thought, but not what she believed. She was positive during those few seconds when she clung to the buoy that he was looking to kill her.

And then Steven probed into the fisherman who had rescued her. When did she first notice him? Could he have gotten a look at the Jet Ski and the rider? Did he say anything to her, or did she say anything to him? He was surprised when she told him that Diego Cabanas had lifted her out of his boat, and carried her into the bait shop. That he had ridden in the ambulance that the shop owner had called, and was next to her right up to the moment when they took her into the radiology area. "He was gone when I came out after my x-ray. The detective told me he had seen him in the waiting room and talked to him. But then he left."

"We're lucky he decided to go fishing," Steven said. "Sounds like he saved your life."

When they reached her condo, he walked her up to her bedroom, gave her the painkillers that she had brought from the hospital. Then he drove to Tara's school and joined the line of waiting parents. He had invited the girl and her mother for a day on his boat, and twice had taken them to dinner, so he knew they would recognize each other. He would tell Tara that her mother had been hit by a boat while swimming, had gotten stitches, and was at home resting. "Nothing serious," he would laugh, "except that you're going to have to do something with her hair. She has a bald spot."

But it was terribly serious. Someone had tried to kill Charlie and had come close to succeeding.

Thirteen

Whether Charlie was underdressed or Tara was over-dressed, they didn't seem to be arriving for the same affair. Charlie was in a straightforward suit, a blended knock-off of linen, in a pale lime so faint that it proclaimed at least her purity if not quite her virginity. She was neat and tidy, but hardly formal, with no jewelry, little makeup, and her shoulder-length hair worn up in a wet look, to cover the bare spot from the head wound. No one would have guessed that she was a bride. "Do you suppose she's wearing her gym shorts under it?" Hillary smirked to her husband.

Tara was in a deep green satin with an off-the-shoulder neckline, revealing athletic, well-tanned shoulders and the beginning of what would soon be cleavage. She had a gold chain hanging around her neck and a matching bracelet. There was a tropical flower in her short light hair. Obviously, she was in a wedding party. "Cute girl," Trish whispered to Gary. "She must take after her father."

Steven, however, was in total awe of his bride. He knew she was attractive because he had seen her in shorts, leotards and, at times, in a simple athletic bra. He was used to her near naked. Now, when she was completely covered, he found her much more exciting. She was truly a lovely woman, not just a lady jock. As his trainer, she had lifted her share of dumb- bells and weights. As his bride, she seemed too regal to even lift a finger.

He ran down the courthouse steps to meet them, and then brought them back up to the foyer where his family and guests were waiting. Charlie, who had seen Steven in shorts and sweatshirts, or bare-chested in the pool with the hair on his shoulders and back matted against his skin, was as- tounded at how handsome he was in his gray suit, blue shirt, and colorful tie. Tara decided that his shaved head was cool, sort of like the haircuts that some of the boys wore to school.

The family waiting to greet the wedding party was nicely turned out. Hillary was in a form-fitting silver silk dress flecked with gray, under a gray waist-length jacket. There were diamonds at her throat, wrist, and fingers, an elaborate pin on the jacket, and sparkling stones in her hair. The provider of all these baubles stood proudly beside her in a dark suit, crisp white shirt and conservative tie, clearly a titan of industry.

Trish's attire was the casual chic of the arty set, getting away from it all in the Hamptons. She wore a knee-length gossamer peach coat over baggy white pants and a dark see- through blouse. A huge black hat with a drooping brim left her just a long cigarette holder short of being eccentric. Like his sister, Gary dressed for his part as a movie mogul in a black suit over a black collarless shirt. Dark sunglasses com- pleted the costume.

They brushed kisses, and then Trish and Hillary fawned over Tara. "What a perfect color for you," and, "your mother's beautiful skin." The girl smiled and turned crimson with embarrassment. Then the party marched down the hall to the chambers of a judge who was also a flag officer at the yacht club.

The ceremony was cut to the essentials. Charlie and

Steven stood front and center, with Tara beside her mother and Matthew standing up for his father. The judge asked if anyone had reason to object to this union, and even though the entire audience could have stepped forward with personal objections, they all stood with smiles frozen on their faces. The judge tried one his favorite jokes. "Doesn't anyone here have some dirt to share? Or are you all sworn to silence?" The smiles never wavered.

Then came the vows, and Charlie and Steven looked lovingly at each other as they repeated the words. They exchanged rings, simple gold bands that Tara and Matthew handed to their parents. By the power vested in him by the State of Florida, the magistrate pronounced them man and wife and encouraged Steven to kiss his bride. They kissed, hugged, and then turned to accept the congratulations of their children. The judge and Matthew signed the documents, and at that point Charlie had a greater claim to all Steven's assets than any of his children. Tara's life rocketed into a higher orbit, and Matthew's, Gary's, and Trish's inheritances were cut in half. Yet, they were still smiling.

A pair of limousines took the wedding party back to the yacht club where a large white tent had been set up on the main dock. Waiters carried champagne and finger foods down from the kitchen, and two dozen guests arrived, some on their boats. Most were members of the yacht club, but the group also included the presiding judge, Steven's personal lawyer and accountant, the doctor who had done his knee replacement, a few of the first executives of his company, Ucandoit, and the company's reigning chief executive officer. The only commoners in the crowd were Maria, his Cuban-born housekeeper, and her husband, who spent a day each week cutting his grass and trimming his foliage. They had agreed to stay at the house along with Tara while the happy couple were away on a two-night honeymoon.

Each guest shook Steven's hand and told him how lucky he was to have landed such an attractive young wife. "Hope your heart is up to this," joked the accountant, and then one of the original executives added that he hoped that it was not only his heart that was up to it. Each told Charlie how beautiful she looked but went quickly to the unusual relationship that led to the marriage. "What a great idea. A wife who already knows how to train a man," the doctor's wife bubbled. "Well, you've already seen him exhausted," the lawyer whispered to her, "so there will be no surprises tonight."

They were amazed that the honeymoon was going to be so short. "Don't be such a cheapskate," a club member teased Steven. "You should take the little lady around the world." Another barked, "Just two nights? It will take that long for your Viagra to work." Charlie came to his rescue, explaining that her daughter was still in school and that she had to be nearby. There were nods of approval from the ladies.

Charlie wanted to believe the guests' obvious joy in her marriage but she sensed the daggers they were hiding behind their backs. *You sure struck it rich,* she imagined one woman thinking. *How much is the old fool paying for his night in the sack?* she thought another lady was implying. The men, she knew, probably saw her as some sort of prize. *Wouldn't I like to be getting a little bit of that?* She knew that no one had any reason to be delighted in her good fortune, and certainly no reason to like her. The best she could hope for was that they might be indifferent, although she suspected that they probably all hated her. Or was she imagining things? Were her feelings simply her own assessment of someone who married without love.

Tara did all that she could to make herself invisible. At first, she stood off in a corner trying to escape the whirlwind of shouted conversation and whooping laughter. Then she slipped up near the combo of keyboard, bass, and guitar that was providing the incidental music, hoping to be taken for part of the group. But all the women now knew that Steve's new wife had a daughter and were dying to meet her.

"Well! Aren't you thrilled that your mother is getting married?" the doctor's wife said. Tara shrugged. "I'll bet you're looking forward to moving into Mr. Armstrong's wonderful

house. Right on the water, with a dock and swimming pool!"
one of the club members gushed.

"I like the house we have now," she said. "I already have a
swimming pool."

She worked her way around the edge of the tent and disappeared behind it, finding a moment of peace at the edge of
the water. Steven's boat reared up in front of her, its bow six
feet higher than she could reach. It held no appeal for her.
What she really liked were the little runabouts that pulled water skiers and tube riders. This thing was an ocean liner, probably much too slow to provide any fun. She wished she had
invited a friend or two as her mother had urged. At least there
would be someone to talk with. But she had been embarrassed at the thought of being seen in what she regarded as an
old woman's dress. And certainly her friends wouldn't want
to get all dressed up for a wedding.

"Oh, there you are." Tara's head snapped around and she
saw Hillary approaching, carrying a glass with a lime hanging over its edge. "Am I finally going to get to talk to you?"
There was no escape other than jumping off the dock. She
forced a smile. "Hello, Mrs. Armstrong."

Hillary was already into a monologue. She told Tara how
beautiful she looked, how perfect her dress was, and how
much she herself wished that she could wear wild flowers in
her hair. Tara returned a compliment in a weak voice, telling
Hillary that "Your jewelry is really neat."

"Now, tell me about yourself," Hillary said, and she began
a line of questioning about Tara's school, the subjects she
was taking, and her ambitions. She asked about her social
life, her boyfriends, and how she was going to stay connected when she moved into a new house in a different
neighborhood. There were constant references to her own
daughter, who was "nineteen and a bit older than you," and
was having an absolutely wonderful life. By implication, her
daughter was someone that Tara might emulate. She was successful at everything, loved by all, and would probably be
entering Harvard Law School in two years. "Wow," Tara

said, trying for the response that she knew Mrs. Armstrong was expecting.

Then Hillary got into the wonderful relationship she had always had with her daughter. "It must be difficult for you with your mother working and being away so much of the time."

Tara said that her mother worked while she was in school, was never away, and that they had lots of time together.

"But when she was away with your new father, or had to stay late at his house, that must have been difficult for you. Was there someone who came and stayed with you?"

Tara knew where all this was leading. Mrs. Armstrong wanted to know if her mother had been "doing it" with her new father. Did she stay overnight? Were they away on trips together? She understood that despite the joyous smile, Hillary didn't like her mother and was digging for reasons to tear her down. She answered that her mother picked her up after school every day, and that she was never gone at night or over weekends.

"That's wonderful," Hillary beamed. But without pausing for breath she began probing in another direction. "And what about your father? Do you see him often?"

"No, I don't."

"Just every now and then," Hillary tried.

"Not now. Not then. I don't even know him."

"Does your mother tell you about him?" Her smile was, if anything, more genuine and more loving.

"No. He was just a mistake."

Hillary shifted to a more serious demeanor. "And how do you feel about that?"

"I feel like I don't want to talk about it," Tara snapped, and she pushed past and ran back into the tent. But she stopped short when she realized that she was crying. She couldn't go back to all those people with tears in her eyes. She veered up the gangway that led from the dock to the clubhouse. There had to be a place up there where no one would find her.

Maria saw her and followed her up to the deck where Tara had found an isolated deck chair. She sat down next to her. "You're not enjoying your party," she said, stating the obvious.

Tara shrugged. "I don't know anybody."

"Me neither," Maria agreed, imitating the shrug. "They all smile and say hello, but they're not looking at me. They're looking for someone else to talk to."

The girl shook her head. "It's more than that. They don't like me. They don't even like my mother. So why do we have to be here?"

"Just to help your mother and Mr. Armstrong celebrate. They're the only ones who are important. The others just like to hear themselves talk." She patted Tara's hand. "I'm going back so that Mr. Armstrong knows I like him. You want to go back with me so your mother knows you care about her?"

Tara hesitated, then got up and followed Maria back down to the tent. At least there was now somebody she could talk with.

The party went on for another hour with waiters bringing fresh trays of hors d'oeuvres and topped-off drinks. Then the combo played a fanfare, and Matthew took the microphone. He made a few jokes about his father telling him the facts of life, and that it was now his turn to give advice. "Don't get so involved with your honeymoon that the boat washes up on the beach." Gary followed by naming some of the titans in Hollywood who had married young starlets. He mentioned one who had died on his honeymoon, "but he was eighty-seven at the time and shouldn't have even climbed the stairs to the bedroom." Trish allowed that the marriage was made in Heaven because "Charlene really likes the edgy paintings that Dad so loves."

Then someone thrust the microphone into Tara's hands. She swallowed visibly, and then managed, "I just want you to be happy," which brought a grateful hug from her mother.

Steven thanked his guests. Charlie said something about how welcome they made her feel, and even managed to look touched. Then the newlyweds waved over their shoulders as they walked up the companion way to the yacht. They were still waving from the afterdeck, standing above the name, *Idonit,* as the boat moved out onto a crimson sea.

Fourteen

Charlie got her first glimpse of the honeymoon suite when she went below to change into cruising clothes. The owner's stateroom was done in brass and bright-work with polished wood decking. The king-size bed was backed against a forward bulkhead. Hatches to either side led into a huge clothes locker and giant bath. The shower was built into the prow of the boat so that its sides narrowed and rose higher as it went forward. The whole setup was bigger than the master bedroom suite in her condo.

There were built-ins all around, two serving as his and hers dressers with mirrors mounted above, one as a pop-up cocktail bar, another as an entertainment center linked to satellite broadcast. The curtains and bedspread were a beige fabric that depicted navigation charts. Each of the two port-holes on either side was covered with the pilot chart for a Caribbean harbor. The bedspread displayed the Leeward Islands, from Anguilla to Marie Galante. Her travel bag was resting on Saint Kitts.

She picked out an outfit of white slacks and a navy blue shell, sandals, and a hair band, and changed in the head.

When she went back up, Steven was in the pilothouse with his captain, going over the course to Nassau. The whirlwind honeymoon was to be a ten-hour cruise to the Bahamas, a full day ashore in Nassau, and then a return trip on Monday. Certainly a thrilling introduction to her new life in the yachting set, but hardly enough time to find out whether she could love this man, whether it mattered, or whether she had made a life-shattering mistake.

Steven set her up in a deck chair where she could watch the sunset over the stern and went below to change out of his suit. There was a crew of three to tend to their needs, and one of them, a young deckhand who doubled as a waiter, was instantly at her side with a flute of champagne on a silver tray. He also set down a plate of toast points, a jar of caviar, and a small dish of chopped onions. She had already met the captain, who was a full-time employee even though he didn't live aboard the boat. And she had heard Steven and the captain discuss their pleasure in the chef who had been hired for the journey. Apparently the captain had complete responsibility for the yacht, and hired crewmen and tradesmen as needed.

Her husband came back up in slacks and a sport shirt carrying a tall drink. He was wearing a baseball cap with the name *Idonit* embroidered on the crown and an admiral's "scrambled-egg" decorations on the peak. He settled beside her.

"You know, I don't even know what you like to drink," he began their first married conversation. "I should have asked. I saw you drinking champagne at the reception and I told them to bring you some more of it. But do you like it? Would you rather something else?"

She shook her head. "I don't drink much of anything except bottled water. But the champagne is festive, and I feel festive. So it was a good choice."

"I'm glad that you feel festive. It must have been a tough afternoon for you, being gawked at by all my friends." He corrected himself. "Not friends really. *Acquaintances* is more like it. People I know and have worked with, a few business associates, some of the people I've met at the club. No one I would call a really dear friend."

"They were all very nice to me, even though I don't think most of them liked me."

He seemed shocked. "What do you mean? They're crazy about you. Or, at least they will be when they get to know you."

"Do you think they really want to get to know me?" Her expression said that it was a serious question.

"Of course they do. You're the youngest, freshest, most exciting woman at the club."

"Young . . . fresh . . . exciting, that should make all the women hate me," she laughed. "And the men won't come near me for fear of their wives. You have to face it, Steven. The people who know and like me don't own yachts, and they don't have big houses on the water."

"We'll do things with your friends, too," he assured her.

Charlie knew that wouldn't work well either. Her friends were either health freaks or parents trying to survive their teenage children. An unfettered millionaire would only make them mad. But she didn't want Steven to sense the loneliness she was beginning to feel. "We'll both have to work on it," she said reaching out and taking his hand.

The dinner was another surprise for her. Not that Charlie had expected to be fed out of an ice chest, but she expected some compromise in the confined space and unsteady footing of a boat at sea. Some sort of prepackaged meal like the ones she prepared when she got in late and Tara had an evening event at school. Instead, she was treated to haute cuisine, from oysters as appetizers through brandied pears for desert. In between, a Dover sole was boned, prepared, and sauced at the table. Three different wines were poured, and a cart of cognacs and cordials was rolled out with coffee.

"I *have* to see this kitchen," she announced to the chef, and he led her out of the formal dining room to a stainless-steel kitchen with a six-burner stove, three ovens, giant freezers and refrigerators, and a hanging collection of at least two dozen pots and pans. There was a six-foot cutting board, a food processor with a blade the size of an airplane propeller, and a cabinet with at least fifty different serving dishes.

"God, this is amazing . . . ," she said, softly as she breathed out the air she had swallowed.

"If you'd like to cook something here," he said, gesturing that she had complete run of his kitchen.

"I'd still burn the toast," Charlie said sadly.

Did people really live this way? Private yachts with world-class chefs, and a full wine cellar to help pass the hours between one watering hole and another. There was no way she could feel at home in such foreign surroundings. And what about Tara? Would she have to send the girl off to a few years of finishing school before she could let her go out with her new friends. No one had ever boned a fish in front of Tara, or asked her what vintage she preferred with her oysters. They had, on occasion, treated themselves to an evening at a clam bar where they ate clams out of the shell on a kraft paper table cloth. Digging in with their fingers, and pouring the clams down their wide open mouths was part of the fun. Lovely as all this was, it wasn't going to be easy explaining to Steven that she liked things a lot simpler, and convincing Tara that all she had to do was be herself.

"What do you think?" he asked eagerly when she returned to the table.

"I'm overwhelmed. I thought . . . I don't really know what I thought, but this wasn't it. I guess I expected that cruising would be something like camping. You know, roughing it a bit."

He was downcast. "I overdid it, didn't I? I wanted everything to be perfect. But it's not always like this. Most of the time I help out as the navigator. In port, I even handle the lines. Generally, I don't bring a chef. I just whip something up for myself and the others."

Charlie put a finger to his lips. "It was wonderful, and probably the most thoughtful thing that has ever been done for me. It's like the champagne, Steven. We just need a little time to get used to one another."

They returned to their deck chairs. The last trace of the setting sun was gone, leaving only a dim glow in the western sky. Overhead, the night was jet black, sparkling with layer upon layer of stars. Steve put his arm around her and drew her close. "It's a little chilly," he announced. "Should I get you a sweater?"

But that would be postponing the moment she was dreading. Sooner or later they would go below together into the owners cabin, get undressed, and slide into bed. She couldn't sit out on deck for the entire night. It was their honeymoon, and she was supposed to be as eager as he was. All she was supposed to be thinking of was the conjugal bliss that awaited them. Instead, she was wondering how she was going to make it through to morning without him realizing that he couldn't make the earth move.

"No," she answered to the offer of a sweater. "We'll just sit here for a few minutes, and then we'll go down to bed."

"Okay," Steven answered, his voice cracking.

Charlie wasn't afraid of sex. She had been active—obviously too active—in her younger years, and she had entertained a few serious boyfriends when Tara was a child. But as a single mother, struggling with menial jobs, she became a target for the wrong kinds of men. There were her fellow losers; guys with nothing to offer who figured that Charlie had nothing to lose. A little fun, a couple of drinks, and a few laughs to break through the desperation. Neither of them were going anywhere, so they might as well have a little fun along the way.

There were also the big-man wannabes; men a few years older who sported a shirt and a tie, wore a pager, and had titles like "manager" and "supervisor" or "regional director." They all told her she was too good to be hustling tips in a diner, and hinted at the promise of a better life. One thought he might be able to get her a clerical job in his office. Another talked about his company's training program that came with medical coverage. Still another offered to put her up in a better apartment in a better part of the city. Each thought he would be good for her. Most got around to adding that their wives didn't understand them.

Charlie had accommodated some of them, but then she had recognized the similarity in their stories. They were all playing con games, and she was inevitably the mark. The only thing she could trust was the love she had for her daughter, and none of the adventurers wanted to think about the needs of a little girl.

The decent men were put off on their first date. A young daughter. No husband who had died or left her for another woman. She might be dangerous with a needy brat that could cost them money, and a jealous lover who might knock down the door and cause a ruckus. It was better to look for a woman who wasn't so encumbered than to take the risk of a nasty affair.

Her job in a health club had led to schooling as a physical therapist. That had given her respectability that she had never enjoyed before. More important, it gave her the means to move to a better neighborhood on her own, and begin offering Tara all the things that a young girl needs. She stopped thinking that she needed a man to save her.

She had been in a few recent relationships, but had always used the utmost discretion to assure that they never became known to Tara. She hadn't brought the men home, nor had she joined them when it meant being away from her daughter. And for those reasons, none of them amounted to anything.

But now, with her husband, everything had to be different. If he had proposed an affair, or an arrangement where she might live in luxury, she could have easily declined. *Been there, done that!* But this was marriage, a lifelong pledge to blend their lives into one. She couldn't rationalize its ending before it began, as she had done with other lovers. Nor could she block off sectors of her life as "out of bounds." She knew that her marriage would work in the countless details of daily life. She knew it would work for her daughter as well as herself. What she had to do was make it work in bed.

She had been thinking about this moment since she had stepped into the *intimates* shop to find her bridal night attire. Because she was a pajama person at home, she started at a table of silk pajamas and found a few styles that just might work. There was a black pair of gauzy material that would give her complete coverage and yet be provocatively transparent. But once they provoked her partner they would be difficult to get out of. Besides, Charlie didn't think they would survive a washing regardless of what the label promised, and she wasn't dressing for a one-night stand.

"A special occasion," the store clerk asked solicitously.

No, I came in here for something to wear to the office, she thought, but she managed a polite smile. "Very special," she said, embarrassed to admit that she was a blushing bride.

"Have you looked over here?" the lady suggested, and led Charlie to a section of outfits that would generally be delivered in a plain brown wrapper. There were gossamer negligees, scanty bras, thong panties, lacy garter belts, and net stockings. Colors favored the reds and blacks, but there were also tiger skins, polka dots, and cupids. Trims were bunny fur, fringe, and imitation Russian leather. *These would go nicely with handcuffs,* she mused, but all she said was, "Not *that* special."

"Perhaps if you tell me what you're thinking."

"I'm thinking this isn't going to be easy," Charlie answered, and left to find another store where she wouldn't be dressed like a hooker.

Her second foray was into an upscale department store where she came right out and admitted that she was looking for something to wear on her honeymoon. The saleswoman brought her a collection of whites that included feathered robes, long gowns, and string-tied pants. This took her in the opposite direction. She didn't want to put Steven to sleep, and she wasn't about to admit that white wouldn't be appropriate. "I'll think about it," she promised. What was there to think about? Stores didn't stock night wear for single mothers in their mid-thirties who were marrying for the first time to someone twice their age. The choices of untouchable virgin, harlot, or whoopee doll didn't fit her situation.

She had been passing a simple dress shop when she spotted a nightgown in the window. It was black, or deep purple, which was as vampish as she wanted to be. It fell below the knee, which was modest yet not discouraging. The top was loose with thin straps over the shoulders. It could easily be slipped down or lifted up as the situation demanded. And it was made of shimmering satin, which announced the special occasion. It was a gown, not a costume. It said nothing about her other than that she was a woman with a good figure. It promised nothing more than "what you see is what you get."

Charlie went into the store and held it up to herself. "Perfect," she announced, and she bought it without even trying it on.

"Let's go to bed," she prompted Steven, relieving him of the chore of saying that the moment had come. "It is getting chilly up here."

"Okay," he answered with feigned aplomb.

He stopped at the head of the steps. "Should I bring down a bottle of champagne?"

"No," Charlie answered. "I don't want to drink any more."

Fifteen

———

"T hen are we all agreed on the detective?" Matthew asked, scanning the people who were seated around a patio table.

"It has to be someone good," Gary said. "We don't want . . ." He stopped abruptly as the waiter approached with another round of drinks. Matthew and Hillary were drinking gin and tonics, really gin over ice with a splash of tonic for disguise. Gary had a rum and Coke, heavy on the rum. Trish had something blue in an enormous stemmed glass, with a peach slice hanging over the edge.

"We don't want some gumshoe who will fall through a skylight and give everything away," Gary finished after the waiter was out of range. "Maybe I ought to get someone from Hollywood. The guys out there have all kinds of experience with maritals."

"I don't care where he comes from as long as he knows what we need," Trish said. "I want pictures of her in bed with whoever it is that put her up to this. I want to be able to throw her a bone and tell her to get lost."

They had been sitting on the yacht club deck since the

boat had disappeared around the tip of the barrier beach, coming to grips with their new situations. There was no prenuptial agreement. All their father had said in response to their hints and urgings was, "I'll think about it." He had made vague promises about talking it over with his lawyers when he got around to it. None of them dared suggest that, once she had a wedding ring, his new bride might not be all that cooperative. Their worst-case scenario was that they would all have to find legitimate employment, and take in a bit on their lifestyles. Their best case was that they would be able to adjust to the prospects of a smaller inheritance—much smaller.

Matthew seemed to be the least at risk. Even if his father sold a good portion of his stock, he would probably keep enough shares to have some say in the operations of his company. That meant that Matthew would remain his man on the spot.

Hillary didn't see it that way. Steven, she told the others "would go to cash," to lavish a lifestyle on his loving wife. Matthew could be out on the street in a matter of months, and she wasn't about to risk everything just to please some trophy wife.

Trish insisted that she had the most to lose. "She doesn't have to do anything except to tell him that she prefers seascapes, and he'll stop buying my artists."

Gary saw his problems as much more immediate. They were all talking about what could happen in the future. He had a movie ready to shoot. He couldn't put it on the back burner. "That's not the way things work in Hollywood. You lose momentum on a project and everyone jumps ship. An actor first, and then maybe the director. Then everyone senses that the film is in trouble and no one wants to admit that they had even heard of it."

Over the second round of drinks, the women had gotten very nasty. Trish claimed that all the guests she had spoken to had covered their mouths and rolled their eyes. "They all know that she's after his money, and they think he's blind not to see it." Hillary had whispered that even the daughter knew what her mother was up to. "When I asked her how she felt about her new father, she said she didn't want to talk about it. She was practically in tears when she ran away from me."

The men had been more resigned to their fate. Gary said that he would call his father as soon as Steven returned from his honeymoon, and admit that his situation was desperate. "Maybe I can get to him before she gets to see his bank account." Matthew said that all he could do was keep telling the lady that Steven's interest in Ucandoit was the fountainhead of all she hoped she might do for her daughter. He planned to find many ways to phrase the message—don't sell!

It was over the third round that they had hit on the idea of hiring a detective. They couldn't sit back and wait to be robbed or disinherited. They would have to find hard evidence to persuade their father that his exercise manager was only interested in his money. They needed proof that she was cheating on him, and that she actually had another lover. They had to find friends and associates who had heard her say that she was going to take the old fool for all that he was worth.

"Isn't that what private detectives do?" Trish had asked innocently.

"Well, now we're getting somewhere," Hillary agreed.

Matthew had objected. Wasn't it a bit sleazy to spy on their father? Besides, wouldn't they risk losing everything if he should happen to find out? It was then that Gary decided that Matthew was against the idea only because the danger to him was least. And that was when Matthew agreed to go along if they were all in complete agreement.

Now, with their fifth round of drinks, they began wondering if even a detective was enough. A proper investigation might take several months. Their father's new wife wasn't a dummy. You couldn't expect her to get caught red-handed a week after her honeymoon. Could they risk that much time?

Gary didn't think that he could. "The next time I show my face in Hollywood, I better have a check in my hands. By the time some detective gets around to developing his pictures, I could be as dead as John Wayne." Trish didn't have much time either. "I've got a wall of paintings that I was counting on Dad to buy. I mean, it's great art. He'll double his money in a year or two. But if he doesn't buy them now, they're going to start getting discounted."

"We don't need a detective," Hillary interrupted. "What we need is a hit man." She looked around at the shocked faces that stared back at her. "That was just a figure of speech," she apologized. "What I mean is that we have to move quickly. We have to get her before she gets into your father's bank accounts."

Matthew looked at Gary. "Do they have hit men in Hollywood?" he asked.

Sixteen

———

S teven led her to the cabin door and then came up with an
excuse about needing to have a word with the captain. He
was giving her a moment of privacy for undressing and
preparing herself, an obvious gesture that Charlie appreciated.
She went into the head compartment, folded her clothes as she
took them off, and then dropped the nightgown over her
naked body. Then she posed at the mirror, turned around as far
as she could see, slipped one of the straps off her shoulder,
and took a few steps to see how the gown moved. She liked
what she saw, a well-proportioned woman showing just
enough skin to be interesting without being obvious.

She folded her clothes, dropped her underwear in the
hamper, and stepped back into the cabin. Steve had not yet
returned, so she used another moment to hang her things in
the locker. Then it struck her that she needed to find a way to
make an entrance. She didn't want to be in bed, or even sitting on the edge of the bed when he returned. Lovemaking
was best when it began standing and led up to the point where
one or the other eased the partner between the sheets.

But she couldn't be simply standing in the middle of the

cabin, wringing her hands. It shouldn't be so predictable that she was ready for his embrace. Events should simply be allowed to happen, to flow from their first sight of one another into greater and greater intimacy. She could go into the bath and then make an entrance when she heard him back in the cabin. But he would probably knock before he entered, and she might not hear him if she wasn't in the cabin. Charlie began to regret that he hadn't come inside with her. One of them could have changed in the cabin and the other in the head. Then their coming together would have been perfectly natural and completely unrehearsed.

She heard him on the steps coming down from the bridge. He coughed as a warning and paused before knocking on the door. Charlie turned to her dresser, leaned toward the small mirror and began the motions of brushing her hair. She heard his fingertips tapping against the door. "Come in," she said in a voice low enough so that it wouldn't be heard by the captain or the crew. Then she posed with the brush in her hand as if she had been caught a bit off guard.

Whatever Steven had intended for that moment was lost at the sight of her. He might have unpacked his pajamas and excused himself into the head. Or he could have gone into the locker and put on a bathrobe. Instead, he stood open-mouthed until he was able to say, "My God, you're beautiful."

"You've seen more of me before," she said, alluding to the hours they had spent together in gym outfits.

He swallowed. "It's not the same. Not the same at all."

He went to her, took her in his arms, and kissed her fully on her open mouth. His hands slid down her sides and explored the curve of her hips. He was already breathing hard when his hands came up to her breasts.

Charlie wanted to be just as passionate as he was. She began undoing the buttons on his sport shirt, got impatient with the buttons, and pushed the shirt up over his chest. He responded by slipping the straps off her shoulders and pushing the gown down to expose her breasts. Then he drew her tight against him, skin touching skin.

The next few moments were more spontaneous than Charlie could have hoped. He threw off his shirt and unzipped his slacks. She pulled off the bedspread while her gown dropped to the floor of its own weight. She stepped out of it and slid between the sheets almost at the same moment when he was slipping in beside her. They were into each other's arms.

Charlie's body responded perfectly. When he touched her she was completely taken by the pleasurable sensations. He was gentle, and she found that exciting. Her breasts were tingling and the space between her legs was soft and receptive. Even though it had been nearly a year since her last venture, she recognized the predictable physical response and enjoyed the mounting sensations of intimacy.

There was no doubt in her mind that Steven was enjoying every touch of their bodies. He seemed to be doing his best to bring her to his own level of excitement. But then he was suddenly over her and into her and gasping for the breath he needed to sustain his momentum.

Then it was over. He slid to one side, sucking air through his clenched teeth. "Wonderful," he managed to say several times between breaths.

"You're wonderful," Charlie responded. They lay silently for several minutes simply holding hands. He was thinking of the wonderful moment he had just celebrated. She was congratulating herself on her nightgown. It had been exactly what she intended.

"Charlie," he asked softly, "did I really light you up?"

"You're a fantastic lover," she said, and squeezed his hand.

He chuckled, but then asked seriously. "But you didn't completely . . ."

"No," she said. "But we have lots of time to work on that. And every day won't be as stressful as this."

Should she have faked it, she wondered? Manufactured a cascade of sighs and screams? Pretended to be lost in a frenzy of passion? Instead, she had played it as truthfully as she could. She had enjoyed the physical sensations of lovemaking. And for at least a few moments, she felt close to climax. But the fact was that she was relieved when it was over. She felt no desire to cling to her husband, had no need for a repeat performance, no interest in offering sexual temptation when they awoke. Those feelings, she supposed, were reserved for people deeply in love with one another. As she had suspected, she was not deeply in love with Steven.

It must have been obvious to their wedding guests. Most likely that was why she had felt their hostility and imagined their scorn. And sooner or later it would probably become obvious to her husband. He had told her that those kinds of feelings would grow over time. Charlie hoped that they would. Because, if they didn't, her marriage would truly be a fraud, and she would have made a terrible mistake.

In the morning, she slipped out of bed while he was still sleeping, dressed in the closet, and tiptoed out of the cabin. In the galley she begged a cup of coffee and a glass of juice from the chef, and arranged it with a flower on a silver serving tray. She carried it back to the cabin and waved the cup close to his face until he began sniffing at the aroma. Steven woke up with a smile.

Charlie sat on the edge of the bed while he sipped at his steaming coffee. "Is this another of the benefits of marriage?" he asked.

"After a while it will be the only one you care about," she teased.

Steven set his tray on the night table and reached out for her. Charlie slid up closer to him. At that moment, the captain's voice rang down on the intercom. "We hold Nassau dead ahead, Mr. Armstrong. We can be tied up in twenty minutes." It was a polite way of asking the newlyweds if they wanted to be up on deck in twenty minutes, or should he cruise around in circles for another hour.

Steven looked pained, and played with her shoulder strap while he tried to decide. "C'mon," Charlie said, pulling away from him. "We'll be back here tonight."

They stepped off the boat onto the dock of a huge marina with slips for more than a hundred boats. Charlie was dazzled. She had thought her husband's seventy-five-foot motor yacht was excessive—too big for fun-filled cruising. Now she was looking at ocean-going yachts twice as big as *Idonit*.

Ships, really, with uniformed crews kept busy with the vessels' ceaseless maintenance.

They came out of the marina onto West Bay Street, where the shops were small, the merchandise tropical, and there was a hint of the city's old, lawless character. Steven pulled her into an open-front restaurant that offered tables outdoors on the quay. They had a breakfast of grilled fish and poached eggs, a combination that Charlie found delicious even though it was a bit bizarre.

They went into native shops where he had her try on colorful native skirts with wide-necked blouses. "Beautiful," he announced and reached for his wallet.

"Are we going to a costume party?" Charlie teased.

She had the clothes she was wearing packed in a shopping bag, and left the store in her new outfit. At the next stall, he added a wide-brimmed straw hat.

They went out to Paradise Island, where they gambled together for two hours, winning at first and then watching their stack dwindle and finally disappear.

They had lunch on the patio of a hotel, overlooking the beach. "Beautiful," she said, taking in the white sand and the stylish sunbathers.

If she liked the beach, he insisted on giving her the beach. "I'll take a cabana."

She laughed and shook her head. "I can't! My bathing suit is back on your boat."

"So, we'll get new ones," he said, taking her hand and leading her into the hotel's shopping mall. "I want you to get the skimpiest bikini they have."

Charlie had to steel herself even to come out of the dressing room. There was no way she was going to wear the suit out on a public beach. But Steve was thrilled with the look and was already reaching for the bill.

"Steve, I wouldn't let my daughter out in a suit like this," she protested.

"She doesn't have your figure," he said.

Charlie's first step out of the cabana was frightening. But by the time they reached their beach lounges she was getting comfortable in the environment. She stole glances at the other sunbathers, and decided that if she wasn't one of the best, she was at least competitive. Steve's joy at having her on his arm was obvious.

After their swim, he took her back to Bay Street, to a jazz bar that served a dozen different kinds of martinis. Their next stop was a backstreet restaurant where they ate bouillabaisse with bibs tied around their necks. By nightfall, Charlie was feeling tired, sunburned, and maybe a bit giddy from too much to drink. The foot that the Jet Ski had smashed was throbbing in pain.

Steven didn't offer her a moment of privacy when they got back to the boat, and Charlie didn't bother with the nightgown. They shed their clothes and fell so naturally into bed together that Charlie thought they had crossed some kind of threshold. If the first night had been nervous for both of them, the second seemed casual. Again, she enjoyed his love-making, and took satisfaction in his growing passion. She received him with a strong sense of excitement and felt his nearly frantic climax. But she wasn't responding. Charlie moved in an effort to reignite herself, but at nearly the same moment Steven groaned and slumped to the side of the bed.

"Charlie, you're going to kill me," he said.

"I hope not. There are still lots of things that we have to do together."

He hesitated. Then he asked mischievously, "Did the earth move?"

She smiled. "How can you tell on a boat? Maybe it was a wave instead of the earth. But I loved it, Steven."

He was asleep almost immediately. Charlie eased out of bed, and found the slacks and blouse that had been wrapped in the store. She dressed silently and slipped out of the cabin.

They were already under way. The captain had taken in lines as soon as they were aboard and had cleared the harbor in order to make a mid-morning return to the yacht club. Charlie went up to the after deck where the chairs were still arranged the way they had been on her wedding night. She slouched into one and put her feet up over the rail. Nassau, towering over the fantail, was ablaze with activity. Paradise Island could have been a carnival. Reflections of every color shimmered across the water all the way to the boat. The frothy wake changed its tint every second.

Her honeymoon had been nothing like she expected, but then again, it hadn't been completely predictable. She had worried that she wouldn't be able to make it through the first night. There had been images of them groping in an awkward silence and then turning away from one another. None of that had happened. On the other hand, Charlie had been reasonably sure that she could form a relationship with a man she admired, enjoy his company, and satisfy his desires. All of that she had done.

But looking back on the sight of their first intimacies, Charlie had a nagging feeling that she had made a mistake. Even in her worst moments, when she could barely manage a room in which to raise her child, when she had counted her tips out on the dresser and dug into her pockets to see if there might not be another crumpled bill, she had been determined to rescue her life. The love she had felt for the man who abandoned her was locked in her heart like a picture in a locket. Someday, she would love another man in the same helpless way. The locket would snap open, and all the feelings of life and joy that she had suppressed would explode outward and color the world for herself and Tara.

In marrying Steven Armstrong she was admitting that she had lost faith and lost hope. She had grasped for security and given up the delicious dangers of living. Instead of holding onto the edge of possibilities for another day, another hour, or even another second, she had let go and dropped easily into the safety net. The explosion of color that she had dreamed for her daughter and herself was fading into the wake as the lights of Nassau began to grow dim.

Seventeen

Charlie expected the worst from her daughter when she and Steven returned to the house. It had been obvious that Tara had suffered through the reception and that she had felt abandoned when her mother waved good-bye from the yacht. If things ran true to form, she would be silent and brooding, blaming her mother for her unhappiness and letting her suffer in her guilt. Generally, this silent retaliation would go on for a day or two until Tara got tired of being gloomy.

But her greeting was bright and cheery. Tara rushed down from her room, threw her arms around her mother, and kissed her cheek. Then, to Steven's amazement, she gave him a peck of a kiss and a big smile. He couldn't have been more delighted. The moment seemed to seal his place in his new family.

"I missed you," Tara said to her mother. "Did you guys have a good time?" She instantly blushed at the question she had just asked as if it had been as blatant as "How was the sex?" But Charlie covered for her by launching into the wonders of Nassau, describing the shops, the restaurants, and the beach. Then she presented the gift she had brought from the same shop where Steven had gotten her the native skirt and blouse. Tara rushed off to try it on and returned to model it with a runway walk.

It was nearly unbelievable, Charlie thought. They had been away for really only a day, yet the girl seemed to have grown a full year. She was completely confident in her new house, moving from room to room with none of the hesitancy of a guest. She even stole a piece of last night's dessert from the refrigerator, and ate it over the counter-top sink. Then she took both Charlie and Steven on a tour of her room. It was casually neat, not ready for white-glove inspection, but nothing like the mess that she had usually left at home. Her CD stack and compact boom box were on top of her dresser with the speakers on either side. Her desk, about twice as big as the one at the condo, was neatly arranged with her books across the back, her notebooks set to one side, and her pens and pencils in a Toby jug that her mother had given her for her twelfth birthday. Charlie raved about the layout, and praised the posters Tara had chosen to hang.

The only thing she didn't see was the collection of teddy bears that Tara kept on her bed. She was sure that she had brought them over to the new house, and yet the girl had decided not to display them. She was about to ask where they were, but she caught herself just in time. Her daughter had obviously made a decision about the way her new life would begin, and it didn't seem wise to have her explain herself.

Maria made a point of cornering Charlie so that she could heap praise on her lovely daughter. She told how Tara had helped her prepare the Sunday meal, and how much they had enjoyed a traditional Cuban dish. Charlie nearly fell down when she learned that her daughter had gone to church with Maria and wanted to go back the next week. Steven gave a shrug. "I didn't know Maria went to church. If it's a problem for you, I'll tell her to forget next week."

It wasn't a problem. It was just something that Charlie had never thought about. She couldn't remember that anyone in her family had ever gone to religious service, and she had never gone herself. "No, if she wants to go, fine. Who knows? Maybe I'll start going with her."

Steven suggested an afternoon of water-skiing off the sixteen-foot whaler that was docked at his house. The three of them changed to bathing suits, Charlie choosing a one-piece instead of her new bikini. They swabbed on sunscreen and motored out into the bay. Tara went over the side first, was towed up to a wobbly start, and skied nicely in the boat's wake. She even broke out across the wake into the unruffled water near the side of the boat. Charlie went over, and let her husband and daughter explain the starting position even though she remembered it from years before. She fell on her first attempt, and then took a header on her first attempt to jump the wake. But her natural athletic abilities took over, and she was soon riding back and forth across the white caps that the boat was kicking up.

Looking ahead, she saw Steven driving and Tara in the stern of the boat tending the tow line. Steven was laughing and Tara was waving enthusiastically. *This is going to work,* she thought. *I'm going to make it work.* It was really up to her. Steven was beaming. He hadn't stopped smiling since she had agreed to marry him. And Tara seemed eager to embrace her new life. Apparently she had broken through all the reservations about her mother marrying a much older man and was welcoming her stepfather into her life with open arms.

Charlie was the only holdout. She could enjoy Steven's company, respect his generosity, and even share his bed. She could even put up with the indicting glances that his friends aimed at her, and whispers that called her a gold digger and even a tramp. What she couldn't do was give her heart to him. Lovers should blend seamlessly so that neither one could think of herself or himself without thinking of the other. Charlie was conscious of the space between them, and had to fight the instinct to jump away whenever their bodies touched. She felt the loss of her dreams, and was constantly aware of the compromise she had made. At times she felt she was lying to him with her every kiss and embrace, even though she had done her best to tell him the truth.

Maybe, as Steven had predicted, love would come with time. Maybe love wasn't the way you felt, but rather the things you did. So, she would do her best for everyone's sake. She would try to make the marriage work.

Eighteen

———•———

Sergeant Toomey arrived at the house the next day.

"You look fine," he told her. "Much better than when you had your head laid open. Marrage must agree with you."

"The only thing that still hurts is my foot. I think I'll have to go back for another x-ray."

But she didn't favor it at all when she walked across the foyer and led him out to the pool deck. She opened the refrigerator and offered him a cold beer. He reached in and helped himself to a soda and then followed her to an umbrella-shaded table. "Very nice," he said, taking in the patio with its outdoor kitchen, the forty-foot pool, and the view down the waterway. "It must be a great way to live."

She sensed a note of censure in his tone. Was it that he thought he knew exactly why she had married her husband? Or was it just the natural contempt for people who lived ostentatiously? "It is a bit over the top," she admitted, trying to suggest that she wasn't caught up in her newfound wealth. But then she wondered why she should care in the slightest what the police sergeant thought of her.

"When is the next triathlon? Because if you're entering, my money is on you."

"I'd be ready to right now," she answered, "but I wouldn't be able to run on this." She stretched out her leg to show the discoloration in her foot. He glanced at her ankle, and then took in everything that showed below her shorts. Charlie dropped her leg quickly. She didn't know why she felt suddenly embarrassed. She lived her whole life in one kind of gym outfit or another.

"Well, it looks as if you were right," he said as he settled into a deck chair. He drank from the bottle, and then added, "Apparently it was no accident. The guy was out to get you."

"You found him?"

He shook his head while taking another sip. "We found the Jet Ski. It was rented from a water-sports shop on the bay. Taken out before 9:00 a.m., and returned an hour later. Actually just a little more than an hour. He was charged for two!"

"How do you know it's the right one?" Charlie asked.

Before Toomey could answer, Tara burst out onto the deck in a bikini, and took two steps toward the pool before she saw that her mother had a guest. She pulled up instantly. "Oh, excuse me. I didn't know anyone was here." In the middle of the sentence she folded her arms across her chest as if she realized how bare she was. Then she turned back to the door.

"It's all right!" Charlie said to stop her from leaving, and then introduced Detective Toomey. "He's investigating my accident," she explained.

Toomey stood and shook hands with the girl. "Don't let us spoil your swim."

"That's okay! I can come back later." She was already backing away and seemed anxious to escape.

"I didn't know you had a daughter," he said as soon as Tara was gone.

"She keeps me busy," Charlie answered without any further explanation. Then she repeated her question. "How do you know it's the right Jet Ski?"

Toomey explained that the clerk in the store remembered

the guy in the wet suit. Why would anyone need a wet suit when the water was seventy-five degrees? The police had lifted the boat out of the water and the forensics people had found blood stains on the tow ring. It was the same blood type that was indicated on Charlie's emergency room charts.

"And the man?" Charlie asked.

"We got a description, but it could have been a lot of people. Sun-tanned, blond hair, big arms and shoulders like a bodybuilder. Probably some beach bum. He paid cash, so there's no bank card to follow. The driver's license he left behind was a phony. We got some prints from the registration form he signed and from the countertop, but we can't be sure that they're his." Then he interrupted himself to ask, "Do you remember if he was wearing gloves?"

"Oh God, let me think." She decided he wasn't. "I think I remember his hands on the handlebars."

Toomey studied her for a second. "Then he must have wiped it clean on the way in. We couldn't find a print anywhere on it."

He finished his soft drink and looked around for a place to put the bottle. He found none, so he set it back on the table. Then he stood to leave.

"So, what's next?" Charlie asked. "Is that as far as you can go?"

"Oh no! We'll keep digging. We have prints to process and at least a general description." He held out a hand to say good-bye, but quickly retracted it. "One more thing! I was curious that the clerk thought our man was a bodybuilder. You work in a gym, don't you?" Charlie said she did, and told him about her work schedule. "So maybe he knew you from your health club?" he asked directly.

She thought about her recent assignments. Most of her aerobics class were women, although there were a few men from time to time. But she didn't remember anyone who would be taken for a bodybuilder. There were lots of hard bodies in the weight room, but she rarely went in there and didn't know anyone by name. The weight room manager had frequently said that they ought to get together, but it seemed more like a running joke between them than a serious interest. She had never done anything to give him the impression she might be available. "It's possible," she finally decided, "but I can't think of anyone in particular."

"How about the neighbors at your condo? Or people with children your daughter's age? Has anyone shown a particular interest in you or the schedule you keep?"

Charlie was shaking her head before he finished. "No, no one," she said.

"Any former boyfriends?"

"Not for a very long time."

"Were you married before?" he ventured with reference to the daughter he had met a few minutes earlier. "Maybe an ex?"

She didn't want to go into her earlier life. "No one," she said forcefully enough to indicate that she wanted to end the guessing game.

Steven slid open the door and stepped out onto the deck. "Sergeant?" he said in a tone that indicated he was surprised to find the police in his home. "What brings you here?"

Toomey offered his hand in greeting, and then took Steven through everything that had been uncovered concerning Charlie's accident. He summed up her answers to the questions he had been asking and concluded with the leads they were still pursuing.

"So, you think that he was a hired killer?" Steven said, drawing the obvious conclusion. The sergeant shrugged. "Most likely."

"And that's it?" Steven wondered, echoing Charlie's earlier question.

"No. We'll keep digging. There doesn't seem to be any *personal* angle, so we'll take the next logical step and 'follow the money.'" Steven seemed confused, so Toomey continued. "We'll look into people who stood to gain financially from Mrs. Armstrong's death."

"My children?" Steven asked.

Toomey nodded. "Each of them would have millions of reasons to hire the assailant." Armstrong was about to protest but Toomey continued. "It's routine in this kind of investigation. We don't suspect anyone, but we have to follow every possibility. People do strange things when money is involved. Particularly large amounts of money."

The policeman took his leave and Charlie saw him to the door. At the last second he turned to her and said, "You don't seem shocked that we would be investigating Mr. Armstrong's children. Did any one of them seem particularly . . . hostile?"

"They were all friendly and welcoming," she said. "I don't think any of them objects to our marriage."

To Toomey, it sounded like a very proper answer. He guessed that she wasn't as certain as her husband was that the Armstrong children wouldn't kill for half their inheritances.

Charlie went upstairs to put on a swim suit for what had become a daily boat ride with her daughter. Tara, on her way down with a robe over her bathing suit, met her at the top. "What do the police want?" she asked.

"Just following up on the man who ran me down," she said. "Nothing important, but he *did* leave the scene of the accident, and that's against the law." She would have started into a lecture on the necessity of obeying the law, but her daughter seemed completely satisfied, and bolted past her on her way to her delayed swim.

"Some hunk!" Tara said.

"What?"

"The police sergeant. He was a really good-looking guy. I'd leave the scene of an accident if I thought he'd be investigating me!"

Charlie watched her daughter vanish through the door and out onto the deck. She was surprised that Tara would notice. Sergeant Toomey was old enough to be her father. But then she realized that the girl wasn't talking about herself, but was saying that he would be a good match for her mother. Once she thought about it, Charlie had to agree. *He is good-looking,* she admitted to herself.

Nineteen

Even though he couldn't believe that any of his children would have tried to harm his new wife, Steven put through a call to each one of them. He got Trish in her Manhattan gallery, and told her that Charlie's attacker had been a hired killer.

"The poor dear," Trish said. "Someone from her earlier life, I suppose. I've always thought that all that exercising and sweating was unwholesome, and you know the kind of people that hang out in gymnasiums."

She was so far from being concerned that Steven couldn't believe she could possibly be involved. Then she switched instantly to her own worries. "I don't suppose you've had a chance to look at the photos I sent you of Charles Eiffel's work?"

"Charles who?"

"Charles Eiffel. Like the tower. I sent you four pieces that you really should buy. The work is magnificent, and he's going to be very big in the next year or two."

He remembered the pink mailing envelope with the postcard-size reprints of paintings that looked like Jackson

Pollock knockoffs. "Oh yeah, you're right! With the wedding and whatnot I haven't looked at them. And now, with Charlie in danger . . ."

Trish gasped. "Charlie's in danger?" Steven repeated the story and Trish sounded as if she was amazed. "You mean it wasn't an accident?"

He knew his daughter hadn't paid much attention to the first half of the conversation. All she was thinking about was selling her damn paintings.

When he called Matthew, he got an "away from my desk," recording and left a message. A few minutes later his son called back. Steven could hear men's voices laughing in the background. "Where in hell are you?" he asked.

"At the club. We're just headed out for a round of golf."

"It's Tuesday, for Christ's sake," Steven snarled. "Why aren't you in your office?" Then he told his son about the hit man.

"My God, that's terrible!" Matthew said, his voice filled with concern. "Do they have any idea who was behind it?"

"No, not yet. Do you have any ideas?"

"Me?" Matthew sounded dumbfounded. "How would I know? One of her health club friends, I suppose."

"What makes you say that?"

There was a moment of silence. Then Matthew said, "I don't know. Just a guess!"

"A very good guess," Steven answered. "The guy was a bodybuilder or a weight lifter."

More silence. Then Matthew excused himself, pleading that he was already late on the tee. "I'll call you tonight," he promised.

When Steven called California to speak with his younger son, Courtney Davis answered. "Just a minute, Steven," she said. "I have to get a towel." He knew she wasn't in the kitchen doing dishes, so he guessed he had caught her in the swimming pool. When she came back to the call, he asked for Gary, and when Courtney told him that Gary was out, he asked her to have him call back.

"Any message?" she asked.

"No . . . well, yeah. You could tell him that we have more information on Charlie's accident."

"Oh, what happened?"

He was surprised. This was already the longest conversation he had ever held with Gary's latest arm decoration. He told her the story as briefly as he could.

"Do they have any idea who it was?" Courtney asked. She sounded crestfallen with concern, but then again, she was an actress.

"They're closing in," Steven said, making it sound as if an arrest was only hours away. "And then they'll find out who was behind it."

"I'll tell Gary as soon as he gets here," she said, and then went into a long explanation of why she wouldn't dare call his office. The new picture was at a critical stage of development. Everyone loved the screenplay—she dropped the names of Hollywood icons—and the most important stars—more names—were lining up to play the leads. Gary was in an all-day conference, but she knew he would want to tell his father all the exciting news. She gushed several compliments to Steven about how important he was in Gary's life and how they talked about him every day. Then she sent her regards to Charlie and prayed that her terrible ordeal would be over quickly.

Steven stared at the phone for several seconds after Courtney had hung up. *Where does he find these dingbats?* he asked himself.

He was relieved that he had no reason to suspect any of them. But he was reminded once again of how self-centered his children were. Trish had used his call as an opportunity to push her paintings. Matthew was more concerned about his tee time. And Gary's live-in had spent most of the conversation kiting the movie that she was hoping to star in. He had to admit to himself that all of them would go to any length to push their own interests. They were equally plausible as villains.

Matthew found his wife at the club pool, in a bathing suit, playing bridge with the ladies. He came close, whispered her name, and told her that he needed a word with her.

"You can see that I'm busy," she answered, keeping her concentration on her cards. He waited until the end of the hand when she gave a giant sigh of exasperation, pushed back from the table and went to him. "Honestly, Matthew, I hate it when you break in like this. What's so damn important that it can't wait?"

He told her about his father's phone call. She didn't lower her sunglasses until he explained that Charlie's accident had been arranged. "Who was it?" she asked.

"A professional thug. They're trying to find out who hired him."

Her eyes widened. "And he called you? Why would he call you? Does he think that we're involved?"

"I don't know," said Matthew. "But I said it was probably one of her health club friends, and it seems I came pretty close. The thug was a bodybuilder. I didn't like the way Dad told me that I had made a very good guess."

"You mean he thinks you know the man who tried to kill her?"

"I don't know."

"You don't know? For God's sake, Matthew, this is too important for you to be guessing. If he thinks we were involved he'll cut us off at the knees."

"So what was I supposed to say? 'Gee, Dad, I hope you don't suspect me.' Wouldn't that start him wondering why I was protesting my innocence?"

Hillary pursed her lips as she considered their jeopardy. Then she asked, "Did he call your sister, or your brother?"

"I don't know. Neither of them called me."

She wrung her hands. "We have to find out. We have to know whether he was probing them as well as you."

Matthew tried to correct his wife. "He wasn't exactly probing."

"He caught you knowing something you wouldn't have had any way of knowing unless . . ."

"It was an idle comment. When he thinks about it he'll see that it wasn't important."

"I'll bet it was Gary," Hillary decided. "He needs money right now. He doesn't have time to persuade Charlie on the wonders of Hollywood."

"If he needs money, why would he have her killed? What's he supposed to do, have Dad write a check on top of her coffin?"

Trish called minutes later wondering if her father had called Matthew and told him about the attack on his wife. Then she wondered if Matthew felt that Steven was trying to find out which one of them had done it. "Do you think that it might have been Hillary? You remember her on the plane. She was nearly crazy with the thought that Charlie would cut us all out of our inheritance."

"Hillary?" Matthew was enraged. "For God's sake, Trish, do you think Hillary would know how to hire a hit man?"

Gary was despondent when he returned home to his Beverly Hills estate. "We're at a dead stop," he told Courtney. "Ira says that if we don't find financing within seventy-two hours he'll bolt to another project."

"What did you say?" she asked.

"That he could go take a flying fuck! I can replace Ira in a minute."

Courtney sagged, and had to put her hand on a chair to keep her balance. "You idiot! Didn't you talk to your father today?"

Gary said he hadn't, and then Courtney told him about the call and Charlie's hired killer. "Your father was nosing around, wondering if we knew anything about it."

"Us? How would we know anything about it?" But even as he said it, his eyes focused on Courtney. "You don't know anything about it, do you?"

"That's not the point!" she screamed. "The point is that your father is too upset to talk about financing the film. You've got to get to him. Tell him that you're shocked to hear about his damn bimbo, but that you have to get financing for the picture right now. Don't you understand, Gary? This whole project is going right down the toilet. And let me tell you something. I'm not going down with it."

"Damn it, Courtney, someone tried to kill my father's wife."

She rolled her eyes. "Like you give a damn!" Then she stormed off to the bedroom and slammed the door behind her. Gary heard the key turn in the lock.

Twenty

Charlie's reaction was more direct than Steven's was. Toomey had given them a good description of her assailant. He was a bodybuilder, perhaps someone who knew her from her health club. Whether he had been hired, as the sergeant had speculated, or had acted on his own out of some romantic fantasy, he was the one they had to find.

She knew where to start. Every member of the club had a photo ID badge. The pictures were taken when a new member joined, and assembled into a plastic tag. A duplicate was attached to the membership application. All she had to do was go through the application files, and borrow the photos of muscular men. She could take the pictures to the marina where the Jet Ski had been rented and ask the manager to look for a match. If he found the man in the wet suit who had rented the boat, then the case would be pretty well solved.

Her only problem would be getting to the files. They were in the manager's office, and someone was in the office all the time. Charlie would have to go into the building after hours. Her plan was simple. She would go into the building late on a night when she wasn't working so that she wouldn't have to sign in and sign out. Then she could hide while the spa was shut down for the night. Once everyone was gone, she would have the run of the place.

She chose Thursday, a night when Steven would be late playing cards with his fellow yachtsmen at the club. The game usually lasted until midnight, so that gave her plenty of time to get the photos and return home. Just in case he was early, she wrote a note telling him that she had needed something from the health club and would be right back. That was the story she told Tara when she went to her room to say good night. "I'll just be a few minutes, an hour at the most." She knew the girl would be asleep in minutes.

Her car started reluctantly, and stalled twice as she backed it out and turned it around. Steven was right about her getting something more reliable, particularly if she was going to continue working evenings. She curb-parked around the corner from the entrance so that her car wouldn't be the last one left in the parking area. Then she walked through the front door waving casually to the receptionist and mumbled that she had forgotten something. The woman looked up for the time it took to recognize Charlie and then went back to her magazine.

Charlie went into the locker room and changed into her gym togs. Then she walked across the exercise area where a few people were struggling on stair-climbers and bicycles. There was no one working on the weights, which was a break because Tom Renthro, the weight room manager, would have talked with her until closing time. She went to the pool where one older man, wearing goggles and a swim cap, was doing laps. As soon as he was turned away from her, she pushed open the door to the equipment room and slipped in.

The stench of chlorine hit her immediately. There was an automatic system that fed the chemical into the water as needed, and it was leaking slowly into a small puddle on the floor. An electric pump motor was whining next to her ear. *Not a pleasant place to wait,* Charlie thought, but certainly secure. No one would look for a member in the equipment room when it was time to close. She settled onto a cardboard carton of water filters and waited.

Within minutes, she heard the "closing" announcement. A short while later the lights flickered and went out. She checked her watch. *Give it fifteen minutes.* By then, everyone would be out of the building. Her problem was that the chemical fumes were stinging her eyes and making them water. She decided to wait in the darkened swimming area, stepped out the door, and found a seat in the bleachers where she listened to the gurgle of the filtering system.

There were noises from other parts of the building—voices of the staffers as they left and the slam of doors behind them. Everything went deathly still in just ten minutes, but she decided to wait a bit longer just in case there was a straggler. Finally, she let herself out into a dark hallway, vaguely illuminated by the red "exit" lights. Once inside the management office she was able to close the blinds and turn on a desk lamp. Then she started through the membership records.

She could move quickly, flicking the files open with her fingertips and taking a quick glance at the photos. It took only a second to breeze past each woman and older man. She paused only at the younger men, recognized the face and filled in the body that went with it. But she came to a dead stop when there was a broad-shouldered man she didn't recognize, or one of the beefy denizens of the weight room. She took the time to check the listed height and weight and if it seemed a fit she slipped the photo out of the file. It took a bit more than an hour to scan the entire membership, and she came up with nine photos, including the weight room manager. She was putting them into an envelope when she heard the bang of the heavy hallway door. Someone had come in and let it slam behind. Charlie snapped off the desk lamp and dropped behind the desk. She heard voices coming toward the office door.

The latch clicked and the door swung open. The overhead lights snapped on.

"Here?" a woman's voice asked.

"No, not here," a man's voice said. "In my private office. Come on."

She recognized his voice—her boss who managed the facility. His office door was directly in front of her where the desk she was crouched behind would offer no concealment.

"I don't think I like this," the woman said.

"C'mon. I've got some stuff in there that you'll like." He was talking to her as if she was a child.

"What kind of stuff?"

Charlie didn't dare breath. The conversation was coming from the other side of the desk that she was hiding behind.

"Drinking stuff and smoking stuff," her boss said.

She giggled. "I thought this was a health club."

"It is. But I don't belong. I just run the place."

The girl laughed again. "Okay, but I really can't hang around. I've got to meet some people." She walked around the desk. Her white slacks and highheel shoes were inches from Charlie's face. The man's casual boat shoes followed her.

Charlie lifted her eyes. He was reaching around the young lady to push open his office door. "Stay as long as you like," he said. She started to turn back toward him. There was no way she could miss a woman kneeling just a few feet behind him. But when he snapped on the light, something in the private office caught her eye.

"Oh, this is very nice. It's like an apartment. You work here?"

He was easing her forward. "Glad you like it." He never turned around but simply reached back and swung the door shut behind him. Charlie drew her first breath since she had heard their voices. She took the envelope from the desk and stepped silently to the outer office door. She turned the handle slowly and crept out into the hall, leaving the door open behind her.

She was surprised to find the streets so dark and empty, and for an instant worried that her car might not start. But as she pulled away she felt a sudden euphoria—the comedown from her paralyzing moment of fear. Risk and danger were exciting. The chase was pure fun. She couldn't wait to run the photos past the marina manager.

Charlie went the next morning as soon as she had left Tara at school. The boat rental office was a wooden building at the end of a pier, surrounded by a flotilla of small outboards and sailboats. The manager was out on the dock, hosing down his inventory. Charlie waited to catch his eye and then followed him inside. He was smiling pleasantly until she spread her photos on the counter.

"Oh God, another cop." He turned away in despair. "What is this, the fourth time? I already looked at your pictures."

"Not these pictures," Charlie snapped. "And I'm not a cop. I'm the one who was nearly killed."

He turned back. "You're the swimmer?"

She nodded.

"Sorry," he said meekly. "It's just that the police have been all over me. They took my boat . . . my books. They shut me down for two days." He bent over the photos and began studying them. "They're in here every other day with a photo for me to look at." While he was complaining, he pushed one of the pictures back toward her.

"Is that him?"

"No. That one is too dark."

He slid another photo to her, and then three others. "None of these guys look anything like him." He gestured to the remaining mug shots. "It could be any one of these. They're all something like the guy I remember."

Charlie's spirits sank. The remaining faces had little in common except that the men all had light complexions and bull necks. It was obvious that he had no clear recollection of the man who had rented the Jet Ski. She gathered up the pictures, forced a smile, and thanked him for his time.

"I'm sorry," he said. "I didn't pay that much attention to the guy. He was just another customer."

She walked heavily up the gangway that connected the dock to the parking area. It had all been for nothing, and now she faced the problem of putting the pictures back into their files without being discovered. She was unlocking her car when she noticed a man waiting in a parked car at the far end of the lot. He was in sunglasses and an open-collar sports shirt. What caught her attention was his size. He was broad-shouldered with a wide neck.

Charlie tried to memorize the car without appearing to be looking. It was a light-colored four-door sedan, no different from a million other automobiles in South Florida. It looked American, maybe a Chevrolet or Pontiac. There was no license tag in front. But it pulled out of its row and followed her out of the lot. She drove slowly, glancing up at the mirror. The car was behind her, keeping an inconspicuous distance. Was it coincidence, or was he following her?

She took a right turn into a commercial street and looked back to see the car turn behind her. Then a left. She seemed free for a moment but then, once again, the car appeared. Charlie thought of slowing, giving the driver an opportunity to catch up and pass her. But if this was the man who had tried to kill her, she didn't want him pulling alongside. Instead, she slammed down on the gas pedal. The Toyota hesitated but then quickly built up speed. The other car fell back, but was still in view.

Charlie made another right turn, this one fast enough to set the old tires screaming. She flashed past a construction site, saw a small street to the left, and rocked into another sharp turn. She knew the man following her hadn't seen where she had gone, but before she could enjoy the thought she realized she had made a terrible mistake. The street ahead was blocked with barriers, protecting construction cranes that were sitting idle. She hit her brakes and skidded to a stop.

The car stalled. She tried the ignition but got only a growling sound. She shifted from neutral to park and tried again. The engine coughed but didn't catch. *Damn!* Should she get out and start running? Or give the car a minute and try starting it again? There was no place to go except back down the street she had just entered. *Give the car one more try.*

She saw something in the mirror and turned to look. The car she had been running from had stopped at the end of the street, and was hesitating as the driver decided what to do. Then it nosed into the street and began rolling slowly toward her. She could see the driver, masked by his sunglasses. His shoulders seemed to fill the whole windshield.

Twenty-one

Sergeant Toomey stepped into the conference room at police headquarters and shook his head in despair. "What in hell did you think you were doing?"

Charlie sipped from the paper coffee cup that her pursuer had brought her as soon as he had delivered her to Toomey's office. "I was trying to find the man who attacked me," she answered.

"What were you going to do if you found him? Make a citizen's arrest?"

"I was going to bring the information to you."

"Why didn't you just tell me about the pictures? I could have saved you a lot of time."

"Why didn't you tell me you were having me followed?" she countered. "You could have saved me one hell of a fright."

"Irv wasn't following you," Toomey answered. "He was guarding you. I asked him to keep an eye on you."

"Well, you could have warned me. When he started down that street toward me I thought I was going to end up in the construction site as part of a foundation."

"Would you have agreed to a bodyguard?"

"Of course not! Why would I need one?"

Toomey rolled his eyes. "Because someone tried to have you killed, and whoever it is might try again."

Charlie suddenly felt ridiculous. She had been out on her own looking for a killer. Thank God she hadn't found him. "Okay, it was dumb of me," she admitted. "And thanks for trying to protect me. I guess I owe you an apology. And your friend Irv, too. I'm sorry I kicked him."

"He'll get over it," Toomey said with a smile. "And I'm going to have him stay with you. So don't shoot him, or anything like that." She promised and then got up to leave. "Not yet," he said. "I have some pictures for you to look at."

Toomey took her through a book of photographs, even though she reminded him that she never saw her attacker's face. But the photos were secondary. What he really wanted to do was get her reaction to the dossier he had assembled on all her stepchildren. The evidence he presented was frightening.

Matthew's high standing in the business community was based entirely on Steven's backing. One executive at Ucandoit had told him off the record that if Steven ever sold his stock, Matthew would be out on the street within an hour. He had also learned that Hillary wasn't beloved at their country club. She was included only because of Matthew's financial clout. The conclusion was that Charlie was clearly a threat to their status quo.

Trish's gallery business, according to Toomey's investigation, was a charade. Her father was her biggest and most consistent customer, and even with his help she was still running up debts that she would never be able to repay. Imagine how frightened Daddy's Little Girl must be now that Daddy had found a new little girl!

Gary's position was nearly as bad. In a community where everyone tried to use everyone else's money, it was only his father's money that made him a player. Charlie was surprised to learn that the house in Beverly Hills was really owned by

Steven, and that despite claims to the contrary, Steven's interest in Gary's last movie had yet to earn him a penny.

"But none of this involves me," Charlie protested. "Steven never talks to me about his business dealings. I don't care whether he subsidizes his children or not. I have no input at all. So why would I be a problem for any of them?" But even while she was protesting she realized that her indifference wasn't important. What was critical was that she was an intrusion into their family, and that she might bring changes to the way the family functioned. And, of course, there was the estate. Her arrival on the scene cut each one's potential inheritance in half. "Fifty million dollars is a very credible motive," Toomey had reminded her.

Charlie picked up Tara and one of her girlfriends and brought them home for an afternoon of water-skiing.

"Where have you been?" Steven asked casually.

She decided to omit her adventures as a private investigator. "At police headquarters. Sergeant Toomey had more pictures for me to look at. No one I recognized."

"The guy is probably out of the state by now," Steven said.

Charlie explained that she had raised the same point with Toomey but that the sergeant thought her attacker was local. If he hadn't been planning on staying in the area, he wouldn't have needed the visor and the wet suit. "He has some more leads that he's running down," she said, and let it go at that. There was no need to tell her husband that the investigation was focused primarily on his children.

The girls raced past in their swimsuits and Charlie went out to the dock to join them. Within minutes, she was speeding over the bay with Tara and her friend skimming along behind her. She enjoyed watching the girls' antics, but resisted their pleas that she go even faster. There were other boats in the bay and she had to be careful not to get too close to anyone. But it was hard for her to keep her mind on her task. She kept thinking of the detailed files that Toomey had developed on Steven's children.

It made sense that each of them would resent her and

maybe even fear her. They could all figure out that Steven's fortune had been at least part of her motivation for marriage. From there it was an easy leap to the notion that she wouldn't want him wasting it on anyone else.

As Toomey had shown her, they were all used to nearly limitless access to their father's wealth. Each one of them had developed a lavish lifestyle that depended on Steven maintaining the status quo. Her arrival was a change that could only bode problems.

But try to murder her? Hire a hit man to run her down in the water? Was any one of them that desperate? Charlie couldn't believe it. Even if they hated her, how could they possibly inflict such grief on a father who had loved them so generously? There must be something she could do to reassure them that Steven never discussed his finances with her, and that she had no intention of squandering their inheritances.

It was a week later when Toomey called. He had someone in custody—an unemployed lifeguard who had drunkenly boasted that he was paid five thousand dollars to "get rid of some bitch." He had, he claimed, "run her over with a Jet Ski."

"Can you get down here right now before someone bails this bum out? I want you to pick him out of a lineup."

Charlie reminded him that she had never seen the man's face, so that there was little chance she would recognize him. Besides, she had promised to take her daughter water-skiing. But Toomey wanted her to at least look at him. "You go water-skiing every day. This is important! There may be something obvious that you'll remember." She agreed reluctantly, made peace with a disappointed Tara, and dressed in a skirt and blouse.

She stuck her head into Steven's office. "Can I take your car?" she asked.

"I gave you your own key," he reminded her. He had insisted she stop driving the Toyota when he learned that it had been stalling on her. Steven wanted to get her a new car immediately, and she had agreed to start looking. She wanted something much more modest than what he would buy her. She backed the car out of the garage, and waved to him when he appeared at the window. He smiled and waved back. It was obvious that he enjoyed watching her go through the daily routine of being his wife.

Toomey came down to the front desk to meet her and took her to the office where he had shown her the files on Steven's children. "I'm hoping that you'll find something that identifies him. If you pick him out of a lineup then we can hold him. We'll add up all the years in prison that he's facing and throw a scare into him. Then we'll offer a break if he tells us who hired him.

Charlie nodded that she understood his plan and agreed to study the men in the lineup. "But I doubt I'll recognize anyone," she said once more. She stood with Toomey at a window while five men were marched in on the other side of the glass. She could immediately dismiss the black man because she had remembered the bare hands on the handle bars. They were white hands, she was sure of that. Another of the men was too slender. He couldn't have weighed 120 pounds, and her assailant had been broad-shouldered. A third was pale, certainly not someone who had ever sat atop a lifeguard stand. That left two men, both about the same height and both with light hair. But one had the wide neck that she always noticed on the weight lifters in the gym. The arms extending from his sport shirt rippled with muscles. Of the two remaining, he was much more likely to be the bodybuilder.

"Take your time," Toomey advised. "If you want them to turn around or move in some way . . ."

Charlie was suddenly aware of exactly what was happening. The lineup was a fraud. Toomey had already told her that the man they were looking for was a lifeguard and that he was built like a weight lifter. She had no trouble picking out the man who fit that description because none of the others came close. But she wasn't there to identify the man that the sergeant had described. She was supposed to pick out the one who had assaulted her. She had no idea whether the figure in the black wet suit had been suntanned, or whether he was overly muscled.

"Based on what I remember of the man on the Jet Ski . . ." she started.

He cut her off. "Don't overrationalize this. There are always reasons to think that it might not be the one, particularly when you're trying so hard to be fair. Just your gut reaction! Is one of these guys familiar?"

Charlie knew that he wanted her to pick out the bodybuilder. He had staged the lineup so that his man would be the only choice. And she thought she knew why. If she identified him, Toomey could at least throw a scare into the man. It might take an hour or even a day for a public defense lawyer to challenge the lineup and get him released, and in that time the man might be tempted to name his employer for a chance to walk away from his problems. She decided to go along.

She pointed. "That one. The big guy in the middle."

Toomey referred to the number that the bodybuilder was standing under, and Charlie confirmed her identification. Neither of them could look the other in the eye when he walked her out of the police station and helped her into her car.

Twenty-two

Maria answered the telephone and then buzzed the phone out by the pool. Steven was about to dive in, and he was annoyed at the interruption. But the call had to be for him. He had just watched his wife drive away, and Maria would certainly know that Charlie wasn't at home. She wouldn't be ringing the pool phone if the call was for Charlie.

He answered gruffly. "Yeah!"

"Mr. Armstrong?"

"Yeah!"

"This is Perry, the assistant dockmaster at Blue Water. There's a problem with your boat that you need to look into."

Idonit was tied up at the Blue Water Yacht Club where he paid princely membership and docking fees. He expected the dockmaster to take care of problems so that he wouldn't have to look into them. "Where's Earl?" he asked, referring to the dockmaster who serviced his boat.

"He's out sick," Perry explained.

"Did you call my captain?"

Perry said he had but that no one had answered. He had left a message.

"Can't it wait until he gets back to you?"

"I don't think so, sir. She's taking on a list."

Steven's eyes widened. "I'll be right over," he said. The only reason a boat would list was if it was taking on water. He wasn't worried about his yacht sinking. At the dock, there was only five feet of water under the keel. But if salt water got into his generators, he would be facing a major overhaul.

He ran up to his room, pulled jeans over his bathing suit, and put on a golf shirt and a pair of sandals. He took his keys from his dresser and was halfway down the stairs when he remembered that Charlie had taken the Cadillac. He had no idea whether her old Toyota was running or where she kept the keys. Then he remembered the Whaler that was waiting at his dock. It would take a little longer, but he could motor down the waterway from his house to the club. He went out to the dock, and took the mooring lines aboard with him. Then he fired up the engine, and turned out into the channel.

There were several small boats making their way down the waterway. Steven pulled into line. He would have liked to put on a little speed but they were in a no-wake zone all the way to the inlet. He cruised along, listening to the dull groan that came from his engine. He wondered if his yacht might be flooded before he even got there.

Then his anger began to peak. The club had a dozen dock hands to service the boats. If his yacht was listing, why hadn't someone gone aboard with a pump and a hose and pumped out the water that was coming aboard? Why hadn't someone checked his electrical panel and figured out why his bilge pump hadn't turned on? The club had mechanics and engineers on staff. Why in hell were they calling him to come down and solve the problem? All he could do would be to marshal the dock crew. What did he know about sea cocks and flow valves?

He also paid his captain handsomely to be on call twenty-four hours a day. The man wore a pager and carried a cell phone, so how come he didn't answer? The boat was his responsibility. He was the one who should be rushing to the yacht club.

The boat ahead turned into the channel that led through the barrier beach and out into the open water. Steven saw his opening and pulled back on the throttle.

He saw the flash, although he would never know exactly what it was. He felt the fire that seemed to burn right through his back. He even heard the first crack of the explosion before his ears were blown out and his whole world went silent. Steven Armstrong's last sensation was that he was flying, arcing out over the water like a pelican that had just lifted from the surface. Then there was nothing. Nothing at all.

The explosion struck the air like a gunshot, echoing down the waterway and rattling the windows on the waterfront homes. Then there was a roar as a fireball belched out in every direction. Finally, a mushroom of inky smoke that curled in on itself as it raced skyward.

The boat simply vanished, replaced by a blot of blackened debris that burned in a pool of flaming gas. The fire spread outward, sizzling whenever it touched the water. Only gradually did it allow itself to be extinguished by the lapping waves.

The first instinct of people in the nearby boats was to duck. They heard the explosion and felt the shock wave. Instantly, they feared for their lives. But within a second they were back up, peering over their decks at the blot of burning debris. Some turned toward the fire, thinking that there might be survivors in the water. Others knew that there could be no survivors.

People dashed out onto their pool decks and terraces. The flash had illuminated their homes like a lightning bolt, and the impact had rattled their walls. When they recovered from their shock, they could see the tower of flame out on the water and they rushed out to assure that they were eye witnesses to the disaster. Some scanned the water for swimmers, or floating bodies. There was nothing. Just a fire that was slowly extinguishing itself.

It was more than an hour later that an officer on a police boat, crisscrossing the area, saw the body floating beneath the surface. The crew lifted Steven Armstrong aboard and laid him out on the deck. Considering the force of the blast and the ravages of the fire, Steven's body wasn't badly mutilated. His face was unmarred, and his limbs were intact. He was still in his jeans and golf shirt, with his wallet stuffed into the side pants pocket.

The damage was all to his back. The seat of his pants and the back of the shirt were gone, the scorched edges seared into the burned flesh. His thighs were open to the bones. The back of his head was caved in as if he had been struck by a blunt instrument. But still, the police were able to retrieve his laminated driver's license from his wallet and compare the picture with the dead face in front of them. They would, of course, await the medical examiner before confirming his identity. But they had no doubt that the dead man was Steven Armstrong, and that he had been killed in a violent explosion.

Charlie was returning from Tara's school when she saw the police cars in the driveway. "What's going on?" the girl asked.

"Shhh!" Charlie told her, as if Tara's question was impolite. She sensed something was terribly wrong. The police didn't send three cruisers to solicit donations for their youth programs.

Her first thought was for Steven. Words like *heart attack* and *stroke* came to mind. He was always pushing himself, whether it was on his treadmill or in his pool. She had often warned him that he pushed too hard.

Then she remembered Maria. Could she have fallen? Was there a kitchen accident? But those things would bring an ambulance, not a herd of police cars.

She was startled that there was no emergency medical vehicle. So it couldn't be a medical issue for either her husband or her housekeeper. Police were involved in criminal matters, and she had just left a police station over a criminal matter. Had someone come for her? Was it the same people who had tried to have her killed in the water? Had Steven shot someone, or had someone shot Steven?

An officer opened the car door for her and tried to lead her into the house. But Charlie ran around the car to put an arm around Tara. She led her daughter into the house, kissed her on the forehead, and told her to go to her room. Whatever had happened, she didn't want the girl to see the results. She didn't want her to hear the hard facts of a disaster without being prepared for the worst.

A uniformed police lieutenant and a Coast Guard officer were waiting in her living room with solemn expressions on their faces. She glanced around quickly, spotted Maria standing in the kitchen doorway, and realized that Steven was missing.

"What's wrong?" she asked, and she looked from one face to the other.

It was the Coast Guard officer who stepped to her. "There's been a boating accident," he said. "We believe your husband was involved, and that he was killed." He put out his hands, ready to catch the woman if she should fall.

But Charlie showed no sign of collapse. "Are you sure? Because he had no plans to take his boat out. He wasn't even going to the yacht club."

Now the police officer came forward and explained that they couldn't be completely sure until they had the medical examiner's report. But the circumstances indicated that the victim was her husband. At some point they would ask her to identify his body.

"What kind of accident?" Charlie wondered.

The Coast Guard officer answered. "An explosion. Probably from trapped gasoline fumes. The entire boat was destroyed without a trace."

"The entire boat!" He face registered disbelief. It was a huge yacht, with multiple decks and dozens of internal spaces. How could it vanish without a trace. "The *Idonit?*" she asked.

There was a moment of confusion. "What was that?" the police officer demanded. Charlie responded by describing Steven's yacht. She had just described the stateroom when the officer held up his hands. "No, this was a small boat. An open Whaler, or maybe a small runabout."

She thought about the Whaler that was tied to their dock, and stepped quickly to the window so that she could see down to the water. The boat that she and Tara would probably have taken out within the next hour was nowhere in sight. Then, without warning, she felt as though she might faint.

Twenty-three

Charlie looked through a plate-glass window at the blue face of her late husband. She nodded.

"Is that the body of Steven Armstrong?" a policewoman asked so that she could fill out the form on her clipboard.

"Yes. That's my husband."

The policewoman held the clipboard in front of her. "Could you sign here, please?" She did, putting an end to any official doubts as to who the deceased was. Charlie had no doubts as to how he had died. Someone had tried to kill her, and gotten Steven by mistake.

"I was supposed to be in that boat," she told Sergeant Toomey when he came to the house to express his condolences. "Tara and I took it out nearly every afternoon. She liked to ski off the back.

"It might have been an accident," he told her. "Boats are finicky! Gas fumes get trapped in the bilge. Exhaust lines get clogged. Sometimes just the hot sun on the gas tank . . ."

"Sergeant, do you really think that this is a coincidence? I agreed to marry a multimillionaire. A few weeks later, someone tried to run me down in the ocean. Then, when I'm married, the boat that I should have been on blows up. Don't you think it all might be connected?"

"Yes, I do," he admitted. "But as of now, we still don't know for sure that it wasn't an accident."

She rolled her eyes. "I was getting ready to take Tara out when you called. My first thought was to go water-skiing, and then come down to your office when we got back. You sounded as if it was urgent, so I decided to skip the boat ride." Charlie reached out and grabbed his hand. "If you hadn't called, I'd be dead. And the worst part of it was that Tara would have been blown up with me." A thought suddenly struck her. "My God, you don't think that they wanted to kill Tara, too?"

"Who wants to kill you?" he asked.

For the first time she told him what she had long suspected and what she knew that he suspected. "It has to be his children. One of them, or maybe all of them."

"Are they coming down for the memorial service?" Toomey asked. She nodded. They had all called and told Maria that they were flying in the next day. Not one of them had asked to speak to Charlie. "I'll be at the service," he told her. "Maybe you can introduce me to them. I'd like to put some faces on the files I've been developing."

He called her back late that night while she was sitting in the living room with her daughter. She had described the terrible accident, told the girl that her stepfather hadn't suffered and that he had looked very peaceful when lying at rest. Tara was stunned, more by the abrupt change in her life than by any strong feelings for Steven. He had been a nice man, kind to her and her mother. But he hadn't yet become her family.

"It wasn't an accident," Toomey told her. He described the laboratory work that had found traces of dynamite on the shards of the boat. There were also witness accounts of the violence of the blast. The amount of fuel aboard couldn't have caused such instant devastation. "The good news is that Steven never knew what hit him. The medical examiner said that he was dead before he hit the water. He probably never even knew that he was burned."

"Thank you," Charlie said quietly, her eyes on her daughter. She had already decided not to mention the evidence of a planted bomb. She would simply confirm that Steven's death had been painless.

"I was wondering," Toomey continued. "Do you have any idea what your husband was doing in the boat? Where he was heading?" Charlie told him what she had been able to learn from Maria. There had been a phone call. It was a man and he said it was urgent. Mr. Armstrong had spoken briefly with the caller, then dressed and left in the boat.

"Why in the boat?" he asked.

"I had the car," she answered in a bitter tone. She explained that she had come to use his car whenever he didn't need it. "Mine is a wreck. We were going to get a new one."

She wondered, too, where Steven had been going. What was so urgent that he couldn't wait for her to return? Maybe one of his friends or business associates would know. She would be seeing them all at the next day's memorial.

Charlie dressed the way she felt, wearing an unadorned gray sheath, black heels, and a simple gold chain that matched her wedding band. She was sad, somber, and restrained, but not in the numb state of mourning that would require a black dress and an opaque veil. Tara wore a dress of deep blue, and no jewelry other than the studs in her ears. Both felt awkward accepting condolences.

Steven's children arrived together in a limousine that had carried them from the airport. On the flight down they had been alternately numb from shock and shouting in rage. Trish had been the loudest of them, certain that it had been no accident that killed her father, and unhesitating in accusing Charlie of murder. "Her swimming accident was a complete sham," she told the others. "She wanted people to think that someone was after her so that no one would suspect her of killing Dad."

Gary had been the most somber. Ira Straus had mentioned his interest in another project, which had driven Courtney to the medicine chest for a hit of Valium. Gary thought that Ira was simply tightening the screws, but Courtney had left the house and vanished in search of another sponsor. He hadn't heard from her in two days.

Matthew was solemn and dignified, but Hillary was plainly bitter. "I warned you what she was up to," she said over and over again. "Now she has it all. We're going to end up begging our stepmother for an allowance."

A minister was brought in to lend a spiritual tone to the service. Standing behind the urn of ashes that was displayed on a clear glass pedestal, he read all the verses suggesting that life was never over, but only changed. Then he held one hand in the air and led a prayer of gratitude for the "wonderful life that Steven has lived."

The judge who had married them delivered a eulogy in which it would have been difficult to distinguish Steven from St. Francis. Steven's lawyer spoke of his charitable activities. Matthew spoke for the family and listed the many wonderful moments that Steven had enjoyed with his children. Then the mourners adjourned to the yacht club where a champagne brunch was waiting.

Charlie sat at a central table where all Steven's friends and associates could pay their respects on their way to the eggs Benedict. Matthew came to her so that they could exchange condolences. "At least he wasn't alone," he said of his father, which was as close to a compliment as any comments she received. Trish took a moment to suggest that she had exactly the right painting to be hung as a memorial to her father. Gary allowed that it was "a dark day indeed."

Sergeant Toomey hung on the periphery of the ceremonies, making small talk with friends and family. He was completely candid about his relationship with the deceased, and his role in the police investigation. Several theories about the explosion that had killed Steven were whispered into his ear.

"Accident!" Steven's accountant mocked, rolling his eyes. "A month ago, Mrs. Armstrong didn't have enough money in the bank to qualify for a free toaster. Now she can buy and sell us all. You think that's an accident?"

"He was an old fool," one of the club members told

Toomey. "What did he think? That an attractive young woman really found him irresistible?"

The lawyer commented that Steven hadn't had the time to rewrite his will. "That little girl is going to walk off with a fortune for a month's work."

Gary told the detective how Charlie had turned his father away from the family. "The first thing she did was make damn sure that none of his money left the house. She wanted it all." Hillary said that if the police weren't going to do something about it she would have to hire a detective to find the truth. "Legally, she can't inherit a penny by committing a crime." Matthew mentioned that his stepmother was now a major stockholder in a national corporation. "You can bet our corporate lawyers are going to look into this."

As far as Sergeant Toomey could tell, Charlie didn't have a friend in the house. Nearly everyone harbored suspicions that she had killed Steven. Those who wouldn't go that far, were at least in agreement that she had married him for his money and that it had paid off quickly. The women who brushed a kiss on her cheek weren't likely to invite her for cocktails any time soon. The men who held her hand wondered cynically whether Steven had gotten his money's worth.

There was, however, a commercial side to the tragedy. Charlie was now in control of Steven's legal and accounting affairs, both of which represented sizable retainers for the firms that handled them. The lawyers and CPAs oozed sympathy for her tragic loss. Yacht club officers had no desire to redeem Steven's bonds for cash and hastened to reassure her that she was a member in good standing. But, on the other hand, there was a large commission to be made for handling the brokerage on *Idonit,* and individual board members offered to relieve her of the burden of maintaining such a large yacht. Two realtors pushed their cards into her hand. "If you decide that it's too painful to go on living in his house." The head of the brokerage firm that handled Steven's trades made a point of reassuring Charlie that he would be more than happy to continue managing the portfolio. The president of the small private bank that the deceased had used had a tear on his cheek when he consoled the widow.

People might detest her, envy her, and even whisper accusations of murder. But she represented income to many people as well as to Steven's children. All the mourners had reason to tread lightly.

She came home to an empty house, switched from her dress to a bathing suit, and plunged into the pool where she swam laps for over an hour. She dragged herself out of the water exhausted, but at the same time refreshed as if the swim had washed away the hypocrisy she had sensed during the day. There wasn't one true friend she could turn to. Every expression of sympathy she had heard had been tainted by financial interest.

So what was next for her and her daughter? Go on with the new life she had chosen? She could leave everything in the hands of the people who had managed Steven's affairs, stay right here in the house with its wonderful view of the waterway and all its magnificent facilities, and go on with the job of raising her daughter. Now she had the means to assure Tara a wonderful future, but that was only a part of what the girl would need. She would also need Charlie's guiding hand to keep her from all the temptations she would confront. That was the most important thing. Before, Charlie had accepted the responsibility but lacked the resources. Now she had the resources, but that didn't relieve her of the responsibility.

Or, maybe she should sell the house and move back into the condo that she still owned. The financial pressures she had experienced would naturally be eliminated. She could pay off the mortgage, get the new car, and take all the trips and vacations that had been beyond her means. That would probably be a more realistic environment for raising a teenage daughter, and it might be a more comfortable environment for her. That would, of course, be Tara's choice. She missed her friends and their activities. But she would be graduating into a different school in just a few months. Nothing that Charlie did could buy her daughter more years of the same situation she had known.

Another possibility was that she pick up and move to a different part of the country and make a new beginning. She had no links with South Florida, and since her daughter faced change, maybe it should be a big change. She had fantasized other lives for the two of them when no other lives were available. Now that everything was possible, maybe she should consider a horse farm in Virginia. Tara loved horses, although that was when she was much younger. Or maybe a town house in a major city. She could only imagine the schools and cultural activities that were available in New York, or Chicago, or San Francisco.

She had to make decisions concerning the money, and for that she needed help. She had no experience in investments beyond the little she gathered in playing Monopoly with Tara and her friends. She didn't understand how much of Steven's estate was hers and how much belonged to others, nor did she know how such matters were generally resolved. Dividends, capital gains, deferred income were a foreign language to her, and she doubted the bookkeeper who prepared her tax return knew much about them either. But where should she turn for help?

Could she trust any of the unctuous professionals who had promised to take care of her interests? Who could help her decide whether Trish's paintings were a good investment or just colorful junk? Or whether Gary had a box office smash or a film that would go straight to video? A widow with money was like fresh meat in a shark tank. Was there anyone who could guide her through the feeding frenzy that was about to begin?

Don't rush into anything, she advised herself. *Just take it one step at a time. And keep a sharp eye out for someone you can trust.*

Twenty-four

―――――

Sergeant Toomey turned in his report on Charlie's hit-and-run investigation. The case had come to a dead end. The suspect he had brought in for questioning hadn't provided any useful information because a court-appointed lawyer had whisked him out of police custody before Toomey had time to broach any deals.

"He's the guy," Toomey told Captain Frank Jennings. "The clerk at the Jet Ski rental shop thought he recognized him, and the lady picked him out. If I could have kept him long enough to throw a scare into him, I know he would have told us who was behind it."

The captain scanned the report and tossed it into his out basket. "Keep track of him," he advised. "He'll probably get involved in something else, and you'll have another shot at talking with him."

Toomey lingered. "Aren't we finished?" the captain asked.

"I think you ought to put me on the Steven Armstrong investigation," Toomey said. "The two cases are related."

"Richie has that one," the senior officer answered, referring to another detective sergeant, Richard Lionetti. "Talk to him."

"But it could be the same guy, still working for the same person." Then Toomey laid out his case. Someone wanted Charlene Armstrong dead because she had become Steven's wife and new heir. Whoever it was had hired the lifeguard to kill her in a boating accident, but she had escaped. They still wanted her dead, so the lifeguard, or someone like him, was hired to blow up her boat. And that would have worked except for the odd set of circumstances that put Charlene in Toomey's office when she was supposed to be motoring out into the channel. Steven, he insisted, wasn't the intended victim. It was Charlene, and she was still in danger.

Captain Jennings nodded. "Could be," he agreed. "So talk to Lionetti."

"But if it's the same case, then it's still my case."

Jennings raised his hands in a dismissive gesture. "Richie has been working on it, and he might as well stay on it. Just tell him what you know."

The next morning, Sergeant Lionetti called at the Armstrong house for his first formal interview with the widow. She recognized him as one of the police officers who had been waiting for her with the terrible news of Steven's death. In fact, she thought she remembered that he was the one who had caught her when she began to fall.

They sat in the kitchen with a fresh pot of coffee. Lionetti was older than Toomey, with a Mediterranean complexion whereas Toomey was Nordic. His dark hair had thinned to the point where he might be called "balding," and a paunch was beginning to curve out over his belt. But like Jerry Toomey, Richard Lionetti was obviously a policeman. He wore gray trousers over black loafers, and a fresh white short-sleeved shirt with dark blue tie. There was a bulge at his hip where his holstered pistol was concealed, and an identification card was clipped to his shirt pocket. Most telling was the black leather notebook.

His questions began in the morning when she and Steven had gotten out of bed. What had they talked about? Did they mention their plans for the day. Did he know that she had taken her daughter to school? Did he know which car she had used? What had he done while she was gone? Did they talk together when she came back? She told him that they had breakfast together, and that he had spent the morning talking with his broker, and going through his exercise routines. He had seemed happy. She hadn't noticed anything that would indicate he was concerned.

After lunch, they had gone swimming in the pool. She had gone to her health club for the aerobics class that she taught. Then she had driven to school to pick up her daughter, and come directly back to the house. No, she hadn't talked to her husband other than to tell him she was taking the car.

She was planning to take her daughter out in the boat. They did that quite often in the afternoons. He nodded and kept writing in a very precise hand that seemed designed to get every possible word onto the page.

"And then Sergeant Toomey called about the suspect he wanted me to identify." She hesitated. "You know that he was investigating a boating accident I was . . ."

"Yes, I'm aware of that, and I know that he telephoned you and asked you to come down to our office."

He flipped back and forth in his notebook. "You had earlier described your assailant as being completely covered in a wet suit. Hood. Face mask." She agreed. "So then why would you have thought you could identify him?"

"I didn't," Charlie answered. "That's what I told Sergeant Toomey. But he thought there might be something I would remember and it seemed important."

He nodded and made another entry. "And that's when you told your husband that you were leaving and taking the car? That was the last time you saw him?"

"Oh," she said remembering for the first time since the explosion, "I did see him again. He was in his office window and he waved down to me."

"Waved as if he wanted you to stop so that he could talk to you?"

Charlie hadn't thought so at the time. "It was just like, 'Hi.' A friendly wave with no particular meaning. But that's where he was when I left. In his office."

Then the interview turned to Charlie's experiences with the boat. How many times had she taken it out? Was it always at the same time of day? How much did she know about the mechanics of the boat? Had she ever sensed any malfunctions? Had she ever mentioned that something wasn't right with the engine?

She said that they had probably used the boat two or three times a week, and answered "yes" that they always took the boat out after she brought her daughter back from school. As for mechanics, she had no idea how the engine worked. All she ever did was follow the few simple steps that Steven had shown her. "Open the fuel valve, squeeze the primer, set the engine in neutral, and hit the start button." She adjusted speed with the throttle and steered with the wheel. The engine died when she turned off the ignition. "No, there had never been a problem and never anything suspicious about the engine." She had no idea what could have gone wrong.

Maria had served a second cup of coffee when Lionetti brought up Steven's schedule. Did she have any idea why her husband might have rushed off in the boat? Did she have any thoughts on where he might have been going? Had anyone mentioned that they were expecting to meet with him? She said no to every question. Why Steven had been out in the boat was a complete mystery to her.

Then, when he had finished his third cup of coffee, the detective brought up the most disturbing questions. Had she been aboard the boat in the last few days working around the engine?

"Of course not," Charlie answered. "I told you I don't know anything about the engine." She also found herself denying any knowledge of explosives or that she had any friends or associates who worked with explosives. No, she had no idea of the terms of her husband's will, but yes, she understood that she would certainly inherit a major share of his estate. Charlie was beginning to resent the whole line of questioning when Lionetti asked her whether she would be willing to take a polygraph test.

"A lie detector? You think I'm lying?"

"No, not at all. I'm not even suggesting it. I'm just asking that should it ever come up whether you would be willing to take one?"

She weighed the question for several seconds. "It would depend on why it came up."

"Is that a yes or a no?" he asked as if he were trying to check a box on a license application.

"I guess you'd have to call it a maybe."

Charlie wasn't at all pleased about the overall tone of the interview. When she walked the detective to the door, she spelled out her own theory on the cause of her husband's death. "Remember, Sergeant, I was the one who was supposed to be in that boat. I'm the target. Steven was a bystander . . . an accidental victim." He gave a quick nod and flashed the suggestion of a smile, seeming to say, *I already heard that one.* His reaction sent a chill through her.

As she drove to her aerobics class, she went back over the options she had been considering. Staying in the house now seemed out of the question. Her obvious enjoyment of Steven Armstrong's wealth was an advertisement for her motive. It made her look guilty, and even feel guilty. She gave a quick thought to escaping on the yacht while she made up her mind. But she knew she couldn't even board a boat named *Idonit.* The title on the stern read like a confession. Leaving the country, or even the state, would also be taken as an admission of guilt.

Was she being paranoid? No one had accused her of anything. The questions Sergeant Lionetti had asked were just establishing a basis of fact for his investigation. Except the series of questions about her knowledge of the boat's mechanics. And explosives! That was damn near an accusation, unless they asked everyone near the case those questions. He hadn't seemed skeptical of her answers. She had seen him write "no" after each of her answers. But what about the lie-detector test? Was that also a question that they asked every witness? Or was he implying that he didn't believe her answers? Had she made it look as if she had something to hide when she didn't agree to the polygraph test? *I should have been anxious to clear any suspicion,* Charlie berated herself.

She walked into the health club where her class was already assembling.

"Hey, Charlie!" It was the weight room manager, coming to intercept her.

"Hi, Tom," she answered.

He touched her shoulder and turned her away from her students. "I thought you ought to know that the police were asking about us."

"Us?" Her face went wide with surprise. There was no "us."

"You know! Stuff like how well did we know each other and what sort of things we talk about?"

"What did you say?"

He sneered, and poked her conspiratorially. "That we're friends. That we work together. That you can't keep your hands off me." Tom thought he was being amusing.

"What else?" she demanded.

He saw that she was serious. "They wanted to know if I ever told you that I was a Green Beret in the army. Did you know that I was a demolition expert?"

"A what?" Charlie knew exactly what he had said and what he meant because she remembered that he had told her the first time he made a move on her. He had bragged that he had been in the Special Forces, and that he was an expert in rigging booby traps.

"I can torch your car so that the insurance company will never know it," he had teased. "They'll buy you a new car." They had both laughed at the idea.

She stood stunned, her hands up to her mouth, while he reminded her of the time when he had told her about his expertise.

She was deathly quiet when she retrieved Tara from school, and didn't attempt small talk on the way back home. "You okay, Mom?" the girl finally said.

"Oh, sure. There's just a lot to think about."

"Like what?"

She didn't want the girl to know what she was thinking about. Maybe this was all part of a routine investigation. Probably it would all go away. Then she rescued herself. "I was wondering what we ought to do next. Any thoughts about where we should live? Stay in Steven's house? Move back to our condo?"

Tara gave her a *why-should-I-care* shrug. Charlie was surprised that she hadn't jumped on the opportunity to go back to their old place. Maybe she was getting to like luxury, waterfront living.

When they got home, they went for a swim, and did multiple-lap races over the length of the pool. Charlie wasn't going all out but still was delighted that Tara kept up with her. Her daughter was changing every day, becoming less the child and more the adult. How much longer would they be together, she wondered. A few years at the most.

They were toweling off when Maria brought her the phone. She whispered, "The police," hoping to keep the word from Tara, but Charlie's moment of anxiety was obvious.

"Sergeant Lionetti!" she said as a greeting.

"It's Jerry! Sergeant Toomey!" the caller answered.

"Oh, I'm sorry. I thought I'd been passed on to a new investigation," she explained. Then she asked, "Any news from your front?"

"You are involved in the new case," Toomey told her. "I tried to keep it all together, but the geniuses down here don't understand that you're the victim in both cases. So, I'm on the outside looking in."

"I see." Charlie tried to make it sound routine for Tara's benefit. "So from now on I'm supposed to talk with Sergeant Lionetti."

"No!" Toomey said. "You don't want to talk with anyone. What you have to do is get yourself a lawyer."

"A lawyer?" Charlie nearly laughed. "Don't I already have half a dozen lawyers?"

"I'm talking about a criminal lawyer, not one of your corporate guys. I shouldn't be telling you this, but you're about to become the subject of a murder investigation, and from now on you don't want to talk with anyone unless your lawyer is with you."

She could no longer hide the fear that she felt. "I'm the subject. . . ."

"That means the department thinks that you set the bomb, or hired someone to set it. What they're trying to do now is build a case that they can take to the district attorney. They're barking up the wrong tree, but you don't want to do anything to help them. So you need an attorney. Do you know anyone?"

"No. The only lawyers I know are the ones that Steven used."

"I'll get you some names," Toomey promised. "And I'll keep the screws on that lifeguard. If I can get something on him, I think he'll give us some answers."

Charlie felt out of breath. She couldn't find the words to answer.

"Are you all right?" Toomey asked.

"I think so."

"Keep your chin up," he encouraged her. "We do some dumb things down here at police headquarters, but in the end we usually get it right."

"Thank you, Sergeant," she managed.

"Jerry," he said. "My name is Jerry."

She thought of Mr. Armstrong, who kept asking her to call him "Steve."

Twenty-five

The lawyer's name was Brad Troxell, and his office was in a second-class commercial building in North Miami. It was a decent building, right near the Bay, but far removed from the downtown business district where most of the region's heavy hitters had their office suites. Charlie introduced herself, and the Hispanic receptionist rushed off to announce her. A few seconds later, Troxell came into the lobby.

Like Sergeant Toomey, he was a young man, probably her age, and fair in complexion. He was short, certainly no more than five-eight. His eyes were blue, and his blond hair was in a dated crew cut. He wore the local business uniform of a short-sleeve white shirt and tie. But instead of the conservative dark tie that seemed de rigueur among all of Steven's business associates, his featured a colorful drawing of Mickey Mouse.

"Mrs. Armstrong," he said and then introduced himself as Brad. "C'mon in," and he turned his back so that she could follow him into the corridor and then into a conference room. There was a large oval table of light wood, surrounded by a dozen metal-framed director's chairs. Each chair was a different pastel color. The room looked nothing like the dreary dark wood offices Steven's lawyers worked in.

"I was going to beg off until I recognized your name," he said as they were getting seated. "Your husband was the Steven Armstrong who was killed in that boating accident."

"Yes," she said, "except it wasn't an accident."

He brushed past her comment. "And you were referred by Sergeant Jerry Toomey?"

"That's right."

Troxell laughed. "I don't usually get referrals from the police department. Most cops think I'm a bastard. But I know Jerry Toomey, and he's a very bright policeman. I've had him on the stand a dozen times, and I've never been able to shake him." They were seated, and he opened a folder that had been waiting in front of his chair. "You think you may be charged with your husband's murder. . . ."

Charlie leaned into the conversation. "That's what I've heard. And the first thing I want you to know is that I didn't . . ."

He cut her off with a chop of his hand. "Don't!" She stopped speaking abruptly. "Don't say anything about the alleged crime. I don't need to know, if there was a crime, whether you're innocent or guilty. It's not my business to know, and I don't make any judgments. Judges and juries do that. All I do is make sure that you have the full protection that the law provides."

"But it's important to me . . ." Charlie began, but once again he stopped her with a raised hand. "Mrs. Armstrong, at some time in the future, if this case ever goes to trial, I may ask you if there's anything you would have to say under oath that would hurt your case. I'll ask that only if it's necessary to decide whether we should allow you to testify and subject you to cross-examination. But I'll never want your opinion as to whether you are guilty or innocent. As far as I'm concerned, you are as innocent as every other citizen until you are proven guilty in a court of law. And even then, there's always the possibility of appeal."

She found herself smiling. He had just explained the rules of a game she didn't understand. She had to credit Toomey for telling her that she needed a good criminal lawyer.

Troxell began with an explanation of the criminal process. The police, he said, could investigate anything they wanted to, and they could arrest prime suspects by presenting a body of evidence to a court. But it was all speculation until they got an indictment by a grand jury and charged someone with a specific crime. "You're a long way from being charged with anything."

Charlie repeated the questions Lionetti had asked her. Troxell didn't seem at all concerned. "You answered truthfully. You don't overhaul boat engines and you don't build bombs. If I had been there I would have told you to answer those questions truthfully."

She mentioned her anxiety about the lie detector test. "I probably should have seemed more cooperative. More willing to vindicate my story."

"I'll want you to have a lie detector test," Troxell said. "To determine whether a polygraph would help our case or hurt our case. If it helps, we'll demand one. If it hurts, we won't allow one under any circumstances. But there's no rush. The ball is in their court and we don't have to do anything until they make their play."

Charlie smiled. Her sense of relief was obvious. She had found someone who understood the game and would keep her abreast of the ever-changing rules. She stood and extended her hand.

"Don't you want to know how much this is all going to cost you?" Brad Troxell asked.

"I suppose I should," Charlie answered. "Can I afford you?"

"With your newfound wealth, you certainly can," he answered. "I'll be billing you a thousand dollars an hour for every hour I work on your case. Plus expenses, and plus fifteen percent to cover the time of my office staff."

She laughed at his chutzpah. The man had no shame. "I could get you into great physical shape for only a hundred an hour," she said.

"Deal!" he announced. "You work to keep me healthy and I'll work to keep you out of jail."

They were on their way to the elevators when the receptionist ran up behind them and pressed a message into Troxell's hand. He looked at it before he pushed the elevator call button. "Hey, it looks like I'm going to send the first bill."

Charlie was puzzled.

"Your stepson, a Mr. Gary Armstrong, is down at the police station with evidence against you. It seems your husband told him that he thought you were planning to kill him."

"What?" Her eyes were wide with fright. "That can't be."

He turned the note toward her. "It's from Sergeant Toomey. Apparently he's looking out for your interests."

Charlie called Toomey's office as soon as she returned home.

Twenty-six

"This is Mrs. Armstrong," she said as soon as Toomey picked up his direct line. "I just wanted to thank you for helping."

"Sure! Only don't call me here. I'll give you another number."

She was surprised at his secretiveness. "This is beginning to sound like a spy story. Is someone watching us?"

"I'll call you back," he said, sounding even more ominous, and he clicked off. She went to the kitchen, took out a bottle of water and carried the remote handset out to the deck. She was hardly settled into a chair when the phone rang.

"It's okay now. I'm outside on my cell phone."

"What's going on . . ."

"*We're* not being watched," Toomey told her. "*You* are. And if they find out that I'm working with you they'll land on me for compromising a police investigation. So we have to be careful."

"Who are *they*? Who's watching me?"

"The police," he said, "from the commissioner down to Richie Lionetti. And there are more wolves joining the pack every day." She took a deep breath that was audible over the phone circuit. "Look, we've got to get together. But it can't be down here. Some public place where no one will pay attention."

She thought for moment. Maybe the beach pavilion where she had started her practice swims. But then she seized on something simpler. "Why not here? My house-keeper is here, and my daughter most of the time. The house is pretty secluded."

He took a few seconds to think. "Okay," he decided. Then he asked, "How about ten tomorrow morning?"

"I'll be here," Charlie promised.

She thought that he had arrived early when she pulled back into her driveway at 9:20 the next morning and found a dark car parked at her door. But it was Detective Lionetti who stepped out and came to meet her.

"Oh, Sergeant! Good morning. I wasn't expecting you," she said glancing around, looking for Toomey. She noticed two vans parked around the turn of the driveway. "What's happening?"

He was very formal, nothing like the polite, indifferent policeman who had slouched in her kitchen drinking coffee. "Mrs. Armstrong, I have a warrant to search these premises." He handed her an envelope. "My men are already inside. You're free to enter, but please don't do anything that would interfere with their work." Charlie was speechless, so he asked, "Do you understand?"

She nodded. "Can you tell me what you're looking for? I may know where it is."

"No, ma'am, I'm not allowed to say. We may be taking lots of things, but we'll try to be neat and put everything back in place."

She went inside and found Maria sitting at the kitchen counter, looking small and frightened. She was terrified of police, who, in her neighborhood, usually came on immigration matters. She ran to Charlie.

"They just came in!" Maria explained. "They showed me a paper and then started bringing in vacuum cleaners and mops."

"It's all right, Maria. It's part of their work to find out

what happened to Mr. Armstrong. You're not in any trouble."
The housekeeper began sobbing, and the two women embraced. But Charlie knew that *she* was in trouble. Toomey had told her that they were watching her. Now they had moved inside her house and, from the sounds upstairs, even into her bedroom.

Toomey, she suddenly thought. He was on his way here. Would he recognize the cars and the vans and drive away? Or would he come in to play some role in the search? She found herself hoping that he would come in. The house was already alive with people who wanted to prove that she had murdered her husband. Except for the frightened woman she was cradling, Toomey was the only one who was on her side.

But he didn't come to the house, and she could only guess why. Maybe there was information about the search at the police headquarters when he came into work. That would have alerted him to stay clear. Maybe he tried to call and warn her. But she had been out, taking Tara to school. He wouldn't know how to reach the phone in her car. Or he might have seen the traffic in her driveway as he pulled up and been scared off. Obviously, he couldn't allow himself to be caught "obstructing a police investigation." But still, Charlie kept glancing at the door, hoping that he would stumble through it. She felt more alone, more abandoned than at any time since Tara's father had abandoned her. She needed a friend, and Toomey seemed to be the only friend she had.

The police went through the house like a cleaning service, moving from room to room, vacuuming, dusting, wiping, collecting their findings in plastic bags. One of the officers sat at Steven's desk, logging in each bag as it was brought to him. Lionetti appeared from time to time to give a direction or ask a question. He passed Charlie several times without glancing at her.

"Should I put on a pot of coffee?" she asked as he walked by, hoping he wouldn't miss the irony in her voice.

"No, thank you, ma'am," he answered. "We brought our own."

They spent a great deal of time in her closet, seeming to

focus on her casual clothes and sports wear. A pair of her running shorts and a pair of jeans each went into a plastic bag.
They were two hours in Steven's basement workshop, which
was equipped with almost every kind of tool that Ucandoit
sold. As far as she knew, Steven had never used any of them.
She had borrowed a few of the simpler devices—hammers
and screwdrivers—to put shelves in Tara's bookcase and to
hang a few pictures that she treasured. She had never touched
the power tools, afraid of cutting off a finger.

She suddenly remembered her lawyer, Brad Troxell, but
when she called his office she was told he was out with a
client. She left word for him to call back. Twice she thought
of calling Toomey on the private number he had given her. It
would be helpful to hear a friendly voice, and Charlie was
growing desperate for a word of encouragement. But there
wasn't anything she could say to him without fear of being
overheard. Maybe they were listening in on the household
telephones.

She went out to retrieve Tara and decided to take her on a
shopping expedition rather than have her walk into her room
while her things were being searched. She called when they
were finished but Maria told her in a stage whisper, "They
still here, Mrs. Armstrong." She decided that they would stop
for a latte before going home even though she could tell that
her daughter had figured out that something was wrong.
Charlie finally had to tell her that the police were at the
house going through some of Steven's things. She didn't get
at all specific, and pretended to be annoyed at the waste of
police time. When she called again, Maria told her that they
had just left.

"Anything there that Tara shouldn't see?" Charlie asked.

"No. They cleaned up everything. Better than I do!"

Troxell had called while she was out, and she got back to
him right away.

"No kidding?" he said with a chuckle. "Seems like they're
lining up their heavy artillery."

"This isn't funny!" she snapped into the phone. "It's up-
setting. I'm scared to death!"

He apologized. "I know it must have seemed like an invasion. But a search warrant is no big deal. They probably found out what kind of toothpaste you use, and how often you vacuum your rugs, but not anything important. And if they do find something that they want to call evidence, they have to tell us all about it."

"Isn't there something you can do?"

"Sure! I'll call Lionetti, remind him that I'm representing you, and that I want to be informed whenever they plan to question or search you. It was rude for them to just show up on your doorstep and wrong of them to start the search before you were served."

"You don't seem concerned," Charlie said. It wasn't as much a criticism as an observation.

"There's nothing to be concerned about," Brad Troxell answered. "Don't worry. If there's ever a reason to worry, you'll be the first one I tell."

Twenty-seven

T rish and Matthew flew down in the evening and joined Gary at the bar of his hotel. They greeted each other politely and settled down at a booth in the far corner until their drinks had been delivered. Then Gary launched into the presentation he had made to the police.

"Dad told me that he had made a mistake, and advised me not to make the same mistake myself. He said that Charlie was in it for the money and asked me if it wasn't the same with Courtney. 'She'll bleed you to death,' he warned me."

"But that doesn't mean she was planning to kill him," Matthew pointed out.

"Maybe not, but it certainly shows that he was on to her," Gary defended. Then he added that his father had been much more specific in a later call. "He said he was afraid to turn his back on her."

Trish rolled her eyes. "You've been watching too many movies," she said to her brother. "That could just as easily mean that he was afraid that something might happen to her. She pulled that boat-attack stunt and he bought into it. He thought someone was trying to kill her."

They looked to their big brother for his opinion. Matthew took a moment to play with the stirrer in his glass. "It could mean any number of things," he decided. "But let me give you a few facts that you might not be aware of."

Trish and Gary leaned in closer to the conspiracy.

"You remember how Hillary was pushing for a prenuptial agreement? Well, even though they were already married, she thought there should be a legal document that spelled out exactly how much our stepmother would get in the event of Dad's death. So, just to get her off my back, I called Dad. I explained that the way things stood, a relative of Charlene's that he didn't know might walk off with half his estate. He said that he hadn't thought of that, and promised that he would talk to his attorney."

They were all breathless with anticipation. Had their father taken legal action to protect their interests?

"I checked with his lawyer," Matthew said. "He and Dad had discussed a legal property settlement that would have put limits on her inheritance. He had drafted something that he and Dad were supposed to discuss."

He sat back as if he had just trumped an opponent's final ace. The others were suddenly deflated. "But nothing was signed?" Gary asked. Trish was even more dismissive. " 'They were going to discuss'? Jesus, Matthew, that means nothing. Absolutely nothing."

"But suppose she knew," Matthew interrupted. "Suppose she knew she was about to be cut down to size. Wouldn't that give her a reason to act quickly?"

They sat together until well past midnight, organizing the details of Charlene's ruthless murder of their father. By the time they tottered off to their rooms, they were in complete agreement as to the case they would present to Steven's lawyers.

In the morning they met Albert Mays, in the offices of Jason, Mays, and Harrington, the firm that had represented their father's interests. Albert wore a dark, pin-striped suit made of a light cotton blend. At his level, suit coats were expected even in the tropical heat of South Florida.

The attorney explained that he and Steven had indeed discussed a legal document that would define the new Mrs. Armstrong's property rights. He had suggested it, arguing that at a minimum he should rule out any possible claims by his wife's family, and Steven had told him to "draft something up and I'll take a look at it." But he cautioned that anything their father might or might not have intended to do was irrelevant to their interests. He also explained that any such document would have been a contract between Steven and Charlene, and that there was no reason to believe that Charlene would have signed such an agreement. Basically, he was telling them that they didn't have a case that could be presented in civil court. "In a criminal case, however, it's a different story," he announced, lifting their spirits. "Your stepmother would lose all claim to the estate if it was inherited through a capital crime."

"You mean if she murdered him?" Trish asked.

He nodded. "Or, if she was part of a conspiracy to commit murder."

Gary jumped into the discussion. "Then let's accuse her of murder."

Mays began a lecture on the difference between a criminal case and a civil tort. Only the district attorney could accuse someone of murder, and he couldn't do that until the police had gathered hard evidence. It was his understanding that an investigation was in progress, although he had no idea of the outcome. He advised them to take their evidence and accusations to the police.

Sergeant Richard Lionetti provided an eager audience. He interviewed each of them separately and then all of them together, writing furiously to keep up with their comments. Gary was quite sure that his father feared that Charlie would murder him. He had no specific evidence other than what he thought he had heard his father say. Trish knew that the attack on Charlie had been a setup. But her only backup was speculation that nobody would have reason to kill a nobody. Matthew was more logical. He had no hard evidence but he had been assured by his father that Charlie would sign a property-settlement agreement. "Who else had any reason to kill him?" he asked.

Next the three children of the deceased met with an editor of the leading Fort Lauderdale newspaper. They didn't accuse their stepmother of anything. But they made it clear that their father's death was suspicious, and was the subject of an intense police probe. The editor sensed a possible Pulitzer Prize for investigative reporting. At worst, he should come away with a true-crime book on the heiress who had murdered her husband. He began calling around to see what the police and the district attorney were up to. He also phoned Charlie to ask her how she felt about being the subject of a police investigation. She slammed the phone down but then collapsed into a chair. Toomey had warned her that the wolves were gathering, and now they seemed to be everywhere. Where was he now that she desperately needed a friend?

She was startled when the doorbell rang. Maria had gone home and Tara was already in bed. It was much too late for casual callers.

Twenty-eight

————

Toomey stepped in as soon as she cracked the door, taking a fleeting glance back at the street to make sure he hadn't been followed.

"God, I'm glad to see you," Charlie said in a burst of relief. "Where have you been?"

He lifted her chin with his fingertip, leaned in, and kissed the tip of her nose. "I've been watching your back," he said. "What did you ever do to get so many people mad at you? I've seen serial killers get less attention from the department."

"A reporter just called me," she told him as she led him into the kitchen. "He wanted to know how it felt to be suspected of murder."

Toomey was at her refrigerator, his head bent down into the shelves. He came up with a bottle of beer and held it up to Charlie, asking for her permission to take it. Her expression said *Of course! Help yourself.*

"If they're already setting up the newspapers, they must be feeling pretty confident," he said while he located the opener. Then he asked, "How was the search?"

"Humiliating!" she snapped. "They went through everything as if I had no right to privacy. I saw one of them going through my daughter's underwear. Why in hell did he need plastic gloves?" Suddenly, she was crying, bawling breathlessly like a baby. She had endured worse indignities during her many years as a single mother, but for some reason the plastic gloves hit her harder than anything she could remember. It was as if she and Tara were dirt, and their intimate possessions too tawdry to touch.

Toomey was at her side, his arm around her shoulder. "Take it easy, Charlie. I know it was insulting. But it's over. They won't be back. If they need anything, I promise I'll warn you. I swear to God I won't let this happen to you again."

She took his consoling hand and squeezed it tightly. *Don't leave me,* she thought. She had never needed protection before. In her most troubling times, all her thoughts had been about protecting her daughter. But now she felt completely vulnerable to forces that had sprung up all around her. He was the only one who seemed to believe her. Charlie struggled with her sobs and slowly regained her composure. When she looked up, Toomey was sitting across from her holding both her hands.

"Why did they take my clothes?" she asked. "What do they expect to find?"

"Nitrates," he answered as if it was obvious. "The boat was blown up by a bomb, so they're trying to find out who made a bomb."

"Me? Make a bomb?"

"Of course it's ridiculous," he said. "If you wanted a bomb you'd buy one from a professional. Probably even have a pro install it. Lionetti knows that. He's just going through the motions."

"That's why they took the tools," she said, suddenly aware of the significance. "They think I made a bomb in my basement."

He laughed at the notion and shook his head in disbelief. But a second later he was back to being serious. "Did you know that Steven was having an agreement drawn up that would have limited your inheritance?"

Her instant bewilderment told him that she really didn't

know. "It's like a prenuptial that spells out exactly what you'd get if something happened to him. Except you're already married so you wouldn't have to sign it if you didn't want to."

"If Steven had asked me to sign something, I wouldn't even have read it. But he never told me about an agreement, much less asked me to sign it."

"The police are making a big thing out of it. Your stepchildren are insisting that it's the reason their father was killed."

She was still baffled. "Why would Steven need an agreement? He didn't owe me anything."

"Yes, he did," Toomey corrected gently. "Once he married you, he owed you a lot. I think he wanted it to pacify his kids. They were all screaming that they needed a piece of paper to protect their interests."

"But he loved his children," said Charlie. "He would have given them anything."

"They weren't worried about him. It was *you*. They were afraid that when he died you would control the estate, and that you most certainly wouldn't give them everything. They wanted the agreement to assure that you wouldn't be leaving with half their inheritances."

Charlie seemed to deflate. "I look like I'm guilty," she conceded. "I used to worry that I looked like a tramp who had married for money. Now I look like a murderer who killed for money."

"That's only the way it *looks*," Toomey said to reassure her. "There aren't any facts. In the end, it will be the facts that count." He finished off his beer, and banged the bottle down as if it were a gavel. "What we have to do is find the facts that point to someone else. The way to prove that you didn't do it is to find the person that really did do it. Someone wants you dead. Probably one of Steven's children, maybe all three of them. They hired that beach bum to run you over in the water. It was a good plan. Maybe your body would never turn up. Your husband would know you went out to practice for a swim competition. Your clothes would be in the beachside locker. It would be very obvious that you had drowned. And if the body did wash up, it would bear all the marks of being hit by a boat. A terrible accident. They would figure that the boat captain didn't even know he had hit anything and just kept going."

"Let's not talk about my body washing up," she said seriously. "I don't like to think about what might have happened."

He went on as if he hadn't heard her. "So then they hired someone to blow up the boat. I think it had to be someone local, because whoever did it had to know that you were the only one who used the boat. And they knew that it was in the water at night, tied up to your dock. So, our friend in the wet suit, or someone just like him, swam to the boat, climbed aboard, and wired in the bomb. A pretty sophisticated bomb, because it didn't go off as soon as the engine was started. It had some kind of timer on it. Or maybe a radio control."

"But we can't prove any of that," Charlie pointed out.

"We have to," Toomey said. "Otherwise you're going to trial. And even if you win, you'll be a marked woman for the rest of your life. 'There she is, the gold digger who murdered her husband,'" he said, imitating the kind of abuse she and her daughter could expect.

He stood abruptly. "I better get busy. I'm not going to catch any bomb throwers sitting here and drinking your beer."

Charlie followed him to the door. "Jerry, I don't know how to thank you. You're the only one who's on my side."

"First I'll find out which one of your stepkids is behind this. Then we can talk about thanking me." He started to leave but stopped abruptly. "Oh, I have something for you." He pulled a cell phone out of his pocket. "If you need to reach me, use this. It's cloned onto a government account, so they'll never trace it back to you. It already has my number. All you have to do is press 'redial.'"

He stepped out into the darkness, again glancing about to be sure that no one would see him. Then he walked away to a car that he had parked at a distance.

Charlie retraced their conversation as she climbed the steps to her bedroom. She liked everything about Sergeant Jerry Toomey. He was her age or maybe just a bit older. He had an easy way about him and talked in plain English. She even remembered that Tara had referred to him as "a hunk," which was the highest praise possible in her teenage vocabulary.

Most of all, she liked him because he was helping her. He was the only one standing between her and a jury of her peers who would start off hating her because she had ripped off her aged husband for a couple of hundred million dollars. She turned his cell phone in her hand and understood that he would be there whenever she needed him.

Twenty-nine

It was Brad Troxell who was waiting at her door the next morning when she returned from school. "I'm running up some billable hours," he said as a greeting, and then told her that he had a few things to discuss. He had called, gotten Maria, and found out when Charlie would be returning.

He suggested the deck where they would have a little more privacy, indicating Maria, who lurked in the distance, with a nod of his head. She offered coffee, but he opted for tea. She went into the kitchen and put together a tray that she carried back out to the deck. They sat at a table topped with a colorful umbrella.

"One of the prosecutors called me in last night," he began. "It looks as if they are going to the grand jury for an indictment."

She felt her breath catch. He had told her that an indictment was far away. Now it was closer than he had imagined. "What do we do?" she asked.

He seemed uncharacteristically morbid. "There's nothing we can do. We don't get to play in this game."

He spoke slowly as he laid out the facts of the criminal

justice system. The public prosecutor presented all his evidence to the grand jury. The jurors reviewed the evidence and decided whether there was sufficient cause to accuse Charlie of a crime. It they decided that there was, then they returned an indictment, and that became the basis for a criminal proceeding.

"Don't we get to challenge the evidence?"

"Not at this point. As I said, this part of the procedure is the district attorney's show. In theory, if he doesn't have enough evidence, then the jury can refuse to hand down an indictment. That would end any proceedings against you. But generally, the grand jury just rubber-stamps the prosecutor. The jurors don't know whether you're guilty or not because they haven't heard your side of the story. So they figure that the truth will come out in a trial. They can indict on pretty slim evidence."

"What evidence could they have?" Charlie demanded. "I know you don't like to hear this, but I didn't kill Steven."

"I believe you," Brad Troxell insisted, "even though it makes no difference. My professional opinion is that they don't have enough evidence to make a case. What they have is a damn good public relations opportunity."

Troxell opened his brief case and took out a pad. "First they have the motive. A lot of people can understand killing a husband or a wife for a hundred million. It's done every day for a lot less. So when Steven's children say that he was afraid you were going to do him in, they'll be very credible. Add to that the lawyer who will testify that Steven was in the process of drawing up an agreement that would have severely limited your inheritance."

"I don't care about the money," Charlie interrupted.

"Mrs. Armstrong, where am I going to get jurors who are ready to believe that someone doesn't care about money? In a monastery in Tibet? I wouldn't even bother explaining that the money was no motive for you. It's incredible on the face of it.

"Next, there's the opportunity," he continued. "You were with your husband every day, and you had sole use of his speedboat for hours every week. No one had a better opportunity to rig a bomb in the boat."

She was squeezing her hands together to stop them from shaking. "I don't know anything about rigging an explosion," she said through clenched teeth.

"Yeah, but I figured they would get around that by saying you hired someone to do it for you. Then I would argue, 'Who? Who is going to testify that you paid him to rig a bomb?' But unfortunately, they now have a more direct link between you and the explosive."

Her breath caught. She looked completely bewildered.

"They found some blasting caps in your basement. And they found residue of nitrates in the clothes they took from your closet. So they can make a case that you inserted the caps into sticks of dynamite. Add to that the two witnesses they have who say that they saw you working around the engine of the boat the evening before the accident."

"Dynamite? On my clothes? That's crazy! I never handled dynamite in my life. I'd be frightened stiff to go near the stuff."

"That's what I'd tend to think. But there you were working with a Special Forces veteran who's specialty was blowing things up. And there are people from your gym who think you and he were pretty tight."

"That's a damn lie! I never even had a drink with him. We never had a conversation that lasted more than twenty seconds."

"Sure, but you won't be able to tell that to the grand jury. And the prosecutor will allude to your relationship with an explosives expert. They won't put the guy on the stand because, as of now, he isn't cooperating with them. But they'll have plenty of time to lean on him."

He turned over the next few pages of his legal pad. "That's about it. That's what they're taking to the grand jury."

Charlie shook her head. "Is there any good news?"

"Oh sure," Troxell said as if there were an abundance of it. "Our argument is that the bomb was meant for you. Jerry Toomey is working that angle. He has to get the guy who attacked you frightened enough to tell us who hired him. Believe me, Toomey knows how to frighten people. That could lead to the person who arranged to have your boat blown up. And, of course, Jerry will testify that he called you down to the station house and, but for that call, you'd have been the one in the boat instead of your husband."

"It doesn't sound like much compared to what they have," she observed.

He shrugged. "If we find the real killer, then all the conjecture means nothing." He paused for a moment, and then as if he just remembered, he blurted out, "Oh, and I want you to have a lie-detector test."

"What? You said . . . don't tell me that you're starting to have doubts."

"Not at all. I need to know what kind of witness you'll make if I have to put you on the stand. There's no rush, and you'll take it with my operator in my office."

Charlie looked at him warily. "What if he asks me if I killed my husband and the machine says I'm lying."

"Then we won't let you testify, so you won't be subject to cross-examination."

She sat perfectly still for nearly an hour after her lawyer left. Sure, there was a lot of money involved, so her motive was obvious. Add to the obvious that Matthew, Trish, and Gary would probably testify to their misgivings about her and their father's fear that she might kill him. But how in hell did they find bomb parts in the basement? Steven had never mentioned any project that might need explosives, so there was no reason why he would have brought them into the house. And dynamite dust on her clothes. That was just crazy.

It had to be a setup, Charlie reasoned. Someone with access to the house had brought those blasting devices into the basement. It could have been done at nearly any time. She was away for long stretches of each day, and Steven was in and out. Maria was on duty, but a good part of her work day was spent at stores, buying the food and household supplies. Anyone with a key could have come in and had the run of the house for an hour or so. She guessed that all Steven's children had keys. They might not have needed a key. Steven left the sliding doors out to the pool deck and the dock open most of the time.

There was also a chance that the police had invented the evidence. They could have brought the blasting caps in with them so they could find them, and they could have added evidence to her clothes any time after they took them from the house. Weren't the police very close to Steven's big-deal lawyers and bankers? Couldn't her stepchildren had paid off the right people? Might that be the reason that the one investigator who believed her story had been taken off the case?

It began to make sense to her. Whoever had tried to kill her to keep her away from the family fortune had gotten Steven by mistake. But now, they could accomplish the same thing by getting her convicted of murder. If they could prove that she had killed Steven, then she would lose all claim on the money, and would be safely out of the way in a jail cell. But who? The children were the most likely candidates, but which one of them? The only one trying to find out was Toomey, and he had to be very careful to keep a distance from the case. She felt completely helpless, a victim who had no line of defense.

Tara! Charlie's thoughts shifted to her daughter. How could a young girl, not yet really sure who she was, handle this? The pressure was going to be enormous. Her mother would be accused of murder in the newspapers and on television. The amount of money her mother had married into would be bandied about with another zero added each time the figure was mentioned. Steven would become a figure of public ridicule, an old fool who had walked blindly into the snares of a scheming woman. Tara's whole world would become tawdry. The most intimate details of her private life would be hung out on the line for the amusement of the neighbors. She would be hounded on the streets by television reporters thrusting microphones into her face. The supermarket tabloids would invent stories about her. In school, she would be the target of every imaginable adolescent cruelty.

But even in her dark brooding, Charlie had no idea of how quickly it would all come true.

Thirty

S he was on the front page of the next morning's newspaper, standing beside Steven in a photo that had been taken at the wedding, under the headline, "DA Seeks Murder Indictment of Trophy Wife."

The murder charge being sought in the mysterious death of her multimillionaire husband was announced in the lead paragraph. Their recent marriage, with emphasis on the discrepancy in their ages, was paragraph two, and estimates of how much she had earned by bringing only a few months' satisfaction to the older man was paragraph three. From there, the story portrayed their two lives, his as a successful businessman and community leader, hers as a single mother who performed in leotards at a local gym. There were brief statements by Steven's mourning children who had flown in to testify before the grand jury. The public prosecutor, who presumably leaked the story, had no comment.

Afternoon television news gave fifteen seconds to a reporter getting brushed off by the prosecutor on the courthouse steps, and then eliciting "It's a very difficult day for the family" from Trish as she was being rushed past. The reporter then turned to the camera and sympathized with the anguish of a family betrayed.

Maria took Tara to her home where she could live until Charlie could make another arrangement. "Can you keep her away from the television set," Charlie begged, "and maybe the newspapers?"

"In my neighborhood, it's all in Spanish," Maria reminded her. She would be as well protected there as in a foreign country.

"I haven't been charged yet," Charlie complained to Troxell when she arrived at his office for the polygraph. "What's it going to be like when I'm indicted?"

"A little more hysterical," he answered. "They'll begin leaking details of their case against you. Every time interest starts to die out they'll leak another piece of evidence. We'll be months getting to trial, and you'll be a headline at least once a month."

"Jesus," she said as a prayer more than as a profanity.

"On the plus side, movie producers and publishers will be all over you, offering millions for rights to your story. Get the money up front, because it won't be worth nearly as much if you're found innocent. And if you're found guilty, they won't have to pay you at all."

She didn't like Brad Troxell's cynicism, or the breezy manner in which he ignored her obvious pain. But maybe he was trying to toughen her up for the ordeal ahead. Maybe he was telling her that if she expected sympathy from any quarter, she shouldn't get her hopes up. The polygraph operator began hooking her up to the machine at about the same time that Trish was sitting down before the grand jury.

The morning session of the grand jury had been filled with expert testimony by the medical examiner—Steven's death had been the result of massive trauma and severe burns, inflicted by a bomb explosion no more than a few feet behind him—and by the forensics experts—the explosion had been caused by highly volatile nitrates, and not by the accidental combustion of fuels carried aboard the boat. Sergeant Lionetti had vouched for the authenticity of the blasting caps found in the Armstrong basement and for the clothing taken from Charlie's closet. Then police laboratory experts had linked the clothes to the type of explosive that destroyed the boat, explained the role of the blasting caps, and mentioned that Charlie's fingerprints were all over the tools that held traces of the explosive material.

Now that Steven's wife had been scientifically linked to the bomb that killed her husband, the prosecutor was moving to establish her motive. Trish, wearing a black knit coat over black pants, dabbed at her eyes with a hankie as she described the close relationship she had with her father. "His mind was failing," she told the jurors. "He had once been logical and objective, but in recent months he had become sentimental and lonely," she explained. "He made no sense at all when he tried to describe his reasons for marrying a woman thirty years his junior. It was as if she held a spell over him."

"The last few days he was plainly frightened," Gary testified. He had talked with his father several times in the days leading up to his death. "He knew he had made a mistake, and he was coming to realize that it was all about his money. But he was afraid to cross her. He was sure that she would react violently."

"Were those your father's exact words?" the government attorney asked.

"No," Gary answered. "His exact words were, 'I'm afraid to turn my back on her.' "

Matthew testified that he too had sensed his father's desperation. "Everyone had advised him that all Charlene was after was his money. I had personally pointed out that they had absolutely nothing in common. But he was irrational, almost as if he were on drugs. He didn't figure things out until after the marriage, and by then it was too late."

Steven's attorney told the jury that Steven had indeed tried to "rectify the situation." He explained the property settlement that he had drafted, which would have limited the new wife's claim on the family assets. "If she didn't sign it, he was going to move to have the marriage declared null and void. In effect he was going to ask the court to eliminate her legal rights because she had lied about her reasons for marrying. It wasn't a valid marriage contract."

The jury's reaction to all this was visible. One woman cried along with Trish. The men scowled when they heard how much money the grieving widow was likely to get. They rushed off to the jury room to hurry to a verdict. Would they be asking for additional information to aid their deliberations? One attorney leaned over to the district attorney and smirked that "the only thing they'll be asking for is a rope."

In a less formal setting in another part of the city, Charlie was gradually becoming annoyed at the repetitive questions being asked in a bored voice by the polygraph operator. He was a rotund figure with a bald head and sagging jowls. He asked questions without any intonation that might indicate he cared about the content, and without even glancing up in anticipation of an answer. All his attention was focused on the paper scrolling through his machine where he made marks and notations with a felt-tip pen. Charlie felt that if she were to let out a bloodcurdling scream, he would simply note it in his squiggly marks.

The questions came in no logical order, veering suddenly from "Do you live in Fort Lauderdale?" to "Have you ever handled high explosives?" They were impersonal, like her social security number, and extremely personal, like whether she had been intimate with any man since her husband's tragedy. Some questions were repeated several times for no apparent reason. Others were reworded to give them a slightly different meaning.

"Are you a licensed physical therapist?"

"Yes."

"Are you a licensed driver?"

"Yes."

"Do you know your deceased husband's approximate net worth?"

"No."

"Did you have sex with your deceased husband?"

"Of course."

"Is that 'yes'?"

"Yes."

"Do you teach an aerobics class?"

"Yes."

"Did you have sex with your deceased husband before you were married?"

"No."

"Do you have a daughter?"

"Yes."

"Have you ever handled explosives?"

"Oh, Christ!"

"Just yes or no, please."

"No."

She tried to interpret the swaying needles that were etching lines on the paper. Sometimes one would jump wildly while the others stayed calm. The next question would set them all into gyrations. She thought that since she was answering every question truthfully, that the traces should always look the same, but that wasn't the way the machine wanted to work. She couldn't even decide whether it showed one pattern for objective questions, like her telephone number, and another pattern for personal questions about her sex life.

Charlie switched from trying to fathom the machine's output to looking for a change in the operator's expression. It seemed logical if he was interpreting the wobbly lines, he would react to an indication that she was lying. She even salted in a few bad answers to test her theory. "Did you have breakfast this morning?" he asked. Charlie answered "no," even though she had toasted a muffin to go with her cereal, and had eaten two helpings of fruit. The needles moved in another indecipherable pattern. His face showed not even a flicker of activity.

"That should do it," he finally said, setting down his felt tip and turning off the machine. For the first time he showed a human smile. "Not too bad, I hope?"

But when she asked him how she had done the mask dropped back over his face. "It all has to be studied," he mumbled, and then began disconnecting the wires that probed her body.

Troxell was waiting for her when she came out of the room. "How'd it go?" he asked.

"It all has to be studied," Charlie parroted. "What's next?"

"Next is the trial," he said. "You've been indicted for the murder of your husband."

"Already?"

He glanced at his watch. "Over an hour ago. The grand jury returned an indictment in less than an hour. The prosecutors will bring it to court tomorrow and get a warrant for your arrest."

"Prison!" Her color drained.

"For an hour or so. I've already arranged for a bail bond. You can pay it off tomorrow, as soon as you get out."

"Will the police come and get me?" Her fear was growing by the second.

"No, I'll drive over to your place and pick you up. I've already told the DA's office that you'd turn yourself in whenever they're ready."

As he was walking her to the elevator she suddenly asked, "Could we swap cars, just for an hour or so?"

He seemed unsure so Charlie explained that she wanted to drive to a friend's house and visit with her daughter. "There were people following me when I came here. I don't know whether they were police or press reporters, but if they're waiting to pick me up when I leave, I don't want them recognizing me."

He still didn't seem to understand. "I don't want anyone to know where my daughter is. I want all this kept away from her."

She drove Brad Troxell's Beetle out of the ground-floor garage and right past the sedan that had followed her Cadillac earlier in the day. She wondered whether they would follow Troxell in her Cadillac right into his driveway before they realized they had been taken. Then she headed west into the older part of the city where Spanish had become the official language. She followed Maria's directions through a neigh-

THE STEPMOTHER 183

borhood of well-kept, old-style ranch houses, with tricycles in most driveways. Maria's car, a newer model of the one Charlie still owned, was parked at her address.

The house was sparsely furnished with pieces of various styles, acquired as needed rather than to fit any sort of decorating plan. Tara came from one of the bedrooms and stood still while Charlie rushed to embrace her. "Hi, Mom," was the best she could manage and even that lacked enthusiasm.

"Are you all right?" Charlie asked.

Tara responded with a shrug.

"I suppose you've heard . . ." Charlie suggested.

"Sure," her daughter answered. She pointed to the television. "It gets all the stations."

"None of it is true! Not one word! I swear to you, it's all crazy."

"I know," the girl said as if it was no big deal. Then she added, "Can I go home now?"

Charlie pulled her down next to her on a sofa. "I was thinking it might be best for you to get away for a while. The newspapers and TV are going to get awful, and all the reporters will be trying to talk to you."

"I know," she said. "It's okay."

"You don't want to go back to school," Charlie suggested.

"Yes, I do. They're my friends, Mom. They'll be cool."

Was she completely naïve? Charlie wondered. Didn't she realize how cruel her classmates could be? Or, had she suddenly grown up? Was she saying that she wasn't afraid to face down her critics?

"Let's give it a few days," she decided. "Let's get through the worst of this, and then we'll decide what we should do."

Tara shrugged as if to say "Whatever!" But then she added, "I just don't want to run away, okay."

Charlie hugged her. She didn't want to run away either.

Thirty-one

There were reporters gathered outside the gate when Charlie approached the house, and her first instinct was to drive right through them. There would be more than a little satisfaction in sending them diving for cover. She owed them a bit of embarrassment for the torture they were inflicting on her. But she could almost write the next day's headlines, about the crazy woman who mowed down anyone who got in her way. The problem with battling the press was that they always had the last word.

She drove past the house, unrecognized in her borrowed Volkswagen Beetle, continued down the street, and turned at the corner. But turned to where? She couldn't drive in circles for the rest of her life.

She thought of the condo that she had left when she moved into Steven's house. It was listed for sale but there wouldn't be any realtor activity during the night. She glanced at the keys dangling from the ignition key. *Damn!* They weren't her keys. Her condo latchkey was on the key ring that she had given to Brad Troxell when they traded cars. Then she remembered the spare key she had buried in the flowerpot that stood next to the entrance. It should still be there.

Charlie checked and rechecked her mirror as she made random turns to the right and left. There was no one following her. Toomey's man had appeared behind her from time to time, or in the next aisle when she was shopping. But he wasn't with her now. She headed to her condo and killed her headlights as she coasted to a stop in one of the visitor slots. Then she walked to her unit so that there wouldn't be a car parked in front. She dug a hand into the flowerpot, swore when she couldn't feel the key, and began sifting the dirt out onto the step. It was half empty when she felt it, and she plucked it out in triumph.

The house was dark, illuminated only by the fading sunlight that was coming in around the blinds, but she could still make out the silhouettes of her furnishings and the steps that led up to the bedrooms. Tara's furniture had been moved to the new house, but her room was still intact. The bed was neatly made and there was a change of clothes waiting in the dresser draws. She started the water into her bathtub, and poured in an extra measure of the aromatic salts she kept for special occasions. Then she found a bath sheet in the linen closet, undressed, and stepped into the sea of bubbles.

The water was refreshing. She had been charged with murder and found guilty in the court of public opinion. Then she had owned up to her most personal secrets in the grueling ordeal of the lie-detector test. Finally, she had been driven from her own home by a lynch mob of reporters. The bath seemed to lift the stain of the day out of her pores and float it away.

Charlie slid down low so that water lapped at her chin. She closed her eyes and tried to let her mind go blank. The tension in her body vanished as she breathed deeply. She began to drift into a quiet zone where there were no accusations aimed at her, no howling mobs crying for her head. If only she could stay right here until it was all over.

She didn't know if she had really fallen asleep. If she was asleep, she had no idea how long it had been. All she knew was that the light that had been seeping through the window had faded completely. She was in a dark space, nearly weightless, with no physical points of reference. Then she heard it—the sound that had probably wakened her. The rear screen door that led out to the kitchen deck had been swung open and was tapping against the side of the house. Someone was fitting a key into the rear door lock.

She eased herself slowly out of the water, and wiped the suds off her body, trying her best not to make a sound. It couldn't be the realtor working after hours. The only key the agency had was to the front door. Who? Reporters who had tracked her down? Or maybe the police were still investigating her, looking for more damning evidence. Charlie wrapped the bath sheet around her, tucking the loose corner under her arm. She stepped out into her bedroom, reached for the doorknob, and thought better of it. She was in this mess because someone had tried to kill her. Maybe they were still trying.

She heard the click of the deadbolt-lock as clearly as if she had been standing right next to it, and then the grunt of the door breaking the friction with the doorjamb. She heard the back door swing open.

The house was dark. She had left none of her things downstairs, so there was every chance that the intruder wouldn't know that she was home. A reporter might be turned away. The police, of course, would search every corner and crevice. In fact, if their last search was typical, they would focus most of their attention on her bedroom. An assassin would come up the stairs expecting to find her asleep, or in her bath, exactly where she had been. She had to get out of the bedroom, and she had to do it now before the intruder reached the bottom of the steps, where he would see her as soon as she stepped out of her door. Again she reached for the doorknob, and again she was stopped, this time by the sound of a footstep on the hard tile floor of the kitchen.

Where in the kitchen? If he was still near the door, or back near the laundry alcove, he wouldn't see her trying to escape. She could make it to the storage closet at the end of the hall, and maybe even to the fold-down ladder that accessed the small attic. But if he were at the counter, or near the dining room entrance, she would be crossing directly into his line of sight. Once more she backed slowly away.

Another footstep, this one muffled as someone stepped from the kitchen tiles onto the carpeted floor of the dining area. Thank God she hadn't made a run for it. She would have been seen instantly. A light flickered under her door—a flashlight searching the lower floor. The intruder was getting his bearings. He could see into the small living room, and certainly notice the stairs to the second floor. The light snapped off, and for an instant Charlie felt secure in the darkness. But then she heard a familiar creak. The intruder had put his weight on the first step. He was on his way up.

She glanced about quickly. There was the bathroom that could be locked behind her. The lock might hold long enough for her to get out through the window over the tub. Or at least long enough for her to scream. She leaned in that direction, and then remembered that the tub was still full of sudsy water. She could never get a foothold.

Under the bed! But was there room? She had stored all kinds of things under her bed. If she pushed in from one side, she would push enough boxes and storage bags out the other side to give her away.

Another noise sounded, this one from the middle of the stairs. Someone was climbing slowly and carefully. He would be at her door in seconds. The door wasn't even locked. Charlie backed past the open slider of her closet and pushed into the clothes. With a fingertip, she pushed the door over just as she heard the bedroom door latch turn. Carefully, she slid back through the hanging suits and dresses until she found the space between the clothes and the wall. She heard her bedroom door swing open. There was silence. He was in the doorway staring into the dark room. Charlie squeezed against the closet wall and stopped breathing.

The flashlight snapped on. She could see the lines of faint light on the closet ceiling as the light filtered through the louvered doors. They flickered as the beam turned into the far corners of the room and panned across the closet. A footstep crunched into the carpet. He was heading for the bathroom.

The water! He was looking at a tub full of water, still warm and still alive with suds and bubbles. He would know that she was there, in the house, only a few minutes out of the bath. He would know that he hadn't missed his opportunity. She heard another footstep crush the pile of the carpet. The light reappeared. The door slid open. Through the clothes, Charlie could make out the outlines of her attacker behind the glare of the light. A hand reached for the clothes hanging in front of her face.

She lunged forward, aiming a punch at the shadowy face. She felt her knuckles hit the point of a chin. The man toppled backward. His flashlight dropped to the floor and bounced across its own light. Charlie darted out of the closet, never even looking at the man who had fallen to one knee. She bolted past him toward the door.

A hand clutched at her ankle. She pulled it free, but then another hand locked around the other ankle. She tried to kick but had no leverage. Then she lost her balance and fell back onto the bath towel that hit the floor just an instant before her.

"You bastard!" she kicked out with the free foot and felt it land. She was able to break the grasp on her other foot and then tried to scamper to her feet.

"Charlie?" Her attacker was no longer fighting her. He was getting to his feet. "Dammit, Charlie! Is that you?"

"Jerry . . . Sergeant Toomey," she answered.

"Oh, for God's sake." He reached for his flashlight.

"No, wait! I'm not dressed."

He lifted the lamp and snapped it off. Charlie pulled the towel around her and went to the wall light switch. Toomey was standing in front of her with blood spreading from a split lip. He looked at her and shook his head slowly. "I was beginning to think that I was going to find your body."

"What are you doing in my house?" she demanded.

"Looking for you," Toomey answered. Then he asked, "What were you doing in a closet?"

"Hiding from you."

He started to laugh at the absurdity. Charlie's reaction was just the opposite. As her fear drained from her, she began to cry. He took her in his arms, rocked her for a few seconds, then paused and let her slip from his grasp. "I'm sorry. I shouldn't have done that. It wasn't very professional."

Charlie touched his bloodied lip with her finger. "Did I do that?"

"No," Toomey smiled. "I had it when I came here." He gestured to the bedroom door. "I'll be downstairs. Come down when you're ready. There are things we have to go over."

Charlie began shivering as soon as he closed the door behind him. She took a fresh towel, dried herself, and dressed quickly in jeans and a long-sleeve sweater. He was at the dining room table with the overhead lights turned low, and he stood as soon as she started down the stairs.

"Once àgain, I have to apologize," he said as he pulled a chair out for her. "I'm not supposed to let these things get personal."

Charlie smiled at him to show that she wasn't angry. "It's okay. And I'm sorry I punched you. God, I was scared."

"I knew you were here someplace when I saw Brad's car. It figured, since he showed up at headquarters driving yours. I knocked. I rang the bell."

"I was under water," she said. "Or maybe just asleep. The first thing I heard was someone opening the back door."

"All the lights were out, but I heard someone moving upstairs. I thought it couldn't be you. You would have answered the door."

"But what brought you here in the first place?"

"When Irv told me he had lost you, I went by your house. I saw the press corps gathered and knew you wouldn't want to run the gauntlet. This seemed like the most logical place."

He apologized again, and Charlie insisted that no apology was necessary. "You may be the only friend I have right now. Or at least the only one who doesn't think I'm a murderer." He settled into the business at hand.

The lifeguard who had driven the Jet Ski had a long string of aliases, and was currently calling himself Max McGraw. He was a leg breaker for some of the area loan sharks and rented himself out as "security" for celebrities visiting Miami. Some of the celebrities were Hollywood types who had worked with or around Gary Armstrong, so that was a possible link. He had also worked as a security guard for one of the local Ucandoit branches. If Matthew had asked a local manager for the name of a tough who could do him a discrete favor, Max might have come to mind.

"Now here's an interesting twist," Toomey said, as he searched through his notes. "Guess who Max McGraw worked with just over a month ago." He didn't wait for Charlie to answer. "This guy!" and he produced a postcard-size picture of a painting resembling a wad of bubble gum that had been stepped on.

"What guy?" she asked.

He turned the card over to reveal an emaciated young man aiming a spray can at an easel. "This guy, the artist. He had a show in Miami and hired Max McGraw as a bouncer. What's interesting is that your stepdaughter, Trish, represents him in New York. So that's one more connection to Steven's children. Any one of them could have hired him to run you down."

"Or put a bomb in my boat," Charlie added.

Toomey winced. "I don't think we can go that far. Max has never done anything with explosives, and he wouldn't be anyone's first choice to make a sophisticated bomb. But it stands to reason that whoever hired him is probably the same person who hired a demolition expert."

She nodded. What he was saying made sense.

"Now, tell me about Tom Renthro?"

"Tom? The weight trainer at the health club?"

"That's him," he said. "The guy that the prosecution thinks might have done a bomb for you. What I'm thinking is that maybe someone else hired him."

"That's ridiculous. He's a teddy bear. Tom wouldn't hurt anyone."

"He was a Green Beret," Toomey said. "That's not the same thing as a Sister of Charity. He was trained to hurt people, generally by blowing them up."

She swallowed. Toomey was right, of course, even though she had never thought of Tom Renthro as a deadly force.

"Did you ever date him?"

"No, I never dated him!" There was anger in her voice. Too many people were prying into her private life.

Toomey caught her resentment. "Sorry, but it's important. Did he want to get together with you?"

"He asked," Charlie conceded. "But it was more like a running joke. I never took him seriously."

"Could that have made him mad? Could he have resented that you chose a wealthy man over him?"

She slammed her palms on the table. "How should I know? He never pressed it. He never stalked me or anything. It's a dumb question!" As soon as she said it, she regretted it. Why was she taking out her anger at all the questions she was being asked at the one person who was on her side. "I'm sorry," she whispered.

Toomey outlined the only plan that was available to him. One way or another, he was going to get something on Max McGraw. Then he was going to squeeze hard until the life-guard told who had hired him to run down Charlie.

He stood to leave, and then as an afterthought asked her if she wanted to get something to eat. She said no, but then hesitated when she remembered that there was no food in the house. "Is it safe for us to be seen together?" she asked, alluding to the possibility that he could be charged with obstructing a police investigation.

"No one will see us at the place I'm thinking of."

Thirty-two

H

e was true to his word. They drove crosstown until they were on the edge of farm country, and then followed a dirt road through sugar cane until they reached a farm house. Toomey cruised up next to it, blew the horn, and blinked the headlights. "Where are we?" Charlie wondered.

"My aunt Pearl's house," he said as if nothing was out of the ordinary.

The woman who came out on the porch probably wasn't his aunt, because she was an ebony black who probably traced her ancestry to Haiti. She wore a long skirt with five or six bands of color and a blouse that was intense orange.

"Aunt Pearl, this is Charlie," he said as they climbed the wooden steps to the porch.

The woman smiled with perfect teeth, and then broke into laughter. "You don't look like no Charlie," she said, and then she wrapped her arms around her new guest.

Inside, they sat in upholstered chairs at a round dining room table. The lamp above them was a Tiffany imitation with fringe hanging from its edges. The plates were heavy china from a diner, and the tableware was an assortment of various knives and forks. Pearl set a bottle of sour mash on the table along with a collection of jelly glasses. "Blackened redfish be all right?" she asked. Then she broke out in a belly laugh and added, "It better be 'cause that's what I got."

When she disappeared into the kitchen, Toomey explained that Pearl told fortunes in a downtown shopping mall. The police used to harass her, but then he asked them to back off, and Pearl was eternally grateful. "I stash some of my witnesses out here," he said. "None of them have ever been harmed, but there were a couple who kept coming back for the cooking."

Charlie was laughing at the absurdity of the arrangement. An hour ago she had been cowering in a closet, her life slipping away. Now she was sitting at a table with a fortune-teller who bribed her police protectors with Cajun cooking. Her orderly life had taken several hairpin turns, and she couldn't be sure exactly where she was.

Toomey talked to his Aunt Pearl during the dinner, mostly about people and events that Charlie had never heard of. Occasionally he turned to her to explain the coded language. "Mother Margaret wasn't really Jelly's mother. She ran a whorehouse down by Homestead. Jelly was the piano player."

Charlie tried to follow along, nodding and smiling when it seemed appropriate. Mostly, she was into her food, enjoying a highly seasoned fish with red beans that didn't want to be ordinary beans. She had almost finished when she realized that she was completely relaxed. It wasn't the sour mash, or the oversized meal. It was the company of people who were obviously good friends, and had a thousand shared moments to recall. She was part of a family, a membership that hadn't been hers since she was a teenager. She wished that Tara were here, listening in.

Pearl got up to clear the plates and Charlie jumped up to help her. Pearl did her dishes in a plain porcelain sink, and Charlie dried with a thick cotton towel. Toomey stayed in the dining room, sipping the sour mash and puffing on a Cuban cigar. When Charlie came out of the kitchen, she had to smile at the ease with which he became head of household.

"Relaxed?" he asked her.

"Perfectly," she said, "for the first time in God knows how long."

"You can stay here," Toomey said.

Charlie smiled. "I'd rather you took me home."

As they drove, he regaled her with some of Aunt Pearl's more outrageous ventures. She had been hauled into court and brought before the judge. Within seconds she was shaking from head to toe moaning, "Oh my God, I feel it bad, real bad." Then she told the judge there was a demon hovering over his bench that had come to take him away. She could see its fingers tightening around the judge's heart. "You can feel it, your honor. I can tell that it's hurting you something terrible."

"Damned if the judge didn't start holding his chest. He was having an angina attack and fumbled a nitroglycerin tablet out of a bottle and put it under his tongue. But Pearl told him that no itty-bitty pill was going to save him. He needed to be in the hospital right away. Next thing he was doubled over gasping for air, and Pearl began wailing some chants that are supposed to drive away devils.

"The medics rushed in," Toomey continued, "but before they could get to His Honor the judge sat up straight with a puzzled look on his face. His color came back and he announced he felt better. His chest pain was gone. The medics said it was because his nitroglycerin kicked in, but Pearl said it was because she had driven off the demon."

Charlie was laughing out loud, reaching the point where she was having trouble taking a breath. "Stop!" she begged, holding up her hand. Then she managed to get in, "You're making this up."

"Honest to God," Toomey said, smiling. "But the best is yet to come."

"I don't think I can laugh anymore," she warned.

"The prosecutor gets back to presenting the charges, basically that she was running a fortune-telling scam where she pretended to communicate with the underworld. So Pearl began staring right over the top of the judge's head. You could see the judge glance up, trying to figure out what she was looking at. Then he realized that the demon was coming back once more to take him away. 'Case dismissed,' he yelled and he banged the gavel hard enough to drive away any kind of spirit. So Pearl walked off without so much as a fine."

They were both in high spirits when he fitted her key into the front door. He followed her in, turned on the dining room lights and looked about. He repeated the routine in the kitchen and then made his way up the stairs to the bedrooms. Charlie opened the refrigerator to confirm that it was empty. She couldn't even offer him a beer. In the cupboard she found an unopened can of coffee and saw that the can opener and coffee maker were still on the counter top. She was measuring tablespoons of coffee when he came down into the kitchen.

"I'm making some coffee," she said. "It's the only thing I have in the house."

"No," he said politely. "You must be exhausted."

She put her arms around him and kissed him gently on the lips. Then she backed away. "It was a rotten day, but a wonderful evening," she said. "Laughs have been few and far between lately."

Toomey pulled her back into his arms and kissed her passionately as he crushed her against him. Her lips parted and his hands traced the curve of her waist and settled at her hips. The kiss went on for several seconds, and after they caught their breath, started all over again. She knew he was excited, rapidly approaching the point where it would be difficult to stop him. But she didn't want him to stop. She wanted him to love her the way she hadn't felt loved in such a long time. He was the one with enough sense to break away from the embrace.

"This time I'm not sorry," he said.

"I wasn't sorry the last time," Charlie answered.

He smiled sheepishly. "I wasn't either." Then he added, "But it's probably best if I get out of here and let you get some rest."

"I don't need rest," she said, slipping back into his embrace. "I need you." He pulled her tight, his hand slipping up to her breast. Charlie pulled back for the second it took to lift her sweater over her head. Toomey turned her and steered her toward the stairs.

Thirty-three

He was gone when she woke up. The bedsheet that she remembered in a tangle, was smoothed up over her. The pillows were in perfect order.

He had gotten up, dressed, straightened out the bed, and left without making a sound. *Just like a detective,* Charlie mused. But she wished he had stayed. She relished the thought of waking up in his arms, slipping free, and then engaging in a pleasant tug of war for the covers. She would have loved sitting across the breakfast table, smiling softly at the memory of the moments they had shared.

She sat up, and noticed her clothes—the jeans and sweater, the bra and pants, even her shoes—stacked neatly on her chair. That wasn't where she had left them. As best she could remember, the sweater had come off at the foot of the stairs, about the time she had gotten his shirt unbuttoned. They had been halfway up the stairs when her bra went over the railing, followed by his shirt that floated down from the next step. She had stepped out of her jeans on the landing while she was undoing his trousers. They had left their underwear somewhere between the door and the bed. It seemed that he had gone through the house and picked up everything. Then he had vanished without a word.

Charlie stretched in bed and considered letting herself fall back to sleep. She felt sexy and was in no hurry to leave the bed where she had felt so loved. Not just loved, but loving. The night had been a new experience that she couldn't remember ever enjoying—a sense of needing and having at the same instant a feeling that no matter how close she was to someone, it would never be close enough. It was what she had given up hoping for when she decided to marry Steven Armstrong, and exactly what had been missing when they made love, or when they were close together. She had never felt a spontaneous urge to reach out and touch Steven just because he was near.

But she jumped out of the bed, showered quickly and got back into the clothes that waited on her chair. She had to get moving, first to Maria's house where she would pick up Tara and take her to school, and then back to Steven's house where she hoped the press that had been at her door might have gone on to newer scandals.

From there, she needed to pay a visit to her lawyer. He had seen the indictment, been apprised of the evidence, and had probably read the results of her lie-detector test. What was his plan? Toomey had been very precise in stating what he was going to do in order to save her. Shouldn't Troxell have a similar plan for how they were going to prevail in court?

But even while she was walking to her car, Charlie knew that she was avoiding the most pressing issue. How was she going to manage her newly realized love for the police detective? She knew she wanted to see him again, in fact over and over again. She wanted him to fill the long-term gap in her life so that she would never be lonely again. But at the same time, she knew that it would be madness to be seen with him.

The press would go crazy with the story of a woman who had seduced one man for his fortune and another to cover her crime. They would come up with a nickname for her, something like the Black Widow. The reporters in her driveway would become the kind of crowd usually associated with a sports event.

A jury would be even less sympathetic. Jurors would begin each court day by looking at her and reminding themselves that shortly after her husband had been killed, she had started an affair with one of the police officials involved in the case. It would seem only fair that she be punished regardless of the details of evidence that were being argued in the court.

There was also Jerry's career to think about. Sleeping with the accused had to be a lot worse than simply interfering with a police investigation. His superiors would be outraged to learn that he was leaving police headquarters, where her case was being discussed, and rushing to her bed, where the case most certainly should not be discussed. Add to that the fact that he was stalking a witness who had been turned free because of his excessive zeal, looking for any excuse to entrap the man, and it would be easy to make him into a rogue cop.

And there was Tara. Her daughter already suspected that she had sold herself to the highest bidder. Tara knew that her mother had married Steven, at least in part, for the benefits his marriage could bring to their struggling family. Then she had been confronted with the allegation that her mother might be a murderer. How could Charlie tell her that she was now sleeping with the man Tara had described as "a hunk"? Even more difficult, how could she make the girl believe that it was true love and not just another attempt at manipulation?

Last night had been a salvation from the private hell she had endured since Steven's death. She didn't know if she could make it through months in that same hell with no one to comfort her and love her.

Tara was waiting at Maria's with the few things she had brought with her already packed in her backpack. Charlie settled her into Troxell's Beetle, explaining why she had borrowed her lawyer's car. "I'm already in hiding," she said, "But I don't want to force you into hiding. So tell me. Where do you want I take you?"

"To school," Tara said without hesitating.

"It won't be easy," her mother cautioned. "You'll hear a lot of things. People may not be very nice to you."

She shrugged. "I can't stay in the house forever."

When did she get so strong? Charlie marveled as she turned toward the junior high school. Then she realized that neither could she stay in hiding forever. She would drop the girl off and then head home to face whatever might be waiting.

She passed silently through a gauntlet of half a dozen reporters and one television crew, pausing only for the time it took her to unlock the front door. Half a dozen tape recorders were thrust in her face, and when someone tried to move them away it was only so that the camera man could get a clear shot of her profile.

"Any comment about the charges that have been filed against you?"

"Is it true that your husband was going to cut you off without a cent?"

"How much are you worth right now?"

"Why have you and your daughter gone into hiding?"

Charlie ignored all the questions until she was inside her doorway. Then the reporter from the television station tried to step through after her. Charlie pushed her back and slammed the door against her foot. The woman bellowed. Through the closed door Charlie heard her screaming that she had been assaulted. "You saw that. She pushed me. Do we have that on tape?"

She went to the phone, called Maria and told her that she could take the day off. Then she phoned Brad Troxell. "I think there may be another indictment against me. I just shoved a newslady."

He laughed. "Technically, she's not supposed to be on your property. So I doubt you'll be sued. But you can't win that battle, Mrs. Armstrong," the attorney advised. "They show you with your hand in front of the lens, or pushing them out of your house, and it looks as if you're guilty of something and trying to hide it. Actually, your best bet is to call the police."

They made a date for that afternoon when he promised he would have some good news to share with her. Once again, Charlie had to push through the waiting reporters, although by this time there were only a few of them left. The television lady had gone and taken her camera with her. She ignored the barrage of questions, nearly caught a hand with a tape recorder when she closed the car door, and drove determinedly through her gate. All she could think of was how difficult it was going to be for Tara when they returned from school.

Troxell made her comfortable in his conference room, and returned with bottled water and his case file. "I have good news and bad news," he began.

"Start with the good news," Charlie answered. "I need a break from all the bad news."

He opened the file. "Well, for starters, the police have been unable to link you to the blasting caps. As far as anyone can tell, that batch is still at a distribution center in Atlanta. We'll challenge that evidence on the basis that it has no link to the crime. They could have been put there by your husband, or left behind by the builder. They prove nothing, and bringing them into court could unfairly prejudice a jury."

"Is it the same for the tools?" she asked.

Troxell winced. "No, because your fingerprints are on the tools. But I have a bomb expert who will testify that you can't make a bomb without using wire cutters and strippers. And your fingerprints aren't on the wire cutters that were taken from your house.

"The next bit of good news is that the people who claimed to have seen you in the boat, working on the engine, are contradicting one another. One says you were wearing a bathing suit, and the other thought you were in a blouse and jeans. One thought the boat had an outboard and you were working near the stern. The other thought it was an inboard engine and said you were in the center of the boat. I doubt the prosecutor will even call them because they would get cut up badly in cross-examination."

"What's left of their case?" Charlie asked, hoping that there would be no charges left for her to answer.

"Well, the motive of course. You still profited handsomely by your husband's death. And the opportunity. Even you admit that you had full run of the house and free access to the boat. And then, there's the bad news."

She braced herself. *Here it comes,* she thought.

"Your friend at the health club, Tom Renthro, says you did ask him about explosives."

"That's a lie!" she snapped.

"The police have been leaning on him," Troxell continued as if there had been no outburst. "He has a history of drug involvement, and he may be afraid that if he doesn't cooperate they could make his life miserable. But he does have times and dates when he says the conversations took place."

"He joked once about blowing up my car so I could get a new one. But I never asked him about making a bomb," Charlie insisted. "I never even . . ." she began but then trailed off. "Oh, Jesus!"

Troxell waited.

"I did say something once, but it was in a different context." She tried to recall the moment exactly. She had finished her class and was in the ladies' sauna. Renthro was in the men's sauna on the other side of a wooden wall. He had called through, "Is that you in there, Charlie?" and then teased that he was coming in to join her. It had been another of his ongoing suggestions that they should get together, a line that neither of them took seriously. She had answered back that her door was locked, and he had replied that a lock couldn't stop him. "I can drop this wall like a curtain," he had called and then pounded his side of the wall over her head. Later, when they had both dressed and were leaving, she had chided him for not being able to break down the wall, and Renthro had responded that all he would need was a bit of Semtex, or something like that. She had asked what it was and he told her about a plastic explosive that could be worked like putty.

"I listened, and I may have asked him a couple of questions," Charlie told Troxell. "But I didn't know what he was talking about. We were both walking to the parking lot and it was just conversation."

Brad was staring at her so intently that she was becoming uncomfortable. His expression seemed to say, *You don't really expect me to believe that!*

"That's the truth!" she insisted. "Besides, that has to be almost a year ago. I don't think I had even started working with Steven at the time, so I certainly couldn't have been planning to kill him."

"You never spoke about it again?" Troxell asked.

"Not that I can remember."

He seemed satisfied, and added that in any event plastic explosive was not what was used to kill Steven. But there was one more item of bad news he had to bring up. Steven had, indeed, been preparing an agreement that would have defined her inheritance. "There's a draft, with your husband's notes handwritten in the margins."

"I knew nothing about that," Charlie insisted.

"Would you have signed such an agreement?"

"Yes," she said defiantly, but then added, "I suppose so, depending on what it said."

"It would have limited you to a quarter of the estate, and probably cost you fifty million dollars."

"A quarter of his estate would have been very generous. I would gladly have agreed to a lot less than that."

Troxell wrote a note confirming that the existence of the agreement would not have been a motive. If his client knew that she was getting fifty million dollars, why wouldn't she agree?

"What about my polygraph test?" Charlie wondered.

"It was fine. My expert thinks that you were telling the truth when you said you didn't kill your husband. You were also telling the truth when you said that you were about to take the boat out yourself."

"Well, that's it, then," Charlie announced. "It proves I didn't do it."

"It's not admissible," he reminded her. "But I will leak it to the prosecution. It might give them second thoughts."

"They could do their own lie-detector test," she suggested. "We know it would show that I'm innocent."

"No, they would just pick the parts that helped their case and ignore the rest."

Charlie was incensed. "Jesus, don't the police want the truth?"

"The police are sure they know the truth already. What they want is evidence to support what they think they know."

She slumped in her chair. It seemed that she was guilty until proven innocent, and Sergeant Toomey was the only one looking for proof that she was, in fact, innocent. "At least I'll be able to testify in my own behalf," she said, trying to salvage something from her ordeal with the polygraph.

"Maybe," Troxell allowed.

"Why 'maybe'?"

"Because you didn't tell the truth on all the questions. Or, at least, that's what our expert thinks."

She could feel the heat of her anger. "When did I lie?" she demanded.

"When you said you didn't care about your husband's money. On all those questions the needles apparently went into spasm. My guy thinks you cared a great deal."

Her chin lowered. "I didn't mean that I didn't care at all. It was always one of the considerations. But it wasn't the only thing I thought about."

He seemed to accept her explanation. "The machines aren't all that subtle. But you can imagine what the prosecutors would do with that bit of information in cross-examination. Jurors wouldn't take kindly to a woman who married just for money, even though it probably happens every day. It doesn't fit the traditional picture of what nice girls are supposed to do."

Charlie could see the problem. It wasn't so much a case of what she had done as what the jurors thought she might be capable of doing. "Did I lie about anything else?" She emphasized the word *lie* as if it were an exaggeration all by itself.

"Yeah, one other place of note. He asked you if you loved your husband, and you answered that you did."

"I did love him," she insisted.

"The machine doesn't think so."

"What does the damn machine mean by *love*?"

"It means whatever you mean by *love*. All the polygraph tells us is when you think you're lying. So whatever you meant when you said you loved him wasn't true."

She couldn't argue. The machine was right. What she meant by love was the consuming feeling she had discovered with Jerry Toomey. She had never felt that with Steven.

Thirty-four

G ary Armstrong could hardly believe the sudden turn
of fortune. Only a month ago his movie deal had
fallen through, and his live-in Barbie doll had vanished. Now there was a new deal being built around him, and
Courtney had come crawling back in total remorse.

Gary, the industry's bottom feeders realized, owned the
rights to a great story. *His* story, about a young man who sees
his father seduced and murdered, and fights a long uphill battle for justice. At a minimum, it was a three-part television
special. If the case was as sensational as it promised to be, it
might even be big screen. A name producer had hired a hot
young screenwriter to do a treatment, and handed Gary a
hundred-thousand-dollar advance against two million dollars
if the story went into production. Each day, Gary met with
the screenwriter, David Becker, and described the loving
family that the young woman had invaded. He described his
father's infatuation with the younger woman and how she had
fanned it into pure lust. Then there was the old man's realization that he had been played for a fool and his frantic efforts
to reverse his foolish decision. It became a race between his

growing disgust and the woman's determination to destroy him while she was still the heir to a fortune. On each of the following days, Becker brought back several new pages of movie script that they edited and enhanced together.

Ira Straus, smelling a new project, restarted the old one. This was no time to show disrespect for Gary's talents. And Courtney Davis, knowing that there would be a part for the young seductress, drove her car back into his garage. "It was all so emotionally shattering," she told Gary. "Your father being murdered was more than I could handle. I know it was cowardly of me, but I had to have some time alone."

He took her into his arms. "I thought you had left me," he sighed into her ear, and she reacted with hurt. "Leave you? Gary, I'm in love with you. You must have known I'd be back." He was smart enough to be suspicious of her motives, but too smart to throw away a whole night of Courtney trying to make amends.

He had flown cross-country three times, to brief the police investigators, to testify before the grand jury, and then for a rehearsal of his probable testimony with the District Attorney's people. Gary had no evidence to support the contention that Charlie had murdered his father, but he knew that his future depended on a quick trial and a guilty verdict. Hollywood wouldn't want to make a movie about a seductress who hadn't killed her wealthy, geriatric husband. And Courtney probably wouldn't hang around waiting for his next break. His testimony became more and more inflammatory, reflecting the evil tone of the screenplay. He completely convinced himself that Charlie had killed his father even though he was sure that she had never planted a bomb.

Trish, too, found her father's ghastly murder good for business. As an eyewitness to a sex scandal, she was suddenly in demand for cocktail parties and dinners both in Manhattan and out in East Hampton. She found herself at the center of conversational gatherings eager to hear the sordid details of her father's seduction. "My stepmother," she said with great sarcasm, "may be nothing but a beauty-school dropout, but she certainly outsmarted my father, who was

one of the world's most astute businessmen. My brothers and
I aren't going to let her get away with it."

In the course of the conversations, Trish liked to mention
her father's collection of great art, now "in the hands of a
woman incapable of appreciating true beauty." And when her
audience inquired about the paintings she would rhapsodize
over the artist. "Thank God there were some that I wouldn't
sell even to my own father. At least that bitch can't get her
hands on those." At which point a subtle bidding war would
start, and Trish would leave the party with one or two assured
sales.

Like Gary, she had made a few trips down to Florida to
meet with the prosecution team. After each session, she returned home with fresh tidbits for her cocktail circuit that led
to new sales. She and the artists she represented were suddenly hot properties. There was no way to estimate just how
much a dragged-out, steamy trial might mean in dollars and
cents.

But there had been no upside to the tragedy as far as
Matthew was concerned. After a suitable period of mourning, the directors of Ucandoit had gotten back to business.
Could Matthew guarantee that his fondly remembered father's block of stock wouldn't suddenly be dropped on the
market? That would be a disaster for the stock options that
many of them held. And if not, exactly who would be voting
the shares? Matthew? Steven's wife? Trustees? Matthew had
none of the answers. His father's last will and testament was
tied up in probate court because it hadn't made the legally required provisions for his wife. The wife was tied up in criminal court and might never have control of the stock. His
father's executor could only wait until the court matters were
decided.

Over a seemingly friendly lunch, the chairman asked
pointedly whether Matthew had any control of the stock.
"Well, of course none of them will do anything without con-
sulting me," he answered, but he had to admit that he had, as
of yet, no legal control of the shares. He sensed that he was no
longer the indispensable leader he had been a few months ago.

Hillary was in a state of shock, alternating between denial and despair. Two martinis before dinner were no longer enough to guarantee her a good night's sleep, and a bottle of prescription sedatives appeared on her night table. "We can't go on like this, not knowing from one day to the next whether we're rich or poor." The "we" she talked about included herself and their daughter, Lisa, who might be dropped from the social register if Daddy's funding faltered. Matthew, in Hillary's thinking, wasn't a victim, but rather the cause of all their problems.

"I told you what she was after the first time I heard about her," she kept repeating. "Didn't I see it coming? Didn't I warn you? And what did you do about it? Absolutely nothing." Matthew found himself wishing that he could get his hands on another bomb. How difficult could it be to connect it to the ignition in Hillary's Mercedes?

His testimony before the prosecution lawyers hadn't been nearly as dramatic as that offered by his brother and sister. But he could say honestly that he had harbored great misgivings about his father's marriage and had warned him of the impending disaster. He recalled telling Steven that he and the girl had nothing in common. "It wasn't just their ages, but their total lifestyles. She was a failure—a single mother with no career goals and no prospects. Dad was a responsible family man and business leader."

He agreed with Gary and Trish that his father had seen too late that the marriage had been a terrible mistake. "Dad finally admitted that all she loved about him was his money," he said, taking liberties with his father's exact words, "and he was taking steps to protect his estate." No, he had no factual knowledge that she had killed him, but neither was he surprised when he learned of his father's violent death. He recalled his first words after learning of the explosion. "She got him."

Sergeant Toomey had called in favors from ex-policemen in New York and Boston, and was paying the retainer of a private detective in Los Angeles out of his own pocket. He had them looking into the affairs of the Armstrong children, searching for a link between any one of them and Max McGraw. Mc-Graw, he kept reminding Charlie, was the only known link to the attempt on her life. If they could find who had hired the lifeguard to run her down in the water, they would probably find who had ordered the bomb on Steven's boat.

McGraw was the focus of Toomey's personal attention. He dabbled with the other cases assigned to him, letting other detectives take the lead. Most of his working hours were spent tracking McGraw. He intercepted his mail so that he could check on the numbers he had called or that had called him. He intimidated anyone who spent more than a passing moment with his target. If Max had bragged once about being paid to run down a swimmer, he might boast of his exploit again. But the lifeguard seemed to know that he was being followed. He stayed clean as a whistle. *He has money,* Toomey realized. He had been paid at least the up-front amount for the hit, and that was what he was most likely living off. Once he was out of money he would probably go back to his illegal ways.

Toomey thought of possible frame-ups. He could plant drugs in Max's apartment and then phone in an anonymous tip. That would get him into police custody, but it was unlikely that he would end up as the case officer. Then, he would have to make a deal with another detective to bring pressure on Max with no assurance that he wouldn't be turned down. He also considered locating a new witness or beefing up the testimony he already had. The store owner who had rented Max the Jet Ski had thought he was the one, but wouldn't make a positive identification. Could he be persuaded to be more certain? Or what about the guy who happened by on a fishing trip? Maybe he could be encouraged to identify the man who had been cutting tight turns around the buoy. Toomey knew he was thinking like a dirty cop, but he was getting desperate for a plan that would win Charlie's freedom.

He had been with her at the condo several times. Twice it was mid-morning while Tara was at school, and once in the afternoon when Tara stayed at a friend's house. Toomey knew that it was dangerous, but he also knew that she needed to see him. His was the only investigation working for her and she needed even the smallest scraps of encouraging news. She also needed the embrace of someone who cared for her.

At one meeting he had asked her to check through Steven's bank statements. Was he getting regular payments from anyone? That might give someone a reason for wanting her husband dead. Had he paid significant amounts to someone she didn't know, or drawn money out in cash? That might imply that he had paid someone for a "special service." Charlie had been hurt by the implication that Steven might have been involved in the attack on her, but Toomey argued that they shouldn't assume anything. "Lot's of times the things you rule out end up being important," he had told her.

He had also quizzed her on any and all the people who might have placed the phone call that got her husband to take out his boat. The police had absolutely no idea who had made the call. No origination number had been forwarded to the local telephone exchange. All they could do was guess at what had been so urgent that he couldn't wait for his wife to return with the car.

On each occasion, Charlie had gradually lost interest in the details of his investigation, and switched her attention to the investigator. She had long since stopped believing in fairy tales, and had even given up her illusions about the knight on a white horse who would scoop her up into his arms. But the police sergeant had become her only source of hope. All she read in the papers were accusations. A television true-crime series had presented her as a seductress even though none of the clips they had of her looked at all seductive. Her own defense counsel sometimes acted as if he personally believed she was guilty. Toomey was the only one who believed in her.

She found herself taking his hand and holding on tightly as if it were a lifeline that might keep her from drowning. She longed for the moments of security she found in his embrace. At one meeting she had held on when he kissed her good-bye, unwilling to let go and return to the isolation of Steven's house.

"I shouldn't stay," he had told her.

"I know," Charlie had agreed, but still she hung on.

At another meeting, when their embrace had become passionate, she had pulled back from the brink. "Just stay here with me, talk to me, hold my hand." That was what she had needed at the moment—a friend rather than a lover.

Once, on the afternoon when Tara was away with a friend, they had moved calmly up the stairs to the bedroom. But even then she had relished the moments lying quietly in his arms more than the moments of ecstasy.

Always, when he was leaving her, he put his fingers under her chin. "Keep your head up, Charlie. We're going to put all this behind you. You didn't do anything wrong, and we're going to make sure the whole world knows it."

At their last meeting, he had given her a list of phone numbers pilfered from McGraw's mail and told her to check it against all the numbers in her husband's directory. If there was any cross match between Steven Armstrong's callers and people who had called Max McGraw, that would be very significant.

Charlie was amazed when she found that there was a match.

Thirty-five

Charlie stuck with her domestic routine. She met Tara and one of her girlfriends at school and drove them back to the house. The two girls took their homework out to the pool deck and spent the afternoon studying while they listened to a disk jockey, gossiped about their school friends and activities, and plunged into the pool whenever the music turned to commercials. Charlie brought them soft drinks, showed interest in their homework, and tried to help with a math problem that went well beyond her own abilities.

She noticed a boat that seemed to linger in the channel, and the two men aboard who kept looking up at the house. The girls were in their bikinis, so her first thought was that they were accidental voyeurs. When one of them lifted a pair of binoculars, she moved her chair to block their view. But when she saw the camera with the long telephoto lens, she realized that there was nothing accidental about them. Reporters, she decided, doing the latest tabloid coverage on the Black Widow at home. She felt rage boiling within her that they would drag Tara and her friend into the story, but she stayed calm hoping that the girls wouldn't notice. She kept them blocked as she read and reread the math problem, pretending to be helpful.

"We'll figure it out," Tara finally told her, embarrassed that her mother seemed to be getting nowhere. At about the same time, the boat moved further down the waterway. She rushed inside and phoned her lawyer. "There are two guys in a boat photographing my house," she snapped.

"It's a nice house," Troxell replied as if he didn't get the significance.

"Can't I stop them? There must be something I can do."

"Stay inside," was his answer.

She slammed the phone down, went back outside in time to see the boat circling back. She had the girls gather their things, and drove Tara's friend home.

When she returned she had a battle with her daughter who didn't understand why her guest was rushed out of the house. Charlie told her about the boat, which only made the girl angrier. "Who cares if they're taking pictures?" she demanded. "Does that mean I can't have friends? That I have to stay inside all the time?" She stormed off to her room and slammed the door with such force that it rattled windows throughout the house. Charlie started after her, but stopped when she saw Maria's expression. The housekeeper's sympathies were clearly with her daughter, and Charlie understood that was exactly where they should be. There was no reason for Tara to go into hiding. She didn't deserve to have her life invaded. Instead, she took a sandwich up to Steven's office and began checking his phone directories for the numbers on Toomey's list.

She started with his desktop Rolodex and within a few seconds identified an area code. One of the area codes that had called Max McGraw was on one of Steven's cards, but the numbers weren't a match. The number in her husband's file was a stockbroker. She found dozens of numbers from the same area code but none that squared with Max's caller.

There was another area code match, this one from another part of Florida. But the numbers didn't jibe. Steven's number was a yacht broker in Tampa. It took her over an hour to go through the entire Rolodex, and find perhaps fifty calls on Max's list that came from area codes on her husband's list. None of the numbers matched. She could phone all of the numbers that had originated calls to her assailant and see if she reached anyone familiar. But the list was long, and the calling would take forever. She decided to go to Steven's computer directory and continue looking for an exact number.

That process took her through the evening, interrupted only when she noticed the light snap off under her daughter's door. She stepped in quietly and sat on the edge of the bed while she apologized for overreacting to the boat with the cameraman. Tara grunted from under her sheet, which was as close to a "you're forgiven" as Charlie could expect. She leaned forward and kissed the top of her daughter's head, the only part of her that was showing. Then she closed the door behind her and got back to the computer telephone directory. She ran another thirty or forty area code matches, and was coming rapidly to the conclusion that both Steven and Max McGraw did business all over the country.

She was down to the letter U when she found it. Ucandoit headquarters, in Boston, had the same area code and exchange number as two of Max McGraw's calls. The numbers were different. Ucandoit headquarters was listed as 3000. McGraw received his calls from 3103. It was the same at the health club. The club number was 2100, but her extension was 2106. The number that called McGraw was most likely an extension from the Ucandoit central switchboard. It was close enough to warrant a test.

Charlie lifted the desk phone and dialed the number. She listened as the call cycled through six rings. Then,

You have reached the office of Mr. Matthew Armstrong,
Executive Vice President of Ucandoit Corporation.
Office hours are . . .

She didn't bother listening to the rest. It was Matthew. Matthew had phoned Max McGraw on two occasions, and Max was the man on the Jet Ski who had tried to kill her.

There was no other explanation why a business executive would be placing a private call to a known thug. Matthew had paid for her murder.

Charlie took the cell phone that Toomey had given her out to the edge of the deck, as far as she could get from the house without leaving the property. She pushed "redial" to reach Toomey's private line.

"I have to see you, tomorrow at nine," she said. She pressed the disconnect button. Toomey would know where to meet her.

She was up early the next morning, and had to hold back to keep from rushing Tara through her breakfast. "Did you hear me last night?" Charlie asked. "I said I was sorry."

Tara shrugged.

"I was furious that these damn reporters were taking pictures of you and your friend. I overreacted."

Another shrug.

"Anyway, it won't happen again, I promise. The truth is that I can't stop them, and I'm not even going to try. So you can invite anyone you want to come home with you. I promise not to embarrass you."

"I don't want to bring anyone home with me," Tara said. She scooped up her books and headed for the car. Charlie followed meekly. Tara would have to hate her for a while before she would be ready to accept an apology. She dropped her deaf and mute daughter off at the entrance to the school, and began the series of maneuvers through the surrounding streets that she used to shake anyone who might be following her. She left her car at a shopping mall and walked to her condo.

Toomey was over an hour late, arriving just as she was about to dial him again. He kissed her as soon as he was inside the door, but with no more passion than a husband coming home from work. "You found someone?" he asked, and made his way to the table where he could spread out his files.

"Someone?" she said, indicating that it was much more than just someone. "How about Matthew Armstrong, Steven's oldest son and my stepson?"

"Matthew?" he asked as if needing confirmation, but then

he added, "I'm not surprised. Matthew is the one most in danger of losing everything. He has nothing without his father's support. The others, at least, have some sort of careers on their own."

"He's the one who has been the nicest to me," she said, but then realized that winning her over was in Matthew's self-interest.

Toomey jotted a few lines into his records. "Okay, so now we concentrate on Matthew."

"Don't we just turn this over to the prosecutors?" Charlie wondered. "If he was dealing with a hit man, then doesn't it make sense that he's the one who was after me?"

He seemed a bit annoyed. "Charlie, I got that phone number by stealing from McGraw's mailbox. I didn't have a search warrant. This will never make it into the courtroom."

Her anger flashed. "Why is it that anything that helps me isn't admissible? They can search my house and take clothes out of my closet, and that's okay. But anything you find out . . ."

He cut her off by waving his hand. "I'll use it to find something legally. Some conversation, or document, that links Matthew to the attempted murder. Better still, something that links him to a bomb maker." Once again, his fingers were under her chin. "Keep your head up, Charlie, I'm going to put all this together."

He stood to leave, but she caught his hand and pulled him back down to this chair. "Jerry, I have to take this information to my lawyer. It's the only thing I have that he can work with."

"No!" Toomey was adamant. "If he brings this to the prosecutors, they'll want to know where he got it. He's an officer of the court. He'll have to tell them."

"He's my lawyer," she argued. "He'll know how to deal with it." He was shaking his head to show that her suggestion was out of the question. Charlie reached for his hand. "Jerry, I'll never tell him how you're involved. But I can't leave you all by yourself, risking your whole career for me. If I tell him, he'll have people look into it. Isn't that better than having you breaking into mailboxes and offices?"

"Jesus, Charlie, I'm doing it for you. I love you."

"And I'm doing it for you because I love you," she answered.

"I want to take care of you," Toomey said.

"You already have," she answered, and squeezed his hand.

He gathered up his papers. "Give it a day or two," he decided. "Let's just both think about it before either of us does anything. If Matthew gets off the hook, you may not have another chance. Don't forget, Matthew has a whole firm of lawyers on his side. All you've got is Brad Troxell."

They left the condo, walking in different directions. On her drive home, Charlie was sinking deeper into despair. She had been excited when she had found Matthew's phone number, certain that it was the case breaker that would set her free. Grill Matthew about what he was discussing with McGraw, and at the same time tell McGraw that Matthew was claiming that McGraw had been threatening him. One of them would get tangled in their lie and implicate the other, and then Matthew's murderous intentions would be out in the open. She could understand why Toomey had to be cautious, but wasn't it possible that his caution was working against her? Was it smart for her to put her life in his hands and his alone?

Thirty-six

Charlie had called her lawyer the next morning, but before he could get back to her she got a call on her cell phone.

Remember where we ate?
Be there at noon. There's something
important you have to know.

It was Toomey, calling on his secure line. He didn't have to identify himself. No one else had the number of the cell phone he had given her. Aunt Pearl's she remembered. But did she remember how to get there? The house was at least forty-five minutes away, and it was out beyond where the streets were numbered. They had been on a dirt road moving through fields of sugar cane, and then he had taken a sharp right turn onto an even smaller dirt road. Charlie thought she remembered, but she wondered why all the mystery. Couldn't they meet at the condo as they had in the past?

When Brad Troxell returned her call, Charlie told him that she had new information to share with him. She wanted to meet him at his office. But she had no idea what time she would get back from Aunt Pearl's house. She asked Troxell could they meet at the end of the day, around 5:00 p.m. She killed time until 11:00 a.m., and then pulled the Cadillac out into the driveway. There were no reporters waiting, which probably meant that her husband's murder had been replaced by an even more distasteful crime. She made her way across town, looking carefully into her mirrors to make sure she wasn't being followed. Irv would have no reason to watch her. He probably knew that she was meeting with Toomey.

She drove on a main avenue with community gates on either side. The entrances were labeled Sea Breeze even though there was no breeze from the ocean; Heron Cove, despite the fact that there was no cove; and The Tides, which wouldn't feel a tide except in a hurricane. Each community was a cluster of cookie-cutter homes that had been carved out of the Florida swamp, and the avenue was crowded with minimalls that served them. Gradually, the developments became fewer, and the roadsides became wilder plantings of grass. Then she was on a dirt road, really a surface of sand and hardpan, that led inland toward the original Florida.

For a few minutes, she thought she was lost. There was a sameness to the long driveways and prefabricated homes that lacked any points of identification. Charlie couldn't be sure whether she had been here before or not. But then there was a rotting billboard that she thought she recognized, and the abrupt edge of a sugar cane farm that looked familiar. She considered calling on the cell phone for more detailed directions, but decided to keep heading west in the hope of recognizing the turnoff.

Charlie was totally absorbed in the road ahead when she heard a crash and felt her car lurch forward. She bounded against the headrest and then forward until her seat belt stopped her. In the mirror she caught a glimpse of a truck grill, headlights, and a bumper. A pickup truck had come up behind her and hit her from the rear.

"Jesus!" She was outraged. "What in the hell is the matter with you?" she yelled into her mirror. The pickup backed off,

a dark-colored truck covered in road dust with a dark windshield that seemed opaque.

The truck was closing on her again, growing more menac-
ing in her rearview mirror. Then it hit her, harder this time,
driving her forward with her front end turning to the right.
She screamed as she struggled for control. But even as she
yelled, Charlie knew that this wasn't a careless drunk. The
driver of the pickup was trying to run her off the road.

She stomped on the accelerator, straightening the wheel.
The Cadillac hurtled forward, pulling away from the pickup.
But she could see the truck quickly add speed and hang not
far behind her. Then there was a turn, a sharp right coming up
quickly. She couldn't take it at full speed. The car would skid
off the road and into the wild tropical growth that came right
up to the road's edge. She eased off the gas and onto the
brake. But the truck didn't seem to slow a bit. It was on her
before she reached the turn.

Another crash! This one lifted her rear wheels off the road
and sent her front end corkscrewing to the right. Charlie was
sure that she was going off the road sidewise into the tight
green foliage. At the last instant, the front wheels bit into the
hardpan and sent the front end into the turn. Branches and
palm leaves broke across her windshield and dragged down
the side. But the Cadillac stayed on the road, swerving into an
even narrower lane between swamp on the left and sugar cane
on the right. In the mirror, she could see the truck rock pre-
cariously. But it clung to the road and was closing behind her.

She reached for the cell phone that Toomey had given her.
All she had to do was push one key and the phone would dial
his cell phone. He must be in the area. He was meeting her
somewhere near here in a few minutes.

Crash! This time she heard the screech of crumpling
metal. The pickup had bashed through the trunk. Her head
snapped back. The cell phone bounced out of the console and
flew to the floor on the passenger side. The truck still held
contact to the rear of her car, and was hurtling her toward a
wall of sugar cane.

She jammed her foot down on the accelerator. Her car

pulled away, breaking contact with the pickup. She caught a glimpse of her trunk lid tumbling away behind her. Now they were on another straight section of narrow sandy road, with the tropical growth crowding in from one side and the cane from the other. Her engine was roaring, and the car's acceleration had her pinned back into the seat. She was pulling away, opening space between her car and the truck. But the terror of the moment had taken over her mind. She wasn't in control. The car seemed to be fleeing on its own.

Another turn came into view, this one to the left. It was familiar. It would be a hairpin and then Aunt Pearl's road would be off to the right. Just turn left, except at the speed she was moving the car would slide sideways and turn over into the sugar cane. But if she slowed, the truck would smash into her from behind.

Charlie backed off the accelerator. The pickup zoomed up close behind her as she was reaching the turn. She hit the brakes and threw the wheel into the turn. The car began to slip to the side, its tires screeching. She held on tight, hoping that the drive wheels would catch and the car would stay on the road. But the pickup was on top of her. In the side mirror she could see the garish grill and the headlights coming right at her. Charlie let go of the wheel and threw her hands over her face. The truck struck the rear door. Air bags exploded from everywhere. The Cadillac lost its traction, slid sideways toward the stalks of cane, then went airborne and flew off the road. Charlie felt it hit as it came crashing down into the foliage. Then she was rolling, the sun visors and the roof sliding under her as her seat turned upside down. Glass shattered and there was the terrible sound of metal tearing apart. Finally, there was nothing. Her world had turned off, leaving her in a blank sleep.

Thirty-seven

She saw light, but she couldn't tell where it was coming from. She was hanging sideways, her torso straining against the seat belt, her head hanging down into the foliage. There were cane stalks everywhere, growing through the space where the windshield had been, and coming through the opening behind the crumpled passenger door. Silvery deflated air bags hung limply from the steering wheel and dashboard. She was a fly caught in a web.

Charlie tried to raise her head, but it seemed too heavy. She rolled her eyes and found that the car was on its right side. The light, what little there was of it, was coming through the driver's window. She felt for her seat belt and pushed hard on the release button. It popped, and she was suddenly turned over in the passenger seat, her legs still trapped under the steering wheel. She dragged herself across the center console, trying to get her feet to the passenger side and under her weight. Then she could try to push the driver's door open.

She began to choke, and was all at once aware of the stench of gasoline. The gas tank had split open and the explosive fuel was soaking into the cane stalks. She knew she had to get out quickly, before something—anything—ignited the fuel.

Charlie pushed aside the deflated air bags and reached over her head for the driver's door latch. She tugged and then pushed, but the door wouldn't budge. Something had bent in the crash, and the door was jammed into the frame. The window! She pressed the control and heard the small motor whirring in the door. The window didn't move; another result of the crash. She turned to the windshield. The glass was gone, but the cane stalks had the opening blocked like bars on a cell. There was no way out, and the smell of the gasoline was getting stronger.

She spotted Toomey's cell phone amid the debris on the passenger side floor. Again, she had to push the tangle of air bags to retrieve it. She pushed the "call" button. *Be there, Jerry. For the love of God, be there.*

His voice came quickly. "Where are you?" He seemed annoyed.

"I'm in the car," she shouted. "It's wrecked. Jesus, they tried to kill me!"

"Where?" he demanded with sudden urgency.

"On the road to Aunt Pearl's house. Or near the road. The car is buried in sugar cane. And there's gasoline leaking."

"Get out right away," Toomey ordered. "Get out of the car."

"I can't! Everything is smashed. The doors won't open."

"How far from the house are you?"

"Damn it, I don't know. One turn, or maybe two. They drove me off the road."

"I'm leaving Pearl's right now. I should be to you in a couple of minutes."

He clicked off before she could tell him to hurry.

The gasoline stench was becoming unbearable. Charlie closed her eyes to keep them from burning, but the darkness was too frightening. She leaned against the passenger seat and began counting the seconds that seemed to be hours.

When she heard a car on the gravely road, she pushed

close to the open windshield and began to yell. The car rolled past but then screeched to a stop.

"Charlie?" It was Jerry's voice.

"Over here," she shouted.

"Charlie, I'm coming." His voice was louder and then he banged against the car frame. She saw his hands against the glass and an instant later his face pulled up into the opening. "Charlie!"

He disappeared from her view and returned with a crowbar. He jammed it in the door and pried bent sheet metal away. He tugged on the door again and again, pulling it open a bit further with each effort. Then it broke free. He put his shoulder to the door and pushed it open. Her hands grasped at his arms. Toomey pulled her straight up as if lifting her out of a manhole.

He took her into his arms and helped her into his car. He dropped the crowbar into the trunk and slammed the lid. As soon as he slid into the driver's seat, Charlie ordered him to "Get away from here!" He pulled away, leaving the overturned sedan nearly buried in the cane stalks.

She recognized Aunt Pearl's house and hurried out of the car to the safety inside. Only when she was seated in a wooden kitchen chair did she notice the bloodstain down the front of her blouse and realize that she had been injured. Pearl tipped her head back and put a wet cloth over her face. "Just a bloody nose," the woman said. "I don't think you broke nothing." She lifted the cloth and amended her opinion. "Split your lip a bit," she added, and went on with her ministrations.

Pearl brought Charlie a glass of rum, assuring her that "this is what you need," but she couldn't handle the taste. She settled for water and then went to a mirror to survey the damage.

"You're lucky," Toomey said over her shoulder. "You should see the car." She had to agree with him. With the blood washed from her face, the only damage she could see was a fat lip. The air bags and side curtains had squeezed her tight at the moment of impact. It was probably the air bag that had bloodied her face.

Pearl chased Toomey out of the kitchen and helped Charlie out of her bloodstained clothes. Wrapping her in a towel, she led her to an open shower on the back porch, just outside the kitchen window. When Charlie had finished soaping off the dried blood and picking grains of glass out of her hair, Pearl appeared with a fresh towel and a garish, oversized robe.

Charlie thanked her. "Jerry has told me a lot about you," she said, and she alluded to some of the stories he had attributed to her. "He sure likes to make up stories," the woman said, shaking her head to protest her innocence. "But he sure is crazy about you."

"You look wonderful," Toomey teased, when she appeared in the living room, wrapped in Pearl's robe. She began telling him about the truck that had suddenly appeared behind her, and he immediately interrupted with questions. Did she know the make of the truck? She didn't. Had she seen the driver's face? No, the window was dark. She hadn't even seen a shape. What about the color? "Black," she said with her first positive answer, but even then she added, "I think!" Her first reaction had been anger, as best she could remember. Some trucker was prompting her to get out of his way so he could pass on the narrow road. Anger turned to fear when she realized that his real intention was to drive her off the road.

Then Charlie had a question. "Why did you want me to meet you out here?"

"Because the police have a stake-out on your condo," he told her. "We can't meet there any more."

"That wasn't the police in the pickup truck," she told him.

"I know it wasn't. And it wasn't Max McGraw, either. Max isn't a factor anymore." Her expression was puzzled, so he explained, "Max was killed last night. Someone shot him in his bed and ransacked his room."

"Dear God," she said, at first reacting to the horror of someone being murdered. But her next thought was for herself. What had she gotten involved in that was getting people murdered? Her husband, the two attempts on her life and now the only witness who might have linked all the violence to whoever was behind it.

"Lots of people could have killed McGraw," Toomey assured her. "He wasn't a very nice person, and he made the wrong kinds of enemies."

"You don't think it had anything to do with me?" Charlie asked.

"I don't know. It might not have. But I don't think you should be taking any chances. I'm going to send a couple of security guards to keep an eye on your place. They're expensive, but you can afford them. They'll rent you a new car, and one of them, probably Irv, will be your driver. And I think you should let your kid's summer vacation start early. Or else get her a tutor. She's too easy a mark for someone trying to get to you."

Charlie felt herself being crushed. What little freedom she and Tara had was being taken away. The house, the cars, the vast inheritance all seemed worthless to her. Wasn't there some way that she could give it all away in exchange for the chance to be herself? How much would it cost to have them leave her alone?

She had only herself to blame. She had married Steven in hopes of a new life, and this was the life she had gotten. Right up to the day of her wedding she had questioned her motivation and berated herself for giving up too easily on the hope of a deep, loving relationship. She had every opportunity to say, "Thank you, Steven, but no. This won't work for either of us." If she had, Steven might still be alive. Certainly no one would have had reason to plant the explosive that was intended to kill her. She and her daughter would still be living in their own house, and Tara would still be spending her days with her friends. Most of all, she wouldn't be living in a prison, watched over by security experts, nor would she have to be driven from place to place in an armored car.

The only good thing that had come out of all this was the man sitting across from her. It was easy to believe that Toomey loved her. He had put his career in jeopardy for her sake. She could even think that he had saved her life. Now, his every thought seemed to be about protecting her and Tara.

It was easy to believe that she loved him. He was the only person she could trust, and she had trusted him with everything—her emotions, her body, and now her very life. She didn't know a great deal about him. Not even as much as she had known about Steven. Did he have an ex-wife somewhere, or a woman living in his apartment? Was he honest, fair, decent? Did he use drugs? Did he extort money? Was he a bully? A racist? There was so much that she didn't know and there were possibilities that she wouldn't let herself consider. At this moment, the only thing that mattered was that he was there for her in every way that a man could be there for a woman.

They stopped by the wrecked car where he retrieved the cell phone. Then he drove her back to the city where he transferred her into a car driven by Irv. On the way, he told her to claim that she had lost control of the car when she contacted her insurance agent. "Don't get into the truck or being run off the road. The last thing you need is to be involved in another police investigation." Toomey squeezed her hand as she transferred from his car to the back seat of the other. She whispered a prayer of thanks when there were no reporters waiting at her gate.

"What happened to your mouth?" Tara gasped as soon as Maria delivered her home.

"I had an accident with the car," Charlie lied.

"The radio?" Tara asked, going instantly to the part of the accident that affected her.

"Gone, I'm afraid. It sort of got blown out of the dashboard when the air bags deployed."

"Air bags!" Tara now understood the seriousness of what her mother had made sound like a fender bender. "Are you sure you're okay?"

"Okay," Charlie said. "Let's go for a swim."

Thirty-eight

T hey're called pretrial motions," Troxell explained. "We move to disqualify some of their witnesses and evidence, and the prosecutor argues that they should be allowed."

"Do I have to be there?" Charlie asked.

"No, but a show of interest in your case might be helpful." Brad was in his usual laid-back mood that gave the impression that he didn't care one way or the other.

"It's the reporters and the television cameras," she said, shivering with a moment of contempt. "I don't want their microphones in my face ever again."

"We'll drive into the parking garage and go up in an elevator. Their only shot at you will be through a closed car window."

He began outlining the arguments that he would make in court in support of written motions that he would have already submitted. The judge, he pointed out, would probably make up his mind before he heard the arguments. Troxell's first motion was going to ask that the case be dismissed for lack of evidence. Nothing that the prosecutors were offering connected her with making or planting the explosion that killed Steven Armstrong. "The judge won't grant that because he would be debunking the grand jury, but it's a formality that we have to go through."

Next, he wanted severe restrictions on what Steven's children could discuss under oath. Their feelings and intuitions, he would argue, were irrelevant, and anything they had discussed with one another was tainted as hearsay. All they could testify to was what they had seen, which was nothing, and what their father had told them individually. And even that was open to interpretation. "We'll win this one," he told her. "There won't be any crying children telling the jury that they knew you had married him for his money."

He also wanted the court to throw out the tools that had her fingerprints on them. No one could link them directly to the explosion, and there were any number of innocent reasons why Charlie might have used them. Their very presentation gave them importance in the evidence chain that they didn't deserve. Brad rocked his hands over and back and told her that this motion could go either way.

"Do it without me," Charlie decided.

"Okay," he said and then told her that there was one more thing. "Steven's daughter has petitioned to have paintings taken from your house and returned to her."

Charlie smiled. "Tell her to back her truck up and take them all. It may be great art, but to me it's like Tara's finger painting that I used to hang on the refrigerator."

"Her claim is that your husband never paid for them so they shouldn't be tied up with the rest of the estate," Troxell said. "You really should go through Steven's records and see if he did pay for them. They may be valuable and you have rights."

"I'm not going to make the five o'clock news over some paintings that I never liked. I don't think Steven liked them either."

The lawyer offered to serve as intermediary so that Charlie wouldn't have to talk to her stepdaughter. "Oh, for God's sake, tell her to call me," Charlie answered. "There are armed guards in the house who will keep us from fighting."

Two days later, Trish called the house in a burst of friendship and understanding that took Charlie by surprise. "I'm so pleased that you have no problem with my taking the paintings," and "Will your daughter be there? I'd love to see her again." She arrived in a chauffeured SUV, dressed in a beige outfit with a floppy green hat, and pecked at both sides of Charlie's face. She accepted an offer of iced tea, and sat out on the patio overlooking the waterway. Charlie remembered her testimony before the grand jury that portrayed her as money-mad, and Steven as fearing for his life. She wondered what she and Trish would ever find to talk about.

"I've always loved this house," Trish said, leaning back in a deck chair. "I don't suppose you'll want to keep it once everything is settled."

"It may not be mine to keep," Charlie answered. "I could well be in jail. Or maybe even . . ."

"Oh, don't even think such a thing," Trish said. "I don't think the case will go to trial. I certainly have no desire to testify against you."

Charlie was dumbstruck. Trish had already testified against her. What in hell was going on?

"In fact, I might switch sides. I could certainly tell the jury that my father truly loved you. I mean, as I've already said, he was a bit eccentric. But that doesn't mean that he was afraid of you."

"That would probably be very helpful," Charlie allowed.

"And, as I say, if this house becomes a burden, I'll be more than happy to take it off your hands."

So that was it, Charlie thought. She's hedging her bets. She's angling to be my friend in case I get off. The bitch is trying to outflank her brothers if I end up making a settlement.

"Well, to the work at hand," Trish said downing her tea and jumping to her feet. She went to the door and summoned her chauffeur. Together, they started through the house collecting the paintings. Two hours later, she had eight paintings boxed and stacked in the SUV. Again she kissed Charlie on both cheeks. Before she made her whirlwind exit, she said once more, "And remember, if you want to get out from under the house, I'm ready at a moment's notice."

Toomey called her to tell her he was coming to the house. Irv would drive him through the gate in the trunk of the car. He needed to see her, and he needed an opportunity to go through Steven's papers. He planned to spend the night in Steven's office, and then leave in the trunk when Irv drove Tara to school.

"Are you sure Irv wants to get so involved?" she asked.

"Yeah, Irv owes me big-time."

That was the side of Toomey that made Charlie uncomfortable. A lot of his friends, Aunt Pearl not the least of them, were involved in some sort of unsavory activity, and seemed to owe him favors. Probably that was simply the way police work was handled, but she worried that Toomey seemed to respond to rules of his own making. It wasn't a big thing with her. He had already proven himself to be a loyal and selfless friend. She couldn't have made it through the past months without him. But it did leave a few dark stains on her otherwise pure white knight.

He came after nine, arriving at the top of the basement steps with an oversized briefcase. He said hello to Tara, who was snacking in the kitchen. But he stopped at the doorway, avoiding the lighted room with open windows. Tara smiled and said she was happy to see him. In her mind, he was still a genuine "hunk."

He and Charlie talked business on the way up the stairs. There were papers he had to check. He was getting close to some answers. But once they were behind the closed door of Steven's office, he swept her into his arms and kissed her with a ferocity that made her knees wobbly. "God, I've missed you," he said.

"I missed you," she answered. But she forced some space between them. "Not here where my daughter is," she said.

"I wouldn't think of it, Charlie."

"You were looking very interested in that couch," she said, tipping her head toward the leather sofa that lent a homey effect to Steven's office.

"It's a nice couch!" he smiled. Then he picked up the

heavy briefcase and went to Steven's desk. "C'mon, we have to talk." He sat in Steven's chair and Charlie perched on the edge of a side chair.

"These are worksheets from Matthew's accountant," he said, kicking the bulging briefcase he had set under the desk. "Did you know that your little boy was helping himself to company funds?"

"Matthew? Stealing? But he owns the business."

"*Embezzling* is a more accurate word. I'm no banker, but from what my friends in Boston tell me, he had a cozy deal with the construction outfit that builds the Ucandoit shopping centers. He paid them twice, and they kicked back the overcharge. It all adds up to about ten million dollars he was putting aside for a rainy day."

"Why? He's a very wealthy man who could only get wealthier. He'll inherit much more than that."

"Why?" Toomey repeated. "Maybe plain old greed. Maybe he wanted to stop being his daddy's puppet. Most likely he just couldn't wait to get his hands on the inheritance. He was going through every cent that he was paid."

She was puzzled. "It doesn't make sense."

"It does if his father found out. And it makes even more sense if Steven told his new wife. That kind of information could land Matthew and the construction company honchos in prison. And add this to the plot. Construction outfits generally know where to get explosives and they certainly know how to use them.

"What I'm thinking, Charlie, is that Matthew didn't much care which of you got into that boat. Both of you had to go. That's why they're still out there trying to put you away."

She sat silently for a moment. All along she had been asking herself what she had gotten into. Why did her marriage to Steven Armstrong mark her for death? Of course Steven's children would want to block her from the inheritance. But bombs? Pickup trucks crashing into her? None of them would know how to arrange such things.

She had thought of Gary. He lived in a world of fantasy and fiction where convoluted murders were a favorite story line. He could certainly imagine the special effect of a boat exploding, or the terror of being bashed by a truck with blacked-out windows. But did he have the courage to go along with the imagination? Trish didn't fit the role of mad bomber, and Charlie couldn't picture her even associating with someone who drove a pickup, much less taking him into her confidence. Matthew, she had thought, always had the strongest motive. But he was a boardroom executive, a business suit and tie, a country club playboy. Hired assassins and bomb makers wouldn't go unnoticed in his circle of friends.

But bring in a bid-rigging construction company, and suddenly things came together. The builders had nothing to fear from Matthew. He was part of the scheme. But Steven would certainly blow the whistle. And if he told his wife, then both of them would have to go.

"What do we do now?" she asked Toomey.

"Now we have to prove it." He kicked the briefcase again. "Nothing in here can be used in court. We're not supposed to steal anyone's records anymore than we can steal their telephone bills. But if your husband was on to this swindle, then it ought to be somewhere in his papers. That's what we have to find. Because his papers are now your papers, and you have every right to take them to a judge."

"I'll bring you up a beer," she said as she started for the door.

"Make it a pot of coffee. We're going to be pulling an all-nighter."

Charlie helped Tara wrap up her homework and gave her the next day's spending money. In the process, she explained that Sergeant Toomey was going through Steven's papers, looking for records that would help prove she was innocent. "It's part of the police investigation," she said.

"They work all night?" the girl asked suspiciously.

She revealed a bit more. The prosecutors weren't looking for this information so Sergeant Toomey had to do it on his own time. "He's a true friend," she said, and then added that he was the only one she had.

"I like him a lot better than the cop who drives me to

school," Tara said as she strapped her books into her back-pack. "That guy gives me the creeps."

"Irv? He's a friend of Sergeant Toomey's," Charlie said reassuringly. "What don't you like about him?"

"He's always looking at me in the mirror," she said. "I feel like he's undressing me with his eyes."

"I'm sure that's just your imagination," Charlie answered even though she was suddenly horrified that a grown man would be ogling her not-yet-grown daughter.

"It's *his* imagination that scares me."

As Tara went off to bed, Charlie stared after her. Jesus, was there anyone she could trust?

Thirty-nine

S he returned to Steven's office after her daughter was
asleep, and found Toomey sitting behind stacks of file
folders. He was leaning back in her husband's chair
glancing at the papers in his lap.

"Steven kept all that," Charlie remarked in surprise. "I
thought he was retired."

"Your husband was a man of affairs," the detective said.
"This is just the paper. I haven't started on the computer
files yet."

"Anything so far?"

Toomey shook his head. Not yet. Then he pointed to a
gray metal file box that he had placed on the table next to the
sofa. "Do you have the key to that thing?"

Charlie went to the box and lifted it by its metal handle.
"It's a strongbox," she said.

Toomey chuckled. "I know what it is. What I want to know
is what's in it?"

She set it down. "I've never seen it before. Where did you
find it?"

He leaned forward and pulled out a deep desk file drawer. "Right in here, under some of these files."

"I've been through his desk a dozen times and I never noticed it. I have no idea where the key is."

Toomey said that he had already tried all the keys that he found in the desk. "Anyplace else where he might have kept it?"

She went into their bedroom and searched through his dresser, his night table, and the leather box where he kept his cufflinks and tie pins. When she returned, Toomey was making progress through the next stack of files. "I found it," Charlie announced, holding up a small key that had been in with Steven's jewelry. Toomey nodded but went on with his reading.

"You're husband didn't have much fun," he announced. "This is pretty dreary stuff."

Charlie sat on the sofa, moved the strongbox to her lap and inserted the key. But it wouldn't turn. She twisted harder until she thought it might break off in the lock. "Sorry, wrong key," she announced.

"Well get a letter opener and break it open. It's probably nothing but since he kept it locked separately, it might be important."

She stepped up to the desk, and bent over the open drawer to look for an opener or a pair of scissors. "I really have missed you," Toomey said, his hand moving across the curve of her bottom.

She sprang away from the desk. "Watch yourself, I'm armed," and she brandished the scissors. Then she went to the sofa and began working on the strongbox. She tried to force the blade of the scissors under the lock but it wouldn't fit. Then she tried it under the hinges, again without success. "I can't get this damn thing open," she announced.

"That's why they call it a strongbox," he said. Toomey put down his current stack of papers, took the box, and set it on the floor. He hammered the point of the scissors under the lid with the base of his hand, and pried the metal apart. Within a minute, he had broken the lock. He opened the box. Inside, there were several folded pages.

"Looks like letters," Toomey said and handed the box to Charlie. She unfolded the first sheet, started reading but stopped abruptly. "This may be it. It's a letter to Matthew about funds in some bank."

He had gotten back to the desk but he bolted to the couch and sat beside her. Charlie held the letter as they both read. It was in typeface, written on a computer and then printed out. It looked like an original, but it wasn't signed. Apparently Steven had printed two copies, signed and mailed one, and kept the other. The contents were explosive, certainly worthy of being kept under lock and key.

In the letter, Steven claimed to know about "rebates that should have gone directly to the company." He feigned not to know why the money had been paid to his son, or why it was being secreted in offshore accounts, but was adamant that it be returned immediately. The letter was dated several days before she had accepted Steven's proposal.

The next letter, written the day after her attack, was threatening. Steven voiced his suspicions that the threat to his fiancée might be the work of the construction company, and that he was beginning an investigation. If it proved to be so, he promised to prosecute everyone involved. Further, it noted that the money had not been returned, and set a deadline for "all the funds in question" to be delivered to Ucandoit's treasurer. The deadline was two days after the boat had exploded.

The third folded letter was from Matthew to Steven and, even though undated, was obviously a response to Steven's first letter. Matthew didn't seem shocked by his father's allegations. He referred to past discussions, reiterated that he had done nothing wrong, and claimed that the offshore accounts were part of a legal accounting ploy to reduce his taxes. He promised that they would speak again about this before an upcoming Ucandoit board meeting.

"God, this really nails it," Toomey said, reading over her shoulder. "I was hoping I could find something to back up the evidence, but I never dreamed of anything this specific. Steven knew that Matthew was stealing and was going to turn him in to the directors. That's one hell of a motive for murder."

Charlie was confused. "Steven never hinted at a problem. I knew he was frustrated with all of his children. He told me several times that he wished they would be more responsible, and stop thinking that it was still his duty to support them. He seemed to want them to stand on their two feet. But he never mentioned that there was a problem like this."

"Why would he?" Toomey asked. "It's no big deal to say that your kids still think they're living at home. But to have one of them stealing from the company you built? That's a lot different." He watched as Charlie refolded the letters. "You get these to Brad Troxell first thing in the morning. These change everything."

She wondered. Did they really change anything? She had been indicted for killing her husband in order to stop him from disinheriting her. Did it matter if someone else had a reason for wanting him killed? Matthew's links to the explosive that had been planted in the boat were much less direct than her own. Proving he might have had a motive did nothing to diminish her motive.

Toomey dragged the briefcase from under the desk. "Don't say anything about these records, I'll get them back before they're missed. And put all these files back in place. We don't want anyone to think that we were looking for something. You just happened to find them."

"Why? I don't understand."

"Because I didn't have a search warrant for these records. I just took them. So they can't be used in court, nor will anything we learned from them pass muster. If we found the letters because of what we learned in an illegal search, then the letters are part of an illegal search."

"We committed a crime?" Charlie asked.

"*I* committed a crime. All you did was find the box and open it. With Steven dead, the letters are yours and you can do what you want with them."

His good-bye kiss was perfunctory. He planned to nap on

the living room sofa until it was time to climb into the trunk of Irv's car.

Charlie slumped into Steven's chair. *I just happened to find them,* she said to herself. That wasn't true. The truth was that she didn't believe they were where Jerry said he found them. She had been through Steven's desk and files a half dozen times since his death. She didn't believe she could have missed something as obvious as a gray steel strongbox.

Toomey had just admitted that he had committed a crime. But had he also planted evidence? She knew he wasn't above such a thing. Hadn't he staged a bogus line-up to identify her attacker? Didn't he consider making up charges against Mc-Graw just so that he could intimidate information from him?

Why? Because he didn't see anything wrong with it? Because it was the way real police work was done as opposed to the good cops on television. Because it had to be done if he was to make certain that she would never be convicted of Steven's murder? How wrong was it to help someone he loved? What was so bad about helping someone who was innocent prove that she was innocent? It was the prosecutors and the police who had put together the bogus case. All Toomey was doing was fighting fire with fire.

As Charlie put the files back into the drawers, she started giving her only friend the benefit of the doubt. If he was going to plant evidence in her favor, why would he have to risk breaking into an accountant's office? He could as easily have his friend, Irv, plant it someplace where she was likely to find it. Why would he be searching all of Steven's records if he knew where the letters were all along? So maybe she had missed it. The strongbox could have been there all along behind some papers that were too trivial to bother with. In truth, she couldn't remember specifically that she had dug to the back of that drawer.

She had two choices. Either Toomey had planted it or she had missed it. Then, like a bolt out of the blue, she thought of a third. Trish had been there just this morning reclaiming her paintings. She and her driver had gone through the entire house. They had removed two of the works from Steven's office. Trish could easily have put the box in the drawer, knowing that it would most certainly be found. But, how would she have gotten her hands on the correspondence? And why would Trish want to frame her brother for their father's murder?

. . . .

Forty

————

Brad Troxell read the letters and then read them again.
"These were locked in a strongbox?" he asked. "In your
husband's desk?" Charlie repeated the story as Toomey
had explained it to her. They were under files that she hadn't
moved. She couldn't find a key and assumed that Steven must
have been carrying it when he was killed.

"Well, it's no smoking gun," he decided. "But it certainly
gives us another reason for why Steven was murdered. An alternative explanation can distract and even confuse a jury."

"Will that be our case?" Charlie wondered.

"We don't need to make a case," the lawyer answered.
"All we have to do is shoot holes in the prosecution's case.
There might be jurors who think a son who kills his father is
even worse than a wife who murders her husband. But if
you're asking does this solve all your problems, the answer is
no. We still need a link between the bomb and someone besides you."

Troxell took her to a small Cuban restaurant for lunch and
spent the meal explaining developments in her murder trial.
As he had assured her, the judge had not dismissed her case

for lack of evidence. Even more distressing, the limitations he had imposed on testimony by Steven's children were fewer than hoped for. Basically, they could tell about their interpretations of specific conversations with their father even though they couldn't talk about their feelings. "I don't know what the difference is," he said. "We'll just have to challenge them in cross-examination." The one piece of good news was that the court had barred the tools with her fingerprints. "So now there's no physical link between you and the explosive device. They don't have a smoking pistol either."

Troxell waited until desert to tell her that a date for her trial had been set. "A week from Monday we'll begin picking the jury. The trial will start as soon as the jury is seated."

"God, it's really going to happen," she said as much to herself as to Brad.

"Yeah, and what you have to be prepared for is that the publicity is going to explode. You're going to have reporters hanging out of helicopters right outside your windows. There will be the usual law-and-order nuts with signs demanding that you be drawn and quartered, and the women's groups screaming that there's no crime in killing a husband. You'll spend the days half blind from camera flashes."

Charlie bit her lip and struggled to fight back the tears. It had been barely tolerable since the indictment. Now it was going to get worse.

"There are two things I want to tell you," Troxell said. "First, under no circumstances should you say one word about anything to anyone. You'll be asked everything from how you triggered the bomb to your shoe size. You don't answer. There will be cameras sticking in your face from all sides. Don't look at them, and don't try to push them away. You can't stop them from taking pictures, but you don't want to give them photos of an angry, snarling criminal. You shouldn't even say that you're innocent, or thank anyone who says that you're innocent." He could see that Charlie was beginning to crumble. "Can you do that?" he asked. She nodded, but when she tried to speak no sound came out.

"Next, your daughter," Troxell went on. "She's fair game

and this will be open season. The press will sneak into her school and follow her right into the ladies' room. You'll find them outside your house when you take her to school and waiting for you when you get there."

"I know," Charlie managed without looking up from the dessert she hadn't touched. She explained that Sergeant Toomey had brought in security guards to protect her daughter from harassment.

Troxell seemed concerned. "Are they good? Professional? Because they could get you into a lot of trouble. 'Hired Goons Protect Killer' isn't the kind of headline you want. And, for God's sake, don't let them near the courthouse. But I had another idea."

Charlie lifted her chin. She was eager for some sort of help.

"I'd like to get her away from here," he said, "from now until after the trial is over. I have a sister who lives in Virginia. She's a nice lady, married to a hard-working guy, with two daughters about Tara's age. I talked to her, and she'd be happy to take her in for the duration."

"I don't think she'll go," Charlie said.

Troxell ignored her protest. "You take her from school straight to the airport, and put her on a plane to Dulles. My sister will meet the flight. There won't be nearly as much publicity up there to hurt her, and the best thing is that no one will know where she is. If they ask, you say nothing. I'll put out a statement that she's staying with friends."

It was a good idea. Even though she didn't know Troxell's sister, she knew that Brad wouldn't make the suggestion if he had any doubt about the girl's safety. She trusted him, so how could she not trust his faith in his own sister.

"I'll ask Tara," she said.

Troxell waved to the waiter for the check. "Don't ask her, Charlie. Just tell her. Believe me, it's best for her."

She got into the back seat of the car behind Irv. They weren't even out of the parking garage when she noticed him glancing at her in the rear-view mirror. What had Brad asked her? Were the security people reliable? Professional? How was she supposed to know? Maybe her daughter was safer with Troxell's sister than she was with the hired muscle. She and Tara were living in Jerry Toomey's world, where she knew things weren't always as they appeared.

The mob had returned to her house, now equipped with a truck that had a dish-shaped satellite uplink. Faces pushed against the car windows as Irv kept moving slowly, forcing their way through the crowd without running over anyone. When he raised the garage door, the press and the gawkers followed them inside. Irv left her in the car while he eased them back outside and lowered the door. Only then, did Charlie dare to get out.

"Something must have happened," he said as he followed her up to the kitchen. "They're all back, even the ones we figured gave up."

"The trial date was announced," she said. She turned on the kitchen television in time to catch the district attorney holding a press conference in the courthouse lobby. He claimed to be delighted with the early court date, stating that justice delayed is justice denied. He wouldn't comment on his evidence, nor make any prediction as to the outcome. "A man has been murdered," he said, "and my job is to find the guilty party and bring him, or her, to justice."

She told Irv that there might be reporters at the school. "Please be right at the gate so that you can walk her back to the car. I don't want her fending for herself."

"Don't worry," he told her. But Charlie was worried. She was entrusting her daughter into the protecting arms of a man who had been "undressing her with his eyes." She made up her mind. Tara was going to stay with Troxell's sister.

Maria had made a salad for her lunch, and Charlie took it out to the table on the pool deck. But the boat was back, joined by two others in a small armada. They were sitting no more than fifty yards from the house, bristling with cameras. She retreated to the privacy of the kitchen. A few minutes later, the car returned and eased its way through the throng. Once again, Irv had to get out first and clear the opening before he could close the garage door.

"What happened?" Tara asked. "Why are they back?"

Charlie explained that her trial date had been set. Then she added that this was nothing compared to what they would face once the trial started. She was about to get into her decision to move the girl away, when Tara announced that she was going for a swim.

"That's not a good idea!" Charlie said and pointed out to the waiting fleet.

"Screw 'em!" the girl said nonchalantly, and skipped up the steps to her room. Maria giggled. Charlie shook her head. When Tara returned, she was in a bikini with sunglasses and a big, floppy hat, looking more like a celebrity on a Riviera beach than a girl scarcely into high school. She carried a textbook, a pad of paper, and a pencil. "Test tomorrow," she told them. "I think I'll study out on the deck."

Charlie caught her hand and detoured her into the dining room. "Baby, those people are ruthless. They'll put your pictures all over the papers, and call you the vamp in the making."

"That would help me get a date for the dance," Tara teased.

"Be serious, and listen to me!" Charlie repeated Troxell's description of the total violation of their privacy and the other horrors that awaited. Then she eased into a description of the idyllic family life Troxell's sister enjoyed, making it sound more like a summer camp than a safe house. Tara's eyes began to narrow as she caught the drift of the lecture. Her mother was building a wonderful image of exile.

"I'm staying with you," the girl interrupted.

Charlie recovered. "It's only for a few weeks. Just until the trial is over and these vultures find something else to do."

"Mom, I'm not going to live with some sappy family that I don't even know."

"It's for the best," Charlie countered. "It's all been decided and I've made all the arrangements."

"I'm not going!"

"Yes, you are," She snapped back, sounding more authoritative than was usual in her dealings with her daughter. She generally played the understanding "best friend."

"I'll run away! You can drag me there but you can't keep me there!"

"Damn!" she screamed. "Stop fighting me!"

"Stop treating me like a baby!"

Charlie's hand flew out in an angry slap across the girl's face. Tara's eyes widened in amazement. Then they began to fill with tears. Charlie would have gladly cut her hand off if she could undo the damage. She jumped up from the table and threw her arms around her daughter. "Oh God, I'm sorry. They've got me so crazy! I love you, baby, and I'm scared to death that they're going to hurt you."

Her daughter was frozen like a statue, unresponsive to her mother's grief. Charlie let her go and reached out to touch the red hand print on her daughter's cheek. Tara moved the hand gently away.

"Can I go study now?"

Charlie was crying. The best she could do was nod. Tara got up with her books and walked quietly out onto the pool deck. Even at fifty yards, Charlie could hear the camera shutters clicking. *It can't get any worse than this,* she thought.

But then the telephone rang.

Forty-one

Troxell was mobbed as soon as his Beetle reached the gate. He slipped through the reporters with his head down, ignoring the cameras and recorders exactly as he had instructed her to do. While he waited for the door to be answered, he stared straight ahead, and slipped in quickly before it was half opened.

Charlie waited in the foyer, wringing her hands. He had called to tell her that he was coming to see her on something that had just come up. "Something that you're not going to like." She had been waiting impatiently even though she wasn't sure she wanted to hear the news. Brad led her inside, looking about for a place where they could have a bit of privacy. He settled for the same dining room table that Charlie had chosen for her disastrous conversation with her daughter.

"I have to bring you in for a line-up," he said. "There's someone who the police think might recognize you."

"Who?" There was no anger in her question. Charlie was too stunned to feel any emotion.

"A gun dealer. The man has a store out in sugar cane country that sells guns, ammunition, hunting knives, and stuff. He thinks you may be the lady who bought some dynamite from him."

"I bought dynamite?" She was still numb.

"That's what he says. Of course, he's not allowed to sell dynamite. But he can get pretty much anything you want. Last time the police grabbed him he was selling diamond drill bits for burglar tools."

It didn't make the least bit of sense to her. "Brad, why in God's name would I be going to a gun dealer out in the boonies?

"Well, you can't get dynamite from the cosmetics girl at Saks Fifth Avenue."

"Where is this store?" she asked, stressing her distaste for the kind of store he had described.

"Out on a crossroads, near Plantation, past the Turnpike. It's diagonally opposite a shack that sells belts made out of alligators."

"God, I've never even been out there," she said, but then she corrected herself. "No, that's not true. I was out in that area once . . . no, twice. . . ."

Troxell nodded. "I thought so. That's where you flipped your car, isn't it?"

So he knew about the car and her claim to the insurance company. "I think so," she answered.

"What were you doing out in that godforsaken place?"

It was a logical question, but she didn't know how much she should involve Toomey. He was sticking his neck out for her and she knew she had to protect him. "Visiting a friend. An old woman who lives out there."

"That wouldn't be Aunt Pearl, would it?" he asked.

She didn't know how to cover up the truth. "Yes, it would."

"Well, I don't think we can use her as a character witness," Brad said. "She's had her own run-ins with the police. And her place is less than a mile from the gun shop. I think that's where she buys her ammo."

"But I've never been in any gun shop," Charlie insisted, trying to regain her initiative. "Besides, how could he *not* pick me out of a lineup? My picture has been in all the papers."

"I made that point, but the judge has allowed the lineup. He says we can challenge the identification in court, if he does identify you and if he is called as a prosecution witness. It's possible that he'll pick a different lady, or maybe not pick out anyone. Then the whole thing goes away."

Troxell explained the procedure that would be followed. First, he would look over the other women in the lineup to make sure they bore at least a passing resemblance to Charlie. Same size, same age, and approximately the same coloring. "We won't let you participate if they want you in a lineup with four eighty-year-olds, or if you're the only Caucasian in the group." Then he told her that she should bring three changes of clothes so that she could try to fit in with the overall appearance of the other women. He also suggested that she style her hair differently, and use a different tone of makeup. "Try not to look like your pictures on television."

His final instruction was that she should leave in the morning in the car with her daughter. She could see Tara to the airport and then have the driver bring her to his office. He would get her into police headquarters with as little notoriety as possible.

"Tara doesn't want to leave," Charlie told him.

"She has to," he said. "You can't spend the trial trying to look after her."

"She told me she won't go."

He grimaced. "Look, you're the mother. Don't ask her. Tell her."

"It's not the way we do things," Charlie snapped. "But I will talk to her again. Only it can't be tomorrow. Maybe the next day."

Charlie was obviously crushed under the weight of the day's events. Her face fell into her hands, and she stayed seated at the table when Brad Troxell stood to leave. He reached to her and touched her hand. "I'm sorry. It's not my business to tell you how to deal with your daughter. Just do the best you can."

The best that she could? How could she fight back when everything was coming apart? Maybe buying dynamite wasn't the smoking gun, but it struck her as persuasive enough. She knew how relieved she would feel if he was going to testify that he had sold the explosives to Matthew, or Gary. But how could she think about her trial when she was on the edge of a break with her daughter? She had actually slapped Tara, something that she hadn't done in years. The only time she could remember was when she was still in grade school and had used the curse word she had just learned. The quick slap had warned the girl that "we don't use that kind of language around here," and Tara seemed to realize instantly that she had gone too far. This time, all she had been saying was that she didn't want to live with strangers. She was an adult, and wanted to make her own decisions. Shouldn't she be proud of that? Why would it deserve an angry slap?

Once more, she crept up the steps to the door of Tara's room in order to apologize. But the room was dark, the girl hidden under the bedspread. "I'm sorry, Tara. I'm not myself," she whispered into the darkness. There was no reply.

Charlie tried to present a cheery face as she set breakfast on the table. But when her daughter arrived, she knew that she hadn't been forgiven. Tara's face was fixed, her lips a thin white line. She had made no effort to cover up the outline of a bruise that curled under her eye.

"I'm not hungry," she said by way of greeting. She crossed the kitchen into the living room where she flopped in a sofa and drew a book up over her face. Charlie looked at Maria, who shook her head slowly. *Don't make an issue,* she seemed to be advising. Charlie decided she was right.

In the car, she tried again, beginning with the same apology she had offered last night. "Please forgive me, baby, you know I love you." Her answer was the all-purpose shrug, which Charlie hoped might be the beginning of a conversation. She went on, explaining the painful intrusions into their privacy that were unavoidable. She stressed how difficult such moments would be for the girl, and the added strain that it would put on her. She wasn't asking the girl to leave the family, but just to take a brief leave of absence until the trial was over.

Tara finally spoke. "Is that where I'm going to live if you go to prison?"

Oh God, Charlie had never thought of that. "No, no, don't be silly. I'm not going to jail. It's just for the trial."

There was no response. Tara was suddenly interested in whatever was passing outside her window.

"We'll talk tonight," Charlie promised. "And I won't be such a jerk. We'll talk about it the way we always do."

They reached the school, and Irv stopped as close to the building as he could get. Tara threw open the door and dashed toward the school entrance. Irv started out to follow her, but Charlie told him to stop. "Let her go!" she said, and he got back into the car. *She's already gone,* she added to herself.

Forty-two

Troxell was waiting in the garage below his office when Irv pulled in. He opened the car door for his client and carried the small suitcase with her change of clothes. Then he drove her to police headquarters where he had an associate waiting to escort her to the elevator.

They passed through the detectives' office, two rows of desks with side chairs. There were several men and women working, all in shirtsleeves. Charlie was surprised that two of the women were wearing gun holsters over their shoulders. She saw Jerry Toomey busy in a telephone conversation. Detective Richard Lionetti stood as they reached his area and gestured them through a door into a waiting area. "You want to see these people," he said not as a question but as an invitation for the lawyer to follow him further. Troxell left with him, and Charlie found a lonely seat in the waiting area. There were two green vinyl sofas separated by a chrome and glass table. The floor was a beige tile and the walls an off-white, stained wherever hands had touched them. A chrome ashtray, filled with crushed butts, was under a No Smoking sign.

Captain Frank Jennings emerged from his office, noticed Charlie on his way past, and then stopped to talk with her. "I'm going for a cup of coffee. It's out of a machine, but can I bring you one?"

She was surprised by his politeness. Were all murderers offered a cup of coffee while they waited? But she declined. She had never been able to drink coffee from a machine.

"They go inside?" Jennings asked.

Charlie nodded. "A few seconds ago."

"Well, we'll try not to keep you long," he said and took up his march to the coffee machine.

Just for the rest of my life, she thought. Wasn't his whole purpose to keep her as long as he could?

Jerry Toomey stepped out of the squad room and greeted her as if he had just happened upon her. "The condo, to-night," he whispered under cover of his biggest smile. "We're not staking it out anymore."

Brad Troxell bounded back, gave a "Hi!" and a nod toward Toomey, and turned his attention to Charlie. "The ladies are okay," he said. "Now let's take a look at the clothes."

She was wearing white slacks with a navy sweater, an out-fit that he dismissed as "too stylish." In her bag she had a summery dress, yellow and white, with a peasant top. He held it up and "Hmmmed," as he thought about it.

"Makes her look like a Barbie doll," Toomey offered.

"Yeah," the attorney agreed. He dropped it onto a sofa. "What else have you got?"

Charlie held up her final choice, fitted jeans and a dark, man-tailored shirt.

"That should work," Toomey said.

Troxell turned to him. "You think so?" He turned the out-fit around so that Toomey could see the back.

"Yeah, with a little attitude."

"Okay," Troxell decided. He gave the clothes to Charlie. "Put these on, and could you kind of mess your hair up a bit? The other women aren't quite so neat."

She took the outfit and headed to the ladies' room. As soon

as she was out of earshot, Brad asked the detective, "Did Lionetti show this guy her picture?"

"Don't know," Toomey said. "Richie is pretty straight. I didn't see any news clippings lying on his desk. But he did have the witness alone for quite a while." Then he asked, "How does it look?"

"I have my fingers crossed," was all that Brad could promise.

Troxell joined Detective Lionetti, Captain Jennings, and a woman attorney from the district attorney's office in a room behind a viewing glass.

"Are you satisfied with the lineup?" the DA's representative asked.

"No!" Troxell said. "My client's picture has been in the papers and on television. There's no one else in the lineup that looks like her."

"C'mon! We even brought in outsiders," Lionetti said.

"Your comment is noted," said the woman.

The witness was then brought in and positioned at the center of the viewing screen between the two lawyers. Troxell could easily envisage him selling dynamite not just to women but to children as well. His gray ponytail was pulled through a bright red bandanna that served as a hat. There was a shaggy mustache that disguised his mouth and an unkempt beard that hid his neck. He wore an open vest that showed a full canvas of tattoos on his chest, belly, and arms. Several sets of chains hung from his belt.

The DA's lady instructed him not to make any comment as the women entered the room on the other side of the glass. "Wait until they are all in position, and until they've turned to show you front and back. Then, if you recognize any one of them as the lady who came into your store and purchased dynamite sticks, please refer to her by the number over her head." He showed no reaction. "Do you understand?" she asked.

"Yeah, sure. Let's get it over with."

The door opened, and the women paraded in. Charlie was

second in line, which would have her standing at position number four. Brad had insisted on the placement. Four was his lucky number. At first glance, all the women seemed quite similar, all between five-foot-four and five-foot-eight, all within striking distance of one hundred and thirty pounds. All were Caucasian, three of fair complexion and two dark, but all in the midrange between Nordic blondes and Mediterranean brunettes. Hairstyles were shoulder length or less, with no extreme spiking or dazzling colors. They were even close in age, probably all in their late twenties or thirties. Four were in slacks or dark jeans, and one was in a striped skirt. The tops were different, two sleeveless and two half-sleeved, with Charlie the only one wearing cuffs down to her wrists.

But on closer examination, they were all different. Two favored heavy makeup, and one used none at all. One was flat-chested and two had generous bosoms. Two were narrow at the waist, and one was showing a roll. One was very long legged, and another a bit squat.

Their faces were the most different, if not in structure certainly in expressions. Two of the women were staring ahead with round, open eyes, blank as if they were hypnotized. The lady in the skirt seemed to be trying hard to suppress a giggle. Another of them looked edgy, as if she might have to go to the ladies' room. Charlie was trying to look natural and unconcerned, but her expression came off as being a bit defiant. It suggested that police lineups were no big deal.

"Please lift your heads, ladies," the lawyer said into a microphone, and all of their chins came up. "Would you turn your heads to the left?" Only one turned right and then quickly corrected herself. "And now to the right."

Troxell kept sneaking glances at the witness, but what little was visible of the man's face showed no reaction. He could have been standing on a street corner waiting for the light to change. His eyes were dull and rheumy, as if he had awakened from a hangover, and they were fixed, panning neither to the left or the right.

"Now please turn around and face the back wall." They

did. One of them shifted her weight onto one foot causing a hip to jut out. "Up straight, please," the woman said into the microphone. She waited fifteen seconds that seemed at least a full minute, and then asked the witness, "Is the woman who came into your store, paid you for sticks of dynamite, and then carried them out of your store, one of the women before you."

"Yeah! Sure!"

"Which number is she standing under?"

"Number four. Second from the right."

"Are you absolutely certain that she is the woman?"

"Yeah! Sure!"

Troxell cut in. "Even though it means that you'll be going to prison."

"Huh?" His eyes suddenly found focus. He turned and looked at Lionetti. "What is this?"

"You've just admitted that you sold dynamite, which is a felony crime," Brad said before the detective could answer the witness's question.

The bearded face snapped back to Troxell. "Oh, that. I got a deal."

"That's not at issue here," the prosecution lawyer snapped. "The record will show that the witness identified Mrs. Charlene Armstrong as the woman who purchased dynamite from him in his store."

"It should also show that he got a deal for identifying her," Troxell persisted. "Shouldn't the record show what kind of deal it was? Did it include who he was supposed to pick out?"

Lionetti sprang from the background. "Are you saying I set this up? Because, damn it . . ."

Captain Jennings held out an arm to block Lionetti's charge. "You're way out of order, counselor," he snapped. "You're impugning the integrity . . ."

The DA's lawyer cut the captain off. "This session is over," she said, her voice registering her authority. "We've had a lineup and a suspect has been identified." She came face to face with Brad Troxell. "You ought to know better than to try to screw up a court function. If you have any problems with the lineup, take them up with the judge, in court."

Brad turned and left the room quickly, apparently chastised but secretly glad that he had gotten under everyone's skin. Indeed, he would take it up with the judge. First thing he would do was prepare a motion to have the identification thrown out on the grounds that the witness was drunk, and under the impression that he could get away with selling dynamite by identifying someone.

Troxell tried to put a better face on the lineup as they drove back to his office. "The witness looks like he probably owns the alligator skin business across from the gun shop," he said humorously to Charlie. "Even if they clean him up and buy him a shirt and tie, he won't be very credible. Particularly if they're not prosecuting him for selling high explosives without a permit."

"But he picked me," she answered, unwilling to be distracted from the harsh reality.

"That's right, but . . ."

"And you thought the line-up was fair. Even I thought most of us looked alike."

"Yeah, but there were differences. If he saw any of your pictures, he could have spotted you. None of the others had your features."

When she got to Troxell's office, there was a message from Maria. Tara had never arrived at school. Everyone was looking for her.

Forty-three

B rad Troxell moved quickly, first calling the school so that they could assemble Tara's teachers, and then calling the police to report a possible kidnapping. He then rode to the school with Charlie, who was bordering on hysteria.

She pressed Irv, her driver, for information that she knew he couldn't have. "You saw her walk up to the school. Did she go into the building?" He wasn't sure. Charlie had told him to let her go and had called him back into the car. "Were there reporters at the door? Could one of them have seen her? Did anyone talk to her?" He apologized, but couldn't tell her anything. He had seen Tara start toward the building, but then he got back into the car.

The school principal met them at the entrance and escorted them to the teachers' lounge where the girl's teachers were waiting. She hadn't been at her morning home room, and her absence slip had been sent to the administrative office. There, a secretary began calling the homes of students who hadn't come to school. There were a lot of them, and only one woman had been assigned.

Her English teacher reported that she hadn't been at her

second-period class. And the math teacher confirmed that she had missed the third period. It was after 11:00 a.m. when the secretary finally dialed the house and got Maria on the phone. Maria had talked to Irv who was inside the front door at his security post. He had insisted that Tara was at school, and so Maria had called back, gotten a recorded announcement, and left her number. The secretary didn't call back until the lunch period, and when she was told that the girl was, indeed, at school, she went to find her teachers. It was a few minutes after noon when it began to dawn on the teachers and administrators that something was wrong. It was the principal who had called back to Maria and confirmed that the girl was missing.

"Four hours!" Charlie screamed. "It took you four hours to figure out that she was missing!"

The principal went into his "cover your ass" mode, and mentioned that the school had been informed that Tara was there. "When we called . . ." he began, but Troxell cut him off.

"We'll do better by putting our efforts into finding her. I'd like each of her teachers to give me the names of her closest friends. Then we can call them to see if she went home with anybody."

"We can't give out students' names without a court order, or permission of the parents," the principal said, wringing his hands.

"Start calling them," Troxell said, his voice threatening. "You didn't need a court order to call about absences. Missing is a lot more important than absent." He glared at the teachers until they were all assembled in administration, checking their class lists and beginning to make phone calls.

Charlie was near collapse, racked by her efforts to hold back her tears. She told Troxell to "see if any of her close friends were absent. I don't think Tara would have gone anywhere on her own." He relayed the suggestion.

Toomey raced into the lounge, and Charlie jumped up and bolted toward him. He caught her in his arms, and drew her into a consoling embrace. "Oh, Jerry, Jerry, she's gone. They got her. They took her."

He patted her cheek, then found a handkerchief and dabbed at her eyes. "We'll find her, Charlie," he said with confidence that was contagious. He led her back to his chair and sat beside her. It was apparent to Brad Troxell that his client and Sergeant Toomey were more than passing acquaintances. Toomey had been the investigator when she was run over by the boat, and he had recommended Brad as her attorney when the investigation turned on Charlie. But that was the extent of their relationship as far as Troxell had known. That morning, when the detective had made his suggestions on the clothes Charlie should wear, his attitude had been completely professional. With Charlie sobbing into Toomey's shoulder, their relationship was obviously personal.

"Are the police looking?" Troxell asked.

"Not officially. They have to wait forty-eight hours on runaways unless there's evidence of a crime."

Charlie pulled back in fright. "Forty-eight hours? Jesus, my daughter is missing. . . ."

"That's officially, Mrs. Armstrong," Toomey said, cutting her off. "But the whole squad is looking on their own. When the report came in, I held a meeting. They're looking."

Troxell noticed the change from "Charlie," to "Mrs. Armstrong." The policeman was back in his official mode. But he could see that Charlie had put her complete trust in him. As far as she was concerned, Toomey was her savior, her daughter's best chance.

"Okay, shopping malls. Give me the names of any malls that she likes." His pad was out and he was writing as fast as she could talk. "How about arcades? Video games and that stuff?" Charlie didn't know of any arcades, but she could think of music stores where Tara and her friends listened to CD samples even if they weren't buying anything. Toomey went through a long list of places where teenagers tended to congregate, and Charlie was able to supply some names.

Toomey stood with his list. "I'm going to make some calls to my guys and have them look into these places," he said. Then he told Charlie, "Best thing you can do is get home in case your daughter calls. That's what happens most of the time. The kids get in over their heads and they call home for help."

"She doesn't have a cell phone," Charlie told him. "She wanted one, but I didn't think it was right." She began crying again, because there was no one to blame but herself. She had missed something very important. Sometime in the last few months, her little girl had grown up. Charlie's idea of sending her daughter away had exploded in her face. Her decision that Tara didn't need a cell phone had eliminated what would have been the easiest way to trace her. She nodded dumbly and went to her car with Troxell.

"I think Sergeant Toomey is right," Brad said as they were being driven to her house. "Most missing kids turn up within twenty-four hours trying to find a face-saving way to come home."

"You said I should just tell her what to do. That's what I did and now I've lost her."

Brad felt chastised. "I'm sorry. I'm not married. I don't have children. All I know is what I read in the papers." But he probed. "Sergeant Toomey has been helpful to you?"

"He believes me," she answered.

"I believe you," he told her. "But in my job what I believe isn't important. It's what the evidence shows, and whether the evidence can be presented to a jury."

They sat in silence as the car passed through the gate. The waiting reporters pressed against the glass to see who was inside with Charlie. As he led her up the steps to her front door, a reporter called, "Is it true that your daughter is missing?" She wheeled angrily. The question made it sound as if her daughter's life was worth nothing more than a headline.

"Please, help me find her," she yelled.

Troxell tried to guide her into the house, but she broke away at the top step. "I'll get her picture. You can put it on television and in the papers. I'll offer a reward. You can announce it."

A television camera zoomed right into her face. Brad Troxell tried to turn her away, but she talked directly into the camera. "Tell people! Someone will have seen her. Someone will know. . . ." He pushed her through the door and into the house. Charlie raced up to her room, and came down instantly with a framed portrait in her hand. "Give them this. Tell them to print it, please." He took the picture and stepped out the front door to show it to the press.

Charlie dropped into a living room chair, and Maria was next to her in an instant, offering a whiskey over ice cubes. "It will relax you, Mrs. Armstrong," she said timidly. Charlie swung a hand and sent the glass flying, spilling ice cubes across the tile floor. Then she rolled forward, her head down almost to her knees, and began to sob uncontrollably.

For hours, she sat perfectly still, hardly aware of her own breathing. Shadows fell across the room and the sun set, and soon the house was in darkness. Troxell had walked around her as he telephoned his office, and then the school. Nothing had been reported. None of Tara's friends knew where she was. There was no call from Toomey.

"They took her instead of me," Charlie suddenly said, breaking two hours of silence.

Troxell settled himself on the arm of her chair. "We don't know that. We don't know that she's in any trouble at all."

"When they call, tell them I'll do anything. They can take me if they let her go. If they want money, they can have it all. I don't want any of it. I want my daughter."

He took her hand. "Okay, if someone calls with a deal, we'll make a deal." He wasn't sure that she could survive another hour without knowing. He went out on the deck, ostensibly for a breath of air. There, he used his phone to contact his own doctor.

In Charlie's mind, she was the one who had brought such misery on herself and her daughter. Steven's marriage proposal had been ridiculous, an old man trying to avoid his age by marrying a young woman. She could have said politely that she was flattered but that it wouldn't work. She didn't love him. And then her life would have gone on, with her daughter coming home each afternoon to their small apartment. Instead, she had been drawn to the lure of Steven's money like a moth to a candle. She had been burned terribly.

When the doctor showed up, Irv had to go outside and shepherd him in through the reporters. He coaxed Charlie to the sofa and then injected her with "something to help you relax." Within a minute, she was asleep.

"Tara . . . Tara . . ." Charlie said in her slumber. Even in sleep, there was no peace.

Forty-four

D aybreak slanted in through the plantation shutters.
Charlie tossed fitfully on the sofa, and Brad Troxell
was draped into a chair. Maria tiptoed around the
kitchen, trying to organize breakfast without making a
sound. When the house telephone rang, she rushed to answer it before it could wake Charlie. She listened, and then
suddenly she was screaming.

"He found her! He found her!" She raced into the living
room where Troxell was already out of his chair. Brad went
to the phone while Maria tried to rouse Charlie.

It was Toomey. One of his detectives had spotted someone
inside the condo. Toomey had rushed over and confirmed that
it was the girl. "I can just pick her up and bring her home," he
explained to the lawyer. "But maybe Mrs. Armstrong would
like to come over and talk to her here."

"Mrs. Armstrong is sedated," Troxell began, but he was interrupted by Charlie stumbling into the kitchen.

"No! I'm here. I have to talk to her." Troxell handed her
the phone and planted her into a chair. She was still wobbly
from the drug. "Tara? Is that you?"

"It's me, Jerry. I found her. She's at the condo and she's fine."

"Bring her home, Jerry. Please."

He repeated what he had said to Troxell. He certainly could do that. But he thought Charlie might want to come and get her. "It could all work out better if she didn't have to be brought home by the police."

"Yes, yes. I'll be right there. Thank you, Jerry. I owe you everything. Everything."

She wanted to leave that instant, but Troxell tried to slow her down. Her appearance confirmed that she had just awakened from a drugged sleep, and she was still in the jeans that had been her costume for the lineup. "Take a shower and change," he said, "You'll want to look your best when she sees you." In truth, she still struck him as groggy. A shower and a cup of Maria's coffee would help bring her around.

Irv eased the car through the dense line of reporters. "Did they find her?" "Is she alive?" In the rear seat, Charlie and Brad stared straight ahead. They had reached the main avenue when Irv told them that they were being followed. "Two cars, I think. One for sure."

"Damn reporters," Brad mumbled. He was about to suggest that Irv try to lose them, but decided that it was probably best to let them tag along. Charlie had cried out for the reporters to help her, and she had given them Tara's picture to publicize. They had done just that. The young girl's disappearance had been the lead story on the late news broadcasts. Her picture had been shown over an 800 number, with the anchor intoning that anyone with information could call the number in confidence. His narrative had stressed the link between the missing girl and the woman about to be tried for murdering her husband. Implied was that the murder and the disappearance must somehow be related.

They couldn't just pick up Tara and smuggle her back into the house. There had to be an announcement that the girl had been found safely. There had to be a reason given for why she had run away from her home and school. The reunion ahead would be as good an opportunity as any, and he was probably the best person to talk with reporters. If he could distract them, then Charlie and Tara might not be tormented with cameras and microphones.

They turned into the condo complex and Charlie directed Irv to the door. As soon as they pulled up, Toomey got out of a parked car and crossed the street to join them. But Charlie didn't wait. She raced up the steps, reached for the lock with her key, and then stopped herself. She shouldn't barge in. She rang the doorbell and waited.

"Is there someone out back?" Troxell asked the detective.

"Sure," Toomey said. "If she tries to run, he'll catch her."

Charlie rang a second time. After a few seconds, the door opened a crack. Tara backed into the shadows and Charlie stepped in to join her. She looked at her daughter who seemed frail and helpless, and then swallowed her in her arms. In an instant, they were both crying unashamedly, bawling "I love you," into one another's ears.

The press cars had pulled up and the reporters were charging the doorway. Ben hurried to cut them off and stopped them with a promise that he would have the family's statement in a few minutes.

"Can we talk to Mrs. Armstrong?" a voice demanded.

"She's been up all night. I think she's exhausted. How about I get you a good photo opportunity?"

"What about the girl? Will she talk to us?"

"She's thirteen," Troxell said, making the request sound ridiculous.

The television reporter was setting up on the lawn next door so that Charlie's condo would be in the background. Brad walked in that direction and the press corps followed. He spoke briefly with the TV reporter, stood where she asked, and counted to five so that the sound man could tune his equipment. Then he said, "We're happy to report that Mrs. Armstrong's daughter, Tara, has been found in apparently good health, at the family's apartment. The apartment wasn't being used, and has been on the market since Mrs. Armstrong's wedding, when she and her daughter moved into her husband's house. The girl was simply overwhelmed by the attention and publicity that accompanied the death of her stepfather and her mother's indictment. She wanted to get away from it."

Questions began flying, but Brad went on with his statement. "Mrs. Armstrong will always be grateful to the press and the news broadcasters for your help in locating her daughter. The prompt reporting was important in finding her."

"How did you find her?" a voice demanded.

"There were several leads," he lied. "I can't say anything more than that." He stepped away from the camera and went to join Toomey who, with two of his detective friends and Irv, had formed a cordon to keep the reporters away from the front door.

"What 'several sources'?" Toomey asked.

"I didn't think you'd want them to know that you organized your own police force."

"Good call," the detective said. Then he asked, "Don't you think 'always grateful to the press' was laying it on a bit thick?"

"Maybe they'll take a liking to her when the trial begins."

The door opened, and Charlie stepped out with an arm around Tara's shoulder. Their heads were down, ready to run directly to their car. Brad stepped in front of them and told them to pause for an instant. "They want a picture. It might as well be flattering. He jumped out of the way and the cameras clicked and whirred, catching exactly the right shot of the mother and daughter embracing.

"Jurors follow the news," he whispered to Toomey.

In the car, Charlie apologized over and over again for the slap that had driven her daughter out of the house. Tara said, "It's okay, Mom," after the first apology and then simply nodded at all the others.

When they reached the house, Brad secreted them inside before he came out and repeated his statement to the press. Nearly all of them left. Just one pool reporter stayed at the gate to keep an eye on the house. Brad went inside, phoned his office and then the school to tell everyone involved that the girl had been found. He was going to talk with Charlie, but when he saw Charlie and Tara side by side at the kitchen counter, he backed away without interrupting. He gave Maria his home number in case something important came up. He was going home to catch up on his sleep.

Tara explained herself in bits and pieces. She had been determined to stay by Charlie's side throughout the trial, no matter how bad it got. She wouldn't let herself be shipped away to live with strangers. But after her mother's outburst, she had known she would be sent into exile. She had decided that the only way to stay close to Charlie was to find someplace to hide.

She still had her keys to the condo. She had walked straight down the school corridor and out the back door that was still open for arriving students. Then she had walked to the house and let herself in. When she found that everything had been cleared out, she made a fast trip to the convenience store, bought bread and cold cuts and a six-pack of a diet soft drink. In the afternoon, she had thought about phoning Charlie just to tell her she was all right, but the phone service had been terminated. Charlie promised that she would have her own cell phone before the day was out.

"I'll never send you away again," Charlie said over and over. She told Tara how frightened she had been. "If I lost you, I wouldn't want to live," she said. Then she apologized again for "being so stupid."

The conversation that lasted well into the afternoon was repeatedly interrupted by outbreaks of crying and emotional embraces. The two women couldn't get enough of one another.

Toomey called her on the cell phone to tell her that he had to see her. Charlie glanced back at her daughter. "Not tonight," she said. "I have to be with her tonight. We have to get through the news blitz and then decide when she should go back to school."

"Tomorrow," he insisted.

"At the condo?"

"No, reporters might still be taking pictures of the place. Or it could attract gawkers."

"Where?"

He was quiet for a moment. Then he decided, "Tell Irv to call me. We'll work something out."

"I have to tell you," she said before he could hang up, "how grateful I am. Brad told me that it was you who found her."

"Tell me tomorrow," he answered and broke the connection.

Charlie and Tara sat together to face the intrusion of the early news. The anchor came on with a smile, and over the footage of the two women emerging from the house and embracing on the street, announced the happy ending to what had been an impending tragedy. They cut to Brad Troxell's talking head as he made the statement and expressed the family's thanks. The next shot was of the car pulling away. But he gratuitously added that Charlie had been indicted for the murder of her husband and that the trial would begin next week. The co-anchor, an Asian Latino, added that it must be difficult for the girl and added that she hoped that the story would have a *real* happy ending. *Just maybe,* Charlie thought, *some of the reporters had switched to her side.*

Forty-five

Charlie got into the car while it was still parked in the garage. The morning television news had replayed both of Brad Troxell's appearances, and had shown and reshown the two women exiting the condo. As a result, there was a new gathering of press people waiting to pounce on Charlie and Tara when they left the house. Tara agreed with her mother that it would be best to skip school for a day or two, and Charlie got ready for her meeting with Jerry Toomey.

Irv had become expert at easing out of the driveway through the cordon of reporters. He kept moving, just fast enough so that it would be dangerous for anyone to stand in front of the car, and just slow enough so that no one would get hurt. Once past the gate, he accelerated onto the main street and headed out into the city.

"Where are we going?" Charlie asked.

Irv looked at the address he had gotten from Toomey. "Near the water. Looks like one of the high-rise towers."

He turned into the circular driveway of a twenty-story condominium that fronted the ocean. A discreet doorman

took Charlie's hand and gave her over to an even more discrete elevator operator. Thirty seconds later, she was stepping
into a lavish apartment that had floor-to-ceiling windows
overlooking the coastline as far south as Miami, and sliders
out to terraces that dangled over the Atlantic. Toomey was
waiting on one of the balconies.

He came to her, received her into his arms, and kissed her
tenderly. "God, but how I've wanted to be with you."

"I've needed you, too," Charlie said. "I've been all by myself." She returned the kiss, and then pulled back from him.
"It's like a firing squad," she said. "I'm the one tied to the
post, and no one wants to stand near me. Then Tara vanished. . . ." She threw her hands up as she spun back into the
living room. "I really thought I had gone as far as I could go."

He sympathized, followed her into the living room, and sat
beside her. "When I heard your kid was gone, I could guess
how frantic you were. That's why I lined up the guys . . ."

"Thank God you did. Who knows where she would have
gone next, or what kinds of people she might have turned to.
You saved her, Jerry. I'll be in your debt for the rest of my life."

Toomey waved away the suggestion. "You're not in my
debt. All I did was cut through the red tape and bureaucratic
bullshit. They want to wait forty-eight hours because lots of
kids decide to come home. In forty-eight hours, she could
have been on her way to the Middle East to some sultan's
harem. All the guys knew that we had to move right away."

Once again, she stumbled to announce her gratitude. "It's
just . . . I'll never get over the terror. . . . I'll never be able to
repay you."

He offered her a cup of coffee, or a soft drink. She decided on bottled water and followed him into the kitchen.
"This place is fabulous," Charlie said, taking in the refrigerator stocked with beer and water, the full shelf of glasses, and
the separate ice-making machine. "Do you live here?"

Toomey broke out into genuine laughter. "Wouldn't I like
to? This pad would sell for maybe seven million. I make fifty-
eight thousand. It's a bit out of my reach."

He poured the water and dropped a few ice cubes into the

glass. Then he opened a bottle of beer for himself. "The owner has a half dozen pros working out of here. High-price ladies who each bring in a couple of thousand a night. He pays the mortgage in the first week, and his operating expenses in the second week. The rest of the month is his."

Charlie looked about, suddenly beginning to feel a bit sullied. "This is a . . . house?"

"At night it is, but things are usually slow in the morning. That's why I was able to borrow it."

Once again, she felt the illicit side of his profession. How could she not love the man who had saved her daughter? But how could she love someone who was so close to flesh peddlers? His profession was noble, but it had hardened him and dried up his sympathies.

They were back at the sofa when he told her why he had summoned her. There were new developments that he had to act on immediately. Bottom line, he confided, was that he was going to have to leave the police force.

"You can't!" Charlie interrupted. "It's your life. It's what you do."

"If I stay, I have to play by the rules," he countered. "And if I do, then the real killer is going to walk free, and you're going to take your chances with a jury."

Charlie fell back into the sofa. What was he telling her? Why would the police prevent him from finding the truth?

"I followed the dynamite," Toomey began, "and I followed the money. Someone paid for the dynamite, and someone took the money and delivered it. It made sense that the sale occurred down here. I mean, why would someone buy it in California and drive it all the way here? And then it figured that the stuff wasn't delivered to the same person who paid for it. The one who paid for it would have a motive. The one who picked it up would have the skill to use it. Most likely not the same person. So I began dropping in on dealers and asking about transactions where the money came from someone they didn't generally deal with, and the delivery was to someone they never dealt with." Then he asked, "You with me so far?"

Charlie nodded. What he had said made perfect sense. And he had chosen California as an example, which implied that Gary Armstrong was involved.

"I came up blank until I got my hands on the computer systems guru from the Ucandoit store right here in Fort Lauderdale. He didn't want to help, but he's been selling illegal converters to get people into cable systems without paying. So I had him between a rock and a hard place. And doesn't he come up with a delivery that didn't match the purchase order. The delivery was to our late friend, Max McGraw. And the buyer?" Toomey left his question open, challenging her to guess.

"I don't know," Charlie answered.

"An inter-company order from headquarters. Somebody in the Boston office okayed a voucher that gave Max McGraw eight sticks of dynamite, blasting caps, wire, and a timer switch."

"Jesus!" She could hardly speak.

"So now what I need is proof that the *somebody* is Matthew Armstrong. Then, we'll have it. A clear line between Matthew and the guy who planted the bomb."

"Matthew tried to kill me," she said softly.

Toomey finished her thought. "And blew up his money tree by mistake. Pretty stupid!"

"Pretty sick!" Charlie was left shaking her head. But then she wondered why any of this would demand that he give up his police career. It seemed to her he had just solved the case.

"The problem," Toomey said as if reading her mind, "is that if I take this to the captain, all he'll do is pass a request on to the police in Boston. Then we'll have some cop who doesn't know a damn thing about the case trying to get information out of a company that's probably a big sponsor of charities and arts. The local police won't want to step on anybody's toes.

"I've got to go up there myself. But I can't do that without breaking regulations. That's why I've got to leave the force."

Charlie was still confused. "Can't you take a leave? Use vacation days or something like that."

"I'd be finished," Toomey said glumly. "They have a dozen ways of squeezing you out once you cross them. There was one guy who got assigned to stake out a house where no one lived. He spent four months sitting in his car, waiting for someone to come out the door. He got the message, and turned in his papers."

"I don't want you to do this, Jerry," she said. "It isn't right."

He took her hand. "Don't worry about it. I didn't go to all that trouble to find your kid just so she could visit you in jail. Besides, I want to see you more often than just on visiting days."

Charlie leaned into his arms and began sobbing on his shoulder.

"Hey, why the tears?" he asked.

She didn't know why she was crying. Sadness, perhaps, because of what he would be giving up. It was hard to picture Jerry Toomey as anything but a policeman. Or maybe it was joy because he was giving it up so easily, just for her. He had been with her right from the beginning, and had been her secret source of strength throughout the ordeal. At the very lowest moment of her life, he had been the one who brought back her daughter.

"I love you," she told him, knowing full well what she was saying. He was putting his life into her hands, and now Charlie wanted him to know that he held her life in his.

"And I love you," he answered, holding her even tighter. They kissed, and slid together down onto the sofa.

"Nobody's using any of the bedrooms," Toomey said.

"I think I could use one," Charlie answered. They held their embrace into a room with a king-size bed that used a mirrored wall for a headboard. "This is my first time as a call girl," she said, glancing around at the setting.

"You'd get top dollar, believe me!"

Forty-six

The trial began on a Monday with the selection of the twelve men and women who would decide how the rest of Charlie's life was going to turn out. Each one came to the witness stand and answered questions to determine his impartiality, the prosecution eliminating anyone who opposed the death penalty, and her defense counsel challenging anyone who was already familiar with the case. By noon, only one seat in the jury box had been filled, that by a hotel desk clerk who had no opinion about anything, especially the death penalty.

To Charlie's mind, all the potential jurors fit into two categories—those who would say anything to get on the jury, and those who would say anything to get dismissed. Generally, the difference was an occupational matter. Retirees, and the marginally employed, thought being on a jury was a great way to spend some time. Corporate types, and small business owners, thought that even a day away from their desks would bring financial ruin.

Over a sandwich in the attorney's cafeteria, Brad confirmed her opinion. "The prosecution's job is easy," he told

her. "He wants conservative white retirees who are personally offended that you married Steven instead of them. It
would make sense to them that the only thing you saw in
Steven was his money, and they would have no trouble believing that you killed him to get your hands on it." Charlie
shook her head at the absurdity of the situation. Could she
possibly be found guilty because of the jealousy of other
older men?

"Our job is a little trickier. Logically, I should be loading
the jury with single mothers who can appreciate the tough
road you've traveled. They should identify with you naturally. But identify how? Do they love you because you're one
of them? Or do they hate you because you overcame it and
they didn't? Maybe they're glad to see that you made it to the
top. Or maybe they hate you *because* you made it to the top.
There's probably no way of knowing which they are."

In the afternoon, four more jurors were seated. Three were
the stern-faced retirees that Brad was dreading. But, as he explained to Charlie, he couldn't block them all. He could use
his peremptory challenges to bar some of them. But he
couldn't have them excused for cause just because they
thought they were more deserving of her affections.

The other juror from the afternoon session was a Latina
who worked for an office-cleaning company. At one point she
mentioned that the men in the offices she cleaned were always complaining. "I'm only allowed one minute a desk,"
she said. "You can't clean picture frames when you only got
a minute." Brad seized on her because she would probably be
hostile to the other three.

The evening news had footage of her car entering the
courthouse garage. The paper had an artist's sketch of Charlie and her attorney following the proceedings as jurors were
being interviewed. Her image made her look tougher than
she felt. The story line simply acknowledged that the trial
was beginning and that the juicy parts would be coming soon.
There was also a reference to Tara's running away, and her
mother's frantic eighteen hours. Tara, who had been back to
school for two days without incident, turned down the oppor-

tunity to stay home tomorrow, "just because my name is in the news." She argued that her name was probably going to be in the news every day until the trial was over.

"How are your friends treating you?" Charlie asked.

Tara shrugged.

The next day things moved a bit more quickly. They seated two jurors in the morning, both middle-aged women who insisted they had not followed the story in the newspapers. "Where have they been? On Mars?" Charlie asked while she and Brad were splitting a sandwich.

"Oh, they've followed it," he agreed. "They just want to be on the jury because their soap operas haven't been interesting lately. You're going to be the daily entertainment."

"And that's good for us?" she asked, not following his logic.

He shrugged. "Maybe they'll take you for the heroine."

In the afternoon session, he struck a male juror who when asked what he knew of the case said it was about "a woman who killed her husband for his money." The defense struck two women who clearly did not want to serve and who stated that in every marriage the woman gets the short end of the stick. But they did seat two more jurors, in a silent compromise between the two sides. One was a retiree who spent his time day trading over the Internet. It was obvious that no woman was ever going to get her hands on his money. The other was a woman who taught special education at a local high school. More than likely, Brad thought, she tended to root for the underdog.

That night, there was nothing about the trial on television, and if there was a mention in the paper, Charlie couldn't find it. She and Tara had an enjoyable dinner, made all the lighter by Tara's story of a lunch room liaison in which the girl's note had been passed to the wrong boy. It seemed to Charlie that her daughter's situation was close to normal. They decided to take their desert out on the deck for an evening swim, during which Tara asked if she could get breast implants over the summer so that she would be ready for high school. Charlie kept a straight face while she gave a serious answer, but she loved the distraction that her daughter provided. *Without her, I'd go crazy,* she admitted.

Toomey called the cell phone he had given her and said he was on his way to Boston. "I've talked with some people up there who can help me. I'm meeting them in the morning."

"Jerry, you didn't quit your job, did you?" He had agreed when they were lying in each other's arms, that he would reconsider. "How would I get a pad like this apartment if I had to pay for it?" he had joked.

"No! I just took three days' sick leave. I've got about a hundred of them that I didn't use. But I still think I'll have to. The brass is really going to be pissed when they find out what I've been up to."

They found three more jurors in the next morning's session and then filled the jury box in the afternoon. Seven men and five women, six white, three black, two Latino, and one Asian. Of the whole mix, Brad thought there would be four who would be hostile to a women who had married for money, and three who were probably starting out thinking that Charlie was guilty. Three, he felt, would never convict someone who might face the death penalty. There were two who were a complete mystery. "No matter what they said, they've all been following the story and are thrilled to get in on the action," Brad said cynically. "Let's hope some of them read about Tara being lost, and felt sympathy for you."

He explained how the trial would begin the next day with the judge's general instructions to the jury, and with the prosecutor's opening statement. "He'll summarize all the things he's going to prove and then outline how his case meets all the requirements of a guilty finding.

"I'll defer my statement until we begin presenting the defense's case. That way I can use it to respond to the prosecutor's most damaging evidence. Then we'll go after their points one at a time.

"Our best play at this time is to show them all the other possible scenarios, like you were the intended victim, or that Steven was about to confront Matthew over his embezzlement. In other words, how can they be sure that it's you?"

She answered his question the way the prosecutor would. "Because there's testimony from the man who sold me the dynamite."

"We can discredit him during cross-examination. He has a deal with the district attorney. If he wasn't in the courtroom, testifying against you, he'd be in jail."

"So, the jury will come back and find me not guilty on all charges," Charlie said, more ironically than as a statement of fact.

"They might," Brad said with a smile. "Or they could find that they can't reach a decision. With a hung jury, maybe the state will decide to drop the charges."

"How long will all this take?" she asked. "How long before we know?"

"My best guess is seven days. It could be a lot longer if the jury gets hung up, but not much less."

"Seven days," Charlie said as if she were counting the days left in her life.

"Chin up!" he said, raising her face to his. "We're going to win!"

At home, she repeated all the details to Tara. She explained the case that the prosecution would present, and all the things that were wrong with it. Then she presented Brad's strategy of proposing alternative scenarios that better fit the crime.

"He thinks they were trying to kill you?" she said, repeating the theory she had first presented to her classmates. "Who was trying to kill you?"

"One of Steven's children. Or maybe all of them."

She took her daughter through the financial losses that her marriage to Steven implied for his children. In round numbers, she was able to explain how much each of them stood to lose. Tara was more interested in how much money her mother had married into. She knew that Steven was very rich, but she couldn't begin to understand that her stepfather had been in a totally different class from anything she could have imagined.

"So, there is enough money for everyone," Tara concluded.

"More than enough," Charlie said. She knew that her daughter counted wealth in very modest terms, the ability to buy a new blouse that she really liked. The scale of the wealth involved in Steven's death was beyond her comprehension.

"Then why would they be killing each other if there was already enough for everyone?"

Good question, Charlie thought. How come kids could see the obvious so clearly? "I guess that for some people there's never enough," she said.

The next day, Tara went back to school, ready with an answer for anyone who suggested that her mother was a killer. *She's the one they were trying to kill,* she rehearsed as Irv drove her to school. Brad Troxell picked up Charlie and drove her through the newsmen at the gate.

"Charlie, is Detective Toomey doing some investigating for you?" Brad asked as soon as they were on an open road.

Charlie didn't know how much to say. "He believes I'm innocent. He's been trying to help me prove it."

Brad pursed his lips. "Might be better if he tried to help *me* prove it. The last things we need are surprises."

She felt chastised. Obviously, she should have been telling her attorney the truth right from the beginning. She shouldn't have lied about finding the correspondence between Steven and Matthew as Toomey had suggested. He was entitled to know that Trish had probably planted the letters. "What surprises?" she asked, still trying to cover for Toomey.

"I got an e-mail last night, suggesting that I subpoena some sales records from the local Ucandoit branch. Do you know anything about it?"

"Who sent the e-mail?"

Brad allowed himself a thin smile. "It was from a library computer. I'm guessing it was Jerry because the two of you seem to be very close. Is there anything you can tell me about the records he thinks are so damn important?"

Charlie got her first hint that Brad Troxell and Jerry Toomey weren't the best of friends. But she wanted both of them on her side. "Detective Toomey told me that Ucandoit's local branch had delivered dynamite to Max McGraw."

"The man who you think tried to run you over with a boat," Troxell confirmed.

"Yes. But that's only half of it. The other half is that the dynamite was paid for by the company headquarters. Jerry . . . Detective Toomey . . . is trying to find out who authorized it. He thinks it must be Matthew Armstrong, probably because Steven had threatened to turn Matthew in."

"Interesting . . ." Brad allowed.

"Interesting?" Charlie questioned. "It's more than interesting. It proves that someone else had the dynamite."

"Interesting," Brad repeated, "because we've been assuming that Max McGraw was hired to kill you. But if Matthew's motive was to avoid being exposed, then why would he go after you? It seems that he would have attacked Steven to begin with."

In the courtroom, before the judge entered, Brad went to the prosecutor's table and held a brief conference with the assembled attorneys. Then he and the chief prosecutor went around to the judge's chambers. When they returned, Brad told her that the judge would subpoena the Ucandoit records. "They won't be entered as evidence until the State has a chance to look them over," he told Charlie. "But if they're what you say, they won't be able to keep them out."

The judge, the Honorable Thomas Hoppe, entered and climbed up to his bench. He was balding, red-faced, and portly, not so much a figure of justice as a parody of local political club politicians. His white hair was combed over a bald scalp, which further eroded his image as an honest man.

The lead attorney for the prosecution rose with the old line that "If it pleases the court," and began his statement. His name was Frank Slattery, and he was tall and as thin as a fence slat, perfectly groomed, shaved painfully close, and dressed in a gray worsted summer suit. His ivory shirt had a buttoned-down collar, and a striped tie in the Florida State colors exploded out of a tight knot. He was magnificent, Charlie decided.

Her attorney, by comparison, looked a bit seedy. Like most cotton suits, his blue seersucker seemed unpressed. His dark shirt was melodramatic, and his tie was filled with frivolous images from Walt Disney Studios. If her trial came down to which attorney was most credible, then she would probably be facing lethal injection.

Slattery's pretrial comments were masterly. He told the jury exactly what he was going to prove, he listed the evidence that would do the proving, and then he told the jury what he had proven. In his scenario, Charlie had seduced an unwitting and maybe even senile, fabulously wealthy senior citizen. She conned him into marrying her and then began living off his wealth. But, the man had come to his senses, realized he was being played for a fool, and gone to his attorneys for help. Faced with being cut off from his limitless wealth, the defendant had blown him to pieces. Greed, lust, money, and murder! Isn't that what the jury would expect?

He was brilliant in his closing. "When you look at the defendant, you see a young woman of obvious charm and great physical endurance. That's exactly what Steven Armstrong saw, and when she told him that she loved him, he couldn't believe his good fortune. Take a close look at her, ladies and gentlemen. Does she look like a woman who wanted to spend the rest of her life taking care of an old man, and then have his money go to his children?" If Charlie were on the jury, she would have screamed for vengeance.

Surprisingly, the prosecutor spent the morning proving the obvious—that Steven had been killed by an explosive device planted in his boat. Even though her life was at stake, Charlie couldn't keep her mind on the proceedings. She was more involved with the prosecutor's description of her. A temptress! A seductress! She knew that she was attractive, but not *very* attractive. Somehow she didn't see herself in the role of Delilah.

Had she really tempted and seduced Steven Armstrong? Could the jury actually envision her giving him the pecks, caresses, and touches that would fire his passion? All she had done was help him with his stretching exercises and then monitor his rehabilitation regimen. A man could have done it just as well!

Would they really think that she had wanted the entirety of

his vast fortune? God knows, all she really needed was a better radio for her car. Well, maybe an entirely new car, but nothing that she couldn't afford to pay off over time.

Could they believe that she would know how to put together a bomb? Install the blasting caps, link them to some sort of switch, and then install the entire mechanism in the boat? She was a klutz! Sometimes she couldn't get her electric can opener to work. She always needed Tara to program the VCR.

And then that she would kill someone? Blow him up into little pieces, just to get her hands on money that she already owned?

When the jury members looked at her, the whole trial must seem ridiculous, Charlie thought. And yet, there they were seated in the jury box, listening intently to the forensics expert describe exactly how her husband had died. *He was blown up,* she wanted to tell them. Massive trauma, fractures, burns were all unnecessary details.

With each expert witness, Brad Troxell rose with the same brief cross-examination. "Was there anything in your investigation that might indicate when the explosive had been attached, or by whom?" Each prosecution witness admitted that they had no idea who had set the explosive that had killed Steven Armstrong.

Over lunch, he explained what he was trying to do. "They have to present all this obvious detail because they have to establish that a death occurred, and it was caused by a bomb. I'm just trying to make certain that the jury knows you're not part of the story. I don't want anyone thinking of you when they think of Steven's moment of blinding pain."

Troxell's assistant interrupted them with news that records of the Ucandoit transaction would be available at the end of the day. Brad decided that his team would work into the night, and ordered that accountants be brought in to verify what they were seeing. "As a matter of fact, get someone from the company that set up their data-processing system. The damn computers do all the accounting anyway."

Forty-seven

There were two new spectators in the afternoon session—Matthew Armstrong and Trish Armstrong. Both looked terribly bereaved, Matthew in a deep gray suit and nearly colorless tie, and Trish in a straight black dress with a black lace jacket. She had a white handkerchief pressed to her eyes.

The State's forensic expert took the stand to explain exactly how they knew that a bomb had caused the explosion. He stood with a pointer to show the traces of a gasoline explosion, and the marked differences with a dynamite explosion.

The prosecutor threw him a straw man. "Supposing there was dynamite aboard the boat and that the initial explosion was caused by another factor—trapped bilge gases, for example. Wouldn't that make it look as if the explosion had been the result of dynamite?"

The forensic expert had even been rehearsed in his dismissive smirk. "No, in that case the dynamite explosion would have followed many seconds after the gasoline explosion. This was a simultaneous ignition of the two elements. The explosion had to have been caused by the dynamite charge."

Brad had been trying to look totally bored with the technical evidence, and by the time the questioning ended half the jurors had followed his lead. They were fighting the urge to nod off after lunch. He didn't leave his table for the cross-examination but simply asked, "Does any of this give you any clue as to who might have put the dynamite aboard the boat?" No, there was no evidence on that subject. "How about when the dynamite was put aboard?" No way to tell.

Brad shrugged. "Then I guess you can't be any more helpful," he said, making the recitation of chemical data seem irrelevant.

Charlie's mind had wandered from the presentation, and she had been stealing glances at Trish and Matthew. They seemed comfortable together, sharing the great loss of their father. But if she was right, then Trish had tried to implicate Matthew by planting the damning letters in her father's desk. And, if Toomey was right, then Matthew had hired someone to kill his own father.

Tomorrow, or at the latest the following day, they would take the stand to tell how their father had been seduced, robbed, and murdered. Joined by their brother Gary, who was already on his way from Los Angeles, they would each testify about their father's misgivings, and how he was taking steps to limit her inheritance to the legal minimum. *But he never made it,* Matthew would say. Trish would probably break down crying, unable to speak, but still managing to point directly at Charlie. Gary, with his Hollywood flair, could say, *But . . . poof! up in smoke!* She wondered how Brad planned to attack them.

Next to the stand was Detective Lionetti, who identified several pieces of evidence that had been taken from Charlie's wardrobe, all of which became official evidence in the case. Then he gave way to another forensics Ph.D. who detailed the tests that had been performed on Charlie's clothes. Traces of nitrate had been found on her shorts and jeans and on one of her blouses, the items that Lionetti had presented as evidence. The jury woke up abruptly and their eyes snapped in her direction. If she wasn't guilty, how did she get dynamite on her clothes?

Again, Brad tried to appear unconcerned. "Doctor," he said while still in his chair, "where on earth could this nitrate have come from?"

"Well, certainly from explosive materials such as dynamite."

"How about household fertilizer?

The witness nodded. "Yes, that too."

Brad stood and held up a can of well-advertised plant food. "This product, for example—which the defendant uses and recommended to me—boasts on its label that it contains fifteen percent nitrates. Could that be what you found on the defendant's clothes?

"Not likely," he answered "If you read further, you'll see that there are other minerals—copper, for example—bonded with those nitrates. It's a bit different."

"Did you test for copper?" Brad wondered innocently.

"No, we didn't. We weren't looking for fertilizer, we were looking for explosives."

"Too bad you didn't test for copper and some of these other metals. You might have decided that what you were finding was plant food. Mrs. Armstrong loves to garden."

The judge adjourned for the day, and Charlie walked with Brad out of the courtroom. Trish and Matthew chose a different aisle and never looked over. They were already in the elevator when Charlie reached the courtroom door.

"How did you know that there was nitrate in that fertilizer?" she asked, smiling at what she thought was a major triumph.

"I bought a can," he said.

She stopped him before they reached the elevator. "What if he had tested for copper?"

"I had the whole laboratory analysis. It's evidence that the State has to show us. It never mentioned testing for copper, iron, or any metals for that matter. Like the man said, they knew what they were looking for."

She cooked waffles for dinner because Tara always wanted waffles when there was something to celebrate. The girl flooded them in maple syrup and ate them one square at a time. Charlie told her how the day had gone, with Troxell making the point after each witness that there was no link between the forensic information and her. She told all the delicious details of the nitrate, sharing the fun moment when Brad had read from the plant food package. Her best description of the witness was that he was like a man who had walked into the ladies' locker room. The man just stands there, too embarrassed to move, and covers his privates even though he's not the one who is undressed.

Tara cut and speared another waffle square. Then something occurred to her. "You never do any gardening! Don't we always say that our house is where plants come to die?"

Charlie colored. "The point was that it could have been lots of things, not just explosives."

"Like what?" Tara wondered.

"Like anything. God, I don't know."

She understood that Tara would hold her to a higher standard of proof than the state. Maybe in court all she had to do was prove that the evidence didn't warrant her conviction. Here, she had to prove that she was innocent.

Brad called as Tara was finishing her waffle. "Charlie, do you know how to get in touch with Sergeant Toomey?"

"I have a cell phone that he's on, but it doesn't show the number. He told me it would keep calls from being tapped or traced."

"Well, call him, and have him call me."

"Is something wrong?" she asked.

"No! The records we got from Ucandoit are terrific. But I need his records on Max McGraw. And I may need him to testify about how McGraw was connected to Matthew."

She agreed to contact Toomey. Brad, who usually didn't seem concerned about anything, was clearly tense. She guessed there was some sort of problem that he wasn't letting her in on.

Toomey picked up on the first ring. "Sure I'll call him. I

think I have everything he's looking for on McGraw. But he won't need it. I've pretty much closed the noose around Matthew's neck." She had trouble hearing him. They had a bad connection that caused a regular beat of static. She asked him to repeat part of what he had said, but Toomey went on in a louder voice. "The order for the dynamite was charged to his sales account as if he was providing samples to a big customer. I think he'll crack wide open when Brad confronts him with the information. It was Matthew who did it, Charlie."

Charlie shuddered as she glanced over to her daughter who was loading the dinner dishes into the dishwasher. If Toomey hadn't called her that day, she and Tara would have been motoring down the channel, on their way to doing some water-skiing. They would have died together.

"When will you be back, Jerry?"

"Probably tomorrow. I have to get copies of some of the documentation, and then get the originals back to Ucandoit. It will probably be a late flight."

"I'd like to see you," Charlie said. "If the trial is going to be over quickly, then I want to talk about what comes next."

"I'd like that," Toomey answered. "But maybe you should take this one step at a time." He said something more about letting things settle down, but she couldn't make it out through the static. "No need to rush," Toomey said aloud when she asked him to repeat himself. Then he hung up.

She was disappointed in his answer even though she knew he was right. She was leading from her heart, reaching out to the man who had believed in her, loved her, and saved her. He was using his head, cautioning her that she should get over the emotional strains she had been through before making any important decisions. Charlie wished that he wasn't being so damn logical.

Forty-eight

———

There was a faint trace of light on the eastern horizon,
enough to separate the blackness of the water from the
deep gray of the sky. Manny Fernandez was the only
one on the beach, moving on a meandering course between
the trash containers, just as he did every morning. He paused
to stab a paper bag, lifted it, and dropped it into the sack he
wore over his shoulder. Then he headed for a six-pack wrapper and a stack of empty beer cans. He added these to his sack
and then dumped the contents into the next trash basket. He
had four hours to cover the entire public beach before the
truck came along and emptied all the baskets. Any trash that
wasn't in a container was his fault, and he would hear about it
when he went to the Parks Department for his paycheck.

There was one car in the parking lot, a plain-looking
sedan. There wasn't yet enough light for Manny to determine
the color. Ordinarily, he would circle away. Overnight parking usually meant lovers who had fallen asleep in their embrace, and while the morning lifeguards liked to peek in
hopes of catching an eyeful, Manny was respectful of the
parkers' privacy.

The sun popped up, a small cherry that instantly brought color to the sky. Now Manny could see that the car was blue. He also caught the shape of a person seated behind the steering wheel. It looked like the outline of a man, and the man was looking in his direction. *A supervisor,* he thought. *The bastard is doing a report on me.* He picked up his pace, nearly running between the small mounds of debris that had been left from the day before.

There was one pile right in front of the parked car. Someone had brought a picnic dinner to the beach and left behind a cardboard box full of crumpled paper. Either that, or the snoop in the car had set this up just to trap Manny. The debris was at the top of the beach, near the parking area, and well away from his usual path. Leave it there, and his boss would be all over him.

He rushed up toward the box, gathered it with all its papers, and stuffed it into the sack. He stole a glance at the car to see if the supervisor noticed. It was then that he realized that the man was slumped over the steering wheel.

Manny hesitated. Maybe the guy was sick, or stoned on drugs. He might need help. Most likely he was asleep and would get really mad at someone who interrupted him. He waved. It was a friendly gesture. If the man was conscious, he would have to wave back. But there was no response. One thing was sure—this was no supervisor. He let the bag slip from his shoulder and eased up to the car. Then he tapped on the driver's window. There was no acknowledgment.

The man was in profile, his head resting on the steering wheel. His left hand hung limply into his lap. Manny knocked again, expecting to see the man snap to and sit up abruptly. There was no movement at all. Manny began to think that he might be dead.

He walked around the car, stealing a glance into the back seat. It was empty, which seemed to mean that the man was by himself. Then he came up to the passenger-side window and pressed his nose against the glass. From this angle, he could see the right hand hanging down beneath the dashboard. He could also make out a round hole in the man's tem-

ple and a straight line of blood that came from the hole and
spread out on the shirt collar.

He pulled back. *Jesus!* But then he leaned forward again.
Manny had never seen a gunshot wound before, but he had no
doubt what this was. He reached for the door handle, but
caught himself in the nick of time. What did they always say
on television? "Don't touch anything!" He backed away from
the car for a few steps, then suddenly bolted over the curb
and out onto the beach. He ran as fast as he could toward the
first aid station and concession stand, and used the pay phone
to call the police.

Manny wasn't back to the car when the first cruiser, its
lights flashing, peeled into the parking area. One of the officers used a cloth to try the door handle. It was locked shut.
Two more police cars arrived, and then a white panel truck.
Within minutes there were a dozen vehicles on the scene, policemen and lab technicians everywhere, and enough yellow
tape stretched around to cordon off a construction site.

The police had used a coat hanger to open the door, and
found a man in a gray business suit, dead from a gunshot
wound to his head. There was a .22-caliber pistol on the floor
in front of the passenger seat. Next to him was a suicide note,
printed out in a bold typeface by a computer printer. The note
said that he had made a mess of his life, disgraced his family,
and then killed his own father. The police found a wallet in
the inside breast pocket of the man's jacket. Inside was an ar-
ray of credit cards and $420 in cash. The driver's license
identified the owner as Matthew Armstrong. To the police on
the scene, he was just another nut who couldn't see an end to
his troubles.

Rich Lionetti heard about Matthew's suicide when he
came in that morning. He called the police department chaplain to tell him that the dead man's brother and sister were in
town, waiting to testify against their stepmother. Someone
should let them know. Then he called the prosecutor, Frank
Slattery, and gave him the news.

"What? You're crazy? It can't be?" Slattery said in rapid
fire. "He's my second witness today."

"Not anymore, he isn't." Lionetti smirked. "By the way, he left a suicide note. He admits that he killed his father." Slattery's end of the line went deathly quiet. "You still there, Frank?"

"I'm here. Who knows about it?"

"Just the cops on the scene and the forensics team. But there are a ton of reporters outside looking for an ID, and a story. So it's going to make the early editions."

"Are you sure it's a suicide? Isn't it possible that the man was murdered?"

"It looks like a suicide, but forensics hasn't come to any conclusion. I could call it an apparent suicide."

"Okay," Slattery said. "Now, what about the note? Is it genuine?"

"On the first pass, his were the only prints. The lab is checking the paper and the ink."

"Can you avoid mentioning the note?" Slattery asked.

Lionetti was enjoying the attorney's discomfort. "I don't have to bring it up, but somebody is bound to ask."

"Look, Rich, I need a few hours to run all of this past the judge. Could you just say that there was a note, but that you can't discuss its contents until you hear from the lab? The problem is that if even one newspaper says Matthew Armstrong killed his father, then my case goes down the drain. Even if the note is phony, the publicity would kill us. The judge has to decide how he wants to handle it."

"Sure," Lionetti said. Then he added, "By the way, I really like those new, big flat-screen televisions."

"Screw you," Slattery said. "If you want one, go buy it yourself!"

Lionetti roared with laughter.

Brad Troxell heard from Slattery's secretary, who would only say that "a man who is identified as Matthew Armstrong has been found dead, and the death may be a suicide."

"A suicide? Was there a note?"

"I have no idea," the secretary said, following the script he had been given by the prosecutor. "I'm calling because the trial will be postponed until tomorrow."

"Does this mean you're dropping charges against my client?"

"I have no idea," the secretary repeated.

Trish was reached at her hotel by the police chaplain. She screamed and dropped the phone, causing the front desk to send up a house detective and a doctor. She recovered quickly, and left a message for Gary to call her when he checked in.

Charlie got the news from Brad. "Last night, or sometime early this morning," he explained. "Apparently he shot himself in one of the beach parking lots." She was speechless. Her decision to marry Steven Armstrong had led to a whole series of horrors. But maybe this death wasn't linked to her. Steven had caught his son with his hands in the till, and the son had resorted to murder to protect himself from jail. All of that might have happened if she had never met Steven.

"Where's Toomey?" Troxell asked.

"In Boston," she answered. "He was closing the loop between Matthew and McGraw. He's supposed to be coming back sometime today. Should I call him?"

"You might let him know," Brad said after a moment of thought. "But tell him to keep digging. We may still have to demonstrate that Matthew was tied into the bombing."

"Brad, does this mean that I'm free?" she wondered.

He responded with typical caution. "Not yet! The trial is postponed for a day. It's the DA's call, and prosecutors hate to admit that they were wrong."

She called on the cell phone and this time it took three rings before Toomey clicked on. Charlie blurted out the news, and Toomey told her that he already knew. "I've got a lot of friends at headquarters," he said. Then he added that, "with what I have, and with Matthew turning his gun on himself, I don't think you have much to worry about." Toomey gave her his flight number and time of arrival from Boston. He had to repeat the flight number twice because of the background static.

"Maybe it's my phone," she said.

"You won't be needing it much longer," Toomey asked.

"When this case is over we'll be able to come out of the closet." Then he asked her if she "could spare Irv to pick me up at the airport."

"Maybe I can spare Irv from now on," Charlie said, already beginning to turn her life back to normal.

It was late in the afternoon when Brad called back. "Charlie, we're going back into court tomorrow."

She was surprised, although not at all upset. The case against her may have come crashing down, but still the court probably had to wrap up the details. "Okay," she agreed. "What's the agenda?"

"I'm not sure. I think the DA might want to move for a mistrial."

"Why? Doesn't Matthew's suicide answer all the questions?"

"The prosecutors don't think that Matthew committed suicide," Brad told her. "They think he was murdered."

Forty-nine

Toomey arrived late in the afternoon. Irv had picked him up at the airport, and taken him past the reporters, straight into the garage. He came up the steps smiling as if he had just won an Olympic event, and was amazed to find Charlie in a somber mood.

"What's the matter?" he said. "I thought you'd be celebrating."

She told him that she wasn't out of the woods yet. The prosecution wasn't ready to admit that Matthew's death had been a suicide, or that the note he left behind was genuine. "Brad says that the trial might pick up tomorrow morning as if nothing had happened. Or even worse, they might ask for a mistrial so that they can start all over again."

"They're blowing smoke rings," Toomey laughed. "How are they going to convict you when someone else has admitted to the crime? Believe me, Charlie, the judge will dismiss all charges by ten o'clock."

Toomey explained the evidence that had connected Matthew to both Max McGraw and the dynamite used in the murder. Matthew had sent McGraw a check out of his brokerage account, disguised as a check for cash. Then he had sent a sales order to the local Ucandoit store, transferring funds to the store and letting McGraw pick up the dynamite. "You put that together with the letters he and his father had exchanged over the missing funds and the case is open and shut. Matthew killed his father to avoid exposure. He couldn't put the money back and he had no intention of going to jail."

Tara was in her room, doing her homework, so they had an hour of privacy out on the deck. Toomey helped himself to a bottle of beer, and poured a glass of white wine for Charlie. "You wanted to talk about what comes next," he said as he settled into a chaise by the edge of the pool.

Charlie lounged into the next chaise, setting her wine on the small table that separated them. "I'm beginning to agree with you. It may be too soon for 'next.'"

"No problem," he assured her. "I love you, Charlie, and a few weeks' delay isn't going to change that. I hope you feel the same way about me and that you're not going to change your mind any time soon."

She realized that they *were* talking about what would come next. Toomey was assuming that they would get married after the case was settled and all the pieces had fallen into place. She was exploring the idea herself, and liked the images that flooded her imagination. They could sell Steven's house and his yacht. They could move to a different part of the country, or even a different part of the world. He would find a job, probably in private investigations or corporate security. She might even pick up her own career as a personal trainer. They would disappear from the newspaper headlines and the evening news on television, and enjoy living normal, quiet lives.

Her biggest reservation was not anything about herself but what another marriage might mean to her daughter. Just as Tara's future had been a major factor in her decision to marry Steven Armstrong, it would also be important to any future plans she made. What would the girl think about her jumping from one bed into another? How would she take to still another father? What kind of father would Jerry Toomey make?

She had seen his good side. He believed in her, and was willing to fight for his belief. He had bucked the system and put himself at risk to protect her. He had taken her into his arms and consoled her, proving himself gentle as well as strong. Most important, he had aroused feelings in her that she never had for Steven, or any other man in her adult life for that matter. So, why wouldn't he help create a perfect home for her daughter?

That brought her to his bad side—not evil, but a bit unsavory. He seemed at home in a world of criminals, hookers, hustlers, and snitches. He had no scruples about bending the law, altering evidence, or using strong-arm tactics. His work took him into the city's dark alleys and fetid sewers, and the stench clung to his clothes. It comes with his job, Charlie had often rationalized, even though she knew that most police officers weren't as unrestrained as he was. And that led to the question of what kind of influence he would have on Tara. She already liked Toomey's looks and demeanor. Would she also learn to like his values?

Toomey stood to leave, and then bent down to kiss her on the forehead. He wished her luck in court, and told her he would be following the investigation into Matthew's suicide closely. Charlie walked him to the door and kissed him again. Regardless of his failings, she didn't want him to leave.

She arrived at Troxell's office the next morning, and traveled with him to the courthouse. Along the way, he explained their problem.

The prosecutor could continue presenting his case, but he would soon be talking to a jury that had learned someone else had confessed to the crime. "That isn't the kind of information they're going to be able to keep under cover. It's too incendiary!" Brad told her. "Some of the jurors may have heard about it already."

"Why doesn't he just quit?" Charlie asked. "Why would they want to keep after me?"

"Because the district attorney can't be sure that Matthew actually killed himself. Forensics hasn't had the time to come up with a definite finding." The suicide note was another problem. It was written on a computer, so it was hard to tell if it was genuine. He agreed that the death looked like suicide but warned that it might be several days before a determination was made.

"I think they'll ask for a mistrial. Then they can wait on the forensics report, evaluate the impact, and decide what to do."

Charlie nodded. "So, when it's declared a suicide, then the case against me is over."

"If it isn't suicide, they could bring you to trial again. But if you're acquitted, then no matter what forensics says, they can never try you again. That would be double jeopardy."

Now she understood. "Then we want the trial to continue."

"That's our position, because if the judge tells them to proceed with their case, I think they'll throw in the towel. We have a strong case against Matthew to present, and we may even have his confession. They won't want to risk looking stupid."

The jury had been sent out, and Judge Hoppe brought them all into his chambers, out of earshot of the reporters and gawkers. Frank Slattery presented his case for a mistrial. He was armed with precedents and bar association opinions, and argued that there was no plausible way to keep news of Matthew's death from the jury. "Even if the note turns out to be a fraud, the jury will already be tainted beyond remedy." His solution was to accept the fact that the trial had been compromised, and leave the state with the option of bringing the charges before a new jury.

Brad countered that his defense would present the alternative scenario that Matthew, and not Charlie, had murdered Steven Armstrong. He said that he had ample evidence to prove that scenario no matter how Matthew had died.

"Are you suggesting that this information can be kept from the jury?" Judge Hoppe asked.

"By no means," Brad answered, and smiled at Slattery. "I'll tell them myself if the police confirm that it was a suicide. I'll want the note subpoenaed as evidence." Then he added his preferred solution to the problem. "If the State feels that it's case won't withstand these developments, then I think it should move to acquit. My client has been through more than enough!"

"So, what do you think he'll decide," Charlie asked as soon as they were back in the privacy of Brad's car.

"You never know. The DA won't move for an acquittal until he gets the official cause of death. The judge won't want a mistrial. Maybe he'll adjourn the court and call it back into session when all the evidence is in."

"Oh God! I don't know how long I can keep hanging by my fingertips," Charlie said in exasperation.

"A couple of days would be good for us," Brad answered. "It will give me time to get together with Jerry Toomey and lock up your defense."

Fifty

Tara came up from the garage beaming, and announced that she had been invited to a sleepover. "The whole gang is going to Janet's on Friday night. We're going to barbecue, have a splash party, and then sleep over!" Her voice was up an octave with excitement.

Charlie tried to match her enthusiasm even though her red flags were up everywhere. "Sounds great!" she said. "Are you going to do the cooking or will Janet's father take over the grill?"

"We'll do the grilling," Tara answered, leaving Charlie in the dark as to whether Janet's parents were going to be on the scene. She had learned the art of finding out without appearing to snoop, an essential skill of parenting. But Tara was getting very good at telling her nothing without appearing to be evasive.

"Oh," Charlie began, trying to sound disappointed, "grilling is man's work. You should let the boys do it."

"We can do anything that the boys can do," Tara said, not revealing whether there would be any boys at the party.

"What are you bringing? Hamburgers? Hot dogs? Is there anything you need?"

"We have everything covered," Tara bubbled. "Everything! We'll go shopping on Thursday." So there was no reason for Charlie to phone Janet's mother on the pretense of trying to be helpful.

"Mom?" It was the plaintive "Mom" that usually preceded her daughter's request for something that was out of the question. She gave Tara her full attention.

"Can I get a new bathing suit?"

Charlie knew that she wanted something even skimpier than the modest bikini she was allowed to wear into her own pool. She decided to feign ignorance. "You already have several suits that look great on you. What did you have in mind?"

"A thong," Tara said boldly. Her expression showed pure anxiety.

Charlie kept a straight face even though a smile was hard to suppress. The girl had a lot of filling out still ahead of her. She doubted that there was a thong that would flatter her bottom. "Oh, angel, I'd rather have you wear that around here before you take it on the road."

"But that's what all the girls are wearing," Tara protested with the usual argument.

There are boys at the party, Charlie warned herself. Why else would all the girls be flashing their backsides? "Tara, I don't think that would be the most flattering look for you. Thongs are really for *heavier* women." It was a stroke of genius. Instead of having to tell her daughter that, as of yet, she had no butt to show off, she could imply that the girls who were wearing thongs were really too fat.

"But you said I look great in my bikini," the girl protested.

"Yes, but that covers up a lot more than a thong."

Tara was suddenly downhearted. "Okay, then I suppose I'll just have to wear my old bikini."

Charlie knew she had been played for the fool. All Tara had really wanted was to wear her bikini, and not have to wear her one-piece Speedo. The thong had been nothing more than a stalking horse. "I think that would be better," Charlie said, knowing that she had learned nothing and had already surrendered on her daughter's attire. Parents who thought they were smarter than their kids were the biggest fools of all.

Brad phoned her with the court's decision. The trial was adjourned for three days. When the judge decided what to do with *People v. Charlene Armstrong,* he would know whether Matthew had killed himself and whether the suicide note was genuine.

In the evening, Irv returned from an errand and had Jerry Toomey with him. Toomey settled at the kitchen counter with a bottle of beer and a handful of peanuts. He seemed right at home when Charlie came down from her after-swim shower. She told him that the trial had been postponed, but that she was still the defendant in a murder trial. They weren't out of the woods yet.

"You're worrying too much," he said, squeezing her hand. "Trials go through all sorts of starts and stops. But when there's a confessed murderer, that usually ends it."

"Brad says," she started, but Toomey cut her off.

"It doesn't matter what Brad says. The medical examiner will come in with a ruling of probable suicide. The lab geniuses won't be able to tell who wrote the note, but the assumption will be that it was the deceased. The DA will be happy to close the case."

Charlie didn't know who to believe. Toomey was ready to celebrate. Brad Troxell wasn't sure of anything.

"Did you meet with Brad?" Charlie asked, remembering that Troxell had wanted to see the evidence that Toomey had gathered.

"Yeah, I showed him all my notes. He has everything he needs."

"God, but I wish all this were over."

Toomey smiled. "You're home free. Now we have to begin the rest of our lives." He kissed her gently on the cheek, but then his arm was around her shoulders and he was pressing hard against her mouth. Charlie returned the kiss and was hungry for more.

"Hey, Mom!" Tara had walked in on them, and had the sense to back away from the door. Now she was announcing a new entrance, giving her mother and her boyfriend time to compose themselves. "Oh, hi, Sergeant Toomey!" she bubbled as if nothing had been going on. He nodded, Charlie smiled. "I need help with the math," Tara said. "Do you have a minute?"

Toomey announced that he was just leaving. Charlie protested that she really wasn't very good at math. Tara turned on her heels and said that she would work it out for herself.

"Are you any good at math?" Charlie whispered into his ear as she was letting him out the door.

"I can only count up to thirteen," he answered, and then he kissed her good-bye.

She went to Tara's room, knocked, and waited.

"I figured it out," Tara said, indicating that her mother's help was no longer needed.

Charlie eased the door open a crack. "May I come in?"

Tara was stretched out on the bed, her chin propped up on her hands and elbows, the math book under her nose. Charlie eased in and settled on the edge of the bed, trying to focus all her attention on the book. "What was the problem?" she asked.

"Nothing," Tara answered, pretending to be totally involved in her homework.

Charlie tried again. "I'd like to know. Maybe it's something that I can understand."

Tara relented and explained the algebraic equation, what she hadn't realized, and how she finally got to the answer. Charlie lost her on the first parenthesis. "It's a good thing you weren't counting on me," she said, getting up to leave. "I have no idea what you're talking about."

"Mom?" Her daughter's opening to a serious conversation

stopped her at the door. "Are you . . . and Sergeant Toomey . . . you know?"

Charlie wasn't ready to face the issue yet, but ready or not there was no avoiding the conversation. "Sergeant Toomey has been helping me prove my innocence. He's been a true friend and I'm very grateful to him."

Oh God, what a stupid thing to say. As soon as the words passed her lips she wanted them back. She had made it sound as if she was repaying the man with sack time. First she was sleeping with a man for his money, and now she was doing it for protection. She went back to the bed. "We've been working very closely, and I have become very fond of him." She took a deep breath. "Maybe even in love with him."

"I thought so," Tara answered, and turned nonchalantly back to her algebra.

"How do you feel about that?" Charlie asked, pressing the issue. Predictably, the girl shrugged. The gesture seemed to say that she had no feelings one way or the other.

"Tara, I want you to understand something. I'm not going to make any commitments until you and I have talked everything over. You're number one in my life. Everything else comes after."

There was a long moment of silence before Tara suddenly raised up in her bed and threw her arms around her mother. Then she was crying, pouring out a deep sorrow or an unspeakable joy. Charlie had no idea which it was.

"I'm sorry, Mom. I'm so sorry!"

Charlie pulled back in shock. "Sorry for what? You haven't done anything?"

"I've messed up your whole life," Tara managed beneath gasps for breath. She rolled out of the bed and raced into her bathroom. The slam of the door set the windows rattling.

Charlie sat staring at the door, and listening to the sobbing behind it. Wouldn't the girl ever understand that none of this was her fault?

Fifty-one

Toomey sauntered into police headquarters, bought a cup of coffee from the machine, and stood at his desk while he sorted through his in-basket. He looked up when Rich Lionetti arrived, smiled broadly, and asked, "Hey, Rich, how's your case going?"

"Screw you!" Lionetti answered.

"I told you that you were chasing the wrong suspect," Toomey went on. "Good thing the guy left a note! Otherwise you'd still be trying to convict the lady." Then he got in another good-natured dig. "You were able to read the note, weren't you?"

Lionetti turned to him. "This whole thing stinks. I'm not buying this suicide bull!"

"That's what makes you such a great detective, Rich. The killer writes you a note and tells you that he did it and you're too busy to read it."

"Yeah?" the detective answered as he picked up a folder from the top of his desk. "Why don't you read this, Jerry? It's the medical examiner's report. See if you can spot the missing evidence."

Toomey took the report. "Just pulling your chain, Rich." He settled into his chair with his feet resting on an open drawer, his coffee in one hand and the medical examiner's report in the other. He didn't try to decipher all the medical jargon that the examiner had dictated while he was dissecting Matthew's body. All he needed were the summary conclusions.

Matthew had indeed died almost instantaneously from a single .22-caliber bullet fired into his brain. The entry wound was on the right temple, a small round hole burned on the inside by the heat of the muzzle blast, and contaminated at its edges with gunpowder residue. The lead projectile and the gunpowder matched the properties of bullets found in the cylinder of a pistol on the floor of the car. Ballistics tests established that the projectile had been fired from that pistol. The position of the body and the proximity of the weapon suggested a self-inflicted wound. Matthew had likely raised the gun to his head and fired. As he slumped forward against the wheel his right hand fell limply, probably striking the car's central console and transmission lever. The gun came free and fell to the floor on the passenger side. The report noted that there were no powder residues on the victim's hand, which normally would be expected on the hand of someone who had just fired a gun.

"Seems like a no-brainer to me," Toomey said.

"So, if he shot himself, how come there's no gunpowder on his hand?" Lionetti demanded."

Toomey chuckled. "C'mon Rich, the gun was a .22-caliber. What's it got, a quarter of an ounce of powder? It's not as if he fired a magnum."

Lionetti spun in his chair. "You're really knocking yourself out to get this lady off. What is she, your squeeze?"

"I don't like sending pretty ladies to prison. It makes it harder to take them out to dinner." He went back to the report and read the forensics section.

When the bullet had struck, there had been an instant spattering of blood. Then bleeding stopped when the heart stopped. There were droplets of blood on the windshield, on the dashboard, the roof fabric, the seat, and the central console, consistent with the assumed position of the victim.

There were, however, no spatter marks on the right sleeve of the suit.

Further investigation showed an absence of spatter marks on the passenger seat. Nor were there any marks on the note that was found on the passenger seat. Judging by the distance of the blood on the dashboard from the assumed position of the victim, similar spatters should have appeared on the passenger seat.

Toomey sat up straight. "Rich, I think you're on to something." He swung his feet down and walked to Lionetti's desk. "What do you think. Someone else in the car?"

"That would explain it. Somebody sitting next to the victim put a gun to his head and shot him. Then he wiped his prints and pressed on Matthew's prints. He dropped the gun on the floor, got out, put the note on the seat, locked the door and left."

"You said 'he.' Do you think it was a man?"

"No," Lionetti answered. "But if I said 'she,' I figured you'd attack me from behind."

Toomey laughed. "Mrs. Armstrong isn't the lady I'm thinking about."

Brad Troxell also had a copy of the police report when he arrived at Charlie's doorstep, wearing khaki slacks and a colorful sports shirt. "Yeah, there's a bit of a problem," he said when he recognized her anxiety at his unscheduled appearance. He agreed to a diet cola and went with her out onto the deck.

"Okay, what's wrong?" she asked as soon as they were settled.

"The police have some questions about Matthew's death," he told her. "They've decided that it wasn't a suicide."

Her disappointment registered, and he noted her reaction. Then he opened his briefcase and took her through the medical examiner's report and the findings of the police forensic lab. Charlie listened carefully, having Brad repeat some of the conclusions. When he finished, he cautioned her not to let herself get down. "We still have the man with a gun to his head, and we still have a suicide note. The odds are that the judge won't want all of the details of the forensics team cluttering up his trial. My guess is . . ."

"He couldn't have killed himself," Charlie said, interrupting the lawyer. Brad raised his eyes. What in the report, he wondered, had made her so positive that the suicide was a fake?

"Matthew was left-handed," she said.

"What?" Brad didn't understand the comment.

"Matthew was left-handed," she repeated. "I remember noticing that he signed the wedding documents with his left hand. He had his arm hooked over the top of the paper so that he wouldn't smear the ink. And at the dinner, he insisted on sitting at the end of the table where he wouldn't be bumping elbows with anyone."

"So, he was left-handed," Brad said, beginning to understand the point that she was making.

"A left-handed person would have a hard time shooting himself on the right side of his head," she said. "It doesn't make sense."

"You're right," Brad decided. He tapped the report that lay in front of him. "Nobody asked whether he was right-handed or left-handed. I never gave it a thought." He stood, stepped to the edge of the pool and looked down at the bottom through the crystal clear water. "But that's not the only thing that doesn't make sense. Like where did Matthew get the gun?"

Now Charlie was the one missing the point. "Where?" she wondered.

"He flew down yesterday on a commercial flight. You can't bring a gun aboard an airplane. So he didn't bring it from Boston."

"Maybe he got it here. In Florida, you can buy guns in a barber shop."

"But you can't at his hotel. Matthew went from the airport to his hotel and from the hotel to the courthouse. Then he and Trish went back to the hotel. They had dinner and a drink at the bar and then they both went up to bed. It was after ten, and it would certainly be a problem for an out-of-towner to find a gun for sale at that hour."

"When did he go out?"

Brad shook his head. "No one knows. His car was in an open lot so he didn't have to check it out. He had no calls. No one at the desk saw him leave. He went up to bed at ten o'-clock and turned up dead in a beach parking lot seven hours later."

"Then he was murdered," Charlie concluded. Her face fell into her hands. "Dear God, what else can happen?"

Brad returned to the table. "Charlie, can you account for every second the night of the murder? Every second between ten o'clock and six the next morning?"

Her eyes flashed. "Jesus, do you think . . . ?"

"I don't think anything. I'm just looking at every crazy theory the prosecutor can come up with. When he announces to the judge that his witness was murdered, I don't want him hinting that you were probably involved."

She took a deep breath. "Yes, I can. There's a security guard who sleeps at my house. He has the keys to the only working car. And there are at least two reporters sitting at my gate. The only way I could get out would be by swimming."

"What about your checking account? Have you paid any-one a substantial sum of money? Or made out a big check to cash?"

"Brad, you know better. I can't write any checks without going through Steven's lawyers. Isn't that how your bills get paid?"

"I know," he agreed. "But I need you to go through every-thing you do. Is there any way that even by the furthest stretch of imagination, they can claim you were able to cause Matthew's death?"

She was ready to scream. How could he be pounding her with these questions when he already knew that Matthew had been defrauding his company? When he knew that Matthew had paid McGraw and arranged for the delivery of the dynamite? "Didn't Sergeant Toomey answer all these questions?" she demanded. "I didn't arrange for the explo-sives. Matthew did!"

He chose his words carefully. "Toomey's evidence has some problems. Some of his documentation can't be substantiated."

"What?" Charlie was wide-eyed, and beginning to feel cold despite the heat. "It isn't true?"

"Charlie, the letters you gave me between Matthew and his father. Tell me again exactly how you found them?"

"In Steven's desk. I just happened to be looking through some files. . . ."

"What files?"

She pounded a hand on the table. "I don't remember what files. Why are you asking me this?"

"Because all the letters were written on paper from the same ream. And that shouldn't be if Steven was writing from down here and Matthew was writing from Boston. It looks as if the same person was writing both ends of the correspondence."

Charlie's hands gripped the edge of the table. She had never mentioned her suspicion that Trish might have planted the letters when she came to get her paintings. And she certainly wasn't going to admit that Toomey had found the locked box and told her to open it.

"Did you really just find those letters?" Brad asked.

She took a deep breath. "Yes, but I don't think they were there when Steven died." She then spilled out the story of Trish's request to get back her paintings. Brad remembered advising her that she didn't have to surrender them because they were an asset of Steven's estate. "I'd been through that part of his desk before, and I don't see how I could have missed a metal safety box. I don't think they were there before Trish came, but they were there after she left." She was careful not to mention that it was Toomey who had actually found them. She knew that his reason for being at her house was to check some records that he had stolen. She didn't want to implicate him in a burglary.

"So Trish might have planted the evidence against Matthew," Brad mumbled to himself. "And Trish was the last person to be with Matthew before he disappeared from the

hotel." He looked at Charlie. "Trish certainly could have gotten him out of the hotel without a phone call. They could
have agreed to a meeting over dinner, or she could have simply knocked on his door."

"But why?" Charlie asked.

"I suppose there could be a lot of trouble between them.
Sibling rivalries are usually kept within the family. Or maybe
she wanted to protect her money. That would get us back to
her planting the bomb in order to kill you."

"But why plant evidence against Matthew? And why kill
him?"

Brad threw up his hands. "I don't know. Maybe Matthew
knew about her. Or maybe they were in on it together. All
we're doing is speculating on the possibilities." He paused to
think, and then said, "But there's the same problem with
Trish being the killer that I have with Matthew committing
suicide. Where did she get the gun? She didn't bring it down
from New York, and she couldn't have gotten in at the courthouse or the hotel."

She went to the kitchen, and brought back a bottle of wine
and two glasses. Brad pushed his soft drink aside and took
the corkscrew. "None of this makes a lot of sense," he said
while pouring the wine. "There has to be something that
we're all missing." He raised his glass and clinked it against
hers. Then they both fell into a moody silence that he finally
broke with a question.

"Do you have complete confidence in Jerry Toomey?"

"Of course," she answered without hesitation. "He believed me right from the start, when that boat tried to run
over me. He has always been there for me. Wasn't he the one
who put me in touch with you?"

He nodded. "I have a lot of respect for him. But he does
push the envelope. I wouldn't put it past him to plant evidence if he thought he was helping a friend, or putting away a
criminal."

Charlie knew where he was leading. "Jerry was in Boston
that night trying to find hard evidence that Matthew author-

ized the explosives. Irv didn't pick him up at the airport until yesterday afternoon."

"I know he didn't kill anyone," Brad said. "But I'd like to know that all the evidence he came up with is genuine. He wouldn't be helping us by embellishing it. Like the Ucandoit transactions he claims prove that the dynamite went to Max McGraw. The document says it went to McGraw Construction, a very legitimate company that never heard of Max McGraw. It was authorized by the company's sales department, but that doesn't prove that Matthew was behind it."

"You think he's making it up?" Charlie challenged.

"I think he's grasping at straws, which makes him a great friend but also a very bad witness. If we have to take this stuff into court, I don't think it will stand up."

She was on a roller coaster, rising to heights of optimism and then hurtling down into pits of despair. Only hours ago, she and Toomey had been celebrating her victory, and wondering when they should begin planning their future. Now she knew that Matthew had not taken his own life, that his confession was probably bogus and the defense she had been counting on wouldn't hold up in court. Once again, prison was staring her in the face.

Fifty-two

"T rish?" Toomey said in disbelief when Brad Troxell suggested that she was his best candidate for Matthew Armstrong's murder. "Jesus, I have to admit that she never showed up on my radar. She's a flake, for God's sake."

Brad had asked Toomey to his office to discuss the gaps in the evidence, and Toomey had admitted that his search might have been overzealous. "The letters pointed to Matthew," the detective said, "so I was looking at Matthew. But if the letters are phony, then I should have been looking at all of the Armstrongs."

Toomey admitted that he had acted on a tip that Matthew was in financial trouble. His assumption had been that Matthew didn't want Charlie dabbling in the family fortune and had hired McGraw to kill her. "There was a cashier's check drawn on a Boston bank, for God's sake. Who else in Boston would be paying off McGraw?" So he had focused on Matthew's activities, and maybe made assumptions that weren't justified. But Trish? Who could have figured on Trish?

"So what are we going to do, counselor?" he asked after he had admitted his failings.

"Try to get her acquitted right now, before the trial goes any further. Or, if we have to go back into court, do my damnedest to confuse the jurors. I think the best thing you can do will be to testify about Max McGraw. We can't bring up the police lineup, but you can certainly share the information you gathered, confirm his attack on Charlie, and get in your telephone call that kept her from taking the boat out. Then we'll go back to the line that she was the intended victim."

"You think it will work?" Toomey wondered.

"It's not as good as a suicide note, so just pray that we don't have to go back to trial."

Toomey got up to take his leave. "In the meantime, I'll see what I can find out about Trish."

"Jerry . . ." the lawyer warned.

"I'll be careful. I won't bring you anything that hasn't been checked out."

Brad had already been doing his own checking. He had different people call each of Trish's galleries, and request a quote on a painting. He didn't care about the prices, but he did want the paper they were printed on. If it matched the letters between Steven and his son, or the paper of the suicide note, Trish's guilt would become more than a theory.

Toomey took a direct approach. He knew that in Florida, anyone could get a gun at any time, and began canvassing contacts in the illegal gun trade. When he called back to Brad Troxell he said that "he was up to his knees in assault weapons." But, so far, he had not found any .22-caliber weapons that had been in the trade during the past few weeks. His next stop was going to be at the hotel where "the concierge can get you anything from a woman to an elephant." Toomey reasoned that no gun could have been delivered to the hotel without the man knowing about it and taking his cut.

Charlie was trying to live her life, but all she was doing was going through the motions. The press had reassembled at her front gate hoping for a reaction to Matthew's suicide and, during the last few hours, to rumors of his murder. She couldn't leave the house. Irv was still lurking downstairs for her protection, now primarily from Trish or her agents.

Maria was underfoot everywhere, dusting things she had dusted yesterday, and rearranging the things in the freezer. Judge Hoppe hadn't yet decided when or whether her trial would resume.

Charlie had showered twice, sunned for a while, and gone for a swim. She had done a full physical workout, running uphill on the treadmill and doing enough strokes on the rowing machine to reach Cuba. All the while she had been thinking that someone had to come to the house, or call on the telephone. She needed to know if a killer had been identified. Was she free, or still in terrible jeopardy?

She was worried over what she should say to her daughter. Tara seemed to have come full circle, first blaming herself for all the family troubles, then turning on her mother, and now back to blaming herself. There were valid reasons for her confusion. The girl had been uprooted from one home and thrown into a totally different culture. She had adapted to the presence of a new father. She had been a bystander to not just one, but two violent deaths. Her mother had gone from defendant to acquittal, and now once again back to being the accused. And finally, a new man had been introduced into her life—a policeman who seemed to be working for her mother's favors. How could Charlie help her daughter make sense out of the past few months when they made no sense to her? It was all a terrible nightmare, except neither of them was waking up. They seemed doomed to a path of endless turmoil where every crossroads led to new dangers.

Hang on, baby! We'll get through this, she kept rehearsing. But she couldn't think of the next line. What would she say when Tara asked her how?

Charlie jumped when her phone rang, and the magazine that had been lying idly on her lap toppled to the floor. She was hoping that it would be Toomey, and she was disappointed when she heard Brad's voice.

"I just left the judge," he said. "He heard arguments from the prosecutor and me, and we're to be in court tomorrow morning."

There was a lump in her throat. "How does it look?" she managed.

"It looks confusing, but we'll know tomorrow."

Charlie was biting on her knuckles. "I'm not sure I'm going to last until morning."

"Sure you will! Just get a good night's sleep."

"Fat chance!" she said. She was living a nightmare while she was awake. She was afraid what would happen if she let herself fall asleep.

Tara was in good spirits when she came home, bubbling with news of the sleepover party. Charlie couldn't believe the range of change in her daughter's emotions. The night before she had worried that the girl might cry herself to death. Now it was more likely that she would hit her head on the ceiling.

Charlie let her exude over all the preparations and details. The girls had gone past hamburgers and franks, and were planning to cook lamb chops. And someone knew where they could get a wedding cake for desert. "Does soda go with lamb chops?" she asked innocently, hoping to trap Tara into admitting there would be alcohol. "No," Tara answered without missing a beat, "we're thinking of that bubbly French mineral water."

She knew she should be monitoring the details of the party more carefully. But at the moment, Charlie was too busy worrying how the girl would survive if she had to do her mothering from a prison cell.

Fifty-three

They came into the courtroom and took their seats forward of the rail. There were already reporters and the usual army of onlookers in the gallery. Charlie couldn't begin to guess whether they were on her side or whether they were like racing fans waiting to see a flaming crash. But there was no jury, so she wasn't yet back on trial.

Judge Hoppe took his place behind the bench and then stood briefly to rearrange his judicial robes. Then he began, "We have two motions before the court." During the next ten minutes he summarized the prosecutor's motion requesting a mistrial. Jurors had, indeed, been exposed to evidence other than that properly presented in the court. It was likely that some had heard of the suicide and the note that Matthew had left behind, and were assuming that Charlie must be innocent. The State wanted the option to begin all over again with a new jury after the details of Matthew's death were determined.

He took less time summarizing Troxell's argument. Charlene Armstrong had been indicted, arraigned, and brought to trial. She was entitled to her day in court and the verdict of a jury of her peers. If the prosecutor felt his case had been damaged, then he could press ahead or move to acquit. A mistrial, Brad wrote, would subject her to double jeopardy.

The judge ruled for the defendant. He said that he could eliminate peripheral issues in his charge to the jury. The State could proceed with its prosecution or acquit the defendant.

Charlie and Brad were deathly still as they watched the district attorney's team huddle at their table. How strong was their case? Could the jurors really put aside the thought that someone else had apparently confessed? Could they clean up their star witness, the gun dealer, to make him credible to the jury? Could he withstand the searing cross-examination that would point out that if he wasn't in court as a State's witness he would probably be in jail? Trish and Gary were still left to testify to their father's fears, but they would quickly open the way for Brad to bring up Matthew in cross-examination. And the gym manager who remembered Charlie asking about explosives hadn't actually told her how to assemble an explosive device.

Brad had already weakened the State's forensic evidence. Certainly, they could prove how Steven Armstrong had died, but they couldn't link the explosion to his wife. The only bridge they been able to build was destroyed when Brad read the ingredients of the plant food.

Their case was circumstantial at best, and weak even at that. As sure as they were that Charlie had killed her husband, it didn't seem they had the evidence to convince twelve jurors. Their best hope was a hung jury, which would have the same effect as a declaration of mistrial, but they would expose their entire case in the process.

If it had turned out that Matthew had indeed committed suicide and left a note behind, then they would have been forced to drop the case. But now, might they not have to show that the two crimes were somehow related?

"Your Honor," Brad said after several minutes, "surely the State had time to decide what it would do if you denied the petition for a mistrial. Do we really have to subject everyone to further delay?"

"I quite agree with you," Judge Hoppe said. He turned to the prosecution table. "Mr. Slattery, may we have your decision?"

Slattery rose. "Your Honor, in view of these recent developments, we would like to request an adjournment, with the trial to resume one week from today."

Brad exploded out of his chair. "Your Honor, surely the State shouldn't be allowed to keep my client in jeopardy until some future date when the tea leaves favor their case. Mrs. Armstrong's life has been on hold since . . ."

The judge cut him off. "Of course not, Mr. Troxell." He pointed his gavel at Slattery. "A postponement is not an option, Mr. Slattery. What's your next best offer?"

Again they dove into a conference at the DA's table.

"Your Honor," Brad protested again, but Judge Hoppe motioned him to hold his argument. "Mr. Slattery," he said, "I won't wait any longer."

Slattery stood again. "Your Honor, the State moves to acquit the defendant of all charges."

Brad exhaled and nearly slid under the table. Charlie burst into tears. Judge Hoppe banged his gavel and announced that the defendant had been acquitted. "Mrs. Armstrong, you are free to go. You may reclaim the bail you have posted, and I apologize for the indignities you have been subjected to."

He banged the gavel again. "Case dismissed!"

The reporters rushed from the courtroom. The guests in the gallery broke into clusters of those pleased that Charlie had been freed and those who thought she had just gotten away with murder. Slattery walked over and shook Brad Troxell's hand. He never made eye contact with Charlie.

The reporters were waiting outside the door in a huge semicircle. There were three television cameras focused on the center. Charlie recoiled as soon as she saw the gathering. "Is there another way?" she asked Brad.

"For heaven's sake, don't rob me of my moment of glory," he said. "Do you have any idea how much fifteen seconds of airtime is worth to me?"

For the first time today, Charlie smiled. "Okay, do your thing."

They stepped before the cameras and stared into the lights. Brad rose to the opportunity. "Mrs. Armstrong is very pleased with the district attorney's decision to acquit her of all charges. It has been a long ordeal for her, but she kept her faith in the American justice system. For my part, as I studied all the evidence, I knew that she wasn't guilty of anything. I, too, am delighted with the outcome."

The press shouted questions at Charlie, but Brad waved them away and, along with a court security officer, guided her to the elevator. Minutes later, they were in Brad's Beetle, driving toward her house.

"I don't know how I can ever thank you," Charlie began. She was only now beginning to appreciate his calm, confident demeanor, and his courtroom skills. She was free not because of a jury's decision, but because of his ability to adapt to neck-snapping changes in direction, and use the court to her benefit.

"Wait until you see my bill," he cautioned. Then he added, "Do you know how much more I would have made if they had decided to proceed with the trial?"

Charlie laughed, and then leaned over and kissed his cheek.

When they reached the house, Maria was already celebrating. "I saw it on the television," she said. "I was so happy that I cried. Just wait until Tara finds out. She'll be crazy!"

That would have been Charlie's fondest wish, to have her daughter rush in and throw her arms around her and cry for joy on her shoulder. But most likely the girl would say something trivial, like "cool." Or maybe she'd just shrug. After all, her mind was on tomorrow's sleepover.

Brad accepted a glass of wine, and picked at the hors d'oeuvres that Maria had prepared. Charlie began to tease him over his impromptu statement to the press. "I had full confidence in the American justice system," she said mimicking him. Then she told him, "I was afraid I was going to be railroaded into life in prison."

"People like to believe that the justice system works," Brad said. "They'll take more kindly to you than if I had said, 'My client is thrilled that she beat the rap!' If you trusted the justice system, then you must be innocent. If you beat the rap, then you're a killer on the loose."

"You know, we really shouldn't be celebrating," Charlie said. "The fact is that someone killed Steven. And probably the same person killed Matthew."

"Not your problem," Brad said. "We pay police to solve those problems."

"But it is my problem," Charlie insisted. "Some people tried to kill me. They were still determined to kill me when they blew up the boat I was supposed to be in. And then they killed Matthew and tried to hang Steven's murder on him. Whoever it is, is still out there, and I may still be the target."

"I think we'll know who it is when the paper samples come in," Brad said. "Trish is the logical candidate. Although, when I interviewed her, she struck me as something of a joke. I would have been amazed if she could change a light bulb much less mastermind a bombing."

"Who then?" Charlie wondered. "Gary was never near the house after Steven's funeral. He couldn't have planted those letters."

Irv returned from his school pickup, and Tara came up the stairs from the garage. She was talking about her sleepover before she came into the room, excited because they had collected an "awesome" group of CDs for their party. "This is going to be the best . . ."

She stopped short when she saw Brad in the dining room, together with her mother and Maria, and a large platter of canapés. "Oh, I'm sorry. I didn't know you had company."

Charlie leaped up to greet her. "It's over, baby! They dropped all the charges against me."

"Oh yeah, I heard," Tara said. "It was on the radio."

Fifty-four

Brad Troxell was about to take his leave when Jerry Toomey pulled into the driveway and rang the front doorbell. He, too, was in high spirits and presented Charlie with a dozen roses and handed a bottle of champagne to Maria so that she could pour. "I heard about it when I got back to the office," he said. "Acquitted on all counts!"

He spotted Brad, went to him and put an arm over his shoulder. "You're the best. When Charlie needed a criminal lawyer, you're the first one that came to mind."

Brad acknowledged the praise with a modest nod in Charlie's direction. It was his opportunity to say something flattering about Toomey, but the best he could manage was, "Thank you for the referral."

Charlie returned with the roses in a vase and gave Toomey a thank-you kiss on the cheek. But despite her complete exoneration, she wasn't in a mood to celebrate. "There's still a killer out there," she reminded the detective. "Someone killed both Steven and Matthew, and came close to killing me."

"We'll find him . . . or her," Toomey said. "It's not your problem."

Brad jumped into the conversation. "Exactly what I've been telling her. She's been acquitted. She has no responsibility for anyone's death. There's no reason why she should stay involved."

"Dead on!" Toomey agreed. "Although I do have some information on Trish. She pulled fifty thousand dollars out of her business account and took it as a cashier's check. She's paying someone for something."

Brad stuck his fingers in his ears. "Don't tell me. She may be my next client."

Maria brought in the open bottle of champagne, and half a dozen glasses. There were three of them, herself, and Irv, who was watching the front door. She thought that on such a special occasion that perhaps Tara would be allowed a sip or two. But she didn't return to a party atmosphere. Charlie, Jerry, and Brad all seemed deadly serious.

"Why would Trish do such a thing?" Charlie was in the process of asking.

Maria set the glasses before them but no one seemed to notice.

"Why would she try to implicate Matthew with forged letters?" Brad said, answering a question with a question. "There must have been something going on inside the family."

Maria poured the champagne and began passing the glasses. The moment cried for someone to make a toast. Charlie lifted a glass and gestured toward Brad. "Here's to my attorney who never doubted that we would win." Maria screamed with delight, yelled a blessing in Spanish, and started to drink. Toomey added to the toast. "You're the best!" And he drank to Brad Troxell.

Brad sipped but then set down his glass. "I've never been as happy with an acquittal," he said, "although I have no idea what actually happened. I don't know who tried to run Charlie down with a Jet Ski. Or who wanted to plant a bomb in Steven's boat. Or who would kill Matthew and try to make it look like a suicide. I know who it wasn't." He nodded toward Charlie. "My client doesn't know any more than I do."

"Maybe I should keep Irv around a little longer," Toomey offered.

"No!" Charlie said instantly. "I've spent enough time under house arrest. I want everything to get back to normal."

"It's not a bad idea," Brad told her, siding with Toomey. "Like you were saying, there's still someone out there."

But she was adamant. Having Irv inside her house was as scary as the thought of a killer outside the house. In the morning, she was going to try to get her old Toyota started, and then drive Tara to school just as she had done in her old life. In fact, she would begin making arrangements to move back into the condo that she and Tara had shared.

Brad glanced at his watch and decided it was time to leave. Charlie walked him to the door and once again expressed her gratitude. Once again he reminded her to hold her praise until after she had reviewed his bill. They laughed together and then he closed the door behind him.

Toomey finished his champagne, mumbled that he ought to be leaving too, but then let Maria coax him into one more glass before she carried the tray out into the kitchen. He sat on the sofa with Charlie close beside him.

"I've decided to quit the police," he said casually, but his tone suggested that his decision was firm. "I'm not even going to pursue the leads on Trish. Let someone else find out why she withdrew all that money. I'm sick of peeking through keyholes."

"What are you going to do?" she asked.

"I don't know. Maybe get a boat and go fishing. Or take up scuba diving. I've been living down here for fifteen years, and I've never gone out on the water. So maybe I should learn to sail and just bum around the Caribbean for a while. And, of course, I'm hoping to spend a lot more time with you."

"Not if you're bumming around on a sailboat," Charlie laughed. "I'm shore-bound. I have a daughter to raise."

"She'll be off to college in a few years. Maybe to a young ladies' boarding school before that. Tara won't be hanging around much longer. Then there won't be anything to tie us down."

"I'm not tied down!" she protested. First Tara had cried that she was ruining Charlie's life. Now Toomey was suggesting that the girl was some sort of anchor keeping her from running free. And what was this about a "young ladies' boarding school"? Did he think she was going to push Tara out so that he could move in?

"Bad choice of words," he apologized. "What I mean is that your daughter is pretty well raised. That part of your life is coming to a close. But the truth is that I don't give a damn whether I'm on a boat at sea or in a grass hut on the beach. What I need is for you and me to be together."

That was what Charlie needed, too. Someone who would love her. Someone she could love. But also someone who would love and protect her daughter, and be there to walk her down the aisle when the time came. She would need to spend a great deal of time with Tara and find out exactly how the girl felt about another new man in the family. Toomey would have to spend time with them so that Tara would know whether she liked him or not. As he had told her, there was no need to rush into anything. Just give it time, and see how it all worked out.

He kissed her at the doorway not with the quick peck that Brad had exchanged with her but rather with an intimate kiss filled with longing. "Can we meet at the condo?" he asked. "Maybe tomorrow, while your kid is off at her splash party."

Charlie wanted to say yes, but she also wanted to be at hand if something should go wrong at the party. Tara had always known that if ever she was uncomfortable with what her friends were doing, she could call home to be rescued. "I'd like that. But let me think about it. I hate leaving her without a backup plan."

She helped Maria clean up from their makeshift party, went to her room, and changed into her bathing suit. A minute later, she was swimming laps and making racing turns, letting out an explosion of energy that served to release her pent-up emotions. For the first time since the Jet Ski had raced over her, she felt something of her old self. She showered, and took great delight in dressing in her gym shorts and tank top. Now what she needed was momentary escape from her prison.

Charlie went down to the garage, climbed into her old car, and turned the key. It ground for a few seconds, went through a coughing fit, and then found its legs. Irv rushed down at the sound of the engine and came straight to her window. "Where are you going? I can take you."

"No, thanks! I want to begin driving past the reporters on my own. Maybe I can bore them into going away." Then she asked. "Can you get the door?" He hesitated, but only for an instant. Then he pushed the switch to the automatic door opener, and the panels began rolling up over her head. She eased the car out, thinking that she would like to give Irv a huge bonus when Toomey called him off the job. She was uneasy with him, but there was no doubt that he had taken care of Tara and her.

There was only one pool reporter at the gate and no television cameras in sight. She was a young girl probably just out of college, and made sure to get out of the way while flagging the car down. Her expression went to amazement when Charlie stopped and rolled down her window.

"Mrs. Armstrong, do you have any thoughts on your acquittal?"

"I couldn't be happier. This has been a long, dark passage for me, frightening every step of the way. Thank God it's over."

Fifty-five

She was up early the next morning to have breakfast with Tara and then drive her to school. The girl was shocked when Charlie climbed into the old car, but then smiled when she understood the significance. Her mother was telling her that things were back to normal. The experiment with high living was over. They were going back to the tinny-sounding radio.

"Are we going to move back to the condo?" she asked as they drove through the gate. For the first time in as long as she could remember, there weren't reporters pressing against the glass. She was grinning from ear to ear.

"You should think about that," Charlie said. "This is a great house, and we can get a new boat to put at the dock. You might decide that staying here is a lot better."

"Do you want to stay?" Tara asked.

"I don't much care. All I really want to do is get back to work."

"I'll think about," the girl said, sounding much more reasonable than she usually was.

Charlie thought about Toomey all the way home. Maybe

they could meet at the condo. She didn't want to seem indifferent to all the help he had given her. And, in truth, she was
longing to be with him. The sensible thing for her was not to
rush into anything. But she couldn't deal with the thought of
keeping him away until Tara was no longer under her roof.
Yet, at the same time, she knew that a long-running affair
wouldn't be fair to any of them.

Irv was gone when she returned home. Maria said that he
had gotten a call from Detective Toomey, said good-bye, and
left with the sedan that had been their passage through the
lines of reporters. Charlie resolved to get his address and
send him a check. Tara's suspicion that he was ogling her in
the rear-view mirror was probably more adolescent fantasy
than fact. His constant glances in the mirror were probably a
precaution against being followed.

It was late morning when Toomey called. He had just
talked to his superiors and tried to turn in his badge. They
had urged him to take a month's leave of absence before
making his final decision. "Why not?" he said to Charlie. "I
have nothing to lose even though I'm not going to change my
mind." Then he asked her about meeting at the condo.

"I have to pick up Tara in a couple of hours," she said.

"They could be a great couple of hours," Toomey countered.

"I know. I'd like to see you. But I don't want to be watching the clock."

They both laughed. Charlie volunteered, "Let me call you
later, after she's off to her party. Maybe you could come over
here so I'll be home if she calls."

"I'll pack my toothbrush," Toomey said. They laughed
again.

Steven's lawyers telephoned her just as she was about to
leave to fetch her daughter. With her acquittal, there was no
longer a barrier to her receiving her legal share of Steven's
estate. The will was another matter because of "the circumstances of Matthew's death, which have yet to be resolved."
But even with the uncertainty of the final accounting they
were talking about a great deal of money. Perhaps she would
want legal representation at the signing.

She thought of Brad, even though this wasn't his specialty. She knew she could trust him to look after her interests. It dawned on her just how substantial those interests were. They would be transferring millions of dollars, much more than she would want to deposit in her savings account. Rather than being the wife of a very wealthy man, Charlie had suddenly become a very wealthy woman in her own right. She had no idea how she should handle such assets.

On the way home from school, Tara talked incessantly about the party. The girls had gone back to hamburgers and hot dogs, and stocked up on soda. She introduced a bit of new information in the same happy banter. Yes, indeed, there would be boys at the cookout and the swimming party, but they would of course be leaving before the sleepover. Charlie pretended not to notice the subtle change in the evening's agenda, even though images of an orgy flooded into her head. It would take more than Janet's parents to chaperone all those kids. They would have their hands full saving their home from pillage and destruction. She suddenly wished that Irv were still around to protect Tara.

"I'll be home tonight in case you need me," Charlie announced. "If things are getting out of hand, I can be over there in a minute."

"Mom, it's just a class party. Everything will be cool."

Charlie wasn't reassured. Even in her day, teenage boys had mastered the art of smuggling beer past chaperones. Some of them grew their own marijuana. How much more skilled must they be today? She could picture a pool deck scattered with cigarette stubs and empty beer cans floating in the water. There were bowls of pills instead of peanuts.

"Just remember. I'm only a phone call away. All you have to do is ask if my knee is better." That was the code word they had agreed upon to keep Tara from the embarrassment of calling home for help. If she asked after Charlie's knee, it meant *come and get me*. In response, Charlie would tell her that her favorite aunt had just been rushed to the hospital and that she would pick the girl up on her way to the emergency room. So far, they had never had to use the ploy. But tonight's party seemed a promising candidate.

She helped her daughter pack. It was certainly innocent enough. Her bathing suit, a pair of simple pajamas, her cosmetics, comb and toothbrush. Tara added her latest editions of *Teen* and *In Style*. So far, there was no smoking pistol.

She was reassured when she drove her to Janet's house. Two parents were at home and neither of the boys she saw on the doorstep looked dangerous. If anything, they seemed frightened. She remembered Toomey's comment when she was driving back home. Her work in raising her daughter was pretty much completed. Sooner or later, the girl was going to have to make her own choices.

When she returned, her house was empty. No reporters, no bodyguard, not even her housekeeper. But she was still anxious over what she should say to Jerry. This wasn't a good night to let herself be distracted. And there was always the possibility that should Tara decide to come home, someone would drive her. *It's not the right time,* she told herself, and she picked up the cell phone that was her private link to Toomey. He picked up instantly, showing that he had been waiting for her call.

"Jerry," she began, "I'm a nervous wreck. I don't think this is a good time . . ."

"I understand," she thought she heard him say. But he was garbled by that same repetitive interference she had heard before.

"I'm sorry. There must be something wrong with this phone. I'm hearing that noise again. It's like blasts of static on a regular beat."

"It's not your phone," he told her. "I think there's a short in my air conditioner. I keep getting flickers on my television . . ."

"No, it can't be that," Charlie said. "The last time I heard it you weren't at your house. Remember, you were in . . ."

She saved herself before she blurted out "Boston." Because if it was his air conditioner that she was hearing then he had been home when he said he was in Boston.

He missed a beat before he answered. "Yeah, you're right.

It must be something else," he said. But his tone wasn't at all confident. It was almost as if he was asking a question. She guessed that he, too, had realized his slip.

"So, about tonight," he started, the annoying static still obscuring his words.

"I really can't until I know Tara is safe," she said, and then began babbling about her concerns over the party. "I know it's silly, but I'm scared to death."

"Charlie, we have to talk."

"I know. I'll call you tomorrow."

"No, tonight, before you get any silly ideas. I'm coming over now."

"Please, Jerry. I'm just not ready."

"I'll be there in twenty minutes," he said.

She knew why he was coming. He had stumbled and gotten caught in his own lie. He wanted to explain himself right away before she had time to think everything through and decide what other lies he might have told her.

Fifty-six

It was possible that all he had done was cover for evidence that he had planted, pretending to be investigating Matthew when he was really manufacturing the details of Matthew's crime. She thought of the letters that had mysteriously appeared in Steven's desk. Charlie remembered that she hadn't found them there. Toomey had said he had found them and given her the lockbox to open. He was the one who had planted the letters. That's where Brad would find his matching ream of paper—in Jerry's printer.

But that might not be so. How would he have brought the box into the house? She remembered that the only thing he had been carrying was that briefcase full of worksheets. He had stolen them from Matthew's accountant, and brought them to compare with Steven's records. She remembered the records scattered all over the desk. She had put them away herself. The briefcase had been—where? Under the desk. Toomey had touched it with his toe when he told her what was in it.

But he had never opened it. She had never seen any of the papers it supposedly contained. Charlie remembered its size, and then the size of the lockbox. She gasped. Of course! There were no papers. He had used the briefcase to carry in the lockbox. Then he had given her the box to open so that she would be the one conveying the letters to the court. He wouldn't be at all involved with the evidence against Matthew.

All he had been doing was trying to set her free. Toomey knew that she had been attacked, and knew that she was the victim and not the perpetrator. His motive had been to give Brad Troxell enough evidence to create doubt in the minds of the jurors. But to save her, he had violated every rule of his profession. He had framed someone else with evidence he had fabricated. What if he had lied about being in Boston? That was part of a plan to save her from charges that were equally bogus. The State had dealt with circumstance and innuendo. What Toomey had done was balance the odds.

Did she want to convict him by exposing the fraud? If the letters between Steven and Matthew had come from his printer, then he would be obstructing justice and fabricating evidence. Wasn't it better to just leave it alone? All Toomey had done was set her free, and that was right because she had never killed anyone. Not Steven, and not his son.

She should forget the letters, Charlie decided. There was the suicide note, and Matthew's suicide would slam the case shut. Whether he and his father were arguing . . .

Her thoughts screeched to an abrupt halt. *The suicide note!* What if the suicide note had also come from Toomey's printer? Then . . . dear God . . . then Toomey would have been the last one to see Matthew. Then he would have killed Matthew in cold blood. The spatters of gore from Matthew's brain would have been on Jerry's shirt. He would have been the one who left the note and locked the door behind him.

Why? To save her? Would Toomey have put a bullet into Matthew just to close the loop of the fraud he had built so meticulously? The letters gave Matthew a motive for killing his father. The suicide was his act of contrition. She was free, and there was no one to contest the evidence. Jesus, he murdered Matthew, she thought. And at that instant she knew that she had to run from Jerry Toomey.

Charlie raced down to the garage and backed out her old car. She was terrified that just as she reached the gate, Toomey's car would be coming in. But there was no sign of him. She turned abruptly off the road and into another side street. Then she wove a round-about route back toward the main highway. The question was where could she go? To the police, where Toomey was a member in good standing? Or to the judge who had seemed anxious that justice be done? There was no one she could count on, no one to turn to except Jerry Toomey, who had always been on her side. But if he had killed Matthew . . . if he had been lying to her all along . . .

She thought of Brad Troxell. But she had no idea how she could find him. His office was undoubtedly closed and she didn't know where he lived. Charlie was driving aimlessly, without a plan, and she needed someone she could trust.

She used her own phone to call Information, and then keyed her way through the menus that listed all of the services provided. In the end, a recorded voice told her that if she wanted to hang on, a human being would appear to assist her. She asked the number of Brad Troxell, an attorney who lived in the county. After a few minutes of give and take the clerk told her that the number was unlisted. The best she could do was phone his office and leave a message, hoping that someone was assigned to check the answering machine:

"Brad, this is Charlie. I just found out that Jerry wasn't in Boston the night Matthew was killed. He was here. And I think that he knows that I've found out. He said he was coming to my house, so I ran. Tara is safe at a friend's house, and I'm driving around wondering what to do. Can you help me?"

She left the number of her car phone. Then she drove to a fast-food shop, ordered coffee through the drive-in window, and parked out in the open. There was no reason to expect Brad to call back quickly, but that seemed her only hope. If she went to the police, whom could she talk to? Sergeant Lionetti, who was probably still working for the prosecutor? Or that captain—what was his name?—who had offered her a cup of coffee? Toomey was her link to the police, the only one she had trusted.

Maybe to Trish and Gary. They were still at the hotel, awaiting the release of Matthew's body so they could return it to a grieving Hillary. They had always been her enemies, but maybe when she appeared with information about their brother's death, they would at least give her a hearing.

Another possibility was to go to the house where Tara's party was, under the pretense of coming to help. That would put her in a public place where she could wait for Brad Troxell's call.

Her phone rang and she spilled her coffee in her rush to pick it up. She pushed the talk button. "Brad?" There was a short hesitation before she heard the voice she dreaded. "No, Charlie. This is Jerry. I came over to see you and you weren't home. Where are you?"

She wouldn't tell him. She shouldn't even speak to him. Her finger felt for the "end-call" button.

"Irv just picked up your daughter at her party. He's bringing her home. I think you ought to be here."

"Tara . . . with Irv?" She blurted out the question without even thinking. "Why . . . ?"

"Because we have to talk," Toomey answered. "You're jumping to a lot of conclusions, and I have to get your attention. Running away doesn't solve anything for either of us."

"Don't let him hurt Tara, please. I'm coming home right now. I'll be there in a few minutes. . . ."

"Irv won't hurt her. You see what I mean. You're starting to think crazy. I love you, Charlie, and I love your daughter. But you have to hear me out."

"I'm coming," she yelled. "I just started the car. I'm pulling out of the parking lot." The words were tumbling out in her desperation to assure him she was on the way. All she could think of was her daughter alone in a car with the security guard. She knew Tara must be frightened out of her wits.

How did they get her out of the party? Did Irv just grab her and run? Or did he do something to lure her outside?

Maybe he told the hosts that "Tara's mother has had an accident," and then reassured them that Tara would know him. "I've been driving her to school for the last couple of months." God, she's afraid of Irv, and then she would be more afraid of what had happened to her mother.

Charlie knew she was driving too fast, risking an accident or being pulled over by a policeman. Either would cost her time. She backed off the accelerator and eased into the center lane. *Get control of yourself,* she ordered. If ever she needed to keep her wits, it was now.

She turned onto a side street, and made all of the stop signs until she reached her subsection. Then she was on her street, passing along a path that meandered behind the waterfront homes. When she reached her gate, there was only one car waiting—Toomey's.

"Tara!" she called as soon as she came through the front door.

"Mom!" her daughter's voice echoed through the upstairs hall.

Toomey was sitting on the living room sofa, cradling a bottle of beer in his hands. "She's fine!" he called after Charlie, but he wasn't surprised that she continued past him and rushed up the stairs.

Tara came out of her room, still wearing the outfit she had worn to the party. "Mom, are you okay?"

Charlie enveloped her and kissed her forehead. "I'm fine, baby, just fine."

"Well, what's going on around here?" the girl demanded.

"A problem I have to work out. Nothing serious . . ."

"Then why did I have to come home?" Tara's anxiety was quickly giving way to anger. "Why did you send Irv to pick me up? He said you were hurt. . . ."

"Something happened! I may have to go away and I couldn't go without you."

"Go away where? You're not making any sense."

Charlie begged her. "Please trust me. Just wait up here while I talk to Sergeant Toomey. Then I'll be back. I promise."

Tara wasn't even close to being satisfied. "I don't want to

wait here. If you're okay I want to go back to the party. We've been planning it for weeks."

"Please, give me a couple of minutes. If everything works out, I'll take you back myself, honest!"

She turned on her heel and marched back to her room. "A couple of minutes," she yelled over her shoulder.

Charlie returned to the living room where Toomey was still sitting exactly as she had left him. She sat opposite him but didn't make eye contact. Instead she slumped forward, her chin resting on her hand.

"I told you she was fine," Toomey said. "There's no way I could hurt her . . . or you. I love you, Charlie. I think I've been in love with you since I first saw you, right after you were nearly killed. I knew someone wanted you dead, and I just wasn't going to let that happen."

She responded with a nearly imperceptible nod. "I know. And I fell in love with you."

"I wasn't lying to you, Charlie, when I let you think I was in Boston. I was lying to them—the DA, and the police, and your husband's children. They were trying to get rid of you. I was doing whatever it took to save you."

"You made up the evidence against Matthew," Charlie said. "I never would have wanted anything like that. I didn't want to frame anyone."

"Charlie, Matthew was the one who tried to have you killed. He hired McGraw to run you over in the water. Maybe I couldn't prove it legally, but I know it was true. McGraw bragged about it to his friends. Matthew sent him the money. He wanted you dead so that he could go on picking his father's pocket. And when that didn't work, he had your boat rigged to explode. You were the one who took out that boat. You were the one he wanted blown to pieces. It didn't bother him at all that you always took Tara out with you. He had no qualms about killing the two of you."

She looked up at him. "Did you kill him? Did you kill Matthew?"

"Yes. I did it for you. It was the only way to get you off.

Why should you go to jail because he was a murderer? He
was the one who deserved to be behind bars."

"But, to kill him?"

"I didn't want to kill him. I wanted him to tell the truth. He
could have saved his life by just agreeing to admit what he'd
done. But he laughed at me. He said he'd rather be dead than
be in prison. He wasn't going to confess to anything.

"Believe me, Charlie, it was the only way. I couldn't let
them convict you."

She knew that she had relied on him. Perhaps she had
even encouraged him. He hadn't made any secret of his desire to compromise Max McGraw. She had known that he
might plant drugs or entrap him in a crime just to gain leverage over him and force him to confess. Yet she hadn't
protested. She had remained silent while he shaved the edges
of the law in her interest. Maybe it was too late for her to be
indignant that he had killed to protect her. "It's a lot for me to
swallow," she finally managed. "Give me some time. Can you
give me a week?"

"I can give you all the time you need," Toomey said. "I
love you. I want to spend the rest of my life with you."

Charlie stood. It was her signal for him to leave. "I'll have
to get Tara back to her party."

He didn't move. "Just one more thing, Charlie. You can't
tell anyone about this. No matter what you decide about me,
you can't go to the police with the things I've told you."

"I won't," she agreed.

He lifted slowly out of his chair. "When I called you, you
were expecting a call from Brad. Remember, you called me
Brad as soon as you connected."

She nodded. She had been desperate for a call from Brad.

"Did you call him? Is that why you were waiting for his
call?"

"Yes, I did call him," she said. There was no way she
could get out of admitting that. Then she tried to cover herself. "There's some of Steven's money being transferred to
me. I want Brad to represent me."

"You didn't call him from here," Toomey said as a statement of fact. He pointed to the telephone. If she had called him from the house, the call would still be on her log. "So you must have called him from your car."

"That's right. Is that important?"

"It just doesn't make sense," he said. "You found out that I hadn't been out of town. You figured that I had framed Matthew and then killed him. I said I was coming over and you ran out of the house to get away from me. And then you called your lawyer, after hours, to ask him to represent you in a trust matter?" He paused long enough to let his logic sink in. "What did you tell him, Charlie?"

"Nothing!" she snapped. "I got his answering machine. I left a message for him to call me."

"And you figured he'd call you back right away instead of waiting until he got into his office in the morning. It seems to me that you must have told him something very urgent. Something you knew would get him to call you no matter where he was."

She tried to sidestep the trap he was springing. "Jerry, can we talk about this tomorrow? Or maybe after I get back? I promised Tara that I would take her back to her party."

"Sure, but how do I know you'll come back once you've taken your daughter out of the house? She's the only reason you're here with me now."

Her fear was building toward terror. Toomey knew that she was lying. He knew she had told Brad Troxell what she knew. But she couldn't admit that he was right. That would make Brad a definite threat to the police officer, and that fact would put him in mortal danger.

"You know I'll come back because I said I would come back. You say you love me, but at the same time you're telling me that you don't trust me. Which is it, Jerry, because we can't build much of a life together without trust?"

"I want to trust you," Toomey answered.

Before he could go on, Tara's voice sounded from the top of the stairs. "Mom! The party is half over! You promised!"

Charlie looked at him defiantly. "I promised her I'd take

her back to the party." She walked to the foot of the stairs. "In a minute, Tara. Sergeant Toomey is just leaving."

She turned back to him, the question painted on her face. Was he going to let her go? He answered with a nod. "I'll wait here," he told her.

"Make yourself comfortable," she said. Then she added, "I'll be right back," even though she knew that she would never come back.

Headlights swung into the driveway, followed by the sound of a car door slamming. Toomey eased to the window, glanced down, and saw Brad Troxell's Beetle. He looked back to where Charlie was standing, her hand now up to her mouth to keep her from screaming. "I don't think you can leave now," Toomey told her. "Your lawyer just arrived."

Fifty-seven

Charlie froze when the doorbell rang. She looked uncertainly at Toomey, wondering what she should do.

"Relax," he said. "He knows I'm here. My car is in the driveway. I'll let him in." He walked into the hall and pulled the door open, which put him face to face with Brad. "Come in, counselor. Charlie and I were just talking about what we should do. I suppose it concerns you."

Brad followed him into the living room. "Some mess you've gotten yourself into," he said to Toomey. His tone was friendly, almost jocular.

"So she told you," Toomey acknowledged, gesturing toward Charlie.

"She left me a message. Once I understood it, the rest was easy to figure out."

Brad chose the chair closest to Charlie. He seemed as calm as usual, unfazed by the obvious tension in the room.

"So what are you planning to do about it?" Toomey said.

Brad answered instantly. "Defend you, once you've turned yourself in."

"Turn myself in for what?"

"For killing Matthew Armstrong. The State will probably add *obstruction of justice* for creating phony evidence, but that will be a sideshow. The murder charge is the one we'll have to deal with."

They sat silently until they were interrupted by Tara calling from upstairs. "Mom, the whole party will be over."

"I've got a better idea," Toomey said. "Suppose we keep this whole thing our secret. Matthew tried to kill Charlie, and then he tried to frame her for her father's murder. I killed Matthew and tried to frame him for his father's murder. It seems like a fair trade to me. If it had gone the other way, Charlie wouldn't be here with us right now. I think all of us are happy to have her with us."

Brad had known for a long time Sergeant Toomey was the law unto himself. He didn't much care for the niceties of evidence, and tried to turn cases in the direction he thought they should go. But now he came to the full realization of just how far beyond the law Toomey had gone. He had taken it upon himself to arrest, indict, judge, and pass sentence. He had even assigned himself the role of executioner.

"Jerry, we can't do that," he said. "The whole department is looking into this case. They already know you were stalking Max McGraw. They found out that you were the one who scared up that idiot of a gun dealer. Turning in your resignation didn't get you off the hook. How long do you think it will be before they turn up the pickup that drove Charlie off the road? Or match the paper on some of your reports to the paper used in the letter and the suicide note?"

Toomey's eyes narrowed with the recitation of the evidence building against him.

"It was a great scam," Brad went on, "but it's over. It was you right from the beginning, wasn't it?"

"I didn't know who Charlie was when that jerk tried to run a boat over her." He looked to Charlie for confirmation. She nodded.

"But then," Brad said, "you took over. You had met a nice, attractive young lady who was heiress to more money that you could have ever earned or stolen. It was just as easy to marry a rich woman as a poor one. All you had to do was make sure she got the money, and make sure she fell in love with you."

Charlie's face came up instantly, her eyes suddenly wide open and hard as diamonds. "My God, was it all a lie?"

"Loving you wasn't a lie," Toomey snapped. Then he turned on Brad. "You're saying that I killed Steven, but you have no evidence."

"None at all," Brad agreed. "But I'll tell you what keeps bothering me. None of the Armstrongs would have the slightest idea of how to build a bomb or where to get the materials. And none of them would know anyone down here who could do it for them. So I kept asking myself, 'Who knows every criminal in southeast Florida? Who could have a bomb designed, built, and planted by people who wouldn't dare turn him down?' The more I thought of it, the more I thought of you."

Charlie was watching the exchange between the two men with the face of a judge. She was taking in information, trying to decide what made sense and what didn't. So far, Brad was scoring all the points.

"But I'm not talking about McGraw and Steven Armstrong. Maybe you killed them, or maybe you didn't. The truth is that I don't want to know. What you have to answer for is murdering Matthew and distorting evidence in a police investigation. And I'll defend you. I don't think I can get you off unless the State does something very stupid. But I think I can persuade a jury that it was a crime of passion, and that your sentence should be lenient."

Toomey laughed. "Thanks a lot, counselor," he said. "Do you know what would happen to me if I went to jail? Half the guys there would be people I put away. I wouldn't last a weekend."

"There are prisons outside the state," Troxell started, but Toomey cut him off.

"Bullshit! I'm not turning myself in." He swung his gaze from Brad to Charlie. "The only question is are you two going to keep what you know to yourselves? If you are, then we can all go home happy. If you're not . . ."

He let the question hang. They knew he wouldn't leave anyone around to testify against him. Either they would help him, or he would silence them. He had run out of alternatives.

"Mom . . ." It was Tara's wail from upstairs that made up her mind. If Toomey had to eliminate witnesses, Tara would be among them. The girl knew all the people in the house, and she would certainly know which of them survived. Charlie understood Toomey's imperative. Kill one and he had to kill them all.

"I'm not going to talk to anyone," she said to Toomey. "I'm not sure of anything, and that's the way I want to keep it. I don't want to be involved."

He looked at Brad, waiting for his decision. "If you're going to run, you better get started," Brad said. "There's no way I can lie to a police investigation."

"How much time do I have before you blow the whistle?" Toomey asked.

"My office opens at nine Monday morning," Brad answered. "The police can't ask me any questions until then."

Tara stormed down the stairs, her backpack over her shoulder. "I'm going to start walking," she announced to no one in particular. She turned to her mother. "If you find time to keep your promise, you can pick me up along the way."

"Tara!" Charlie snapped. "Get back upstairs right now!" There was a no-nonsense tone to her voice that startled the two men as well as her daughter.

"No, wait," Toomey interrupted. "I was just leaving anyway. I'll take her to her party." There was a triumphant smile on his face. He had found a way to leave the house with assurance that no one would call the police.

Charlie saw his motive instantly. "No! Don't touch her."

Toomey grabbed the straps of Tara's shoulder bag and pulled her to him. He held her in front of him as he reached behind his back and drew his service automatic. Charlie, who had bounded out of her seat, stopped abruptly when she saw the gun. "Don't! Please don't take her."

Tara began to squirm, but he twisted the straps, tightening his grip. "She'll be fine," he told Charlie, "as long as you stay cool." He gestured the gun toward Brad, who had gotten to his feet and was standing between Toomey and the front door. "You too, counselor. Don't do anything dumb."

"That goes for you, too, Jerry. Adding a kidnapping isn't going to help your case."

"Step aside!" Toomey ordered.

Reluctantly, Brad took a step out of the way.

"Let's go, Tara. We'll get you to your party."

"Mom," Tara managed through her fright. She couldn't struggle. Toomey was using the backpack like a harness, and had nearly lifted her feet off the floor. He started with her toward the doorway.

Charlie leapt at him, screaming "No!" as she attacked. Toomey swung the pistol against the side of her face, but she kept coming and got an arm around his neck. Then Brad jumped into the scuffle, grabbed the gun hand in both of his hands. With his momentum, he was able to bend it up behind Toomey's back. The automatic came free and flew in an arc, landing on the sofa cushions.

Toomey would have flicked his attackers off like flies. But he still had one hand caught in Tara's backpack, and she was pulling with all her strength, trying to get away from him. In effect, Toomey was battling three opponents and was scarcely holding his own. He finally ripped his hand free and threw Tara up against the fireplace.

With his free hand he tried to peel Charlie off his neck, but she clung ferociously, her fingers digging into his neck. Brad still had his other hand bent behind his back and was applying painful pressure. Toomey stamped down on Brad's foot and fired an elbow into his chest. At the same time, he spun out of the handhold, and slammed the back of his fist across the lawyer's jaw. Brad dropped to his knees.

Now he turned his anger on Charlie. With two free hands, he was able to break her stranglehold. Then he twisted her arm and flung her to the floor, where her head struck the base of the table. He turned to retrieve the gun from the sofa cushion, but Troxell bounded up on his back and wrapped his arms around Toomey's neck. Toomey spun around and bucked like a bull, trying to throw his rider, who was hanging on for his life. Toomey bent forward, lifting Brad's feet off the floor. He took a running step and then spun, slamming him against the wall. He heard the air burst out of Brad's lungs. Again and again he used all his weight to drive his adversary into the wall until the hold on his neck weakened. Then Toomey reached back, got a hand on Brad's shirt collar, and peeled him off his back.

He turned on his attacker with his full rage and found him sinking slowly down along the wall. Troxell was winded, battered, and exhausted. There was no fight left in him. Toomey fired two punches in a professional combination, a left hook to the side of Brad's face and then a thundering right smash into the pit of his stomach. Brad's limp body fell onto Toomey's shoulder. Toomey lifted him up. In one motion, powered by his explosive rage, he threw the smaller man into the front window. The thick glass broke into several large sheets, and fell out into the driveway below. Brad went with it, landing with a thud on the pavement. His arms and legs were spread out, his head turned awkwardly to one side. Blood was puddling under his face.

Toomey stood for a few seconds, looking down through the open window frame at his victim on the ground below. He drew deep breaths in his effort to recover from the struggle. Thoughts came slowly, but he understood that everything had gone wrong. Only hours earlier, he had enjoyed the affections of a very wealthy woman. As Brad had surmised, he had risked everything to get the Armstrong fortune into her hands, and then to have her come into his arms. And it had all worked, he thought, until just a few hours ago.

He turned back to the wreckage of the room. Tara was standing near the fireplace, frozen in fear. Charlie was picking herself up from the floor, still dazed from hitting her head. They were both witnesses to the murder he had just committed.

He had to run, but how far could he get? Charlie would be on the phone the second he left. Stealing the girl would do him no good. Even with her daughter held as his security, she couldn't simply stay in her house and ignore the body lying outside her broken window. He had no choice. He couldn't leave two witnesses behind.

But could he do it? Could he systematically execute a teenage girl, and a few seconds later put the gun to her mother's head? Murder wasn't new to him. He had killed Max McGraw when he walked in while Toomey was tossing his apartment. He had blown up Steven Armstrong to steal his fortune. Then he had executed Matthew because all the evidence he had woven into a web was coming apart. But two young women? Could he kill them both just to buy himself a few hours for his escape?

Toomey reached for the pistol that had been resting on the sofa. The gun wasn't there. He lifted the cushion. Nothing! He looked around frantically and saw no sign of it. But then he looked at Tara, who was still standing near the fireplace with her hands behind her back. Her secret was written across her face.

"You better give me that, kid." He stepped toward her very slowly, realizing that if she panicked, she might try to use the gun. "That's a very dangerous weapon," he said with almost fatherly concern. "Why don't you give it to me so that I can get out of here?" Another step. He was almost to her. "C'mon. You don't want to hurt yourself." Carefully, he reached out his hand.

Tara brought the gun quickly from behind her back. It was too big for her hand and her finger barely reached the trigger. But the muzzle was swinging toward Toomey, and it looked as if she was going to fire rather than give up the gun. He slapped at the weapon with the hand he had extended. The gun flew out and bounced across the floor. Tara seized his arm, a feeble grasp that the police officer hardly felt. But when she closed her teeth across his hand, he screamed in pain. He pulled his hand free and grabbed the girl by the neck ready to kill her in an instant.

"Let her go!" Charlie was standing ten feet away, with Toomey's pistol raised in both hands.

He released his grip on Tara's neck. "Put that thing down," he said. Then he smiled. "You don't know how to use it." While he was cajoling, he took the girl by the shoulders and eased her in front of him. "If you shoot, you'll probably kill your own kid. So just put it down. All I want to do is get out of here."

"Then go. Take your hands off my daughter and get out of here."

Toomey had lifted the girl off the floor and was holding her in front of him as a shield. His face was peering over her shoulder. "I need the gun. Just give it to me and all this will be behind us." He was easing toward Charlie as he talked, reaching around Tara to take the weapon.

"Don't come any closer. One more step and I'll fire."

"Charlie, you don't want to pull that trigger. Not when it's aimed right at your daughter. Give it to me so I can leave." He shuffled a step closer.

Charlie had once fired a pistol at a shooting range. Even with the protective goggles, she had turned her head away from the flash. None of her shots had come close to the target. Now she was sighted at two faces, Tara's the closest to her and filling most of her vision. Only half of Toomey's head showed over the girl's shoulder. She tried to lock in on him but the gun was trembling.

"Stop!" she ordered. "For God's sake, you're waving that thing all over the place." He took another step.

Charlie steadied the sight. She pulled the trigger. This time there was no looking away. She saw the flash engulf both faces. The two bodies hurtled backward and crashed to the floor.

"Tara!" Charlie yelled. She dropped the gun and rushed to the two victims. Toomey was on his back, he head tipped up against the edge of the sofa. There was a small hole in his forehead that was beginning to ooze gore. The stain spreading rapidly on the sofa fabric indicated that the wound to the back of his head was much larger.

Tara lay on top of him, held by Toomey's left arm. Her eyes were wide with fright. "Is he . . . ?" she managed as if asking permission to move the arm. Charlie scooped her up and hugged her tight, forgetting that she was kneeling only a few inches from the body of a man she had once loved.

"Don't look, baby. It's awful" Tara shook her head. She had no intention of looking. "Go upstairs and get some bedsheets," Charlie said, beginning to recover from the emotional nightmare. She stood unsteadily, made her way around the body without looking down, and went to the broken window. She saw Troxell lying deathly still in the midst of the tiny lights reflecting from the broken glass. "Oh Jesus!" It was a prayer even though Charlie didn't believe in prayer.

She rushed to the phone and dialed the police emergency. "Two men have been shot," she said, assuming that Toomey had shot Brad. She gave the address and screamed for them to hurry.

Charlie caught Tara when she reached the bottom of the stairs, took the sheets, and sent her upstairs to her room. "Just rest, baby. When the police come they'll want to talk to you." She draped one sheet over Toomey, taking care not to look at him directly. Then she rushed out the door with the other sheet and veered into the driveway where Brad was lying.

When she saw the blood on his face, she thought that he had been shot through the head. She wiped the blood away and was startled to hear him moan. When she pressed her ear against his chest, she could hear his heart. He was alive! There still might be time to save him.

She lifted his head and slipped the folded sheet under it. Then, with a free corner, she cleared the wound, which proved to be a gash across his cheek. There was another wound on his scalp that had already matted the hair on one side of his head. That, Charlie thought, was the more serious of the two. She looked up at the shattered window over her head. He had fallen through, she realized, and his wounds were probably the result of the fall. Either that, or Toomey had hit him with the pistol. Brad was deeply unconscious, but he was still alive. None of his wounds were spouting blood. She let herself hope that he would survive.

She heard the approaching sirens and saw two police cars bracket her gate. Officers ran toward her, one with his gun already drawn. "Where's the shooter?" the first officer demanded. "Is he still in the house?"

"He's dead," Charlie said calmly. "But this man is alive. He needs an ambulance!"

"There's one on the way," the officer said, kneeling down next to her. "It will only be a minute."

True to his word, an ambulance pulled through the gate, and the two paramedics were out and rushing to Brad's aid before the truck had stopped rolling. The policemen went up to the house. Charlie stayed at the site while the medics bandaged the two wounds they could see, started an IV, connected an oxygen line, and carefully slipped Brad onto a gurney.

"Is he going to make it?" she asked one of them.

"Everything seems to be working," the medic said. "They'll know more at the hospital, and we won't lose him on the way." The ambulance started its siren as soon as it cleared the gate.

Charlie saw that there were two more cars at her gate, and when she went back inside, two plainclothes officers had joined the original policemen in looking over the crime scene. One of them was Sergeant Lionetti.

"Can you tell us what happened here?" he asked.

"I can, but not now. My daughter saw all this and she's very upset. I think I should be with her." Charlie walked past them and turned up the stairs.

Lionetti glanced at his partner. His expression said that they should talk to the woman right away. The partner shrugged. He wasn't going to be the one to keep her from her daughter.

Fifty-eight

C harlie sat on the deck of the yacht club and watched
Idonit turn around the buoy and head for its dock. She
wondered what the new owners would call her. Probably something related to their lives the way *Idonit* was related
to Steven's. Something like *Longshot* if they had made their
money in gambling, or *Reward,* if they were celebrating re-
tirement from a lifetime of hard work. She hoped the yacht
would take them on many happy voyages. Her own voyage
had been anything but happy.

Had she kept the boat, she most certainly would have re-
named it. *Idonit* was a bad joke for a person who had been
suspected of murder. *New Start* was a name she had considered. Another was *Wiser Now.* Either would have served the
same purpose—to announce her hope of putting her past behind her and finding a different life for Tara and her. But the
yacht held no meaning for her. She knew she couldn't sail
away from the problems she had created. In her new life, she
would have no need for a large boat.

Tara had been her main focus, yet she had led the girl
through a stormy passage to her adult life. She had survived

abandonment, her mother's bad choices, the grisly deaths of the two men who had been closest to becoming her father, and then the horror of being taken as chattel. Charlie could only hope that her daughter knew how much she was loved. She was determined to be there for Tara until she was no longer needed, a time in the future that she couldn't yet estimate.

Her daughter had been the key witness to the gruesome events that had taken place the night she had planned to spend at a party. She didn't know anything about the conversations that had taken place while she was pacing in her bedroom, fuming at being called home from the sleepover. But from the moment she had come down the stairs determined to shame her mother into taking her to her friend's house, she had been at the center of the violence.

Tara had sat quietly composed out on the pool deck while investigators swarmed through the living room. She had glanced inside only once, when a body bag was rolled out of the crime scene and out to the front door. All the while, she had been telling Sergeant Lionetti and two of his associates everything she had seen and had been calmly answering their questions. They were all amazed at her demeanor and her nearly total recollection of the details of the crime. They had no idea that when she went back to her bedroom, she rolled herself up in a ball of bedding, and barely slept for the next three days.

Charlie had provided the details of the conversation. She told how she found out that Toomey had never left town, of her conversation with him when he told her he was coming over, and of her decision to flee her own house. Then there was the call in which Toomey announced that he held her daughter and her panicky return with no thought for her own safety. She remembered her call to Brad Troxell, and his arrival just as Toomey was about to flee. Toomey had bargained with both of them for their silence. She had agreed; she would have agreed to anything. Troxell had held fast, telling Toomey that he had no escape. And then Tara had entered. Tara's memories of that story had been slow in dissipating. Charlie wasn't sure whether she would ever heal.

The yacht eased up to the pier, and the two crewmen who

had taken her on her honeymoon put the lines over and made them fast. Charlie watched the husband and wife come out on the afterdeck with the yacht broker. They popped a cork, and all drank to the agreement that they seemed to have reached. Charlie knew that she was probably being ripped off, but it made no difference. She had no head for business and no interest in large sums of money. What she really wanted was to be free of the yacht and its attachments to her past.

For a while, she had thought of keeping it for Brad. His head wounds had not been that severe, but in the fall he had broken both legs. That, plus the ribs shattered and the lung punctured in his battle with Toomey, promised a very long period of convalescence. She had toyed with the idea of turning the boat over to him. Was there any better place to recover than on a leisurely cruise through the islands? The sunshine and salt air seemed a perfect prescription. But Brad's doctors had vetoed any such trip. He was still a few operations away from being whole. He faced a long journey of painful therapy.

Charlie and Tara had visited him frequently over the past few months, supposedly to help his recuperation. But the truth was that he was the one being helpful. While his body was broken, his mind was sound and his spirits were high. Charlie's injury had been of little consequence, and Tara had suffered none, but both of them were shattered mentally. Tara was nearly crippled by her feelings of guilt. Charlie was so conscious of her failures that she had no hope that life could ever forgive her. They went to the hospital to cheer up Brad, but each time they were the ones who were cheered.

Sergeant Lionetti had been a frequent visitor to the house, checking one fact or another and telling Charlie of the latest findings in the police investigation. Brad had assumed correctly that it had been Matthew who had tried to have her killed. And while he had guessed at the broad picture, Lionetti filled in the details. Toomey had immediately recognized that the young woman was about to be cut into one of the country's larger fortunes. He had little trouble deciding why people wanted her dead, and just who those people had been. Finding Matthew's telephone call to McGraw had sealed his case.

But Toomey had a much broader agenda then solving the crime. He saw a vulnerable young woman married to a much older man. He had assumed that she had married Steven for his money and decided that he would marry her for her money. That led him to have the boat wired with explosives. The bomb was activated with a radio signal once he had called Charlie and made sure she wouldn't be aboard. He had placed the call that led Steven to take the boat and rush to the yacht club.

It had been Toomey who had invited her out into the sugar cane fields and then crashed a truck into her. Apparently, he meant only to frighten her; to keep her convinced that someone still wanted to kill her. Lionetti could only speculate what must have gone through his mind when Charlie lost control and the big car rolled off the road.

Crazy, she thought, that she could have been taken in by such a man and his mad grasp for money. She still wondered whether she would ever be able to trust herself again.

The new owners of *Idonit* came out on the deck, delighted with their good fortune in acquiring Charlie's yacht. "What are you going to name her?" she asked.

"*Martha!*" the man said instantly, and looked at his wife.

"That's my name," she explained.

They were about the same age, and both showing the mileage of the years. She was no trophy wife. *He really loves her,* Charlie thought, not without a tinge of envy. It must be nice for a man to think that you're the most important thing in his life.

She took the check for five million dollars and decided to stop by Brad Troxell's office on the way home. In the course of his recovery, he had become her financial adviser. While still in the hospital, he had negotiated the settlement of the Armstrong estate, essentially dividing the fortune into four equal shares.

Trish had enlarged her Manhattan gallery and built a new beach house in the Hamptons. She was still losing money, but now it was her own money and she could afford the losses.

Gary's new movie, starring Courtney Davis, had been snubbed by the theaters and gone straight to video. He was hoping that offshore sales would cut his losses to just a few million, which was hardly a dent in his share of the estate. In the meantime, he had launched a new project with Ira Straus for a movie based on a scandalous murder in Florida. Courtney would play the role of the young woman who had touched the whole thing off by marrying an older man.

Matthew's widow, Hillary, had received a sizable insurance benefit that added to her share of the estate. She had bought a Paris apartment for her daughter, and built a new beach house on the Cape for herself. She was still a dominant player at the country club, a much sought-after bridge partner for all the bachelors and widowers who were struggling with their dues.

When the estate was settled, Charlie had allowed herself a few luxuries. She bought the latest-model Toyota, and added the premium sound system. She got a small speedboat, ideal for water-skiing, and a berth at a local marina to dock it. She found a beautiful set of small diamond studs to give to Tara.

She had sold the house along with all its painful reminders. It would have been impossible to go on living there no matter how many coats of paint were put over the bloodstains. The condo, too, held difficult memories of her passionate affair with Jerry Toomey. Charlie had put it back on the market at a reduced price, and sold it immediately. Now they lived in a small beach house near the high school where all Tara's friends were going. She had added a room for her gym equipment with a window that looked out over the surf and a game room for Tara and her guests. Back in her normal setting, the girl was acting normal, which was all that Charlie had hoped for.

Brad was behind his desk, but in his high-back leather chair rather than the wheelchair he had been using. When Charlie entered, he surprised her by standing to greet her. "Watch this!" he said, and stepped around his desk and walked to her. His steps were slow and shuffling, but he was on his feet and moving without crutches or canes.

"That's wonderful," Charlie laughed as she took his hands. Then she pulled him into an embrace. "I'm so happy for you."

He walked her to the sofa and lowered himself gently down beside her. "Still a little slow on the ups and downs," he said, admitting the obvious, "but it's getting better."

"You have to make it better!" she warned him. "From here on, your recovery is completely up to you."

He nodded. "The doctors say that I need to get into therapy. But with my schedule I'll have to have a personal trainer. I was hoping you might be looking to get back to work."

"Me?" She was suddenly flustered.

"That's what you do, isn't it? You help people get back their flexibility, their strength. You push them to work hard, to accept nothing less than a full recovery. Well, that's what I need, a full recovery."

He had her laughing. "I suppose I could, I mean you're right, that's what I do." She looked around at the oversized office. "You could put everything you need right in here. All it has to be is a mat and a table for stretching. A few steps for climbing. When you're ready, we could add a Universal."

He was nodding in agreement. "That's easily done. But no big weights. I don't want anything falling through the floor into the office below."

"I also have a pretty good gym at my house that we could use whenever you're not tied down here in the office. I have a better view than you do, and walking on the beach is great exercise for strength and balance."

"Then it's agreed," Brad said. "You're my personal trainer starting right now."

"Starting tomorrow, maybe. I have to pick up some mats. Oh, and you'll need some gym shorts and sweats." She was really getting into it. "Is there a shower here that you can use? If we work out in the morning . . ."

"In the men's room," he assured her.

"Well, okay, then. What time tomorrow?"

"How about lunchtime? I haven't been getting out anyway." She stood and he reached out for her hand. She helped him up. "Good thing I didn't start today. Once we get started, you'll be getting up by yourself."

"Slave driver!"

"That's what I do for a living."

He walked her to the office door.

"Charlie, I'm looking forward to this. I'm grateful that you're taking me on."

She kissed his cheek. "Wait until you get my bill!"

Read on for an excerpt from
Diana Diamond's next book

THE OTHER WOMAN

Coming soon in hardcover from St. Martin's Press

Pam Leighton should have seen it coming. She knew when John Duke was named a candidate for a position in the administration he would have to tidy up all the messy corners of his life. She was one of those messy corners.

It wasn't that she was naïve. Pam was a reasonably bright college graduate with an advanced degree in economics who held down a responsible research post for a Washington trade association. She knew that married men who wandered from home were usually on short leashes. Deep down she understood that John Duke would never leave his wife, Catherine, no matter how sincerely he claimed that they were no longer in love. Love meant different things to men at different stages of their lives. Maybe his romantic feelings for her were stronger than his feelings for Catherine, but that didn't mean he wanted to leave his wife. Pam had always understood that if push came to shove, she would be the one pushed aside. It was just that, it was hard to believe. Hard, because her two-year affair with her boss wasn't the typical affair.

Pam wasn't a kept woman. She earned her money and

paid her own rent. The only thing she depended on John Duke for was affection. Their relationship wasn't centered on the bedroom, even though it might have been. Pam was a very sexy woman, on the cusp of thirty, when youthful attractiveness softens into mature interests. Her coloring—dark hair with blue eyes—looked like it was the result of the mating of an English stallion and an Italian mare somewhere back in her bloodlines. Her skin tone, high cheekbones, and full lips came from her Mediterranean heritage. Her straight nose and sharply cut jawline were inherited from Nordic raiders. Her figure was a bit too curvaceous for a runway model but without the bounce that draws applause from construction workers. There was just enough flow in her movements to turn heads on the street, and to raise faces over the tops of restaurant menus.

But she wasn't a sex toy. She had no drawer of transparent nightwear, nor were there leather outfits hanging in her closet. She slept in pajamas, or in nothing at all, depending on the occasion. Her bathrobe was terry cloth, her underwear white cotton, and her bras unpadded. When John came to her apartment, she was as apt to smell of a lemon fish marinade as of an exotic Parisian fragrance.

In their typical evening together, they worked side by side in the kitchen, generally sipping the wine intended for the saucepan. They shared a lively conversation over dinner and often fell asleep in front of the television. On weekends, when he was in town, they sat around in pajamas passing sections of *The Washington Post* back and forth before they settled down to the crossword puzzle.

Some evenings, they worked together. The Electric Energy Institute's real business was lobbying government officials to make sure that no legislation hostile to the electric utilities, or regulation distasteful to their executives, would ever be passed. Pam often needed guidance on exactly what politically attractive conclusions her research should yield. John would sometimes ask her advice on a recalcitrant senator. How big a donation was he looking for? How many votes could he deliver?

What they shared wasn't that much different from any marriage between urban professionals. Much more than just casual sex, their affair was a commitment of time, interest, and affection, from which intimacy flowed naturally and guiltlessly. It truly seemed that it would last forever.

They had to be discreet, of course. In the Electric Energy Institute offices, they exchanged greetings in passing that held no hint of affection. "Good morning, Pam!" "Good morning, John," when they met in the lobby. "I'll have those figures you asked for this afternoon" and "Thank you, Pam," when they interacted in the office. If they found themselves at the same table in the cafeteria, they invited others to join them. They never booked luncheon reservations at the same restaurant.

When they had an evening out together, it was never at a fashionable downtown restaurant or at one of the Georgetown clubs. As director of the institute, John was immediately recognizable by most senators, congressmen, and their staffers, as well as power industry executives. As the institute's top researcher, Pam would be recognized by most second-level Washington officials and many of the executives of the institute's sponsoring companies. Both of them were well known to the lobbying industry, with its offices stretching for block after block along K Street. Within hours after their appearing together in the District, it would have been universally acknowledged that they were an item.

Instead, they would often travel north to Baltimore, where they could get lost in the crowds at the harbor. They could drive west to Leesburg, where the county was exploding so rapidly that no one knew anyone. Or they might head south to Charlottesville and join the chaos of student revelers. When business called for them to travel together, they would find separate rooms in the hotel, even though one of those rooms would go unused. Or if Pam was joining John in a major resort city, they would book separate flights on different airlines. The subterfuge bothered neither of them. It was accepted as a necessary arrangement in their relationship, just as a husband might put up with a two-hour daily commute.

Over the two years of their relationship, there had been several close calls. One time, at a resort in the Bahamas, John had excused himself from the dinner table only to run into the president of a sponsoring company in the lobby. While the two men shared a drink at the bar, Pam had slipped away, leaving two untouched dinners behind. They had checked out in the middle of the night. On another occasion, Pam had seen a man from their office at an airport gate where John's flight was arriving. Suggestively, she had led him off for a cocktail. For weeks after, her colleague had hinted around the watercooler that she was hitting on him. Only once had Pam and John been caught red-handed, when they glanced across the aisle of a theater and saw a congressman they both knew staring back at them. Fortunately, the woman with the congressman was from an escort service, and both couples silently agreed not to acknowledge one another.

Pam had been delighted when John told her that his name was in play for a position in the new president's cabinet. He had modestly dismissed the implications. "Lots of names get kicked around. It's no big deal." But it was a big deal. The incoming administration was pro-business, particularly favorable to energy producers. The new Secretary of Energy would be responsible for turning the industry's wish list into public law. More important, she knew that John wanted it. Instead of courting important men, he would be the one being courted. The position would be his entry into public life, with all its social and financial perks. The repute that came from rubbing elbows with the president would lead to book advances, speaking fees, maybe even a university chair. All heady stuff for a man who was a paid flack for a stolid industry.

Pam knew that John would go through a detailed vetting. The new president's team would scrutinize every detail of his life, looking for breaches of the law or of public morality that could embarrass the administration. Ideal candidates had been unceremoniously dumped because the family maid was an illegal immigrant, or because they didn't pay a nanny's Social Security. A vice presidential candidate had lost out when it was discovered he had seen a psychiatrist. A

Supreme Court candidate had been rocked by charges of sexism. More than likely, they would ask John about the state of his marriage.

He would have to tell them about her, because there was every chance that they would find out anyway. From the day his name came up, detectives had probably been following him. A panel truck full of radio equipment was probably homing in on his cell phone calls. More than likely, someone at the post office was watching his mail. But even when he told them, Pam didn't think their affair would be critical. Hadn't presidents carried on affairs in the White House? Weren't congressmen balling their interns? By comparison, her relationship with John was proper and discreet.

He had a lovely wife who presided over a household in Connecticut to which he frequently returned. She was the daughter of a politically connected family that had made its fortune in shipping, running molasses and hardware to the Caribbean, and bringing back rum and slaves. Two of her forebears had served as state representatives to the United States Congress, and two recent presidents had dined with members of the family while campaigning in the state. One of her cousins, Benjamin Porter, was the majority whip in the House. She was known to politicians of every stripe, and Pam had no doubt that her influence had been critical John's selection for a cabinet post. Catherine was at his side in all his official photographs and joined him at important functions, always smiling at him adoringly even though they had separate bedrooms. She was the woman who would be at his side when he was sworn in, and she would be photographed with the president's wife. She was the perfect companion for his public life.

He also had a mistress, who was invisible to the outside world. She had no desire for notoriety, was content to live backstage, and would never do anything to embarrass his wife or jeopardize his public image. She was a perfect companion in his private life. It all worked very well, so why should the administration's inquisitors be concerned? Surely they had more incendiary issues to deal with.

He came to her apartment on a Monday night after spending a weekend in Connecticut, gave Pam a distracted kiss, and opened a bottle of a modest wine they both liked. He put the bottle on the table that Pam had already set, went to the stereo, and slipped in a jazz CD. Then he eased onto the sofa almost as if he was afraid of crumpling a cushion.

"How was your weekend?" she called from the kitchen.

"Okay," he answered unenthusiastically.

Pam knew something was wrong. John always clung to her when he returned from home, demonstrating how much he had missed her. By now he should have poured the wine, toasted to her beauty, and then plunged into the food preparation, taking every opportunity to brush against her.

"A problem?"

"Sure. There's always a problem."

She dried her hands and stepped out of the kitchen. The table was close to the front door, across from the kitchen counter. He was sitting at the far end of the room, tapping his fingers on the armrest in time to the music. She lit the candle, her signal that dinner was ready. "Anything you want to talk about?" she asked as she poured the wine.

He got up heavily, showing none of the zest he usually brought to their table. "No . . . well . . . there is. But not now. It will keep until after dinner."

They began silently, John plainly lost in his thoughts and Pam wondering what dreaded topic was hanging over them. She couldn't take the tension.

"What do you think?" she said, gesturing toward the fish she had served.

"Wonderful! What did you marinate it in?"

His eyes were glazing over before she finished listing the ingredients, but she went on with the details of preparation, trying to keep the conversation alive. "Delicious," he interjected when he realized she had stopped talking.

She tried another tack. "How was the flight?"

"Uneventful," he said without glancing up. "The best kind."

"Did Catherine pick you up?"

"No, she was busy. I took a limo."

"What was she busy with?"

"The usual nonsense. Nothing important."

Pam wasn't going to give up. There had to be something they could talk about. "Let me tell you about my weekend," she started, but she was cut off by the clatter of his fork falling onto his plate.

"She knows," John said, breathing out the words rather than saying them. "Catherine knows about us." He reached for his wineglass and drained it.

"So?" Pam asked. It wasn't a frivolous question. They had often speculated that his wife might already know of their affair and, if not, that she would probably find out. Both of them assumed she would live comfortably with the arrangement, or perhaps demand a divorce. Whichever, it would be a quiet and dignified resolution. Catherine wasn't into scenes.

"So," he answered softly, "she wants this ended."

Pam set her fork down and pushed her plate aside. She felt a cold chill of fear and a knot tightening in her throat. She couldn't even pretend to eat. "How does she want it ended?" she managed.

"Just ended! She doesn't want me to see you anymore." He refilled his glass and then tried to pour a bit into Pam's glass. His hands were shaking. He looked up at her, but he couldn't hold eye contact.

"What do *you* want?" she asked, even though she could already guess his answer.

"What I want doesn't matter. It's what I have to do." He seemed distraught, on the verge of tears.

"What do you have to do?" she asked. He half-turned away from her. "Do you have to give me up?"

He nodded. "That's Catherine's price."

She didn't understand. Price for what? What was John's wife holding over his head?

"Her price for my nomination to go through. Catherine has connections all over the government. If she makes it known that she would rather not have me burdened with the demands of public life, the administration will find a more available candidate. Christ, the only reason my name came up in the first place is that the new people are trying to suck up to her family. They'd love to get her cousin in their pocket."

He jumped up from the table, went to the stereo, and snapped off the jazz combo. Then he sat down on the sofa, this time heavily, as if he were falling into a great, black hole. Pam followed and took a chair across from him. "If I understand you, I'm not sure that I'm being dropped because of Catherine. It sounds more as if I'm losing out to a job in the new president's cabinet."

He shook his head slowly. "Catherine isn't giving me any leeway."

"No," Pam corrected. "It's your ambition that isn't giving you any leeway. You want the job more than you want me."

"That's not true," he wailed. "You know I love you. But Catherine has me by the short hairs." He was up on his feet and pacing in front of her. "I think she knew about us from the beginning. She's been biding her time, playing right along with us, just waiting for the moment when she could crush me like a bug. Now she has it. She pushed my nomination just so she could dangle it over me."

Pam caught his arm and turned him toward her. "If there's no nomination, then she has nothing to dangle over you. Call her right now and tell her you've decided not to join the administration. You'll still have the institute, and we'll still have each other."

"It's not that simple," he answered curtly. "Catherine could make one hell of a scene."

"And drag her illustrious family through the tabloids?" Pam reminded him. "Catherine will never let that happen. She'll accept the present arrangement or arrange a very quiet and dignified divorce. Either way, we'll still be together."

She looked toward the telephone, and his eyes followed. But when he saw the handset on the end table, he turned his head away. "Damn it! It's not just a phone call. It's a lot more complicated."

That was true, Pam thought. She had never been able to

explain why she was in love with John, or why their relationship was the anchor of her life. She couldn't expect him to explain why a short-lived position in the executive branch would be such an aphrodisiac for him. Sometimes people, or places, or titles, or opportunities simply became irresistible. Few people could explain all the choices that had shaped their lives, so it wasn't fair to demand an explanation.

"What are you going to do?" she asked sympathetically. She was trying to help him focus rather than demanding an answer.

"I don't know. It's all so sudden. A few days ago I had everything. Now I'm afraid that I'm going to lose it all."

"Is there anything I can do to help?"

"Just bear with me for a while." He reached across the table and touched her hand.

Pam understood why he wouldn't stay the night. She was even grateful. How could they lie together while each of them was thinking how they were going to live apart? Lovemaking would be artificial. Conversation would be distracting. Sleeping together guiltlessly was a mark of their commitment. Now, the commitment itself was being debated.

She was completely unnerved, unable to find a comfortable position in bed and too distracted to read or watch television. For the first hours of the night she wondered what arguments John was having with himself.

She couldn't picture him in his bedroom because she had never been above the ground floor of his town house. She had been in his living room, dining room, and kitchen when he had given small parties for the staff of the institute. On those occasions, caterers had passed cocktails and canapés for exactly an hour, then served dinner at his long colonial table. Pam had blended in with the other staffers, respectful of her boss and clearly one step down from him in the business pecking order. But often she had found herself glancing toward the stairs, wondering how the second floor was furnished, and what kind of bed he slept in when his wife was in town.

She had guessed a four-poster, probably one with a canopy over the top. The facades of all the homes on his Georgetown street were Federal, pretending to have been built in time for the Adams administration. The interior furnishings were generally colonial, usually with a copper kettle hanging over a seldom-used gas log. John had added to the illusion by hanging prints of the Founding Fathers in elaborate frames. So it was reasonable to assume that there was a washstand with basin and pitcher in his bedroom, perhaps even a long-handled bed warmer resting near the upper fireplace. The four-poster seemed a given.

Was he tossing and turning the way she was, weighing the alternatives and evaluating the consequences? For John, the choices were simple: fame and fortune or love and contentment. The argument was one-dimensional. How much would he give for the power and notoriety of a cabinet position? Were his ambitions worth a brutal separation from the woman he loved? For her, the choices were complex. What would she do if he said he wanted to stay with her? Could she believe that he was giving up the opportunity of a lifetime without resenting the limits on his future that their affair demanded? Wouldn't that resentment grow to frustration and anger and eventually destroy the very love he was trying to save?

What would she do if he told her that it was over and that they had to make a clean break? Could she go on with her life as if nothing had changed, continuing at the institute and seeing him when their business paths crossed? Or should she launch herself into an entirely new life, among different people in a different place?

All Pam had were questions. There could be no answers until John told her what her choices were. She was disposable at his whim, and that fact began to fuel her anger. In a sense, he had already decided she was a burden. What he was weighing now was whether the burden was too heavy for him to carry.

By the time the morning light began to leak through the blinds, she was angry at herself. How could she have loved without reservation when her total commitment wasn't returned? How could she have missed seeing that she was only a part of John's life, and that his sole enduring love was for himself? She knew she should have seen it coming, and that made her mad at herself. She knew that he was concerned only with his future, and that made her furious at him. And yet, Pam hoped with all her heart that in the end he would decide she was the most important thing in his life. She could forgive his wavering. She loved him that much.

He phoned seconds after her alarm clock rang. His voice was exhausted. "I've had a terrible night," he moaned. "Maybe the worst night of my life."

"It wasn't a beauty rest for me either."

"We need to talk."

She winced. "All you have to say is that you don't want to join the cabinet. That's not a lot of conversation. It's just a simple declarative sentence."

He let the opportunity pass. "I think I have a solution," he said without any great enthusiasm.

"Am I part of it?"

"Of course you are. That's why we have to find a place to talk."

"Won't you be coming here tonight?"

John hesitated and then said, "That might be a bit risky."

It was all the information she needed. Being seen with her would risk his appointment. So the cabinet post was the new love of his life. "Okay," she answered. "Wherever you say."

"In my office at the end of the day. I'll find something that we have to discuss and set up a meeting."

The day dragged at a painful pace. Pam pretended to be involved in a study of the industry's finances and let most of her calls go unreturned. All she could think about were the plates that were crashing under her feet, and the giant fissure that threatened to swallow her up. Why was he prolonging her pain? It was obvious that if he had decided he couldn't live without her they would discuss it over dinner in her apartment. The trumped-up office meeting meant he wouldn't be coming to her apartment. And that meant he had decided to abandon her.

But despite the flawless logic, she still held hope that he might choose her. She should have been preparing herself to receive the devastating news with dignity. Instead, she continued to nurture the possibility that he would decide he couldn't live without her.

She saw him in the office dining room, sitting with the public relations director of one of the new energy marketers. His expressions and gestures were all business. If he was torn by the same agony that she had felt since his announcement, John was certainly hiding his pain. She knew he had seen her come into the room, yet he never spared her a glance.

During the afternoon, Pam jumped at her phone whenever it rang, hoping it would be the call to his office. At three o'clock she was tempted to call his personal secretary, Marion Murray, to make sure she was on his afternoon schedule. Marion was her closest friend inside the institute. Their social life was limited by Pam's need for secrecy and Marion's devotion to a woman she lived with, but they had shared an occasional evening at the movies. By four, Pam sat on the edge of her chair with her arms wrapped around herself, staring at her desk phone. When it rang, she jumped as if it was the last thing she expected. She forced herself to let it ring a second time before she lifted the handset.

"Pam, this is Marion. Mr. Duke wonders if you could stay a bit late. He needs to see you, but he won't be free until six." In her role as the director's secretary, when Marion asked "if you could," she wasn't really asking.

"Sure," Pam said. "Any idea what it's about?"

"Not a clue! Whatever you're working on, bring it along."

Did she know? Pam wondered. A personal secretary usually knew even the most intimate details about her executive's life. The phone number of his favorite restaurant and the maître d's first name. His wife's birthday, and the kind of flowers she liked. His haberdasher and his shirt and sock sizes. Pam had always wondered whether Marion knew about her. Was it Marion who bought the wines they shared, and booked the hotels for their out-of-city liaisons? If she did, she would certainly know that Pam was about to be jettisoned.

Marion called back at six. "He'd like to see you now," she said. "I'm leaving, so just walk right in." Pam was relieved that she wouldn't have to face the secretary, but then the woman added, "Good luck!"

She knows, Pam guessed, and she's on my side. "Thanks," she answered.

John stood up when she entered his office. He took a furtive glance over her shoulder to be sure no one was watching before he closed the door. Then he gave her a quick, meaningless kiss and led her to the furniture grouping at the far end of the room. He gestured her to the sofa and waited until she was seated before he took the chair across from her. His manner was all business. Pam felt as if she were on a job interview.

"You can't imagine the agony I've been going through," he began. "I think this has been the most miserable day of my life."

Just say it, she thought. He wouldn't have needed to agonize about how to tell her he was staying with her.

"But I think I've found a way."

She leaned forward to show that she was listening intently, even though she didn't expect the news to be good.

"You know how important a cabinet post is to me." She nodded slightly. "I've come to a fork in the road. In one direction there are unlimited possibilities. Risks, to be sure, but the opportunity to push my career into a much higher orbit. The other direction really leads nowhere. I can go on being an industry flack, but I'll always be a second-team player. I'll always be doing someone else's bidding."

He paused to gauge her reaction. Pam nodded again to show that she had followed him so far. Those were certainly the choices.

"You know me well enough to know I'd never take myself out of the race. I don't have to tell you that I want the opportunity. But the truth is, it won't mean anything unless you're there with me."

Her eyes widened. She couldn't hide her spontaneous smile. John reached across the coffee table and took her hands in his. "The point is," he continued, "that once I'm established in the position, Catherine's connections won't matter. Right now, while I'm a candidate, I'm vulnerable. But a year from now, I'll be established. It won't matter whether I have her support, and no one will care if I show up with a different woman on my arm. This isn't the Vatican! People don't get thrown out of Washington for getting a divorce."

He was talking enthusiastically. He believed he had solved their problem and delivered the good news. But Pam wasn't enthused. "A year?" she asked.

"Maybe a bit more. Maybe even less. We'll just have to see how things are going. But it won't seem long. We'll still be seeing each other."

"How are we going to manage that? Won't Catherine know that you've lied to her? Won't she walk out on you?"

"We'll have to be very careful," he hastened to agree. "We can't be living in the same city or meeting at business affairs. Obviously, I can't be coming over every night. But we can still be together."

"How?" she repeated. But she wasn't completely puzzled. The conversation was beginning to sound familiar.

"I'll get you a place in Baltimore, down near the harbor," he answered. "And I'll line up a job for you on the staff of one of the power companies. The place will be yours, in your name, so you can take it over once you get settled." He paused, giving her a chance to react.

"And?" she asked. Obviously, there was more to his idea.

"We'll get together every time we can. I can easily arrange to have business in Baltimore a couple of days a month. And there will be a lot of travel to places where we can arrange to meet."

She took back her hands and looked away.

"I know it's not perfect," he pressed on. "I won't like being away from you. But it's just for a while. Just until the time is right for me to confront Catherine."

Pam knew when she had heard it before. It had been two

years earlier, when he first told her he loved her and couldn't live without her. He had admitted that a clandestine affair was far from perfect but assured her that it was just for now. It wouldn't be long before he would be able to divorce his wife. She hadn't believed it any more then than she did now. But then she had wanted to believe it.

John Duke had been visiting the Electric Energy Institute when he was introduced to Pam. He was a top executive with a New York public relations firm working to get a rate hike for one of his clients. Pam had joined him in the conference room and briefed him on the rate increases that other utilities had been granted. He had thanked her by taking her out to dinner. In the course of the next two months they had conferenced a dozen times. The dinners had started earlier, with cocktails, and ended later, with his coming up for a nightcap. On the day their business was concluded, John had stayed the night, and most of the next morning.

For the following months, he had seized every excuse to be in Washington, and their relationship had opened up like a flower. He had never lied to her. He had admitted to being fifteen years older than she was, even though he could have claimed a much younger age. He had made it plain that he was still married and had described a relationship that had gone cold, his fault as much as his wife's, and a house that was lifeless since his two daughters had left. "But I'm not a cheat," he had insisted. "I haven't been catting around. You're the first woman I've been with for too many years."

As he had told it, he wasn't looking for anything more than a dinner companion the first time he had asked her out. It wasn't until their third evening together that he realized he loved her. "I found a new life with you," he had told her, and Pam had found no reason to doubt him. The first time they'd slept together he had held her close throughout the night, "afraid that if I let go you wouldn't be there when I woke up."

Then, miraculously, he had been offered the top position in the institute, and he had accepted it with neck-snapping speed. He loved her, and now they could be together all the time. Marriage would have to wait, of course. He couldn't simply destroy his wife, even if he no longer loved her. Besides, she was a powerful woman with important Washington connections. It would take time. He would have to find the right moment to broach a divorce.

"You told me all this two years ago," Pam said.

He bristled. "It was true then, and it's true now. I love you Pam."

"And will it still be true two years from now, when you're offered an even bigger job?"

"What are you talking about? What job?"

"Suppose you're such a wonderful Secretary of Energy that they want you to run for vice president. Catherine will still be a well-connected woman. Will you ask me to wait around for just another few years? And where will you send me to live? Someplace in the Orient?"

"You're not being fair," he protested. "There was no way I could have foreseen this opportunity."

"John, that's what marriage is. It's two people pledging themselves to each other even though neither of them can foresee the future. That's what we should have done two years ago. It's what we should be doing now."

He labored to his feet and paced away toward his desk. "I can't. Not now. I just need a little more time."

"How much more time? Because I'm going to hold you to it. I'm going to sign up a caterer and send out the invitations."

He took a paper from his desk and held it up triumphantly. "Do you know what this is?" She shrugged. "It's the invitation for me to appear before the Senate Energy Committee. The president has named me. That's how close I am."

She rose and started toward him. "Good. You can tell them about me."

He sagged, letting the paper drop to his side. "You know I can't do that." He reached for her hand, but she didn't respond. "I'm sorry. I didn't mean to upset you. Let's just give it a couple of days, and then we'll talk again."

"No!" she snapped. She was surprised at her vehemence. "No," she repeated softly. "Not another couple of days. The decision is right here between us. If you love me, take my hand and we'll walk out together, ready to face all the things that neither of us can foresee. I can't put my life on hold until you have all your bases covered. I can't go on loving you in the hope that someday I'll be a safe bet."

She extended her hand. "Come on. Let's take our chances."

He rolled the paper carefully and held it with both hands. "I can't. If you can just give me some time."

Pam leaned forward and kissed him on the cheek. "Good night, John. I'll see you in the morning."

She was halfway to the door when he called her name. She stopped and turned slowly. "Please," he begged. "Let me get you set up in Baltimore. Or anyplace you want . . ."

She knew what he meant. "You want me out of the institute, don't you?"

He writhed in his embarrassment. "I think it would be best. Even when I leave, I'll still be meeting with the institute. We don't need to be running into each other."

She smiled, the truth of the situation beginning to get through to her. "You even want me out of town."

"No, that's not what I want. It's just . . ." John didn't know how to explain.

"Who then? Catherine? Was this one of her conditions? You don't just have to stop sleeping with me. You have to make sure that you never even run into me."

"She wants a clean break," he mumbled.

Her anger flashed. "But you wanted to hedge it. I was supposed to stay in touch just in case you needed a good fuck!"

"That's not true!" he snapped back.

"Well, you can call and tell her that you did it her way, and that Pam Leighton is gone for good. I'll be back in the morning to clean out my desk."

"Pam, wait!"

But she never broke stride.